A Telegram
from
Berlin

Also by A. O'Connor

A Telegram

from

Berlin

A. O'Connor

POOLBEG

Published 2020
by Poolbeg Press Ltd
123 Grange Hill, Baldoyle
Dublin 13, Ireland
E-mail: poolbeg@poolbeg.com
www.poolbeg.com

A catalogue record for this book is available from the British Library.

ISBN 978-1-78199-730-7

Typeset in Sabon 11pt on 15pt by Poolbeg Press Ltd

www.poolbeg.com

About the Author

A graduate of the National University of Ireland Maynooth and Trinity College Dublin, A.O'Connor is the bestselling author of fourteen previous novels including *The House, The Secrets of Armstrong House, The Footman, The Left-Handed Marriage, By Royal Appointment* and *A Great Beauty.*

He has also written children's books on Kilmainham Gaol, Martin Luther King, James Joyce and the Irish patriot Michael Davitt.

Acknowledgements

A big thank-you to the team at Poolbeg – Paula, Kieran, David and Lee. Also, my gratitude to my editor Gaye Shortland for her dedication. As always, a big thank-you to the book buyers and the readers.

PROLOGUE

SEPTEMBER 1940

As their plane flew over Berlin, Karina looked down at the massive metropolis of four million people stretched out below. There had been an air raid on Berlin two weeks earlier on August 25th which had mainly targeted the Tempelhof Airport. This meant the plane they were travelling in was diverted to a small airfield north of the city. As they disembarked, Karina thought it strange that she had campaigned so long to get there and now she just wanted to get out of Germany as quickly as possible.

A motorcar was waiting for them and, as it drove them into the city, she viewed the familiar sights of Berlin. As she studied the busy streets, life in Berlin did not seem that different to her from what it was before the war. Unlike London and the other British cities that were now being bombarded each night by the Luftwaffe, the Berlin bombings had been sporadic and had not inflicted much physical damage so far. Berlin was at the very far reach of the flight ability of the British air force, making an attack on the city difficult to carry out. Also, the civilian population had not been the target of the air raids so there had been few casualties.

As their motorcar pulled up outside the majestic Kaiserhof Hotel, Karina felt that Berlin was a city at the zenith of its power, bursting with confidence after all the military victories. A city waiting impatiently for a final victory in the war, so it could be established as the new undisputed capital of Europe.

As Karina stepped out of the motorcar, she looked at the Nazi flags hanging over the doorway of the hotel and hid the shiver that ran through her body. The hotel was beside Hitler's Reich Chancellery and across the street from the Ministry of Enlightenment and Propaganda in the heart of the government district. As such, it was a favourite of the Nazi elite, and had established itself as the epicentre of the Nazi social scene.

As they went through the doors they passed a Gestapo officer walking out with a blonde woman on either arm, as they all laughed uproariously at something he had said.

The foyer was gigantic and luxurious and filled with people. As Karina looked around, she realised that the majority of the men were wearing high-ranking military uniforms and there were members of the Gestapo everywhere. There were beautiful women, dressed glamorously, drinking champagne with them at the different tables while a fleet of waiters continually served them. A blonde woman was singing a seductive song in a throaty voice while a pianist accompanied her on a grand piano in the corner of the foyer.

Karina looked through the doors into the hotel bar which was full of people in party mood while, on a landing up a central staircase, impeccably dressed waiters were running in and out of the restaurant, holding aloft trays of food. It was all so different from the atmosphere and mood in London, a city under siege. The war had already been won in German minds.

At reception, they filled in the forms provided and handed them back.

"Thank you so much," said the receptionist. "And if I can have your passports, please."

Karina looked at him. "Why do you need my passport?"

"It is our policy to hold the passports of our guests during their stay. They will be quite safe – they are held in the hotel safe."

Karina hesitated as all her instincts were telling her not to part with her passport. The idea of being in Nazi Germany without it seemed unwise – to the point of being dangerous if her secrets were ever revealed.

"Passports, please!" repeated the receptionist as he held out a hand.

BOOK ONE

AUGUST TO DECEMBER 1939

CHAPTER 1

The aroma of bacon being grilled first thing in the morning always filled Karina Harper with a comforting and warm feeling. It wasn't that the smell awakened an actual hunger in her, but rather brought her back to the days of her childhood growing up in Ireland.

Each morning, the cook and her dedicated team of kitchen maids would be busy preparing the breakfast in the basement kitchen of their stately home, Inishwood. The scent of the bacon would waft up from the kitchen, past the servants' stairs, and travel down the wide tiled hallway and up the wide central staircase which was hand-carved from ancient oak. The scent would drift along the Persian-carpeted corridors on the first floor until it found its way into Karina's bedroom. She would be wakened in her four-poster bed by the beautiful smell and would quickly prepare herself for the day. She would be washed and dressed by the time one of the maids knocked on her door to tell her breakfast would be served in ten minutes. She would then run downstairs and into the dining room where her parents were already seated at the long teak dining table that stretched down the grand ornate room. She would kiss and hug first her father and then her mother before sitting down, and her mother would give the butler the nod to begin serving breakfast ...

Karina woke up and opened her eyes. She blinked a few times as she became more conscious of the smell of bacon being grilled, before sitting up and looking around the tidy but drab little room that was her bedroom. She suddenly felt a terrible sense of loss.

The aroma had once more brought her back to Inishwood. For a few wonderful seconds, as she had awoken from a deep sleep, she had believed that she was back there in her family home. Now fully awake, she was brought back to reality. She was far away and far removed from the glory of Inishwood. She was now in the small house on the edge of Fulham that she and her mother called home.

She ran a hand through her wavy blonde hair as she slipped out of bed and put on the silk dressing gown that was flung across a chair, tying the belt around her waist. She walked over to her dressing table, sat down and studied her fine porcelain skin. She leaned forward, peering, and was happy to see she looked fresh despite having had a very late night. She'd been at a party until two in the morning. It had been held in the Belgravia home of her cousin, Lord Julian Ashton. Most of the guests she knew, or had met before. Julian's guests were the sons and daughters of aristocrats or wealthy businessmen, with the occasional stage actor or writer – or even the occasional visiting movie star who set everyone's heart racing. Karina was in that circle by virtue of being born a member of the peerage. And the peerage would never exclude or turn its back on one of its own, no matter how unfortunate or pitiful their circumstances had become. You were guaranteed an invite into the golden circle – or at least for as long as you were beautiful and young and charming or, failing that, notably talented.

She had lit herself a cigarette when she heard the familiar sound of the drop of post through the letterbox. She got up quickly and rushed out of the room.

Outside the smell of bacon was much stronger. She hurried downstairs to the front door and swooped down to pick up the post. With the cigarette between the fingers of one hand, she riffled through the envelopes, her heart beating quickly. It was the same routine every morning. A rush to the post as soon as it arrived – the rush of adrenaline as she checked the envelopes, silently praying to see the familiar yearned-for handwriting with the accompanying German postage stamp. And then, inevitably, the crushing disappointment setting in as there was no letter from him that morning.

Sighing, she turned and walked down the hall and into the kitchen where her mother was just removing the bacon from the grill. No matter how many times she saw her mother standing over a stove, Karina could never get used to it. It just looked so wrong. She was a tall elegant woman with soft blonde hair who still had the hallmarks of being the great beauty she once was. But her attire was now devoid of the glamour she once carried with aplomb. And what an elegant beauty she had been, Karina remembered. Penny Harper wasn't meant to spend her time over a stove in the same way as Karina was not meant to spend her time over a typewriter. But circumstances dictated. Karina smiled wryly to herself as she remembered a teacher at her school, Miss Simmons, happily declaring that if a girl knew how to cook and type she would never go too far wrong! How depressingly accurate Miss Simmons had been!

"Good morning, Mama," said Karina as she sat down at the table. Taking a drag from her cigarette, she began to open the post.

"Good morning, darling. I was just about to call you for breakfast." Penny came over to her with a plate of bacon and eggs and placed it in front of her, kissing the top of her head at the same time. Even though it was over thirty years since Penny had left New York, to move to Europe to marry Karina's father, her soft American accent was still unchanged.

"Thank you, Mama," said Karina as she put out her cigarette.

Penny waved the cigarette smoke away with her hand and tut-tutted. "I was reading an article in one of my magazines that said smoking may actually be bad for your health, Karina!"

"Isn't everything these days?" said Karina as she looked down at the headline of the newspaper delivered by the paperboy that morning. Yet another warning of an upcoming war with Germany. She picked up a slice of toast and began to butter it.

"How was the party last night? I didn't hear you come in." Penny placed her own plate on the table and sat down.

"I tried to be quiet as I didn't want to wake you. It was good – the usual crowd – Julian was asking after you, as always."

"*Ahh*, Julian! Always such a pleasant boy. He was your father's favourite nephew …"

"His only nephew, Mama!"

Penny ignored this as usual. "I remember when he came to visit us at Inishwood. He was at boarding school and he simply could not believe the freedom he had while he stayed with us, running free through the Irish countryside ..." Her eyes became misty at the memory before she was jolted back to the present. "Anything interesting in the post?"

"Just some party invitations," said Karina.

"Was the Viscount of Suffolk's son there last night?"

"George? Yes, I believe he was."

"I heard it through the grapevine that he is quite taken with you."

"George is the clumsiest dancer I have ever met," said Karina.

"Clumsy dancer or not, he is due to inherit a twelve-thousand-acre estate in Suffolk one day!"

"Well, bully for George! Hopefully he will be able to afford a few dancing lessons when he does!"

"I wish you wouldn't be so flippant, Karina!" Penny gestured around the kitchen. "Look around you – do you want to be here the rest of your life? Or for that matter be a secretary at the Foreign Office forever?"

"I was very lucky to get the job at the Foreign Office."

"Be that as it may, I think you were cut out for better than that, don't you? And, thanks to our connections, you could achieve much better than that."

"By marrying Two-Left-Feet George? No, thank you! I'll stick to the typing pool if that is my only option. It will be safer for my toes!"

"You were twenty-nine this year, Karina!"

"Well, thank you for reminding me, Mama!"

"I just don't want you to squander the opportunities that present themselves to you – just because ... just because ..."

"Yes, Mama – just because what?"

"Just because you spend your life waiting for a letter from Germany that never arrives!"

Karina's eyes filled with tears. "Thank you for that as well, Mama!"

Penny sighed loudly. "I'm sorry, darling. I really am. But how long has this been going on? And how much more of your life can you waste – put on hold – for something that is not real – someone who is not here for you now to have and to hold?"

"Whereas Two-Left-Feet George is? I could never marry for the wrong reasons, Mama. You know that. I guess I'm just like Papa in that way!" Karina was fighting back the tears.

"And I've often thought that he might have been better off without me ... there was nothing for us to fall back on when things went wrong ... and we had to spend our whole lives hiding the truth from everyone. Living a lie almost. And we are still hiding it – now more than ever!" Penny gestured to the newspaper headline.

"Anyway, I simply do not wish to talk about this anymore," said Karina.

"As you wish!" sighed Penny as she picked up the newspaper and began to read.

It wasn't long before she was tut-tutting.

"I see the Irish Prime Minister Mr de Valera has said it is his country's intention to declare neutrality if there is a war with Germany! No surprises there! Their neutrality, I imagine, is the best we can hope for from the Irish! Unlike what they offered us in the last war – treason! They basically attempted to ally themselves with Germany then!"

As Karina looked across the table at her mother engrossed in the article, she could see the bitterness. The bitterness of what had happened that dreadful night all those years ago at Inishwood would never leave them – and had embittered her mother against the Irish forever.

CHAPTER 2

Gabriel Ford sat at the board table at Government Buildings in Dublin as everyone present listened to the Taoiseach Éamon de Valera speak in a grave voice.

"It is not a case of *if*, but *when* the war breaks out, gentlemen. The German aggression looks to be unquenchable. The consequences for Europe will be serious, but it is our responsibility – we here around this table – to protect our nation and our people to the best of our ability."

"The British will be expecting us to be their ally – and not in words only – they will want the ports back," said Tom Kelly, a junior minister.

"The three ports were ceded back to us by international treaty last year," said de Valera, a worried look accentuating his long sharp features. "It is not an option for them to have them back – they are Irish territory not to be used by a foreign power in a game of cat-and-mouse with the Germans."

Gabriel coughed before speaking. "Because of our location in the North Atlantic and still being a member of the British Commonwealth –"

"A very reluctant member and in name only at this stage since we drew up our own constitution and elected a president two years ago!" said Tom Kelly.

Gabriel hid his irritation at the interruption and continued. "The British will not take us declaring ourselves neutral with a pinch of salt. We are risking a full-scale invasion. They could very easily send the troops over our border with the North and overrun us."

"Would they risk a war on two fronts?" asked de Valera.

"They did it in 1916. They came and quashed the 1916 rebellion while mired in the Great War on the continent," said Gabriel.

The men sat in silence for a while.

"It's a sobering thought," said de Valera. "And we are walking a fine diplomatic tightrope of maintaining our independence, so long fought for, and not angering our powerful neighbour so that we risk another war or invasion from them."

"Or even a risk of invasion from the Germans," added Gabriel.

"Highly unlikely they could get an invasion force as far as us!" said Tom, aghast.

"But not impossible," said Gabriel. "May I suggest as well that if it is our intention to remain neutral then a change of envoy in Berlin is probably required. Mr Bewley appears to be an admirer of Hitler and the Nazis – frighteningly so. He has drawn some serious criticism from the British. Someone more neutral is needed, I suggest."

"Yes, indeed – start looking for somebody new for the post," said de Valera. "Worrying times. We'll reconvene tomorrow to discuss strategy. Good afternoon, gentlemen."

As the men got to their feet and began to leave the room, de Valera said, "Gabriel, I need a word with you. Close the door."

"Yes, sir."

Gabriel waited for the others to go and then closed the door.

De Valera had risen to his feet and gone to one of the long Georgian windows which looked out across Merrion Square.

"Such a pity we will have to put our redevelopment of the city centre on hold because of the war," he sighed.

Gabriel looked out at the beautiful Georgian buildings that surrounded the park in the centre of the square. The government had drawn up a plan to knock the entire square down and replace it with modern buildings. The Georgian buildings were now seen as unwanted relics, an unpleasant reminder of British rule, in the same way the stately homes and manor houses of the Anglo-Irish aristocracy in the countryside had been viewed with hatred. Many of those homes had been destroyed during the War of Independence and the Civil War by Irish Republicans in their endeavour to drive the aristocracy out of Ireland.

"Yes, I doubt it would make very good economic sense to start rebuilding the city with a war on the horizon," said Gabriel who had been horrified at the plan to demolish the square. He had secretly always harboured sorrow over the burning of the stately homes around Ireland. He did not share the hatred of the buildings in the same way many of his countrymen did. He could see beyond what they represented and admire them for their architectural beauty.

"If we don't remain neutral, the Germans will probably do the job for us and flatten the whole place with their bombs anyway," said de Valera, moving away from the window and focusing on Gabriel. "Gabriel, you have been doing excellent work in the Department of Foreign Affairs. It is not easy as a new and young country to build up diplomatic relations abroad from scratch."

"Thank you, sir. I only try to serve my country as best I can."

"In the same way your father did – he would be very proud of you."

Both nodded in a moment of sadness and respect for the fallen hero. Gabriel thought of his father – dark and brooding, he was an iconic figure. Gabriel felt he himself was not really cut from the same cloth, being much more the diplomat than the fighter. Nor did he even look like his father with his light-brown hair, fair complexion and blue eyes.

"I am seriously worried about the way the British will try to deal with our neutrality," said de Valera. "I didn't want to say it in front of the others – but we are only getting back on our feet after the destruction of the War of Independence, the Civil War and then the economic war. We are too weak to withhold a British invasion at this point."

"I couldn't agree with you more, sir."

"I want you to go to London and have some meetings with their senior fellows. Figure out what they want from us without us either giving back the ports or becoming a full ally. You are one of our best diplomats – so explore options with them but promise nothing."

"I'll organise a visit and a conference," said Gabriel.

"Very good," said de Valera as he walked him to the door. "I understand that you're finally making an honest woman of Siobhán?"

"Yes, sir. She finally agreed to marry me!" said Gabriel with a smile.

"Not before time. She's the poet's daughter, of course."

"Yes."

"Does she write poetry herself?"

"Not any she admits to! She's quite happy being a teacher. In fact, we are having a small engagement party tonight at Roxford if you're free to join us? Mother would be delighted to see you." Gabriel's parents had fought on the same side as de Valera in the Civil War – the side that eventually was forced to capitulate and accept the Anglo-Irish Treaty.

"Very kind, but I must decline. Too much to do during these turbulent times ... times are always so turbulent ... Your mother is delighted with the match?"

"Yes, you'd think it was she was getting married, she is that excited!" said Gabriel with a chuckle.

"Wonderful woman, your mother. A very brave woman. Terrible what she had to go through. Give her my regards."

"I certainly will, sir," said Gabriel as he nodded and left the room.

De Valera looked at the closed door for a few moments before going back to one of the long windows and staring out again at Merrion Square, his face a mask of worry.

After work, Gabriel went first to his own home, a classical three-storey townhouse in Monkstown with views of Dublin Bay across the road.

Having changed into a more formal suit, he checked his appearance in the mirror. He felt somewhat apprehensive. He had turned thirty that year. It was about time he got married and Siobhán would make the perfect wife. He just hoped he could make her the perfect husband and would never let her down.

Gabriel drove into the driveway of Roxford. It was a beautiful Victorian villa which offered a wonderful view of the sea. It was one of many villas and mansions that were dotted around the hills and clifftops of the south Dublin suburb of Killiney. From the veranda and sloping back garden the whole of the city could be seen as it swept along Dublin Bay. It had been Gabriel's childhood home and also his mother's. Cynthia had inherited it from her father, a doctor, when he died.

Gabriel got out of the car and walked across the gravel forecourt and up the steps to the front door where he let himself in. He could hear a piano playing and his mother's voice singing. He crossed the large hallway and went into the parlour which stretched from the front of the house the whole length of the building to the back where there were French doors and windows that looked out at the sea.

Cynthia was sitting at the grand piano, her fingers running up and down the keys as she sang 'A Nation Once Again' at the top of her voice.

Cynthia was a handsome woman in her early fifties. She had a presence about her that had always commanded respect and admiration. She took great pride in her appearance. Perfectly groomed hair tied back in a bun and tweeds was the image familiar to those who knew her.

"Hello, Mother!" Gabriel said as he walked up to her and kissed her cheek.

She broke off from her playing. "Hello, darling!"

She stood up and walked across to the drinks cabinet where she began to pour herself a gin and tonic. "How did your meeting go with Éamon?"

It amused Gabriel that Cynthia always referred to de Valera by his first name. But then Cynthia knew all the political establishment by their first names. She saw herself as being part of that establishment even though she also felt she had been robbed of her rightful position amongst them by the assassination of her husband during the Civil War. Rory Ford, Gabriel's father, had been a hero of the 1916 Rising. And a hero of the War of the Independence. A name that was held in reverence in Ireland nearly as much as Michael Collins or indeed de Valera himself. Many believed his assassination during the Civil War had robbed the country of one of its best and most capable men, one earmarked as being a future leader of the country. Wherever Gabriel went in Ireland he wasn't too far from hearing praise and worship being heaped on his father. As gratifying as that was, it was not compensation for the fact he had been left without the father he adored at the tender age of thirteen.

He would never forget the day he heard that news. His mother never shed a tear that day or any day after. She sat him down in that very parlour and broke the news that his father had been ambushed and killed by enemy troops. Gabriel would never forget the anguish and loss he had felt. The whole country wept at the loss of another great man. Rory Ford's funeral had been a gigantic public affair, but for Gabriel the whole day had been confusing and overwhelming as he had to stand by his mother's side and shake hands with hundreds of people. Many of the weeping mourners there had never actually met his father. Gabriel had felt so angry, not just because he had lost his adored father, but because he had to share the mourning of his father with all these people, the vast majority of them strangers.

"The meeting went well," said Gabriel.

"Who else was there?"

"Tom Kelly."

"Kelly! Why was *he* there? Kelly wouldn't know how to handle the British at a tea party let alone a war!" Cynthia scoffed as she sat down on the elegant couch and took a swig of gin. "Who else?"

"Austin Farrell."

"Oh, the great war strategist Austin Farrell!" she mocked. "Your father always dismissed him as a lightweight – he used to say that during the War of Independence Austin couldn't find the road to Killarney let alone independence! Well, if that is the calibre of brains we are relying on to keep us out of this war, then God help Ireland! So what has been decided as the next course of action?"

"I am to go to London to the Foreign Office to present our position and indicate our intention to declare neutrality in the advent of war," said Gabriel as he poured himself a drink. "And to try to persuade the British that this is not a hostile act against the British but our right as an independent nation."

"I doubt the British will look at it that way. If I know them – and I do – they will accuse us of letting them down in their hour of need. Be careful, Gabriel. You aren't the first man Éamon has sent to London to negotiate on behalf of the Irish ... and look what happened to Michael Collins ..."

"Mother! Hardly the same thing!" Gabriel said as he took a sip of his gin.

"Why not? History always repeats itself – only with different players." She stood up. "Well, I must go and change."

After Cynthia left, Gabriel went to stand by one of the back windows. He lit a cigarette as he gazed out at the sea which was beautifully calm under a reddening sky. Siobhán and her family would be here shortly. Siobhán disliked the smell of tobacco so he knew he wouldn't get an opportunity to smoke again for the evening.

He had known Siobhán for a few years. As Dev – de Valera – had mentioned, her father was the revered poet Mícheál Vestry. His poetry was fiercely nationalistic and held up as emblematic of the new Irish nation. It glorified the 1916 Rising and the War of Independence. He was also principal of one of Dublin's best private schools, the same school that Siobhán taught in. Siobhán and Gabriel were a great match. Everyone said so. Even Cynthia wholeheartedly approved. She loved the idea of being related to such a poet as Mícheál Vestry. She thought it added to the family's reputation. For Cynthia, family reputation was everything.

Cynthia had herself been heavily involved in the Easter Rising and the later conflicts. Despite being the mother of two young boys at the time of the Rising, she had put her life on the line acting as a courier between the different positions of the Republicans. As he thought of his mother now, all coiffured and perfumed, it was hard for Gabriel to imagine her sneaking through the Dublin streets, dodging enemy fire. But that was what she had done and had been even decorated by the State for her services. She had relished it when Gabriel's father Rory had become one of the great heroes in the later fight for independence. Gabriel remembered that secret meetings were often held in their parlour during the guerrilla war that was waged against the British. All the big names of the revolution had regularly met in their house, plotting and planning strategy. Both his parents had several times nearly been killed, so there was an extraordinary sense of relief for the family after the British troops finally evacuated and the country became the Irish Free State. But when Gabriel's father was then shot during the ensuing civil war, it seemed an unbearable blow. For Rory to be snatched away, just when they thought they were over the worst, was almost impossible to accept.

Gabriel believed that for Cynthia the most unforgiveable thing was that her husband had not been killed by the British. She would have been able to cope better with his death could she blame the British troops – and it would have added to his martyr status. But for Rory to be killed by a fellow countryman was the cruellest cut of all. For her, it was an unspeakably cruel thing to happen. It would have crushed many another, but it did not crush Cynthia. It galvanised her insofar as she saw herself as the guardian of Rory Ford's memory and reputation. Along the way, to Gabriel, his father seemed to stop becoming an actual man but was elevated to iconic status.

Cynthia relished her new role as widow of the hero. She felt robbed of the life she should have had with Rory so in its place she started grooming Gabriel and his brother Tim to take their father's place. It was a big responsibility for them to shoulder. At least Gabriel could now escape Cynthia's constant watchful eye as he lived in Monkstown. But Tim had never moved out of Roxford and, when he had married Tess, she had moved in as well. Gabriel didn't know why they did it and how they endured it as, although Roxford was a very large house, it wasn't large enough to share with a character as domineering as Cynthia.

As Gabriel heard motorcars approach the front of the house, he put out his cigarette and then stood in front of the full-length mirror, inspecting himself. He smoothed down his hair with his hand and left the room to greet his guests.

Siobhán Vestry was twenty-eight years old. She wore her fine blonde hair shoulder-length, had pretty features and was always well groomed. She came across as a woman who was confident and sure of herself without being arrogant. She was a woman that other women automatically liked. She was trustworthy.

As Cynthia led Siobhán around the drawing room that evening, introducing her to any guests who had not yet met her, she wholeheartedly approved of her son's choice of bride. Siobhán was a solid, uncomplicated woman from good stock who would never rock the boat, never let the side down and always put her best foot forward. She would be a great support to Gabriel in his career and produce a fleet of grandchildren for her. She knew how to behave. She was quietly charming without ever looking to be the centre of attention. She didn't flirt and crave men's attention. She only had eyes for Gabriel and those eyes looked at him adoringly. Yes, Cynthia could quite happily hand her son over to Siobhán and know he would be in safe hands.

As Cynthia looked at Tim's wife, Tess, who was at that moment quite happy in the middle of a circle of admiring men, she wished she felt as relaxed about her as she did about Siobhán.

"Now, everybody!" Cynthia called out and clapped her hands for attention. If we could all have a few moments of quiet, we can ask Siobhán's father Mícheál for a few words!" She beckoned Gabriel to her and stood between him and Siobhán with an arm around each.

Mícheál came and stood near them.

"*A Chairde ...*"

Cynthia's smile tightened as she realised he was opting to give the speech in Irish. An ardent promoter of the Irish language, Dr Mícheál Vestry had been going around the entire evening opening conversations with the other guests in the Irish language. Cynthia was sure he used it as a test to see how nationalistic they were. If they could converse back to him in Irish they got the stamp of approval of true patriots. If they could not, then – in the well-used and much-repeated words of the schoolteacher he was – *they could do better!*

As the speech dragged on and on, she looked across the room to her son Tim who had an arm around his wife. Tess was holding a glass of champagne and was not bothering to disguise the fact that she was utterly bored. Cynthia was certain Tess would hardly have a word of Irish nor have any interest in it. As Cynthia studied the faces of all her guests, she wondered how many actually had any clue of what Mícheál was saying – which was why she would have preferred if he had stuck to English for this occasion. Cynthia made a note to herself not to let him to have free rein at the wedding when it came to speeches.

Tess took a sip of champagne and whispered to Tim. "When is he going to finish?"

"*Shhhh!*"

"I will not *shhhh*! Bad enough I had to listen to that shit in school and be bored senseless with his poetry – now I'm to be inflicted with it at every family occasion from here on out!"

"*Will you be quiet!*" Tim hissed and gave her a small pinch on the arm.

"*Owwww!*" she gasped and elbowed him surreptitiously in the stomach.

Cynthia watched the interaction between her son and his wife and raised an eyebrow of disapproval. She had known Tess since she was a child growing up down the road in one of the other smart mansions in the area, the daughter of two wealthy medical doctors. Tim had been madly in love with Tess since they were children and had pursued her relentlessly. Cynthia sometimes wondered had she married Tim because he had simply given her no choice. Cynthia was very fond of Tess – it was hard not to be. She was good-natured, witty, fun, with a vicious sense of humour that was hard not to respond to. Tim had been elected to parliament and was a hard-working and respected TD. Cynthia could not fault Tess as a political wife – she attended all the events and charmed the electorate and the political establishment. On the surface they had everything going for them. But Cynthia did worry about them. They were four years married now and no sign of a child. Where were her grandchildren? And Tess liked herself just a little too much, needed attention from men just a little too much. That vicious sense of humour she had was directed at Tim just a little too much. In fact, if Cynthia had to sum up her opinion of her daughter-in-law it would be in the words that she was in every sense *just a little too much.*

As Mícheál continued with his speech, Cynthia, now sensing he had lost everyone's attention, decided an intervention was necessary. As could be typical of a school principal, he had forgotten he was not in front of a classroom of children.

She moved over to him and cut in as he ended a sentence.

"Thank you so much for those wonderful words and thoughts, Mícheál – after which it is only left for me to ask you all to raise your glasses –" she raised her own in the air, "and to say: *to Gabriel and Siobhán!*"

"*To Gabriel and Siobhán!*" cried everyone as they toasted the happy couple.

Cynthia looked on in contentment as Gabriel gazed down at his fiancée and smiled before kissing her.

"I thought I'd find you here," said Tess as she walked down the steps from the terrace at the back of the house to the garden where Gabriel was standing smoking a cigarette. "Give me one of those, will you?"

Gabriel opened his cigarette case, and proffered it.

She took a cigarette and he lit it for her. She inhaled deeply.

"I needed that after listening to all that shit from your future father-in-law!" she said.

"Now, now, Tess," Gabriel chastised her with a smile.

"Lord save us, I thought he would never stop! And I couldn't follow a word he was saying!"

"Did you ever know any Irish?"

"No! Sure the nuns gave up on me ever learning a word when they found a copy of *Tatler* in my schoolbag!"

Gabriel laughed.

"I don't envy you, Gabriel, marrying into that family with a father-in-law as fond as listening to himself as Mícheál is! I thought I had it bad, marrying into the Fords. But I think I have a new-found liking for Cynthia's silent treatments if the alternative is non-stop verbal diarrhoea!"

"Will you stop now, Tess?" said Gabriel sternly, disguising his amusement.

They had known each other all their lives and so were easy in each other's company. Yet Tess had always felt that, though he was one of the gang when they were young, he was somehow separate from them too. There was something about him that set him apart. She wasn't sure who she had imagined Gabriel would settle down with but, as perfect as Siobhán seemed, she would not have put him together with someone like her.

"Well, it's too late to back out now, Gabriel – you've made it official," she said.

"But why would I want to back out?"

"Well, no more pleasing yourself, no more coming and going as you want. When you are married you throw away all your freedom, all your independence – and what do you get in return? Somebody who snores beside you in the bed which prevents you from getting any sleep and somebody who will always tell you that you are doing whatever you are doing wrong!"

"Ah, c'mon, Tess – there must be some advantages to marriage?" Gabriel said, laughing.

"Well, I haven't found any while married to your brother, so let me know if you come across any while married to the lovely Siobhán." Tess suddenly made a mock-distressed face. "She wouldn't expect you to speak Irish at home all the time, would she?"

"Of course not!"

"Thank fuck for that!"

"But you're very happy with Tim, aren't you, Tess?"

"Oh, deliriously so!" she said with a grimace.

His face became serious. "But you are, aren't you? You two were always meant for each other."

"Of course I'm happy with Tim, Gabriel. He's a nice fella. I could have done a lot worse."

"That doesn't sound very enthusiastic."

"Well, I don't think I gave myself much chance to see if there was anybody else out there, Gabriel. It was just all so easy. Tim was there, he adored me, he ticked all the boxes, well, most of them anyway ..." She stared out at the sea in the darkness.

"Go on, Tess." Gabriel knew he was intruding, knew he was

invading his brother's privacy, but he couldn't stop himself. It was as if he felt Tess could provide him with answers he was looking for.

"I don't know if I ever really fancied him." She turned, looked at Gabriel and blinked several times.

He was amazed to see she had tears in her eyes.

"And I'm not sure if Tim ever really fancied me. Oh, he adored me, worshiped me even. I was the prize he had to have. And he got me ... but ... I tell you one thing, Gabriel ... marriage is for a long time. At least the Protestants have an opt-out clause and can go across to England and get a divorce if it doesn't work out ... but for us ... for us, it's a *life sentence* if it doesn't work out."

Suddenly Cynthia stepped out from the shadows into the moonlight beside them, causing Tess to jump in fright.

"Cynthia! You nearly gave me a heart attack!"

"Sign of a guilty conscience, Tess," said Cynthia.

"You have an amazing ability to appear without anyone ever seeing or hearing you come!"

"I must have learned that when I was avoiding the snipers during the Rising."

"Must have!" said Tess, giving Gabriel a look.

"Gabriel, Siobhán is looking for you everywhere. She's worried about you."

"I had better head in so," he said, putting out his cigarette.

As he walked up the steps, she called after him, "*Best get used to it!*"

He looked back and smiled before heading for the French windows.

"I wish you wouldn't encourage Gabriel with the smoking, Tess," said Cynthia. "You know how Siobhán dislikes the smell of it."

"He was out here smoking before I was!"

"They make a handsome couple, don't you think?" said Cynthia as Gabriel and Siobhán came into view through one of the tall windows.

"Stunning!" said Tess, not hiding her sarcasm.

"Their children will be beautiful," sighed Cynthia with satisfaction.

Tess raised her eyes discreetly to heaven. "I have to say her father nearly had me falling asleep with that longwinded speech he was giving in Irish with nobody having a clue what he was talking about!"

"Yes, I've heard you mention that several times now, Tess, and like all repetition it is becoming boring. Most people could understand him, Tess. Mícheál Vestry is one of our most treasured poets and it is always a pleasure – for most of us – to hear him speak."

"Certainly unforgettable whatever about treasurable!" scoffed Tess. "I heard it through the grapevine that, despite all Mícheál's airs and graces, the Vestrys are just one generation away from poor potato famers in the west of Ireland!"

Cynthia turned abruptly to her daughter-in-law. "Who said such a thing?"

"I can't recall, but it was from a couple of different sources."

"And what if the Vestrys were? It's nothing to be ashamed of. If that is so, it is only because they were kept down by some cruel Protestant landlord."

"I –"

"And I'm surprised by your silly snobbery, Tess Ford. Is this what we fought for? Is that what so many brave Irishmen died for – to get rid of British rule only for us to sneer and create a new social class system of our own?"

"Of course not," Tess said, managing to look suitably contrite. There was no point in trying to argue with Cynthia when she went into this mode – she even regularly gave speeches at girls' schools to inspire them with her own brand of nationalism. The reality, Tess knew, was that Cynthia was more guilty than anyone of endorsing the new class system that had quickly developed in Ireland since independence, placing herself at the top of it.

"Besides," continued Cynthia, "perhaps what this family needs is a good injection of peasant genes. Poor potato farmers from the west of Ireland are some of the best breeders in the world – rare to find one of those families with less than seven or eight children. So if that is in Siobhán's genes, I look forward to meeting all the grandchildren she will give me!"

Tess stared up at the house in silence.

"I naturally always thought you and Tim would give me my

first grandchild … you're running out of time, Tess." Cynthia looked at her pointedly before walking up the steps to the terrace.

Tess turned and looked at the moonlight weave a path across the sea.

"Why is it always the woman's fault?" she whispered to herself, before throwing her cigarette into the grass and making her way back inside the house.

As the piano played and the party continued into the night, Cynthia held court with a group of senior politicians, including Gabriel. They spoke in low voices to make sure none of the other guests would overhear.

"Who is leading the English side in the talks, Gabriel? Do we know yet," asked Tony Fallon, a distinguished senator in the parliament.

"Sir William Baxter, I found out today," said Gabriel.

"That old goat – he lives in the past," said Tony. "He'll treat you as if we are still a colony."

"In a way we still are – at least until we pull away from the Empire fully and declare ourselves a republic once and for all," said Harry Kelly, a private secretary who worked for de Valera.

"This could be our opportunity – if the British are foolhardy enough to have another war with the Germans … it is well said that England's woes are Ireland's opportunity," said Cynthia.

"The British are expecting us to fall into line behind them like the rest of the Empire," said Gabriel. "My main aim over there is to let them know we are an independent sovereign nation whose population is in no mood to fight a war for them … and also to discover the British attitude to us."

"Their attitude will be what it has always been to us – hostile," said Cynthia. "We can't let them bully us this time like they have in the past! Even if they threaten to invade us – we have to stand our ground this time or never hold our own against them in the future!"

The men around Cynthia all nodded in agreement, except for Gabriel. He knew all of them present there in the circle were carrying baggage from their pasts – from the War of Independence and the Civil War. But that was a generation ago and the world had changed. They were fixated on the old enemy, not realising a new terrifying enemy had emerged on the Continent. Ireland was walking a tightrope between the old enemy and the new one in Nazi Germany. In this uncertain new world, it was hard for Cynthia and the others in that circle to understand the dire consequences for Ireland and Europe if Britain failed to contain the Nazi menace.

"Well, Mr Ford, it is official now – you couldn't get out of it, even if you tried," Siobhán said as she held up and admired her diamond engagement ring on the forecourt in front of the house.

"You are the second person to have said that to me tonight! Why does anyone think I want to get out of my engagement?" he said, smiling at her.

"I wonder!"

It was now after midnight and a lot of the guests had gone home.

"Happy?" he asked as he put his arms around her.

"Couldn't be any happier." She smiled up at him. "Except for this trip to England next week. Could Dev not send anybody else?"

"I'm sure he could, but he hasn't. That's the job of a diplomat – to be sent where we are told."

"I know. I'll just miss you, that's all." She held him tighter.

"It'll only be for a few days. And you'll be busy anyway with the new term about to start. You'll hardly miss me."

"I'll miss you every minute of every hour ... and you aren't to be even speaking to any Englishwomen when you are over there – do you hear me?"

"Yes, miss!"

"They can be very fast, you know?"

"So I've heard!" he smirked at her, causing her to hit him playfully.

"And no parties – no alcohol – and no bars! Not allowed – understood?"

"Absolutely!"

She looked at him wistfully. "I do love you, Gabriel."

"Glad to hear it – I don't tend to make a habit of marrying girls who aren't that fond of me!" He winked down at her, causing her to hit him again before they both became serious and they kissed.

* * *

Gabriel stood on the gravel forecourt, waving Siobhán and her family off as they drove away.

It was now well after one o'clock and all the guests had left.

"I couldn't approve more!" said Cynthia from behind him, startling him.

It was true for Tess – Cynthia did have a terrible habit of creeping up on people unnoticed.

"Yes, well, she will do me!" said Gabriel.

"I'm so pleased for you. Goodnight, darling." She leaned forward and gave him a kiss on the cheek before walking across the forecourt and into the house.

Gabriel looked up at the moon in the clear sky and wandered around the side of the house to the back garden. He strolled down to its very end where there was a cliff and a straight drop down to the sea. There were steps in the corner of the garden which led down the cliff face to a beach. He had always thought the place was beautiful and felt lucky to have grown up there.

Now, as he looked out at the sea, he was consumed with a terrible feeling of emptiness, and he didn't know where it came from. He knew he should be feeling on top of the world. His career was flying and he was going to be married to a wonderful girl. His whole future was mapped out for him and he couldn't want more. But if he couldn't want more, than why did he feel so empty? He wished he could figure it out.

CHAPTER 3

Karina was sitting upstairs on a double-decker bus as she made her way to work. She was dreadfully late but that wasn't unusual. The bus was full and as she looked out the window at trenches being dug in Hyde Park she began to fill with dread. They said this war with the Germans, if it came, would be far worse than the last. They said that technical advances since the Great War meant that civilians in London would be attacked by planes that would fly across the Channel at night dropping bombs. The trenches being dug in the parks were air-raid shelters for civilians to hide in. It all seemed outrageously inconceivable to Karina as she stared out the window on that bright sunny August day.

"They ain't going to get me down one of those holes, love, not with my arthritis!" said the stout woman in her sixties who was sitting beside Karina on the bus.

Karina glanced at the woman and couldn't help smiling. "You might have to, for your own safety," she said.

"My own safety! There's nothing safe about going down one of those trenches!" The woman leaned towards Karina and whispered, "I'm lucky, you see – I've got a cellar in my house, so that's where I aim to go if those German planes head over here with their bombs!"

Karina nodded and smiled. "Let's hope it never comes to that … oh, this is my stop!"

She got to her feet and slid past the woman, then made her way quickly down the circular stairs and jumped off the back of the bus.

As she made her way through the busy London streets, Karina

thought of the woman on the bus. She, like millions of others, had thought out what to do if the war came. Every day at the Foreign Office, Karina saw first-hand how the government was making contingency plans. But people were making their own personal contingency plans to keep themselves and their loved ones safe in the coming months – maybe even years. Distant cousins in the country, whom people barely exchanged a Christmas card with, were being contacted to see if children could be sent to stay with them if war broke out. Factories that manufactured hoovers and radios were being converted into munitions factories. Housewives were getting ready to leave the kitchens to take over the running of the country if the men were sent to war. Millions of gasmasks had been distributed to the population. The whole country was mobilising for war and yet it all felt unreal. It felt as if it couldn't really be happening. Everyone was preparing for the worst but hoping for the best. Despite the stoicism there was an underlying feeling of terror as nobody knew what this 'total war' would bring. As horrific as the last war was, for the general population it was one thing to wave soldiers off to the front but quite another to have bombs rain down and destroy people's homes on a nightly basis. Karina had some idea of what that felt like. During the War of Independence in Ireland twenty years before, she had seen first-hand the destruction of her own much-loved home of Inishwood and the killing of a loved one. As she walked along briskly that morning, attracting admiring looks from passersby, all that seemed like another lifetime and a million miles away.

"Good morning, Miss Harper," said the doorman at the Foreign Office as he held the door open for her.

"Morning, Jack!" She smiled as him as she passed him by.

"A late night again last night, Miss Harper?"

"Of course! I was dancing in the Ritz until one!"

"*Tut-tut!*" he said, beaming a smile. "I think we will call you Mrs Rily from now on – because you have the life of Rily!"

Karina laughed as she continued through the busy foyer and up the sweeping staircase, greeting different personnel as she went.

The large office she worked in had two rows of six desks. On the desks were typewriters that were busily being battered by hardworking young women. All the secretaries were a type – young, attractive and from good families. They had all done exceptionally well to get a position there. Karina knew them all and knew that they had one overriding ambition, their reason for getting a job there in the first place: to meet and marry a diplomat. Karina was different from the rest as this was not and never had been her aim. She had taken the job four years before as it paid well and had good holidays and they let her get away with late starts in the mornings – most of the time.

As she reached her desk at the end of the room, she took off her jacket and hung it on the back of her chair. As ever she felt lucky that her desk was situated beside one of the tall windows that gave the room the maximum amount of natural light. From her desk, she had wonderful views over St James's Park.

"Don't bother even sitting down, Karina," said Diana, the secretary at the next desk to hers. "Sir William wants to see you immediately."

"Ah!" said Karina as thoughts raced through her head. "Did he say what about?"

"Your atrocious timekeeping, I daresay!"

"I see," said Karina.

She felt her heart beginning to beat with excitement as she rushed through the maze of corridors towards Sir William's office.

"Go straight in, Miss Harper – he is waiting for you," said Sir William's older secretary who guarded admittance to her boss in the manner of a well-trained Alsatian.

Karina paused at the door and smoothed down her skirt and hair before knocking and entering the room.

"You wished to see me, Sir William?" she said, closing the door behind her.

"Yes, come and sit, Miss Harper," he said, looking up from his papers and beckoning to her.

She walked quickly towards his desk and sat down opposite him. She tried to hide her impatience as he continued reading a letter. She felt herself fill with anxiety.

"For goodness' sake!" he eventually said, throwing the letter into a drawer and slamming it shut. "If that is the level of grammar the Civil Service have in India these days then I fear the Empire is lost already!" Sir William was a notorious stickler for grammar, diction and syntax. A secretary once presented him with a letter he had dictated with a typing error. Sir William's resultant shouting could be heard in Whitehall.

"You wished to see me, Sir William?" Karina said again, trying to contain her nerves.

"Yes – yes. I want you to clear your schedule for next week as I need you to attend a number of meetings due to take place with the Irish. You are to take the minutes. I know you are an eminently suitable choice because of your wonderful proficiency in shorthand but I asked for you specifically as yours is the only handwriting I can read out of all the damned secretaries in here! Times were when a secretary had to pass a handwriting test to get a job in the Foreign Office – not anymore, of course! Do you know, I have noticed that the more young women use typewriters the worse their handwriting becomes! I think the typewriter has a lot to answer for, resulting in sloppy handwriting and shady grammar. Times were, when –"

"The Irish, Sir William?" Karina couldn't contain her anxiety.

"Yes, the Irish are coming over to discuss their role in the upcoming war. Or their lack of a role as they would have it. You can always rely on the Irish to stab you in the back when you need them most! If they would just give us back the three naval ports we handed over to them last year, it would be a start. Of course, they will make life as difficult as possible ... they always do ... I actually think they have got worse since they became independent. Times were, you could at least trust the Irish to do the honourable thing when the chips were down and your back was against the wall. Not anymore of course, not since 1916 –"

"Sir William!" Karina cut in as she felt despair overcome her at his rambling. "I wonder if you have any news on the other matter I discussed with you two weeks ago?"

"Other matter?" He looked confused.

"My transfer to Berlin!" she announced in desperation.

"Oh!" he said, as if suddenly remembering.

"You said you would look into it for me?"

"Yes, I did, didn't I? I don't know why I actually said that – as it's really a non-runner, my dear. An absolute non-runner!"

"A non-runner?" Her heart sank.

"My dear – all our staff in Berlin are trying to get transfers back to London as quickly as possible with this coming war – they are all desperately trying to get the heck out of Berlin. Why on earth would we be sending you, a young slip of a girl, out there at this time?"

"Well, exactly because of that! The embassy will still need secretaries and I am quite willing to go – to replace somebody there who is anxious to come home!"

"Quite admirable but most bizarre! Why on earth would you want to put yourself in the lion's jaw?"

"I just want to serve my country as best I can."

"But you can serve it best by staying here and writing up legible meeting notes for me!"

"But I really –"

"Miss Harper, please! I am not sending a young woman over to Berlin at this dreadful time. We are trying to minimise our staff there not increase it, as if and when war breaks out we cannot guarantee their safety or that they will be treated with any diplomatic courtesy or immunity by the Nazis. Times were, in war, there was a kind of honour amongst thieves. A chivalry almost, but not anymore – oh no, not anymore, when you are dealing with people like the Nazis ... not when you are dealing with those scoundrels ..."

As Sir William droned on about how times past were so much better than the present, Karina looked out the window at St James's Park and almost fell into a trance. She had really thought Sir William would organise the transfer after the last conversation she'd had with him. Now she realised he hadn't even been listening to her properly. And now her one hope of getting to Berlin had been crushed.

"Anyway, you may return to your desk, Miss Harper," said Sir William at last.

"Yes, sir," said Karina as she stood up, deflated, and made her way to the door.

"Oh, and Karina?"

"Yes, Sir William?"

"There will be a couple of evening functions I will need you to attend next week with me – functions being given to try and seduce the Irish into being our allies. So keep your diary clear for next week."

"Yes, Sir William."

"Oh, and Karina – wear something nice – there's a good girl!" he said with a wink.

She opened the door quickly and left.

Karina felt despondent as she tried to catch up with her work. She found it difficult to concentrate. Eventually she managed to make some progress though her mind kept straying.

It seemed like no time had passed before the other girls were standing up and putting on their jackets.

"Oh, you're hardly in and it's time for lunch, Karina! How very convenient!" said Diana.

"I will stay late tonight to get my work done – don't fret about that, Diana," said Karina.

"That really isn't the point, is it?" said Diana as she flounced off with the others.

As the girls exited the room, Karina could still hear her.

"Just because she's Lord Ashton's cousin she thinks she can please herself!"

"And the fact that Sir William is soft on her!" said another girl.

The typist who sat at the desk in front of Karina, Vera, hesitated before leaving.

"Will you join us, Karina? We're going to the new tea room down on the Mall for lunch. Best scones in London, or so they say!"

"No, thank you, Vera – I fear I'd not be much company today."

Vera gave her a sympathetic smile. "Don't mind Diana – she just gets a little insecure at times. She doesn't mean any harm."

"Oh Vera, Diana is the least thing on my mind," sighed Karina.

Vera nodded and hurried to join the others.

As Karina sat there, she reached into her pocket and took out an envelope. She ran a finger across the fine handwriting and the German postage stamp. It was dated May 1939 – three months ago. It was the last letter she had received from Hugo.

CHAPTER 4

Karina sat on her own on a bench in St James's Park, holding the envelope containing Hugo's last letter. She usually carried it with her. It gave her comfort to have it close by. She took out the letter. Looking at it, she was filled with a familiar yearning mixed with fear.

She read it again.

My Darling Karina,

I cannot tell you how happy I was this morning when I received your letter. It made my week. Just the sight of your handwriting fills my heart with light during these dark days. I miss you and live for the day that I can be with you again.

But, first, I must warn you, under no circumstances are you to try to come to Germany as you suggest in your letter. Regardless of how painful this separation is, it is not safe for you to be here. My flat is watched nearly all the time. They stand across the road, in the park, watching. I now only go to the shops once a week to get the groceries I need, and I am followed there and back.

It is now four months since I have had any contact with my publishers – since my writing has been banned. I fear, if you came, it would merely make my situation worse. At best, it would achieve nothing without a visa for me to come to Britain. The answer to our problems is not your coming to Berlin – but for me to get to London. I am continuing in my attempt to negotiate my passage from Berlin with the Nazi authorities. The negotiations are tortuous, soul-destroying. I see they enjoy toying with me. Holding out the idea of safe passage tantalisingly to me and then snapping it away. An element of revenge for my writing. To think a few misplaced jokes about Hitler has resulted in this persecution! They are demanding all my property and possessions as the price of my passage. I have offered them my flat in Berlin and the contents of my bank accounts. But they insist I have more to give them in return for my freedom. I do not know why they call it freedom – it is anything but free to get away from here. I can only continue to try to secure their agreement to allow me to leave, regardless of how much it costs. I fear I will arrive in London with just the shirt on my back.

But, darling, this is where I need you to do your part. As you know, I need more than just the Nazis' permission to leave Germany – I also need a permit to enter Britain which would allow me to transit neutral Switzerland. Have you had any measure of success through your contacts at the Foreign Office, or through your family connections, in trying to get me a permit? Please, my darling, get me the entry permit so I can escape from this nightmare.

I cannot wait to see you and hold you in my arms again like last summer. I love you, Karina, with my whole being.

I had better go out now to post you this letter. I see outside the window the shadowy figures across the street again – waiting and watching. I will leave for the Post Office now so I will be back before dark.

I will write soon,

All my love,

Hugo

Karina held the letter close to her heart as her mind began to whirl with thoughts. She couldn't bear thinking of him living with that daily turmoil. She allowed her mind to drift back to last summer, to that wonderful time when she had met him at a house party in

Berlin. She had been immediately mesmerised by him, the handsome author so witty and clever. He was from an old aristocratic family of which he seemed to be the last surviving member. He was ten years her senior and he seemed so worldly and knowledgeable to her. As she had studied German for years and was fluent in the language, she had read his books previously and loved his writing. She was thrilled when she got to meet him in person and even more thrilled to find he was more impressive in person than he was on paper. He was famous for his satirical writing and, before the Nazis came to power, had poked fun at them in his novels. They were now wreaking their revenge by banning his books and making life as difficult as possible for him. After meeting him that first night, he had invited her to his holiday villa in the Alps the very next day where she had spent weeks and weeks – the happiest time of her life.

At the risk of provoking more disapproval from Diana, Karina did not leave her desk for the rest of the afternoon as she typed away furiously, getting through her workload. When five thirty came, the other girls rose to go but Karina did not move.

"Are you not leaving with us, Karina?" asked Vera.

"No, I'm going to stay and catch up on my missed morning's work."

"If some people got to bed at a normal time instead of staying out partying with their fancy friends, they could be home in time for dinner like the rest of us!" said Diana as she walked past Karina.

Vera made a face at Karina before saying, "See you in the morning, Karina."

"Or the afternoon most likely!" called Diana as she walked out of the room.

Karina continued to type until she felt sure they had all left the building. She then got up and marched out of the room. The building was quieter now, empty of most of the nine-hundred-odd employees who worked there. She walked to the top floor and then made her way to a closed door and knocked loudly.

"Come in!" called a voice.

She went in.

"Oh, hello, Karina," said the friendly voice of Alfred Boland, a senior civil servant at the Foreign Office who worked with the immigration branch. Alfred, with his neat grey hair and kindly thin face, looked the very epitome of Foreign Office efficiency.

"Hello, Alfred, sorry for disturbing you." She smiled as she approached his desk "I just wondered – have you any good news for me? Any news at all?" She fidgeted with her hands.

He gestured to her to sit down opposite him and she did as he bid. He studied the beautiful young woman as he smiled at her. Karina Harper had become something of a pest in recent months. Initially, he had been charmed by her and somewhat flattered by the attention he was receiving from the most beautiful girl working at the Foreign Office. Soon, however, he realised Karina Harper had an agenda. She had pursued her friendship with him for the sole purpose of getting a British visa for a friend of hers who lived in Berlin. And Karina Harper knew no shame, Alfred came to realise. Any time he saw her now he tried to duck away into the nearest room or corridor to avoid her. He found it amusing that he would do anything to avoid the company of such a beautiful woman.

"Karina, I spoke to our chaps in Immigration and there are no extenuating circumstances whereby your friend Mr Von Caspars should be given a permit to come here."

"No extenuating circumstances! How can you say that? His writing has been banned by the Nazis and he is too frightened to leave his flat! He is being watched continually by the authorities there!"

"But that is all hearsay ... there is no evidence his life is in danger ... he is not Jewish, is he?"

Karina gave a little shiver. "No, he isn't."

"So he's not in any real danger."

"Real danger! He is a political opponent of the Nazis and spoke out against them in his books and now they are not going to stop until they get their revenge!"

"Well, we looked at Mr Von Caspars' books and he was hardly making big political heavyweight statements against the Nazis, was he? He merely made fun of them."

"But they have no sense of humour over such things!" Karina put her head in her hands in despair.

"Look, we just can't let everybody into the country who wants to come here, Karina! We will capsize into the ocean if we let all the refugees who want to come here in. Each year for the past decade thousands and thousands of people have been coming to escape fascism on the Continent. As if things weren't bad enough with people trying to get away from Mussolini and Hitler, then we had the thousands who came here to escape the Spanish Civil war. We just simply cannot let them all in and priority must be given to any Jews from Germany who are trying to get here as they are the ones in imminent danger."

"But –"

"As I said, your friend is not Jewish and so he is not a priority. As he's a German, we cannot simply allow him to come here when we are on the brink of a war with that country. He could be a spy, a terrorist, a Nazi himself –"

"*How dare you! He is not!*" She was horrified.

"In the past two years we have refused permits to more Germans than any other nation because, quite simply put, *they are our enemy!*" He hit the desk with his hand to emphasise his point.

"Not all of them!"

"Look, even if we managed to wangle a permit to get him here, it would be of no use to him if the Nazis refuse to allow him to leave!"

"But at least if he had the permit from you, there would be nothing preventing him from coming here once he got permission to leave."

"Which may never happen – let us face facts!" said Alfred. He hated pointing out the hard facts to Karina but he now needed to be brutally honest, not just for her sake but for his as well so that she'd stop harassing him over this issue.

Karina stared out the window at the park. The workmen who had been digging trenches all day were now heading home. Now, young couples were walking through the park in the early-evening sunshine, holding hands and looking very much in love.

"Karina – are you alright?" asked Alfred, concerned at the faraway look in her eyes as she stared out the window.

All her carefully laid plans were falling apart for her that day. She had the whole thing mapped out in her mind. Firstly, Sir William would have got her the transfer to Berlin. Then Alfred would have got her the permit for Hugo to come to London. Then she would have travelled to Berlin with the permit for Hugo and would have persuaded her colleagues at the embassy to secure his exit permit from the German authorities. Now, her wonderful plan lay in ruins.

"Karina?"

At last Karina turned to face Alfred and looked at him for a while before she burst out crying.

"Karina – Miss Harper!" said Alfred, looking horrified. He rose to his feet and offered her his clean pressed handkerchief.

"Sorry – I'm so sorry – so sorry," she sobbed as she took the handkerchief and buried her face in it.

"I know this is a bit of a disappointment for you, my dear, but worse things happen at sea," he said, patting her knee.

"You don't understand! I have been left with no option but to throw myself into the Thames tonight!"

"The Thames!" He stepped back from her, aghast.

"Or from a high building, whichever is nearer on my way home." She stifled her sobs.

"But – but – why should you do such a thing?"

"*I'm pregnant!*" she declared before bursting into sobs again.

"Pregnant!" Alfred was dismayed and horrified. "But – but – by – whom?"

She looked up from the handkerchief before nodding tearfully at him.

"Not – not – not this Hugo Von Caspars you are trying to get the permit for?" Alfred was even more horrified.

She nodded before crying loudly again.

"*Shhh-shhh!*" Alfred waved his hands in the air. "People will hear! They will think I'm the daddy when this comes out!"

"I have no option but to kill myself if Hugo is not allowed to come here! I will be ruined – *ruined, I tell you!*"

"Quite so!" Alfred could see the truth of her words.

"And my cousin, Lord Ashton – he will be ruined too by association!"

Alfred shook his head in dismay as he tried figure it all out. "But how many months are you … gone?"

She pulled her jacket protectively around her. "More than I look!"

"But – I do not wish to be impertinent – but how did this occur with the mother in London and the father in Berlin?"

"As I said, I am further gone than I look and – we conceived when we last managed to meet, a while back now … so you see now why I need him to come here as soon as humanly possible to save me from being a fallen and disgraced woman!"

Alfred's face clouded over as he nodded and went back to sit at his desk.

"Yes, it all makes sense now," he said grimly.

He wasn't a fool – he knew when he was being lied to. This man in Berlin, Hugo Von Caspars, clearly was not the father of Karina Harper's child. How could he be? He didn't know when Karina had last seen this Hugo Von Caspars but she was not showing any sign of pregnancy yet. He knew Hugo could not be the father. The real father, whoever he might be, had done a runner and left Karina high and dry with a bun in the oven. He was probably married. This friend of hers in Berlin was obviously willing to step in and marry her to save her from ruin.

He was shocked by Karina Harper – she'd seemed such a nice girl at the beginning. Anyway, the last thing the Foreign Office needed now was a scandal and Karina Harper was about to plunge the department into a huge scandal with an unexplained pregnancy. She would be bringing disrepute on the Foreign Office just at a time when they needed to be above reproach.

He began to write.

One hour later Karina was walking through St James's Park, smiling with delirious happiness and clutching an entry permit for Hugo to come to Britain.

CHAPTER 5

It was late by the time Karina got home so she had no time to waste. She had a quick bath, changed from her sensible tweed work suit into a slinky gold lamé dress and did her hair and make-up.

"Give Julian my love," said her mother as she kissed her goodbye.

Karina raced out the door. Thirty minutes later she was hurrying down to 28a Leicester Square – the 400 Club. Quite simply there was no better club in London and the 400 had been the number-one club for the upper classes for two decades now. No matter how many times Karina swished through the doors into the opulent splendour inside, she still got that familiar thrill – the thrill of the expectation of a wonderful night ahead with old friends, and new friends ready to be made.

The doormen greeted her as if she were an old friend – in fact, she felt like an old friend of theirs at this stage.

Inside, the 18-piece orchestra was playing and impossibly glamorous couples were on the dance floor. At the immaculately set white-linen-cloaked tables she whizzed past were a mixture of the famous, the rich, the beautiful. She spotted an MP with his mistress. A film star with his boyfriend. A tycoon with his wife *and* his mistress sitting on either side of him – rumours of a strange ménage-a-trois followed the three around like an overpowering cologne that refused to fade away. And all three of them looking gloriously happy!

As she spotted her cousin Julian and his gang she waved to them and hurried towards their table. She walked past Royals and

Mitfords and Churchills and Rothschilds and embraced the usual gang with kisses and hugs before collapsing into an art-deco chair and having a glass of champagne placed in her hand. As she looked around at the party which was just getting into full swing, beyond the glamour and the laughing and the dancing there was something else in the air. The feeling was not that the party would go on forever. The feeling was that they were all living on borrowed time. There was an underlying knowledge that the party would soon come to an end and so everybody must squeeze every bit of life out of it while they still could. Most people felt they should already be at war with Germany and it had only been postponed after the Munich Agreement the previous year. There, in the 400 Club each night, the patrons weren't so much enjoying life – they were waiting for the inevitable and trying to fill their minds with enough food and drink and fun and dancing to distract them from what was to come.

As Karina glanced around the gigantic club, recognising the familiar faces, she wondered grimly how many would still be alive in a year's time.

"My darling Karina, I would like to introduce you to a very good friend of mine, Colonel Maurice Fitzherbert – of the Fitzherbert family of Fitzherbert Hall," said Julian.

Karina turned to see a very dashing man of about thirty.

"If you are such a very good friend of Julian's then why have I never met or heard of you before?" she asked with a smile.

"*Aah* – well, that is a very good question!" said Julian, scratching his head.

"Isn't it just?" said Karina, wondering if Maurice Fitzherbert could come back with a witty reply.

"Well, you do not need to know somebody very long to become a very good friend, do you? I mean to say – you can become a very good friend to somebody within just an hour if the chemistry is right," said Maurice Fitzherbert of the Fitzherbert family of Fitzherbert Hall.

Karina nodded in surprised agreement. "What a very good and truthful answer!"

"In the hope then that we too may become very good friends in a very short space of time – may I have this dance?" he asked, holding out his hand to her.

"Of course," she said, smiling and taking his hand as she stood up.

Julian's mother and Karina's father had been brother and sister. It had been quite a coup for the Harper family for one of them to marry Lord Ashton. Everyone had expected her father to make a similar match. But he hadn't. He had not married into the peerage but had followed his heart. Even though Karina was one of the golden circle, she felt like an outsider after they lost their estate in Ireland. None of them made her feel like a poor relation, but that was what she was. That was why Julian, with her own mother's encouragement, was always trying to set her up with the likes of Maurice Fitzherbert. Marriage to such a man would bring the family back to its rightful position and re-establish the status quo. But, as Julian watched Maurice twirl Karina around the dance floor, he knew nothing would come of it. No matter how many eligible and dashing young men he introduced Karina to, nothing ever came of it and she seemed blind or just not interested in how many of them were in love with her.

It was two in the morning when the party arrived back at Julian's four-storey over-basement townhouse in Belgravia. There were eight of them in total as they noisily walked through the large white tiled foyer and into the spacious parlour where the butler and his footmen had, as usual, left out a fantastic spread of caviar, canapés, chocolates and bonbons.

"Who's for champagne?" asked Julian as he grabbed the bottle from the ice bucket and began to open it.

"Stupid question, Julian! I imagine everyone is!" said Karina as she spread some caviar on a cracker. "I'm famished!" She ate the caviar while eyeing up the chocolates selection.

"*Eat, drink and be merry – for tomorrow we die!*" cried Roger, who was busy putting music on the gramophone.

"Oh, really, Roger! That's such a crass thing to say!" snapped Karina angrily.

"Why? It's probably true!" replied Roger as he grabbed one of the girls and started dancing with her.

"Why do you have to be so flippant all the time?" demanded Karina, her anger not abating.

Roger ignored her as the others began dancing too.

"I think I've just lost my appetite," said Karina to Julian as she turned her back on the table of food.

"In that case, would you like to dance, Karina?" asked Maurice Fitzherbert who sidled up beside her.

She shook her head politely. "No, thank you, Maurice. I think I need some air."

Julian and Maurice exchanged worried looks as they watched Karina head towards the French door that led out to the terrace.

Half an hour later Karina was still out on the terrace smoking a cigarette as she gazed across the London skyline.

Inside the party was showing no sign of slowing as the dancing and high jinks continued.

The door opened behind her and she turned to see it was Julian. He closed the door behind him and came and stood beside her. He too gazed out across the skyline in the warm August night as he reached into his pocket and retrieved his silver cigarette case. Taking a cigarette, he perched it in his mouth and lit it with his gold-plated lighter.

"Has your appetite returned yet?" he asked.

"No!" she said as she took a drag from her cigarette.

"Well, the food is going to go to waste if you don't get in there soon and dig in! Whatever about dying tomorrow I wager there's a good chance there will be rationing once war is declared so we might not be seeing caviar and chocolate for quite some time!"

"I just do not understand how people can treat this whole horrible mess in a flippant way!"

"Well, we often disguise our true feelings through humour, do we not? I wager Roger is more terrified than anyone about there being a war and certainly terrified of dying. He is simply trying to hide it behind bravado."

"I suppose – poor Roger!" She glanced back through the French door at Roger who was dancing exuberantly.

"But it's not just what Roger said that has you so perturbed, is it?"

"No." She shook her head.

"Is it your friend in Berlin again?"

"Yes," she said, nodding. "It's three months now and I have heard nothing from him. I don't know if he's getting my letters ... I don't know if he's dead or alive! The last letter told me he was being followed continuously and his flat watched. I am beside myself with worry!" Her voice cracked a little.

"I know, darling." He nodded sympathetically. She had kept him informed of the situation to such an extent that he wondered why she didn't realise she was continually repeating the same story to him. "I'm afraid I've got nowhere trying to get him a permit to come to Britain either. I've tried all my contacts in the House of Lords and the Commons too. But there is such resistance to letting anyone in these days – particularly a German. Exceptions only being made for Jewish people, particularly children, as you have seen in the press. Have you managed to do anything through the Foreign Office?"

"Ah, but I made progress today! Quite a lot actually," she said, looking excited. "I managed to get him a permit to come to Britain!"

"But that's amazing! How did you manage it?" Julian was astonished at her achievement.

"I was very bold! I pretended I was pregnant by Hugo to one of my bosses and that we simply had to get Hugo to London in order for him to marry me – to save not just my reputation but also the reputation of the Foreign Office and the whole damned Empire if it came down to it!" Karina managed to look both delighted and ashamed of herself at the same time.

"But that's quite ... staggering!"

"Isn't it just?" Karina giggled like a bold schoolgirl.

Julian was not really surprised by this latest stunt Karina had pulled. She was very singleminded when she put her mind to something. Julian, like the rest of the Ashton family, was very concerned about this relationship with a German man she had got herself mixed up in. If ever there a good time to be getting mixed up with a German, this was certainly not it! What's more, the man in question seemed to be mired in political intrigue according to Karina. But at least Hugo wasn't a Nazi, Julian mused. Fortunately, Karina seemed to be avoiding going down the route of that Mitford girl in that way.

"Well, I had to do something drastic after my application to go work at the embassy in Berlin was turned down," said Karina.

"Your application!" Julian's mouth dropped open in shock. "You cannot be serious, Karina! You were not seriously thinking of going to Berlin at this time? On the brink of war!"

"Of course I was! And I still would if I could! I have to get this permit to Hugo!"

"Can you not simply post it to him?"

"Oh, don't be so stupid, Julian! Are you not listening to a word I'm saying?" She was becoming exasperated. "I do not know if he is still at his flat – he is not replying to my letters! In fact, he must not be there. I will have to go there and find him!"

"Yes, of course I see!" said Julian as he studied her beautiful face which seemed lost in thought again. He broke his heart to see her wasting her best years on this man who she could not even be with. She hadn't even given Maurice Fitzherbert a second look all night even though he was making doe-eyes at her.

"I just have to get to Berlin to give him the permit and help acquire his exit permit from the German government."

"Well, what are the chances of that? How you possibly arrange to get him an exit permit? The Nazis aren't letting anyone leave, are they?"

"They are, but it's based on a lot of negotiation and money ... money we don't have."

"Well, I'd like to help, Karina, but we are still paying the death duties after Papa went. And Ashton Hall needs a new roof – a whole new roof! The leaks are so bad now it's like taking a shower every time one goes to the top floor!"

"Oh, I wouldn't dream of taking money from you! You and your family have been so good to Mama and me over the years. I couldn't ask for anything more."

Julian was deep in thought for a while.

"But I tell you what I can do!" he said then. "I shall contact my good friend Eric Von Vassel who lives in Berlin. Eric was up at Oxford with me and he's a jolly good fellow – one of ours. And I will get him to go to Hugo's flat and find out what the blazes is going on."

Karina's face lit up with relief and delight. "Oh, could you, Julian? Do you really think he would?"

"Of course he will. Eric has never let me down!"

She jumped into his arms and kissed him. "Oh, thank you, Julian! Thank you so much! I've even got my appetite back. Let's go in and have some of that caviar and chocolate!"

She linked his arm and they went back inside.

CHAPTER 6

Karina sat at her desk as she and the other secretaries typed away furiously. Mrs Potter, the administration manager, walked in holding a huge volume of papers. She walked down the aisle between the two rows of desks, plonking a large wad of paperwork on each desk. Minutes from meetings, proposals, letters that all needed to be typed up. It was just the constant avalanche of paperwork that descended on the office each day.

"Thank you, Mrs Potter," said Karina as she was handed an encyclopaedia of daily work.

"Oh, and this is your itinerary for the Irish convention next week which Sir William spoke to you about, Miss Harper," said Mrs Potter in her clipped, precise accent as she handed over a sheet of paper.

Karina took the paper and began to read through it as Mrs Potter continued dishing out her paperwork.

"Sorry – excuse me, Mrs Potter!" said Karina, looking up in confusion.

"Yes, Miss Harper?"

"This itinerary – it says the convention is to take place in Oxfordshire – in Great Hankerton Hall!"

"What of it?" asked Mrs Potter impatiently.

"Am I expected to go to Oxfordshire?"

"Unless you have managed the task of taking notes from a couple of hundred miles away, then I expect you are, Miss Harper!" Mrs Potter's voice dripped sarcasm which caused all the girls to burst out laughing.

"But Sir William never said anything about going to Oxfordshire when he spoke to me about this. He suggested I may have to attend a couple of social functions as well – but that was it! I can't possibly go to Oxfordshire for a week! I just can't!"

"Why? Are you frightened the 400 Club won't survive without your patronage for that length of time, Karina?" asked Diana with a smirk, causing the girls to burst out laughing again.

"*Silence!*" snapped Mrs Potter loudly, bringing the room to an immediate quiet. "In case none of you realise, I must point out that we are about to go to war with the Germans and so I really find there is nothing to laugh about at this moment! Miss Harper, I really do not have time to discuss your social diary – but may I remind you – in the words of Lord Kitchener in the last war – your country needs you! And if we are asking our young men to go to the Continent where they most likely will get shot and killed or horribly wounded as they try to liberate the world from Nazi tyranny, then it is not too much to ask of you to travel up the road to Oxfordshire to spend a week in a stately home – am I correct?"

"Yes, Mrs Potter," said Karina demurely.

Mrs Potter had an amazing ability to make whoever she addressed feel humbled and contrite.

"One o'clock, girls – off to lunch with you! And please be back by two. May I remind you we are struggling against the biggest menace the world has faced since the Ottoman Empire's invasion of Christendom several centuries ago!"

"Yes, Mrs Potter!" said the girls in unison.

They stood and began to file out.

Karina sat at her desk, looking at the itinerary in dismay.

"Poor Karina!" said Vera. "Try to make the best of it – as Mrs Potter says, worse things can happen than a week in a beautiful stately home."

"I wouldn't care as a rule, but I have so much I am trying to organise at the moment and I don't have much time to get it all done," sighed Karina.

Vera looked around and then bent down and lowered her voice. "Word to the wise, Karina – keep your door locked at night! Sir

William has a reputation – if you get my meaning! Don't let that wife and seven children he has buried away in Surrey deceive you – he is a notorious womaniser!"

"Good Lord!" Karina was even more dismayed.

"And don't allow yourself to be left alone with him if you can help it – if he suggests you go out to dinner alone as it's easier to takes notes that way – avoid – avoid – *avoid*! I'm sure your excellent shorthand and beautiful handwriting are the reasons being cited for your being chosen to cover the meetings with the Irish. But I imagine Sir William is more interested in your body than your handwriting!"

Karina rolled her eyes to heaven in disgust.

"As we used to say in the Girl Guides – be prepared!" said Vera. "Wearing two pairs of bloomers at all times is what is required, I daresay! Best of luck!" She stood to attention and made a salute before she turned and marched out the door to join the others.

Just then a porter came bounding in and handed Karina a crisp white envelope. "A note delivered to you from Lord Ashton's footman, Miss Harper."

"Oh, thank you, Jimmy," said Karina, taking the envelope from him. Tearing the envelope open, she read the note inside.

Darling Karina,
Can you drop by the house in Belgravia this evening?
Love and Kisses,
Julian

Julian's butler opened the front door when Karina knocked.

"Good evening, Miss Harper," he said as Karina rushed in past him.

"Good evening, is His Lordship in the parlour?"

"No – the drawing room, Miss Harper."

"Oh!" Karina changed direction and hurried to the drawing room which was at the back of the house.

She swung open the door and saw Julian standing at the window, staring out at the back garden.

"Julian! Have you any news? I received your note – have you heard anything from Eric?" She was so anxious and excited that she had dismissed the thought that Julian might have wanted to see her about a completely different matter.

"Darling Karina!" He crossed over to her and hugged her.

"Is it about Eric? Is that why you wanted to see me?"

"Yes." He went over to the drinks cabinet and began to pour some Scotch.

"I don't want a drink, Julian! Will you just tell me – have you any news about Hugo?"

He came back to her and handed her a crystal tumbler of whisky.

"Take it, darling," he insisted.

She took the glass and he led her over to the wine-coloured chesterfield couch where they both sat down.

"Julian! You are making me nervous! Did your friend Eric go to Hugo's flat – yes or no?" she demanded.

"Yes," he said, before knocking back his whisky in one go.

"*And?*"

"It's bad news, old girl, the worst really … I don't know how to say it so I had better just spit it out … Hugo's dead, darling … has been for several weeks … that's why he wasn't writing back to you … there was no answer at the door when Eric called to the flat of the address you gave me … so he spoke to the neighbours who said Hugo had been killed. A road accident … he was crossing the street, the one where he lived and a motorcar knocked him down … he literally didn't know what hit him … instant death … didn't feel a thing … if you have to go, there's worse ways, I suppose."

Karina stared out the window at the back garden as if she were in a trance.

"I'm sorry, darling … so sorry," said Julian as he reached out for her, took her in his arms and stroked her hair.

"It's my fault … all my fault …"

"No! How can it be your fault?" demanded Julian.

"I should have tried harder to get him out – to get the entry permit – he was begging me to get it – what kept me so long?"

"They are impossible to get, darling – impossible!"

"I got it this week, didn't I? If I got it then, I could have got it three months ago or even before."

"But even if you got it, he still had to get the exit permit and it was unlikely he would! No use blaming yourself – you did everything you could to help the man, dammit!"

"I loved him – I would have done anything for him!" The tears started streaming down her face.

"Just a terrible, horrible, unfortunate accident – nobody is to blame," said Julian.

"*That was no accident!*" said Karina, suddenly pulling back from him. "*That was murder!* That motorcar meant to kill Hugo and ran him over! He was being watched and followed all the time! The Nazis wanted him gone because he had criticised them and had worked against them. That's what they do – get rid of people who speak against them!" She took her whisky glass and downed the drink in one.

"There's no evidence of that, darling."

"I don't need evidence – I have his letters – he was terrified for his life, being watched all the time. I know they killed him – they murdered him."

CHAPTER 7

Gabriel had arrived in London with the rest of the Irish delegation and was ensconced in Claridge's Hotel. The conference was due to take place at Great Hankerton Hall, some stately pile down the country and they were due to travel down there the next day. Gabriel had gone through his paperwork that afternoon, before he had gone for a wander around the city, admiring the architecture and looking through Harrods and the other stores.

That evening he had dinner with the other delegates and then everyone retired to their bedrooms at ten. But, as he sat in his hotel room he suddenly felt very restless and found himself wandering down to the bar and ordering himself a cocktail. As he sat on his own at the bar, he had this feeling of yearning to do something different – a yearning for excitement. He had London at his feet and he was suddenly determined to see some of it that night.

He beckoned to the barman.

"Another cocktail, please, and could you recommend some good clubs I can go to tonight?"

It was eleven o'clock that night and Karina poured another whisky into her glass from the decanter.

"Steady on that stuff, old girl. You'll have a thumping headache in the morning," warned Julian.

"Good! I want a thumping headache! I want the headache to thump so loud that I can't even hear my own thoughts," she said as she drank back the whisky.

Julian stood up and walked over to her. He placed his hands on her shoulders.

"Look, Karina, this is terrible – the worst news you could have received. But you are a young, beautiful, intelligent woman and there is a whole life for you to lead. You tried your best for Hugo but now he's gone – but you are still here and you cannot waste any more of your life on this man and this – tragic love affair you entered into."

"*Waste?* I wasn't *wasting* my life on Hugo! I love him! I … loved him … how can I explain it to you who have never been in love? You who see relationships as a commodity to be traded one way or the other!"

"There's no need to be cruel, Karina," said Julian, looking hurt.

Karina blinked back tears. "I'm sorry, you are right, there is no need to be cruel … especially to you, Julian, who have always been such a good friend to me and went out of your way to find out what happened to Hugo for me. I'm just taking out my pain on the nearest person to me … don't take it personally … I think I'd like to go home now."

"Why don't you stay the night here, Karina?"

"No, I really just need my own bed tonight … if you could get your butler to call me a taxi?"

"My driver will drop you home, Karina."

"No, he's probably gone to bed already and there's no need to wake him when I can just get a taxi. A taxi will be fine, thank you, my dear lovely sweet Julian!",

She reached for him and embraced him tightly as she started to cry again.

Karina sat in the back of the taxi, looking out the window. She felt a little dizzy from the alcohol she'd consumed. She could not comprehend the news she had heard and realised she should not have started drinking whisky to alleviate the hurt. And now she felt she needed more alcohol to numb the pain. She needed to be somewhere lively and full of people to distract her from what had happened – even if it was only for a couple of hours. She'd had to

get away from Julian as she could not take his sympathy anymore
and his well-intentioned but ridiculous words of comfort. Julian
had never been in love, that was the truth of it as she had said
earlier. He had no idea what love felt like and what it meant to
have that love stolen.

As the taxi neared her home, she couldn't bear going through
the door into the loneliness of her bedroom. She was sure as soon
as she was alone what had happened to Hugo would hit her and
the pain would be too much to bear.

She tapped the taxi driver on the shoulder.

"Yes, love?"

"Turn around – change of destination – take me to Leicester
Square," she instructed.

She had worn a black dress to work that day and she was
grateful she had as it managed not to look out of place in the 400
when she arrived in. A tweed suit would not have fitted in.

The club was busy as usual. She had never done this before –
arrived into the club without a prior arrangement to meet somebody.
But she was sure she would bump into somebody she knew. She was
hardly in the door when she spotted a friend and went over to join
his table for drinks.

To anybody looking on, Karina looked as if she was having a
ball that night. She went from table to table chatting with different
people, dancing with different men. She could not sit still for a
second because, if she did, she would have to face the awfulness of
what had happened and her world would come crashing down.

To Gabriel looking on, that's how she looked initially – as if she
was having a ball. And she looked to be the belle of the ball. He had
spotted her as soon as she had arrived – the tall, strikingly beautiful
woman who strode through the club as if she owned it. He could
not keep his eyes off her and he became intrigued by her. For as he
studied her intently, behind the smiles and the laughter there seemed
to be a huge sadness that she was disguising. He would catch her
every so often staring off into the distance, looking heartbroken, and
then she would quickly snap out of it and come back to reality.

* * *

As the night wore on, the club began to empty of people. Karina begged her friends to stay longer – just one more drink, one more dance – but they all drifted off after a while.

Another Martini arrived for her as she sat at a booth. She lifted it up and took a sip.

"Do you mind if I join you?" came a voice and she looked up to see a strikingly handsome man standing there.

"Do I know you?"

"No."

"Then why should you want to join me? And why should I want you to join me for that matter?" He looked a little different from the usual types there, a little more ruggedly handsome than the Oxbridge types who populated the 400 Club as a rule.

"Well, because you're on your own and I'm on my own – I'm visiting the city on business – and both of us look as if we aren't ready to go home just yet."

"Where are you from?" she asked.

"Dublin," he said, taking the question as consent from her to join her and sitting down at the booth.

"Oh, I see!" she said and raised her eyes to heaven. She should have known he was Irish but his accent was much less pronounced than that of the Irish she remembered who worked in the house at Inishwood.

"Is there a problem with that?"

"Being Irish? Well, actually there is –" She stopped herself as she was about to give a long litany of personal and political reasons why there were very many problems with being Irish. She didn't need a political discussion that night or to divulge to a stranger the woes of her family's past – that was the last thing she needed. She needed a distraction from her present pain. And he looked as if he could fit the bill.

"No, nothing at all wrong with being Irish," she said.

"Have you ever been to Ireland?"

"No, but I hear it's divine in July! The rain stops for a couple of days then, I understand!" Her voice was dripping sarcasm.

"You should visit," he said.

"I'm afraid I've just missed the dry season. I'll have to wait for next year!"

He studied her and tried to figure out if she was being serious.

"Do you work?" he asked.

"Yes, I work in –" she quickly thought of an alter ego, "Harrods! Perfume counter ... drop in and I'll give you a discount on a present for your wife back in Dublin."

"Oh, I'm not married," he said, thinking about Siobhán.

"Well, that's convenient."

"For whom?"

"For both of us!" she said, finishing her Martini.

"I'm over here on business ..." He was about to say he worked for a brewery as he couldn't possibly divulge the real reason he was there to anybody.

"I'm really not interested – sorry, I didn't catch your name?"

"Gabriel."

"I'm really not interested, Gabriel. All I'm interested in is ... are you a good dancer?"

"I am."

She stood up and offered him her arm.

Standing up, he took it and escorted her out onto the dance floor.

Karina was pleased to find out he was indeed a good dancer. An hour went by and she still had no desire to go and sit down. She just wanted to stay there on the dance floor with this man forever. She felt if she left the dance floor that would be it and she would have to face Hugo's death. As the music became slower, they danced closely together. She found this man – Gabriel – incredibly attractive and she wasn't sure why. It might be that he was Irish and being with him transported her back to the comfort of her upbringing at Inishwood. It might be because he wasn't part of her circle. It might be because she was feeling vulnerable and terribly lonely. It might be because of all the alcohol she had consumed. Despite all the men that had come on to her, she had not entertained one of them. Her loyalty was completely with

Hugo and she would not dream of being unfaithful to him. But now Hugo was gone and she desperately wanted somebody there for the night. She did not want to be on her own that night. And this man was not from her circle – nobody would ever know. He would be going back to Ireland and she would never have to see him again. For once in her life, for just one night, she could do what the hell she wanted and face reality tomorrow.

As she held him close and buried her head in his jacket, tears were trickling down her face.

"Where are you staying?" she asked.

"Claridge's."

"Would you like – would you like me to go back there with you?"

Gabriel stopped dancing and looked down at her.

"Well, would you or wouldn't you? Don't waste my time."

As he tried to fathom her, he was shocked by her proposal. And yet the offer was so tempting. But he was engaged to Siobhán …

"Have you been crying?" he asked, concerned.

"Oh, for goodness' sake!" she said before turning and storming off the dance floor.

He stared after her and saw she had grabbed her jacket and was leaving. He hurried after her as she walked out the door.

Outside, he saw her walking down Leicester Square.

"Wait!" he shouted as he raced to catch up with her.

"Too late! You missed your chance! A once in a lifetime chance!" she said as she marched on.

"Will you wait? I don't even know your name!" He grabbed her arm and swung her around to face him.

They stared at each other for a few seconds and suddenly were kissing passionately.

CHAPTER 8

Gabriel held his hotel-room door open as he turned on the light.

Karina walked in and looked around the spacious art-deco room. After kissing passionately for what seemed like forever on Leicester Square they had shared a taxi in silence back to Claridge's. Now, in the hushed luxury of his hotel room, they both felt awkward.

"Drink?" he asked as he lifted up the decanter of sherry.

"No, thank you," she said as she took off her jacket and sat down on the bed.

He poured himself a sherry and watched her sitting there, resting her head on her right hand.

He came and sat beside her and took a sip of his drink.

"You don't look like much of a sherry man," she said.

"I'm not! But it's all they left in the room."

She reached for his glass, took it and finished off the contents before placing it on the beside locker. They stared at each other and then she leaned in and they began to kiss again.

She could vaguely hear traffic outside in the hushed quietness of the hotel's luxury.

She suddenly pulled back.

"Is anything the matter?" he asked.

"I'm sorry … I think I've made a terrible mistake … I shouldn't have come here tonight. I don't know what I was thinking of." Tears sprang to her eyes.

He looked at her, perplexed. "Are you in some kind of trouble?"

"No." She shook her head as she started to cry. "I just received some terrible news today and I seem to be ... lost."

He looked at her and leaned towards her, putting his arm around her. "Do you want to talk about it?"

She shook her head. "It's too painful."

He nodded as he stroked her back.

"That's why I came here – to try and the numb the pain. I'm sorry – I think I was planning on using you."

"That's alright – feel free to use me as much as you want!" He smirked at her.

She looked at him and managed to laugh through her tears. He handed her a handkerchief and she dabbed her eyes before handing it back to him.

She studied him. "You're incredibly attractive," she said. "If I had met you at a different time under different circumstances ..."

He nodded. "Will I ask the concierge to get you a taxi?"

"No, he most likely knows me and it wouldn't look right for me to be leaving the hotel at this time of the night. I can just get one out on the street."

"I'll walk you down," he said, standing up.

"There is no need. I can find my own way," she said. "Stay."

"If you insist?"

She turned to go and then looked back.

"Thank you," she said.

"For what?"

"For being so understanding." She leaned into him and he put his arms around her again.

"I like your cologne – it's very comforting," she said.

"Really? I had hoped it was irresistibly masculine," he joked.

She giggled as she put her arm around his back and held him tightly. The tears began to slip down her face again.

He sat her down on the bed again and held her close.

Soon her eyelids were getting heavy and she was nodding off to sleep.

Karina blinked a few times and looked around before sitting up quickly. She recognised the art-deco bedroom of Claridge's and her memories came back flooding back ... going to the 400 Club ...

meeting the stranger ... coming back to the hotel with him ... deciding to go ...

She'd had every intention of going home ... but had fallen asleep in his arms ... and when she had woken an hour later one thing had led to another ...

She looked at the sleeping form of the stranger lying beside her. She put her hand to her forehead and shook her head quickly before slipping out of the bed and gathering her silk underwear which had been cast unceremoniously on the thick-pile carpet the night before. She quickly gathered her other clothing, slipped into the bathroom and began to dress. She looked at the huge mirror embedded over the sink in the black-and-white-tiled bathroom. She looked dreadful. Looking at her watch, she saw it was half past six in the morning. She tied back her hair and then tiptoed from the bathroom across the thick carpet to the door. She took one look back at the sleeping form of the stranger before quickly exiting.

Avoiding the lift in case she might bump into somebody there, she used the staircase and raced down to the foyer. She glanced around the corner and was grateful to find she did not know the concierge and luckily there was no doorman there yet. She walked confidently through the foyer with her head held high.

"Good morning, miss," said the concierge as she marched past him.

"Good morning," she said aloofly, trying to disguise her embarrassment.

"Would you like me to call a taxi for you?"

"I'm quite alright, thank you," she said as she quickly disappeared out the front door. Outside on the street, it was just becoming bright and the air was cool. She looked around and then set off down the street.

As she walked she didn't notice the man stepping out from a doorway and following her.

Karina put her key in the front door of their house and let herself in. The familiar smell of bacon was coming from the kitchen.

"Karina? Is that you? I've just put breakfast on. I didn't hear you come back last night so assumed you had stayed at Julian's."

Penny came out of the kitchen, drying her hands on a towel. She stopped short when she saw her daughter and how upset she looked.

"Karina! What's happened?"

"Oh, Mama, he's dead – Hugo is dead!"

Karina raced into her mother's arms.

Karina lay on her bed while Penny stroked her hair.

"It's a terrible shock for you, darling. I will telephone your work and say you can't go in today," said Penny.

"I just can't believe it. Although I knew something must have happened when he wasn't replying to my letters."

Karina was so distraught that Penny was filled with concern for her.

"I know it might be hard to believe now, Karina, but you will get over this. You will move on – you will find somebody else and life will get better again."

"I never want to meet anybody ever again," said Karina, but then she immediately felt guilt over the man she had met last night.

"You are young – you have your whole life ahead of you."

"That's what Julian said."

"He's a wise boy, I always said it. Look what we have been through in the past – after what happened at Inishwood, I thought we would never be able to rebuild our lives."

"And is this what rebuilding our lives is like – *this* – compared to what we lost at Inishwood?" Karina gestured to their modest surroundings.

"We were lucky to get out of Inishwood with our lives. I know this isn't much, but at least we are alive and you have a real chance of becoming somebody again ... by playing our connections correctly."

"I can't even think of the future right now when the present is so painful," said Karina as she started crying again.

"Oh darling!" said Penny as she hugged her daughter tightly.

That night, as Karina prepared for bed, she felt emotionally exhausted and desperate for sleep. She kept seeing Hugo's face in front of her, smiling at her, and tried not to break down crying again.

She went over to the window to close the curtains. As she was about to draw them she spotted a man across the road under a streetlight. There was a fog that evening and it swirled around the figure. She wondered momentarily what he was doing there and squinted against the pane of glass.

He suddenly turned and disappeared into the fog.

Penny suggested that Karina take the next day off as well, but Karina insisted on going in to work. She had the Irish convention coming up and she knew there would be much preparation needed for that. Also, if the truth be told, she needed to be distracted. She couldn't bear spending another day at home staring at the walls. It was for the same reason she had gone to the 400 Club the night after she heard the news, the same reason she had gone back to the hotel with that stranger. She knew she should feel mortified for having done what she did with the stranger – and ashamed of herself. Should feel it showed lack of morals and also disrespect for Hugo. But she didn't look at it like that and she knew Hugo didn't look at life like that at all. He had liberated her from all that bourgeois guilt and dictation of how to behave rightly and wrongly. Karina knew what was right and wrong and did not get caught up on the details. She had needed a distraction in a terrible moment of pain and found one with that Irishman.

As the bus passed Hyde Park, she looked out at the workmen digging more trenches in the park and she allowed herself to think of the stranger she had met at the 400 Club. Gabriel – that was what he said his name was. She'd had a lot to drink that night but she remembered him being incredibly handsome. And he had been very kind and sweet. She imagined they had nothing in common and were from completely different backgrounds and class even – but he had been just what she had needed that night. Little would she ever have thought that an Irishman, after all the pain and anguish that country had caused her and her family, would have rescued her when she felt at such a low ebb.

She got up and quickly descended the steps of the bus as it neared her stop.

CHAPTER 9

When Karina walked into the office, the other secretaries were already seated typing away.

"Oh, here she is! So gracious of Karina to grace us with her presence today!" said Diana.

Karina ignored her, took off her jacket, sat down and began to sort out the paperwork that had been left for her.

"Nice to get a day off without any notice! I wish my conscience allowed me to call in sick whenever I felt like it!" said Diana.

"Not today, Diana, please," said Karina firmly.

"Of course if *I* was out in the 400 Club each and every night like some people, I'm sure I wouldn't be hard pressed to show up to work either!"

"*Diana!*" shouted Karina, turning to face her. "Will you ever give the rest of us a break and just shut up for ten minutes! Ten minutes! That's all I ask for – to hear no words coming from that mouth of yours which, unless it has a slice of cake in it which to be fair is quite often, never stops from incessantly and needlessly talking!"

The whole room went quiet as everyone stopped typing.

"*Oh – oh – oh* – I have never been so insulted in all my life!" said a shocked Diana.

"Really? *Really?* I find it hard to believe you have not been insulted at least twice as much with a mouth as provocative and obnoxious as yours!"

"*Oh – oh!*"

"So if I could just give you some advice for the future and

repeat that marvellous phrase: *silence is golden!* And while I am in process of giving you advice – for goodness' sake, Diana, stop wearing black every blessed day! It makes you look washed out!"

"*Oh!*" said Diana and burst out crying.

"*Karina!*" Vera rushed to console Diana.

"*Miss Harper – if I can speak to you right now!*" came Mrs Potter's stern voice and Karina looked up to see her standing angrily in the doorway.

"For fuck's sake!" said Karina under her breath.

As she left the room she could hear Diana say through her sobs, "She's a bitch, that Karina Harper! A right bitch! And she's always been jealous of me – right from the moment she came here to work!"

Karina raised her eyes to heaven as she followed the administration manager down the corridor.

Mrs Potter swung around to face her. "I heard all that, Miss Harper, every last word! Do you honestly think that now is the time to be giving Diana fashion advice when we could be invaded by the Nazis at any given minute?"

"No, Mrs Potter," said Karina with a sigh. "I just find her extremely aggravating!"

"Perhaps if you didn't hold yourself superior to the other girls, they might not judge you quite so harshly!"

"I do not hold myself superior to them!"

"I don't know why you came to work here, Karina, but certainly it isn't for the love of typing! I've heard all about you – canvassing behind the scenes, trying to get permits for a friend in Berlin and looking for transfers there. I wouldn't be surprised if you were a Nazi yourself – all you upper-class girls are!"

"Do I really have to listen to this nonsense?" said Karina, folding her arms in annoyance.

"I have a good mind to request you be taken off the Irish convention in Oxfordshire – but I can't spare the time to have you replaced!"

"Oh, please do – if you can replace me I'd be delighted!" said Karina.

"Go back to your desk, Miss Harper, and start typing!" ordered Mrs Potter.

"Sorry, Miss Harper!" came a voice.

It was Jimmy the porter.

"A telegram for you!"

"Thank you, Jimmy," said Karina, taking the telegram.

"*A telegram!* Could I ask you to please stop using the porters at the Foreign Office as your social secretaries! Thank you!" said Mrs Potter as she marched off.

Karina walked down the corridor and stopped at one of the wide Georgian windows there that looked out over St James's Park. She often got notes delivered to her workplace about different social events, but rarely a telegram.

It read:

BERLIN

MISS KARINA HARPER

I AM LEAVING THE FLAT IN THE MORNING BEFORE IT IS TOO LATE. I AM GOING TO WHEN WE FIRST MET. POST NOT SAFE.

HUGO

Karina stared down at the telegram in shock. She felt the room spin and everything go black before she felt to the floor.

"*Karina! Karina!*" came a voice.

Suddenly she inhaled a horrendous smell and jolted awake.

She opened her eyes and looked up to see all the secretaries and a couple of the porters gathered around her in a circle.

"Smelling salts! They work every time! I've been carrying a bottle of the stuff ever since I was in the Girl Guides!" said Vera proudly, as she popped her bottle of smelling salts back into her handbag.

"Karina? Karina, you fainted!" said Mrs Potter, whose voice sounded unusually gentle.

"If I were a betting gal, I'd wager it was alcohol-induced! She must be a floating gin palace by now!" said Diana.

Karina blinked a few times and sat up.

"The telegram! Where is the telegram?" she demanded, struggling to her feet.

Pushing the others out of the way, she began to look frantically around until she spotted a paper on the floor and shakily bent down to get it.

She held the telegram in her hands and read it again.

"Hugo! He's alive!" she whispered.

With that, she ran off down the corridor and down the stairs.

"We really are going to have to do something about that girl!" muttered Mrs Potter.

Karina rushed past the butler at Julian's Belgravia home.

"He's in the parlour!" announced the butler as she ignored him and swung open the parlour doors.

Julian was sitting at the desk writing a letter.

"Good Lord, Karina, are you alright?"

"He's alive, Julian, he's alive! I got this telegram from Hugo. It came to the Foreign Office for me today – and look! He's alive!"

Julian picked up the telegram and read it.

"How could this happen? How did your friend Eric get the wrong information? Oh, but, Julian, he's alive!" She clasped her hands together in joy.

"But it can't be, it just can't. Somebody's idea of a practical joke, I'd say." He went crumple up the telegram.

"*Don't!*" she cried, prising it from him. "What are you *doing*?"

"I just don't like somebody making a fool of you, Karina. Hugo is dead –"

"Well, clearly he isn't!" she said, waving the telegram in the air.

"But a telegram can be sent from anybody to anybody. I could send a telegram and sign myself off as the Aga Khan if the mood so took me –"

"Oh, don't be ridiculous – who would do such a crazy thing? And nobody even knows about me in Berlin."

"Oh really? What about all those letters you sent to his flat that have probably fallen into the hands of goodness knows who? You probably mentioned everything about yourself – where you work, who your family are – a very, *very* dangerous thing to do in these sinister times."

"Julian, I want to know who your friend Eric spoke to in the building where Hugo lives – who were the neighbours who told him Hugo had been killed?"

"I'm really not going to bother Eric with this matter again, Karina. He's far too busy and he's already done what he can."

"But – do you not realise the agony I have been going through this past couple of days? For nothing! Hugo is still alive!" She waved the telegram again.

"Hugo's dead, Karina! Get it into your head!" Julian was becoming uncharacteristically angry.

"Stop saying that, Julian!" she said, becoming angry too. "Who is this friend if yours in Berlin anyway? How do you know him?"

"He's just a friend from Oxford."

"So James knows him then? And Sebastian? And Simon too? You were all in Oxford together."

He sat there is silence.

"Julian! Will you answer me, damn you? What is going on?"

He heaved a huge sigh and didn't answer.

She waited, glaring at him.

He sighed again. "Karina … I didn't send Eric to the flat where Hugo lives … I didn't send anybody," he said, his voice low and tired. "I do know an Eric in Berlin but I haven't spoken to him in years and he would never have got into Oxford – not with his grammar."

Karina recoiled in confusion. "But I don't understand – how did you know then about the accident and Hugo being supposedly killed?"

"I made it up," said Julian with a sigh,

"*Made it up!*" Her eyes widened in horror.

"I just could not bear seeing you waste any more of your life on this man who – I'm sorry to say it, Karina – is most probably dead anyway! I don't believe for a second that telegram came from him – where's he been for the past three months if it is?"

"Where's he been? *Well, not in a grave anyway having been knocked down by a motorcar!*" Karina's voice rose so loudly it cracked. "Julian! How could you do such a thing to me? I have been …" tears sprang to her eyes, "*heartbroken* this past couple of days."

"I did it for your own good!"

"My own good?"

"Maurice Fitzherbert was the last straw!" snapped Julian angrily. "He is the last in a long line of eligible, handsome rich men I have introduced you to that you have turned your nose up at without a second thought!"

"But if I was that desperate to find an eligible husband, I'd place a personal ad in the *Evening Standard*! That is not your role in my life, Julian – to marry me off!" She was aghast.

"But, darling, at twenty-nine you'll soon be turning the wrong side of thirty and it will be all over for you. These men want wives to produce children and your window for doing so is closing!"

"Julian!" Her mouth opened in shock. "And so you cooked up this scheme to just simply... kill Hugo off because he was getting in the way of me marrying one of your rich friends? Am I really that much of an embarrassment to you? That, just because our branch of the family have fallen off the tree, you would trample on my happiness to bring us back up?"

"That's nonsense! I told you – I did it so you wouldn't continue to waste your life on an illusion! You are not in love with Hugo – you are just infatuated and you are prepared to throw everything out the window for this infatuation!"

She went and sat down on the chesterfield couch and placed her hand to her forehead as she fought back tears.

"Oh, Karina, can't you see I did it for your good?" He sat down beside her, placing a hand on her shoulder.

She slapped his hand off. "Don't touch me, Julian! I could never believe you would pull such a – *cruel* – stunt on me. To let me believe Hugo was dead – it's *unforgivable!*" Her voice cracked with emotion as the tears continued to fall.

She thought of the anguish of the past couple of days. She thought about the stranger she had met in the 400 Club and how she had gone back to his hotel bedroom and slept with him just out of loneliness and grief, thinking Hugo was dead.

"You have no idea of the trouble you have caused!" She stood up abruptly and went running from the room.

* * *

She slammed her front door behind her and walked into the sitting room where her mother was reading the newspaper.

"Are you alright, darling?" asked Penny, seeing the state she was in.

"I received this telegram from Berlin from Hugo – he's alive, Mama. I just came from Julian's – *he made it all up!* Hugo was never killed by a motorcar! He made it up to try to make me forget Hugo! Can you believe it?"

"Oh, I see ..." said Penny, folding away the newspaper.

"Such a bastard! I will never speak to him again!"

"That's a bit harsh, isn't it?"

"No! I hate him for what he has done." Karina she paced up and down, then halted to look at her mother. "You don't seem that shocked by what has occurred?"

Penny looked down at the floor. "You mustn't blame Julian for it all, Karina."

Karina stared at her as realisation dawned. "Oh, no – Mama! Please tell me you hadn't a hand in this?"

"I suggested the idea to Julian," admitted Penny, her voice quiet.

"*What! How could you do that to me?*" Karina was outraged. "*My own mother!*"

"I did it because I love you and I am trying to stop you from destroying your life –"

"Because like Julian you want to see me to stop 'wasting' my life and to marry one of the chinless wonders he keeps introducing me to?"

Penny stood up abruptly and her voice rose. "No, Karina, you can marry who the heck you want. But this love you profess you have for Hugo is now bringing you into severe danger and you are like a moth to the flame going blindly after it. When you told me you were trying to get a transfer to the embassy in Berlin to track Hugo down I knew I had to take action – drastic action. Karina ... I am Jewish which makes you half-Jewish and you going to Germany at this stage is like committing suicide."

"But, Mama – nobody knows you are Jewish outside our immediate family! Not even Julian or any of Papa's other relatives!"

Penny walked to the window and looked out. "Yes ... we went to such lengths to cover it up."

"I could never understand why we had to keep it such a secret," sighed Karina.

"Back in Edwardian times when your father and I met and fell in love, we knew there would be raised eyebrows about the fact that I was not a member of the peerage nor had any connection with the aristocracy. Bad enough I was an American from an average background ... but we knew how much more prejudice we would face if it got out I was Jewish. Back then we hid the truth to try and avoid any further social snobbery our marriage might cause. Little did we know then that thirty years later in these dark days being Jewish would risk far more than enduring a little social snobbery. Now it has become a death sentence."

"But, Mama, as you say, not even Papa's family know so how would anybody else find out? I would be completely safe in Berlin as nobody would know about my Jewish connection and, besides, I would have diplomatic protection working at the British embassy there."

Penny swung around to face her daughter. "Nobody is 'completely safe' in Berlin these days! And how long do you think that protection would last if war broke out? Karina, this love you have for Hugo is dragging you down a dark and dangerous road. Turn back now, before it's too late!"

Karina held the telegram tightly in her hands. "I can't. I love him and he needs me and I will do anything I have to in order to save him."

The two women stared at each other before Karina turned and walked out.

Penny staggered over to her armchair and collapsed into it, putting her face into her hands.

Karina sat at her dressing table, staring at herself in the mirror, trying to comprehend what had happened. Trying to understand her mother and Julian's actions. She did understand their motives but she still found it utterly cruel. To put her through unnecessary grief by pretending Hugo was dead was hard to forgive, regardless of the fact they were just thinking of what was best for her. What *they* thought was best for her. It wasn't for them to decide that – it was for her and only her to decide. She clasped the telegram in her hands and read it for the hundredth time that day.

BERLIN

MISS KARINA HARPER

I AM LEAVING THE FLAT IN THE MORNING BEFORE IT IS TOO LATE. I AM GOING TO WHEN WE FIRST MET. POST NOT SAFE.

HUGO

Karina realised that the pressure Hugo was under at the flat must have become unbearable and he felt under threat. The telegram was obviously written in a hurry and it was very cryptic and intended not to give any information away. *Before it is too late* – what did he mean by that? Was it that he was about to be arrested? Or did he mean he was frightened of a worse fate? *I am going to when we first met* – the grammar was unusual – was that done deliberately, in order to make it more cryptic? Hugo obviously intended that if anyone read the telegram they would not know where his destination was, apart from Karina.

She distinctly remembered the first time she met Hugo. It was the previous year, the summer in '38 at a party of mutual friends in Berlin. She had taken the summer off work to go to Berlin, on the surface to perfect her German on a course at the university. It also suited her to be out of London for a while as she had been involved in yet another awful relationship. The man, rich and spoiled and childish, would not accept the relationship was over, so she decided three months away would be in order.

She threw herself into the social life in Berlin. She found herself in popular demand, being the glamorous cousin of Lord Ashton, and was invited to many parties and dinners. She had been invited

71

to a dinner party at Felix and Charlotte Friedrich's house the evening she met Hugo. They were wealthy and glamorous socialites, always anxious to fill their parties with new and exciting faces. Karina had been introduced to them by a mutual acquaintance from the university and Charlotte took an immediate shine to her and put her on her guest list for the summer.

The night she met Hugo she had gone there feeling a little melancholy. As she thought of her last failed relationship, she wondered if she would ever meet somebody to settle down with. She was twenty-eight and wondered where her life was going. Her job was really going nowhere. She had no savings. She lived at home, stripped of her inheritance by the dreadful Irish War of Independence twenty years before. And her relationships never seemed to last longer than three months and that by her choice. She just became terribly bored with men after about three months and ended the relationships. So her life then always reverted back to nightclubs and parties and having a rip-roaring social life. "We aren't here for a long time – we are here for a good time!" was Julian's repeated motto which she had enthusiastically followed. But recently that did not seem a very satisfying way to live one's life.

When she arrived at the Friedrichs' party that night, the house was as ever filled with glamorous and interesting people. And then she saw him. A handsome man who was about ten years her senior, surrounded by a small group of admirers. She was immediately drawn to him. Looking back later, she felt she had fallen in love with him on the spot.

"Who is he?" she asked Charlotte.

"That's my good friend, Hugo Von Caspars," smiled Charlotte, noting Karina's interest, and then took her by the hand. "Come, let me introduce you."

It was obvious when they were introduced that he felt the same attraction to her. And, as they chatted, they had found a quiet corner and spoken together for hours, oblivious to everyone else. He was a well-known author and Karina felt she could listen to his opinions on the world forever. He was going to his villa in Bavaria the following morning to finish his new novel. That night when they said goodbye she felt as if she could not tear herself away. The next day he sent a telegram from Bavaria asking when she was going to join him there. She packed her things, abandoned her university course and got the night train to Munich that very evening. She then spent the most glorious time of her life over the following weeks at his beautiful villa. As he wrote his novel during the day she went for walks, then prepared dinner for them and they drank wine into the night. She could have spent the rest of her life there with him.

But he was not liked by the Nazis because of his earlier writings when he had lampooned them before they came to power. He wanted to leave Germany but he was finding it hard to secure an exit permit or a visa for another country.

By the end of the summer she was running out of money and knew besides that she might lose her position at the Foreign Office if she did not soon return. She and Hugo returned to Berlin and spent a few precious weeks at his flat there. Then, with a heavy heart, she returned to London with the understanding they would both try to arrange his emigration to Britain as soon as possible. She would try and secure him an entry permit to Britain and he would try to secure himself an exit permit from Germany. But since then the situation had worsened frighteningly in Germany. Kristallnacht had been unleashed in November of last year – the attacks on Jewish property and people resulting in widescale destruction and deaths. The round-up and placing in concentration camps of anybody who was seen as an enemy of the Third Reich had been accelerated. People like Hugo lived their lives in fear, being watched, and terrified each knock on the door would be the SS coming for them. Hugo's fear and desperation was palpable in the letters he had sent her. The situation had obviously become so bad now that Hugo had fled his flat.

Post not safe – he had said at the end of the telegram. So this was why she had received no letters from him and also it was a warning to her not to try to contact him by post as the mail was obviously being intercepted.

She walked over to the window and gazed up at the stars before looking across at the small park across the road. Suddenly she again saw a man there, standing by the railings looking up at her windows. He was wearing a trench coat and a hat. She strained to get another look and went to open the window. As soon as he did this, he turned and began to walk down the street. She watched him turn the corner. She shook her head and closed the window again. This was the second time she had seen a man there watching the house. It could be just coincidence but she suddenly thought of Hugo's letters and how he said there were people across from his flat all day watching him.

She quickly drew the curtains and sat down shivering. Why would anybody watch her house, unless it was something to do with Hugo? She began to feel very frightened when she thought Hugo's letters might have been intercepted. The people who had been watching and following Hugo now knew about her through the letters they had stolen in the post. They would know where she lived and everything about her.

She went back to the telegram on her dressing table.

He had gone to *'when they had first met'*. So Hugo was with Felix and Charlotte Friedrich. They had been good friends of Hugo's and could hide him in their huge house and have the money to protect him. She felt relieved that Hugo was with them. Now she just needed to get him to London.

CHAPTER 10

Three days later Karina was seated opposite Sir William in a private carriage on a train at Paddington Station. There were four other members of the team in the carriage including Vera, who had at the last minute been added to the party by Mrs Potter. Karina was sure Vera had been added as a back-up in case she herself fell down on her duties after her recent behaviour. There were a further ten personnel from the Foreign Office attending the conference and they were in another larger carriage.

As the others discussed the ongoing talks, Karina was reflecting on the past couple of days. After she got over the shock that Hugo was still alive, she had been flooded with excitement and hope. She had thought she had lost him for good but now she had been given a second chance. And she would not let him down this time. Now that she knew what it was like to feel the loss of him, she was determined not to ever feel that way again. Quite simply, she would do whatever she had to do to rescue him.

Her first port of call had been to see Mrs Potter where she had grovelled and ate more humble pie than she would have ever thought possible – she had to save her job at the Foreign Office and also her place at the talks with the Irish. Yes, she had been distracted from her work of late. Yes, her timekeeping had become tardy. No, she wasn't setting a good example to the others. Yes, she had been very rude to poor Diana who deserved a full and unreserved apology from her (deserved perhaps, but never actually delivered!). And finally, yes, she fully understood the dreadful threat the country was under from the Nazi menace and she realised her tiny, miniscule role as a tiny cog in the wonderful machine of the Foreign Office could not be neglected again for fear the Empire would be lost.

"Why are we still here? Why is this train not moving?" demanded Sir William suddenly as he peered out the window.

"A delay down the line, Sir William," explained one of his deputies.

"Delay down the line! I never heard of such nonsense! Times were you could get on a train at Paddington that was scheduled to leave at nine o'clock and it left precisely at nine o'clock! None of this 'delay down the line' nonsense back then!"

As Karina smiled at him, her heart sank – it was going to be a long few days.

He smiled back at her and, reaching forward, patted her knee. "Did you bring something nice to wear with you, my dear?"

"Several nice outfits, Sir William," she responded.

"Good – good!" He winked at her and patted her knee once more for good measure.

Vera gave Karina a warning look that Karina chose to ignore.

Sir William was a decorated hero of the Great War. He had received a knighthood for bravery at the Battle of the Somme. Married to Edith, with seven children, they lived in a picturesque house in a picturesque village in Surrey.

Did he really, Karina wondered, plan to bed her that weekend?

Four motorcars were waiting at Oxford Station to carry the party the rest of the way to Great Hankerton Hall.

As the car that was carrying Karina and Sir William drove up the long straight driveway, she could see that the hall was a huge Palladian pile of white stone.

"Do we know what time the Irish are scheduled to arrive, Sir William?" Karina asked.

"Who knows with the Irish? They say one thing, mean another. I, for one, am not looking forward to trying to tie them down to joining us in a fight against the Germans."

"Will there be many in attendance from Ireland?"

"Several, I believe. De Valera is sending over one of his head fellows to lead the delegation. Seems a decent enough kind of fellow – there is worse they could have sent, I can assure you! He carries personal baggage though, so one never knows how that may affect the talks."

"Personal baggage?"

"He's the son of one their dead heroes of the Revolution – Rory Ford."

Karina suddenly shivered. "Rory Ford?"

"Yes, you've heard of him?"

"Yes, of course." She shivered again.

The name was famous throughout Ireland and he might be a hero to the country but for Karina, like the rest of the Anglo-Irish class, his name sent a shockwave of fear and revulsion through her. Rory Ford had organised and led the burning and attacks on many of the great Protestant houses of Ireland during the War of Independence and after. He had waged a campaign against the Protestant aristocracy, determined to drive them out of Ireland. Even after all these years, the sound of his name filled Karina with dread.

Sir William noticed her shiver and patted her knee. "Are you cold, my dear? We must see what we can do to warm you up!"

Gabriel led the Irish delegates down a Persian-rugged corridor. They were being shown the way by a butler who stopped when he reached a large oak door.

"This is the meeting room, sir."

"Very good – lead on, my man!" said Gabriel, turning to his give his colleagues a quick cheeky wink.

The butler knocked loudly and theatrically on the door and a moment it later it was opened by a footman.

Inside, there were four men seated at a huge oak table. They all stood as the Irish walked in.

Gabriel immediately recognised Sir William whom he had met previously on trips to London. Gabriel was in two minds whether it was a positive or a negative thing to have Sir William lead the talks. It wasn't that Sir William was obstructive or particularly belligerent. However, he was definitely old school, his character and politics firmly formed in the trenches of the Somme in the Great War. Empire came first for Sir William. He also had an annoying habit of living in and harking back to the past all the time. He had grown up in the Edwardian era and every aspect of him yearned to return to the perceived rosiness of that time.

"Mr Ford, good to see you again and welcome to Great Hankerton. Your rooms are satisfactory, we trust?" said Sir William, shaking his hand.

"Most satisfactory, Sir William. Whatever we may say about the British government, we can never knock them for hospitality!" said Gabriel with a smile.

"Yes, quite!" said Sir William, wondering if that was a backhanded compliment. "I think you have met Henry Prendeville before, and this is John Fellows ..."

There was further handshaking and greeting as Gabriel introduced his side.

Kathleen, the Irish secretary, stood awkwardly behind the Irish delegates.

"And our secretary, Kathleen Heavey ... perhaps she can sit with your secretaries?" suggested Gabriel, turning to look at the two women who were seated at a side table.

His mouth dropped open.

Karina was staring back at him with equal shock.

Then she quickly shook her head at him which jolted him back to reality.

"Yes, your little girl can go join ours," said Sir William. "Off you trot, dear – there's a spare seat at their table."

Kathleen promptly went and sat beside Vera.

Gabriel stood there, still staring at Karina.

"Well, if we all care to take our seats and get the business of the day started?" said Sir William as he and the others began to sit down.

Karina shot Gabriel an angry look and he quickly turned away and joined the others at the main table.

"I think you have an admirer," whispered Vera to Karina.

"Don't be ridiculous, Vera!" Karina snapped back.

As she started to arrange her notepads and pen, she felt hot and flustered. She tried not to look at Gabriel Ford. When she eventually stole a look at him, he was staring back at her.

It was lunchtime and the meeting had been adjourned for an hour. Karina quickly got up from her table and hurried from the room first, in order to avoid Gabriel Ford.

However, he strode after her down the long corridor and quickly caught up with her.

"Well, this is a turn-up for the books!" said Gabriel.

"A turn-up of something, that's for certain!" said Kate as she walked on.

He walked alongside her. "You left that morning from Claridge's without so much as a goodbye."

"Yes, well, you were fast asleep and I had to get to work."

"Yes – work! You never said you worked at the Foreign Office."

"You never asked. And you certainly never mentioned you were over as part of an Irish delegation. You said you were over on 'business', if my memory serves me correctly."

"Well, it is a form of business. And, besides, as I'm sure you are aware, the confidentiality of my visit is very important – I couldn't just reveal it to anybody I met in a club, could I?"

She stopped abruptly and turned to face him. "*Just anybody?* You are a right charmer, aren't you?"

"Well, you know what I mean! Nobody is supposed to know we are over here discussing what we are discussing."

"*Hmm.*"

She glanced down the corridor and saw that the rest of the party had gone in the opposite direction towards the dining room.

She walked on and he followed.

"I was quite worried about you, you know," he said.

"Why on earth should you have been?"

"Because you seemed so lost that night, so unhappy! As if you were trying to escape some terrible pain that had engulfed you."

"Yes, well, in a way that was true. But it was all a misunderstanding –

which has now been sorted out. So no need to fret about me anymore."

"I see! How could something that could cause such upset be sorted out so quickly?"

"I told you – it was a misunderstanding! What I thought had happened hadn't happened at all!" she said, exasperated with his probing.

"So I am correct then? I was a distraction for you for the night?"

She stopped again and faced him.

"Look – Gabriel – I don't make a habit of jumping into bed with strangers, I can assure you."

"Glad to hear it, I suppose," he said.

"I had heard something that shocked me that day. I had gone out to get blindly drunk and then you came along, and one thing led to another. It meant nothing to me and I'm sure it meant nothing to you. I am sure we were convinced we would never see each other again and we would have *never* gone to bed with each other if there had been the *remotest* chance we would *ever* cross paths again ... but here we are, through a strange twist of fate, at Great Hankerton Hall at the same conference –"

"Perhaps it is fate."

"More likely just a bizarre coincidence. But, since we are to be in the same place for the next three days, I suggest we get on with our jobs – try to stay out of each other's way as much as possible – and really – *really* – pretend the whole unfortunate previous episode never occurred! Don't you agree?"

He stood there, perplexed.

"Do you understand, Gabriel?" she asked.

"Yes – perfectly!"

"Excellent! Now, if you would excuse me, I need to type up my notes." She gave him a cold smile and turned and walked quickly away, leaving him to stare after her in bewilderment.

CHAPTER 11

Karina stood beside Vera, each of them holding a glass of wine in the great drawing room. Delegates from both sides were present, being served drinks and canapés by the staff.

"My father worked in the Foreign Office for years and he says more work gets done over drinks in the evening than ever could be achieved over the conference table," said Vera.

"I can imagine," said Karina.

"How are you feeling now after your fainting spell the other day?"

"Oh, perfectly fine."

"I came prepared – just in case!" said Vera, taking her smelling salts from her purse to show her.

"Oh – very pre-emptive of you, Vera!" smirked Karina.

"As I said, 'Be Prepared' is my motto! Have to say, Karina, you nearly scuppered your chances of coming here after your behaviour that day with Diana. Mrs Potter was in a mind to replace you actually *with* Diana ... but, of course, Sir William wouldn't hear a word of it!" Vera gave her a knowing look.

"Indeed!" said Karina as she looked across the room at Sir William who held his glass up to her and winked. She returned the salute to him with her glass and smiled.

"Oh, don't encourage him, Karina, whatever you do!"

"I'm not! But I can't ignore him either! He's harmless enough."

"I shouldn't be too sure of that if I were you! Don't wreck your chances of hooking an eligible diplomat here by having him hovering around you like a bad smell all the time!"

These trips away are like gold-dust to these girls, Karina knew, offering a chance of snaring a foreign diplomat as well as a British one.

"Have you checked out the Irish contingent?" asked Vera.

"Not really," said Karina.

"Oh, you should! There's a couple of contenders there! Gabriel Ford, who seemed stunned on first seeing you, is totally dreamy, don't you think?"

Karina looked over at Gabriel who was talking in a small circle of four but looking straight at her.

"If you like that sort of thing," said Karina.

"Oh, I do and I would ... pity," Vera sighed.

"What's a pity?"

"That he's taken."

"Taken?" Karina asked, turning her head abruptly to look at Vera.

"I checked out his résumé with one of the Irish secretaries. He's engaged to be married."

"Is he, indeed?" said Karina, her voice full of surprise as she looked back at Gabriel. "He's not quite the good little Catholic boy he pretends to be, is he?"

"What do you mean?"

"Eh, nothing. Who's he engaged to?"

"To a schoolteacher, can you imagine? How dull! I can't imagine him with a schoolteacher – far too good-looking to be with a schoolteacher!"

Gabriel was in conversation with a couple of the English delegates. He always found the social aspect of these conventions nearly as important as the boardroom. Once he got to know the opposing side socially, personally, he found it built an element of trust that could never be achieved in a meeting room. Gabriel had found the art of being a good diplomat was best served when they all had a drink in their hands.

"So there we were – the wife and I – driving through the South of France and all these Spanish were suddenly on the road – it was like driving through a flock of sheep," said Henry, an affable diplomat.

"Refugees?"

"Yes, trying to escape Franco. They are all trying to escape some dictator these days and all trying to get here!"

"Difficult for you," Gabriel said, wondering how he could fish for information about Karina.

"And likely to get worse!"

"Well, I hope our negotiations are easy and successful," said Gabriel, knowing full well the opposite was likely to be true.

"Indeed," said Henry dubiously.

Gabriel glanced around. "Well, people seem to be getting on well so far. *Em*, I was talking to one of your secretaries earlier and –"

"The blonde? Vera?" Henry glanced over at Vera and Karina. "Smashing gal – all jolly hockey-sticks and team spirt!"

"No, the other blonde."

"Oh, Karina … not quite the usual type we have at the Foreign Office, but a great girl all the same."

"She seems a little aloof?"

"Only if you get her on a bad day – she can be a sweetheart most of the time. She's a cousin of Lord Ashton."

"*Ahh!*" said Gabriel, startled.

"She's actually Irish – well, Anglo-Irish."

"I see!" said Gabriel, becoming more amazed by the moment.

"The Harpers were a very important and connected Protestant family from the West of Ireland … Inishwood, I believe, was the family seat."

"Ah, yes, Inishwood!"

"Their house was burned down after independence by the locals and the family driven out," said Henry, always glad to remind an Irish diplomat there was wrongdoing on their side as well during the War of Independence.

"It was a fine manor house," said Gabriel, his knowledge of architecture coming to the fore. "What happened to the family after that?"

"Well, like so many of their class they came to England to escape the hatred they were enduring in Ireland. I believe Karina's father died soon after from a heart attack which leaves just her and her mother ... they live in relative obscurity these days, apart from the fact that their aristocratic ties still allow Karina into the 'golden circle'."

"How very ... tragic," said Gabriel who was suddenly overwhelmed by sadness as he looked at Karina.

"Karina's an excellent typist, though, when she shows up to work!" said Henry with a laugh and suddenly noticed that Gabriel was studying her intently. He placed a hand on Gabriel's shoulder and whispered into his ear. "I shouldn't go there, if I were you, old chap ... she's with Sir William for the weekend – if you get my meaning!"

Gabriel looked at Henry in shock and Henry gave him a knowing wink. Gabriel then stared back at Karina who along with Vera was enjoying a loud jovial conversation with Sir William.

CHAPTER 12

On the following day the meeting between the delegates became very tense as it emerged that they were taking two extremely different views of the approaching war.

"We only gave you back the three naval ports last year," said Sir William. "Surely you could lend them back to us in the advent of war!"

"They were never yours to give back in the first place, Sir William!" said Gabriel. "And they were signed over to the Irish Free State by Britain by international treaty."

"But those ports could make all the difference in a war against Germany. We could use them to protect our shipping crossing the Atlantic," said Sir William.

"I'm not denying their strategic importance to Britain, but if we let you use those ports Ireland would not be able to maintain its intended policy of neutrality in a war."

"Well, you can't be serious about this notion of neutrality!"

As Karina took notes in shorthand her anger was rising at Gabriel's standpoint.

"It just would not be acceptable for the Irish people to fight alongside the British in this war," said Gabriel. "The time that has passed since the War of Independence is too short and people's memories are too long. The Irish public would not accept it after the atrocities committed against them by British forces during the fight for independence."

"*Huh!*" Karina said loudly, causing everyone in the room to look in surprise at her.

She quickly put her head down and began scribbling away.

Sir William responded, "The reality is there were atrocities committed on both sides during Ireland's fight for independence, Mr Ford –"

"*Yes!*" agreed Karina a little too loudly, without raising her head, which caused everyone to look at her again.

Gabriel, disconcerted, continued, "You British are just going to have to accept that we are an independent nation and will not come to Britain's aid in a war with Germany."

"*Bastards!*" muttered Karina angrily.

"Miss Harper, are you quite alright?" asked Sir William.

"Yes, sorry, just a slight cough!" She reached forward, took a glass of water and drank from it.

"Well, I don't know what to say," said Sir William, "apart from the fact I'm shocked by the Irish stance and I imagine everyone in Britain will be too. Every nation of the Empire will be expected to do their bit to support the Mother Nation in our darkest hour."

"But we are an unwilling member of your empire, Sir William. The vast majority of our people want a full republic," said Gabriel.

"By the sound of it you plan to take full advantage of Britain's woes with Germany to achieve your republic. Pretty shoddy behaviour if you ask me, Gabriel. Times were you could rely on a neighbour during times of peril."

"Well, times are not what they used to be, Sir William!" said Gabriel.

"Isn't that an unfortunate fact! I really hope Dublin changes its mind – or else we may have to change your mind for you!"

"That sounds like a threat, Sir William? Would you really invade Ireland to get our ports?" asked Gabriel.

"We'll do what we have to do – *anything we have to do* – to win this bloody war!" shouted Sir William as he slammed the table with his fist, making everyone in the room jump.

Karina looked at Gabriel. Even he looked worried by Sir William's words.

The next day, after the round of talks, Sir William cornered Karina in the corridor.

"Karina, dear, I actually need you to take some notes privately for me this evening," he said.

"I thought you might do," said Karina knowingly.

Sir William looked around to make sure nobody could hear. "Actually, my dear, the notes are of a rather sensitive nature – highly confidential – so I'd rather we got away from Hankerton Hall for the evening. There's a restaurant in Oxford we can go to. I've booked us a nice quiet corner table where nobody will overhear us. Is that alright?"

"Perfectly fine! I'll remember to bring my notepad and pen!" She smiled at him.

"Good girl. I'll have my driver come to the forecourt at six." He winked at her and moved on.

She watched him march off down the hall and shuddered.

Gabriel had been watching the interaction from down the corridor, observing the body language between them. Sir William was standing way too close and she seemed to be responding. He remembered Henry's words: "*She's with Sir William for the weekend.*"

Tucked away in a corner booth in a quiet restaurant in Oxford with Sir William, Karina wondered could he have found anywhere more discreet. He must have had a lot of practice at seduction.

As they ate a delicious steak dinner accompanied by a bottle of expensive wine, she had listened to his war stories from the Somme, his stationing in Washington during the roaring 1920s when he joined the diplomatic corps (prohibition had not stopped the fun times, seemingly) and his sojourn in Buenos Aires (Argentinian girls were the best dancers, apparently). As he raced through a second bottle of wine, she followed his adventures from South Africa to India, all the time appearing to be fascinated. She wondered how he ever found the time to father seven children.

Not once had he mentioned the talks with the Irish nor did she have to pick up her pen and notebook which were on the table beside her.

"*A-a-a-africa!*" he declared, his words now becoming slurred from all the wine. "I tell you, my dear, Africa is not what it used to be … t-t-t-times were a man could arrive on that continent with just a-a dream in his heart and a song in his s-soul and make his fortune. Now, it's just a desert and … full of foreigners. More Dutch in South Africa now than in Holland – it's all *Van der* this and *Van der* that …" Once again he filled his wineglass to the top.

It was after midnight and she had ordered a third bottle of wine which Sir William was just polishing off.

"Oh, Karina – I do adore you," he said as he gazed at her across the table.

"Do you?"

"From the f-first moment I saw you – I thought – I thought – there is a quality woman – a woman, indeed, full of quality!" He took her hand and began to rub it.

"You never said – I never suspected!" she said, putting a hand on his and rubbing it back.

"I s-simply had to have you, Karina, I really d-did – from the first moment I saw you I thought – I have to have that girl."

"Really?"

"Let's go back to my room – I have a very big – big – four-poster bed," he said.

She gulped and nodded.

Back at Great Hankerton Hall, Sir William had gone up to his room first.

"We can't let anyone see ush – *shhh!*" he had whispered as he clambered out of the motorcar.

"You go first and I'll follow you in ten minutes," she promised.

"Ten minutes! No longer or elshe I'll send the cavalry to find you!" he threatened as he stumbled across the forecourt to the front door.

Karina walked across the forecourt and down into the gardens where she lit up a cigarette.

"Oh – hello!" came a voice.

She turned to see Gabriel there, also smoking.

"Good evening," she said.

"It's a beautiful night, isn't it?" he said, looking up at the stars.

"Yes."

"You didn't join the rest of us tonight for dinner?"

"No, I had other arrangements," she said.

"Did you go anywhere nice?"

"It's actually none of your business!" she snapped.

"Oh, of course." Gabriel looked embarrassed, angry and hurt all at once. "Goodnight."

He walked away.

She immediately regretted her words. She thought about going after him to apologise but quickly dismissed the idea. He was a stranger, who she had a chance encounter with. He was also Rory Ford's son. Besides, she had more important things to do.

Inside Hankerton Hall she first went to her room where she retrieved a bottle of brandy she had hidden there earlier. Then she made her way through the maze of corridors to Sir William's room.

When she reached the door, she bit her lip and shook her head despairingly before gathering her courage and knocking on the door.

A few seconds later, Sir William opened his door, in his dressing gown.

"My dear!" he said, pulling her in, closing the door and locking it.

He turned and grabbed her by the shoulders.

"I have waited for this moment since I saw you first walk down the corridor at the F-foreign Offish," he slurred as he began to kiss her and fumble at the buttons on her blouse.

"So have I, Sir William," she said as she allowed him to kiss her neck.

"Oh, let's discard with the formalities – you can simply call me 'sir'!"

"Alright – sir!"

"Let's to bed!" he said, pushing her towards the four-poster bed. "F-fortune f-favours the brave!"

"I brought a little nightcap!" she said, raising the bottle of brandy.

"What's thish ... a bottle of original Rémy Martin brandy – 1927! Where did you get this, you little minx?"

"I borrowed it from the wine cellar here," she said.

"Borrowed it?"

"Well – fortune favours the brave!" She smiled cheekily at him.

"It most certainly does!" he said as he looked at the bottle lasciviously.

An hour later, Karina was looking at Sir William passed out naked on the four-poster bed, snoring loudly, the half-drunk bottle of Rémy Martin in his hand. She sighed with relief.

Her blouse already discarded, she continued to undress.

Light was shining through the windows as Karina sat on the bed, nudging Sir William awake.

"*Sir – sir!*" she hissed as she shook him.

"W-what – what?" he said, struggling to wake up and sit up all at the same time. "What the blazes! My head feels as if a full-scale artillery is going off in it – where the heck am I?"

"Great Hankerton Hall, sir."

"Oh yes ..." he said as he shook his head to try and clear it, then winced in pain.

He then focused on Karina who was perched on the side of the bed, legs crossed, dressed only in silk underwear, her hair mussed up and her lipstick artfully smeared.

"Goodness me – Karina, isn't it?"

"Yes!"

"It's all such a blur – the restaurant – the wine – the hotel room – then all blurry and then blank ..."

"Well, it wasn't blank for me, sir, it was wonderful!" she sighed.

"Well, I'm glad you enjoyed yourself, my dear," he said as he desperately tried to recall events from the previous night.

"How could I not when I was with the man of my dreams?" she sighed.

"Yes – well, eh, yes."

"I always wanted my first time to be special with a man as wonderful as you – but I could never have guessed how wonderful it could be!"

"Oh, yes, well ..." he began, feeling embarrassed and confused all at the same time. "What – did you say – first time?"

90

"Yes!"

"But surely – surely – surely not! There isn't a gal in London over twenty-one who hasn't been around the block at least once before, at least the upper-class girls like you!"

"I wanted it to be special with a special man and that's what I waited for and that's what I got – let's do it again!" she said, pouncing on him.

"Wait – wait!" He slapped her away. "Madam – please remember yourself and unhand me!"

"But, darling – that's not what you said last night!"

"Times were a girl used to wait for the chap to make the first move! I do not know what has happened to the modern woman – I blame universal suffrage!"

"I'm sorry – I'm just so excited I can't restrain myself!"

"Yes, yes, I'm sure but ... perhaps later ... my head ..."

She pulled back, looking downcast. "Alright, darling ... later then ... I'll go back to my room ..." She rose to her feet. "But ... when will you tell Edith?"

"*Tell Edith*?" he shrieked.

"Yes, your wife."

"I know who Edith is, for goodness' sake! What the hell are you saying about telling her ... tell her *what*?"

"Well, she will need to know as soon as possible. I'll speak to my cousin, Lord Ashton, today – he knows an excellent divorce lawyer and we can get this show on the road!"

He jumped off the bed and pulled on his dressing gown. "My dear girl, there is no show! Lord Ashston! Divorce lawyer! I can't divorce Edith – she would kill me! And what about the children – we have seven children! The eldest is only nine!"

"I know – I want seven children too! I'm hoping we already made a start last night," she said, rubbing her stomach.

"I think I'm going to throw up!" He began to retch and struggled to control it. "I am in no mood or position to start embarking on a journey that will result in a further seven children – not at this stage of my career, you stupid girl!"

Karina suddenly burst out crying, surprising herself by

managing to produce actual tears. She sat back on the bed and buried her face in her hands.

"*Oh no!*" sighed Sir William. "Times were a girl knew what to expect from a roll in the hay!"

He came and sat on the bed beside her. Taking her hand, he said, "Look, dear, you must see how impossible the situation is. I couldn't possibly divorce – think of the scandal! What would Mrs Potter say?"

"Yes, there is that, I hadn't thought of Mrs Potter," Karina snivelled. "But what can I do? I have fallen madly in love with you. I just can't go back into the Foreign Office and see you each day, knowing you will not be mine."

"Perhaps – a foreign posting? That's always good to be had in these events. You mentioned you would like to see Buenos Aries earlier. Let's ship you off there! You'll love the steak!"

"Berlin."

"Pardon?"

"I already requested a posting to Berlin," she said.

"But there is going to be war, in case you hadn't realised? Your safety would not be assured there."

She started crying again. "I want to go to Berlin!"

"Very well! Berlin it is! I'll sign the papers as soon as I get back to London." He stood up abruptly. "And now, young lady, if you could please return to your own room and allow me some privacy and peace and quiet!"

She got up meekly and quickly kissed his cheek before whispering, "I'll never forget you!"

"Nor I you!"

She gathered up her clothes and walked to the door.

"*Stop! For God's sake put your clothes on!*" he cried and then clutched his head in pain.

"Oh, yes." She pulled on her clothes haphazardly, not bothering with her stockings. "Goodbye, my love."

"Goodbye!"

She walked out onto the corridor, filled with relief and excitement. Her plan had worked.

She closed the door and rested her back against it, closing her eyes and smiling happily.

As she opened her eyes, she saw Gabriel standing there, staring at her in disbelief.

She opened her mouth to say something but no words would come out.

He then nodded at her and continued down the corridor to his own room and let himself in.

She looked after him and then raced down the corridor to her own room. She felt mortified that he had seen her. He would fully know whose room she had come from as he was just down the corridor. He would have assumed she had spent the night with Sir William. Which she had – in a way.

She looked in a mirror. Her face was red with embarrassment, her hair in a state and make-up smeared on her face. What must Gabriel think of her? Spending the night with him in Claridge's a few nights ago and then apparently with Sir William that night.

She told herself it did not matter a damn what Gabriel Ford thought of her. He was practically a stranger to her who was going back to Dublin and she would never have to see him again.

But regardless of how much she kept telling herself it didn't matter, she couldn't help feeling that it did.

"Well, I'm not sure we have achieved much this weekend at Great Hankerton Hall," said Sir William as he shook Gabriel's hand.

All the delegates were out on the forecourt as the Irish contingent were about to leave.

"I wouldn't say that, Sir William – I think we have all found out a lot about each other," said Gabriel as he glanced over at Karina who was standing beside Vera on the edge of the group.

"I would have hoped to be able to go back to Downing Street with some firm good news that the Irish were on our side!" said Sir William.

"I think the British can rest assured we are on your side against the Nazi threat, and I'm sure will help in any way we can that will not compromise our probable neutrality," said Gabriel.

"But, if you are not willing to fight with us, then that – as we used to say in the last war in my army outfit – is all talk and no trousers!"

"An unfortunate turn of phrase," said Gabriel, looking at Karina again. "We had better go or we'll miss our train back to London."

Gabriel quickly shook hands with the whole party and then came to the secretaries.

Vera smiled at him. "A pleasure to meet you!" she said gushingly.

"Likewise!" said Gabriel, shaking her hand before he moved and stood in front of Karina.

"Goodbye, Miss Harper."

She felt herself go bright red as she nodded at him and shook his hand.

Gabriel turned and quickly went to one of the waiting motorcars.

Karina turned and joined the others as they walked up the steps to return to the house. As she reached the top of the steps, she turned to look at Gabriel's motorcar. He was seated at the back and staring straight at her. She stared back as the vehicle moved out of the forecourt and down the driveway.

CHAPTER 13

"You simply can't, Karina! I'm begging you!" pleaded Penny as she watched Karina pack her suitcases.

"I am going, Mama, and that is the end of it!" said Karina as she hastily folded dresses. "I hope to be in Berlin by the end of the week."

"But this is madness! Everyone is trying to get out of Germany and you are rushing there!"

"Exactly! Hugo is desperate to get out and I have to get there to get him out. Hand him the permit which at least gives him permission to come here and then start working from the embassy to get him an exit permit. It's the only way. And if war is coming, then I have no time to lose – otherwise, who knows what the Nazis will do to him under the cloak of war."

"The Nazis don't need a cloak of war to do what they are doing to the Jews there," said Penny and she slumped down on an armchair and began to cry.

Karina stopped packing for a moment and looked at her. The she went over and knelt down beside her.

"Mama, nobody knows my heritage. Nobody knows I am part-Jewish and even if they did they couldn't touch me. I will have diplomatic immunity. I wouldn't be going if I didn't have the safety of the embassy there behind me. With it, I'm untouchable."

"You have that same arrogance – or naivety, call it what you will – that your father had. I begged him for us to leave Ireland when the attacks on the great houses started, but he refused to leave his home. So we waited until that terrible night when they came to get us and drive us out." She began to shiver at the memory.

"I'll be fine, Mama – I know how to look after myself," Karina assured her as she hugged her tightly.

"You father thought the same thing about himself," she sighed ruefully.

Karina left home feeling elated. She walked down the street and waited for her bus.

She closed her eyes and hoped that the arrangement for her transfer to Berlin would be made when she arrived. She had kept the pressure on her seniors all week despite the heightened tension at the Foreign Office due to the ongoing situation on the Continent. True to his word, Sir William had given permission for her to go to Berlin – in fact, as promised, he had signed her transfer papers himself.

She had passed him the previous day. She had been walking down the corridor smiling happily when suddenly he came walking towards her from the opposite direction, an aide either side of him. As he approached, she had switched her expression to looking sad and forlorn, like a lovesick schoolgirl. He had coughed loudly, quickening his pace as he passed her by and she pretended to look longingly at him.

The Germans had made many demands regarding Poland and there was frantic diplomacy being undertaken. As precarious as the situation was, Karina felt optimistic that Britain would be brought back from the brink of war. The same thing would happen as in the previous year, 1938 – everyone predicted war then too. But an agreement, however unsatisfactory, had been reached in Munich and war had been avoided. The reality was that everyone knew just how devasting a war with Germany would be. Nobody wanted it, so diplomacy would have to win out in the end.

The bus came and she jumped on and climbed upstairs to her usual place.

Soon she began to notice that there was a strange atmosphere in the bus. An unusual quietness.

And then she saw the headline on the newspaper the passenger in front was reading. She leant forward abruptly to read it over his shoulder, praying that her eyes were deceiving her. But there it was.

GERMANY BOMBS AND INVADES POLAND – BRITAIN MOBILISES

There was chaos in the Foreign Office that day when Karina arrived. People rushing about, panic in the air. Last-minute diplomacy was being tried but everyone knew the time for diplomacy had passed. Instead, the diplomatic efforts were being redirected to capitals other than Berlin – all the capitals of the Empire, Paris and Washington – to build a strong alliance against the Nazis.

Karina was sure that Dublin was one capital that would not be throwing its weight behind the allies, having witnessed their attitude at the conference she had attended.

Karina had requested a meeting with Mrs Potter but none had come through. She tried to concentrate on her work all day but she found it impossible. She kept gazing out the window at St James's Park, lost in her thoughts. She kept hoping there would be a reprieve from war at the eleventh hour, but she knew it was hopeless. And she knew all hopes of now getting to Berlin and finding Hugo had vanished.

"If I only had one more week, I would have got there – just one more week!" she muttered to herself.

Two days later, a Sunday, and Britain and France declared war on Germany.

As Karina sat at the window in her bedroom, her mother came in nervously with the newspaper.

"I thought you might want to read it," she said, putting it on the dressing table. "I know it might not seem like it now – but you are a lucky, lucky girl that you didn't get over there. I read in the paper that all the personnel at the British Embassy in Berlin have been arrested. The Foreign Office is desperately trying to negotiate for them to come home – that could be you, Karina."

Penny looked so relieved. But the only thing Karina could think about was Hugo. He hadn't been saved. He was now stuck in Germany forever and she doubted she would ever see him again.

CHAPTER 14

The Foreign Office was working very late as crisis diplomacy was being undertaken at every turn. Karina almost didn't have time to think, she was so rushed off her feet. She left work after completing a twelve-hour day. As she felt like some time to think and take some air, she decided to walk home part of the way rather than straight away catching the bus.

As she walked along the darkened streets, a car suddenly pulled up. She let out as scream as she was seized and bundled into the back.

"Secret Service, no need to be alarmed," said one of the men in the car as he smiled at her.

A man carrying files entered the room, marched over to the table and sat down.

Karina tried not to show that she was shaking. After she had been kidnapped off the street she had been driven for twenty minutes to an area in the Docklands and a disused-looking building. She had been marched inside.

She had been told she was not in danger and to cooperate but she feared the worst and could not stop shaking as she sat in a windowless room.

"Miss Harper, apologies for the way you were brought here tonight," said the man.

"How do you know my name? And who the hell are you? The man in the car said you were Secret Service," she said, trying to sound strong.

"Well, we know quite a bit about you at this stage, Miss Harper – you have come to our attention quite a lot recently." He looked through the file on his desk.

"How on earth could I have come to your attention?" she asked.

"Born in Ireland, lives with her mother in Fulham, a girl about town, a cousin of Lord Ashton and a secretary at the Foreign Office ... quite a résumé."

"Why would you be interested in those details about me? So what?" she demanded.

"Well, it's not so much those details we are interested in ... it's the others," he said.

"What other details?"

"That you have been canvassing to be transferred to Berlin. The fact that you actually did manage to get that transfer to Berlin and would be there now if war had not broken out. The fact that you spent the night with Gabriel Ford in Claridge's hotel before the recent conference at Great Hankerton Hall where you were in attendance as a secretary. And the fact that you spent a night with Sir William Baxter while at Great Hankerton during the said conference ... now *that* is a very interesting part of your résumé ... it certainly is of interest to us."

Her mouth dropped open as she stared at him.

She started to laugh. "Is this what all this is? That you think I'm a Nazi?"

"You must admit your behaviour is looking very alarming. This dash to try and get back to Germany before the war ... the fact that you spent a night with both the head of the Irish *and* the British delegation at the recent conference you were working at?"

"But how did you even get this information about me? How did I even appear on your horizon?" she demanded.

"By pure chance. We were following Gabriel Ford and the other Irish delegates once they arrived in London – keeping an eye on them to see what they were up to. We saw him pick you up at the 400 Club and followed you back to Claridge's. We checked you out after that and were alarmed to discover you worked at the Foreign Office. We watched your every move after that."

She shook her head in bewilderment. "But I had no idea who Gabriel Ford was when I met him or when I went back to his hotel. We never spoke about anything political. I never even told him I worked at the Foreign Office – I told him I worked in Harrods! And he told me he was a businessman! I was shocked – completely shocked – when the next week he arrived at Great Hankerton Hall and I found out he was the head of the Irish delegation. I barely said two words to him there after I found out. When he approached me I insisted we keep our distance from each other and pretend the whole thing never happened."

"No secret rendezvous at night? Sneaking into each other's rooms?"

"No! Of course not! And, actually, I'm sure if you have been following me as closely as you say you have and saw me go into Sir William's room at Great Hankerton, you would have seen that I didn't go into Gabriel Ford's as well. And I do not know what kind of girl you think I am – but I'm actually not *that* bad!"

"Ah, yes – your tryst with Sir William. Would you care to explain that to us?"

She bit her lip. Sir William was a tricky one to explain! She was damned if she did and damned if she didn't as far as Sir William was concerned. If she stuck to the story she told Sir William then she would come across as having very loose morals. If she came clean and told the truth then she would portray herself as a dangerous liar prepared to go to extraordinary lengths to achieve what she wanted.

"Miss Harper? Please tell me about your night with Sir William."

"Actually, no, you can't ask me such a question because it really is none of your business! What I do in my own time and with whom is entirely up to me. I've had enough of this – this – interrogation – and now I really must insist on going home!" She stood up abruptly.

"Sit down, Miss Harper!"

"You have no right to keep me here against my will," she said.

"I have every right. Under emergency legislation passed on September 1st – Defence Regulation 18B – your personal freedoms and rights are suspended if you are perceived as a threat to national security. We can lock you up and throw away the key until the war is over."

Karina felt a cold sharp shiver. She was well aware of the new legislation as she had typed up drafts of it two weeks before. She remembered Defence Regulation 18B had been passed to the Foreign Office in preparation for the war in so far as it affected foreign nationals living in the country, particularly Germans and Irish republicans, who could be detained without trial if they were deemed to be working against the British. Karina remembered the draconian laws, though, applied to not just those two nationalities but anyone who was deemed to be a national threat.

She retook her seat.

"How could I be any threat to the nation?"

"By passing information to the Irish, by trying to get to Berlin to the Nazis – by sleeping with an inebriated Sir William Baxter in order to find out confidential information to pass to the Irish and the Nazis."

"Why do you think he was inebriated?" asked Karina.

"Our contact at the conference said he was despairingly hungover the next day."

"But I didn't sleep with Sir William. Yes, I went to his room and encouraged him to get blind drunk, but I did not sleep with him and had no intention of doing so. I pretended to him the next morning that we had slept together in order for him to organise a transfer for me to Berlin. I pretended I was madly in love with him in order that he would send me anywhere to get rid of me as a perceived risk to his marriage and family."

"Well, that neatly sums up the case against you! Whether you slept with him or not is irrelevant – surely you can see that? You are an utterly unscrupulous Nazi agent who deliberately made Sir William 'blind drunk" in order to extract information from him. Followed by blackmailing him into giving you an immediate transfer to Berlin. You're condemned out of your own mouth. Indeed, your 'defence' seems a singularly stupid one."

"That's because I'm not making up a defence! *It's true!* That's what happened and why!" She realised there was nothing else for it but to come clean. "I'm not a Nazi! I'm anything but!" She opened her handbag and took out the telegram from Berlin and handed it to the man. "I am in a relationship with a German man, a writer, whose life is at risk from the Nazis. He has been desperately trying to come to Britain but couldn't get out of Germany. I just managed to finally get him a permit to come to Britain. You can check that fact with Alfred Smyth at the Foreign Office."

"How did you manage to get a permit for this man?"

"I – I told Alfred that I was pregnant and that Hugo was the father and that I would bring disgrace onto my family and the Foreign Office if I couldn't get him over here to marry me," she said, before hastily adding, "I'm not pregnant incidentally. I just made it up to get what I needed."

The man looked incredulously at her.

"Who is this man in Berlin. Hugo ...?"

"Hugo Von Caspars. He's a writer, you see – a novelist. You may never have heard of him. But his writings were disapproved of by the Nazi party. Before Hitler came to power, he satirised him in his writing. He is well known and popular in Germany. He is in grave danger, you see. He was writing to me each week, telling me he was being followed and threatened. Then I heard nothing from him for three months, so in desperation I lied to get him a permit to come here. And then I received that telegram from him last week, begging me to get him out of Germany. So that's when I decided I had to do whatever it took to save him – and I tricked Sir William to get the transfer to Berlin in order to find him and give him the permit and help him get an exit permit from the Nazis. And I was nearly there. I was all packed and ready to go ... and then the war started." Karina looked at him in desperation.

He got up and left the room.

Karina sighed loudly when she was left alone. She looked around at the bare grey room. She didn't know what was going to happen from here. Would they let her go? It was unimaginable they could just arrest her and keep her locked up for the duration of the war. Would they believe her story? She had the letters from Hugo at home to show them if she needed to verify her story.

The door opened, the man walked in and sat again. He flung something down on the table and she saw it was a number of stamped envelopes.

"What are those?"

"I'm sure you'll recognise them for yourself," he said, taking one of them and throwing it to her.

She caught it and studied the front. She immediately recognised the handwriting and the Berlin postmark.

With fury she realised they were her letters from Hugo.

"*How did you get these?*" she demanded.

"We called to your mother's house."

"*Called?*" she cried, appalled. "You mean you searched my home? Went through my things? Went through my personal items?"

The man said nothing.

"How dare you! *How dare you!*" she shouted, getting to her feet. "My mother! She must be beside herself! I'm going home! I will be making a full complaint about what has been going on! You can't do this!"

Karina went marching over to the door and went to open it but to her frustration she found it was locked.

"Sit down, Miss Harper – please – let's not waste any more time unnecessarily."

"Waste more time! But it's you who are wasting everyone's time!" she ranted, her eyes filled with fury. "I'm not the enemy, damn you! I'm against the Nazis more than anyone for what they are doing to Hugo. And as for the Irish – it is ridiculous to think I have been somehow colluding with them after what they did to me and my family – they burned down our beautiful home during their bloody War of Independence!"

"Calm down, Miss Harper. I believe you. But we had to be sure and investigate you fully after what was going on in your life came to our attention. But I believe your story mainly because these letters from Berlin back up what you have said."

Despite her anger, Karina felt a wave of relief sweep over her. She had felt very vulnerable with all her rights stripped away and had genuinely feared that she would be interned for the duration of the war.

She walked back slowly to her chair and sat down.

"You had no right to read those letters – they are of an extremely private nature," she whispered.

"I know – I read them," he said, allowing a smirk to cross his face that made her go red. He opened a cigarette packet and, taking one himself, he offered her one.

She reached forward for a cigarette and he lit it for her with his lighter.

"You should be grateful for those letters – otherwise you very well might have found yourself in the women's Holloway prison tonight," he said.

"For sleeping with Gabriel Ford?" She was aghast.

"For everything you have been doing, Miss Harper! You have been treading a tightrope in very dangerous times."

She inhaled her cigarette and thought carefully. "I really do need to see my mother immediately … you don't understand, she went through a terrible time when our house in Ireland was attacked by Republicans … for your men to arrive at her home and ransack the place will have distressed her terribly."

"Do not worry. She is fine and there was no ransacking. Our men showed up pretending to be from the Gas Board looking for a leak. She is at home, none the wiser about what is occurring."

Karina was hugely relieved and nodded her understanding.

"My name is Kendrick Wells, British Security Services," said the man, holding out his hand to her.

She looked at his hand sceptically, before reaching out and shaking it.

"I would like to say 'pleased to meet you' – but I'm not really!" She took a drag from her cigarette. "May I go home now, Mr Wells?"

"Not yet, Karina," said Kendrick, lifting Hugo's letters and fanning himself with them. "While I was listening to your explanation of events I wasn't sure if you were quite mad or a genius – to go to such lengths to get what you wanted."

"I'm neither, I fear – or at least I hope – I am just trying to rescue the man I am very much in love with … and I would do anything to get him out of Germany."

"Maybe I could help you with this?" said Kendrick.

Her mouth dropped open in amazement. "Help me? Could you really? But why would you?"

"I think you're wasted in the typing pool at the Foreign Office, Karina. I think you have more than showed through your manipulation of very clever and important men like Gabriel Ford, Sir William and Alfred Smyth that you could be an asset to us now war has finally arrived." He put his cigarette out in the ashtray on the table.

"To us? You mean to the British Security Services?"

"Yes," said Kendrick.

"Oh no!" she said, shaking her head and smiling. "You've got the wrong girl! Whatever you have in mind – I'm certainly not the girl for it! I don't even like politics!"

"But you want to help your nation during the war, don't you, as best you can?"

"Of course! But I can best help my nation by getting back to my typewriter at the Foreign Office and keeping on churning out those perfectly typed papers!"

"I think you can do a lot more than that. I think, with your charms and cunning mind, we could make a lot better use of you."

"You are completely overestimating me! Just ask Mrs Potter – she'll let you know quickly how unreliable I am! I'm no asset to winning the war. I just want to enjoy myself in the 400 Club and be with the man I love!"

"But you can't be with the man you love, can you? You can't be with him or speak with him – you don't even know where Hugo is. This is where I can help you. I can use our spies and contacts to try and locate him and – if we can – help him to get him out of Germany if it is remotely possible at this stage."

Karina's eyes widened and filled with tears. "Don't say that unless you really mean it."

"This might be your only chance to rescue Hugo," he said.

"But – but what would you expect me to do?"

"As we expected, but hoped against, the Irish have indeed declared neutrality. As Ireland was always part of the United Kingdom in the past and is now part of the Commonwealth, it never of course had the need to have a British embassy or an ambassador there. The war has changed all that and, with Ireland now determined to go its own way, it's the British government's intention to appoint its first envoy to Dublin. The government feels this is necessary to maintain good and close relations with Ireland during the war."

"But what has all this to do with me?"

"We want you to transfer to work at the new embassy in Dublin."

"Dublin! Oh no, I have no desire to ever put a foot back into that country after what happened to my family there!" Karina shook her head vehemently.

"But, you see, this is what makes you so suitable to go to Dublin – your complete knowledge and understanding of the country and its people. It will give you a natural advantage."

"Natural advantage to do what?" she demanded.

"Ireland is going to be a flashpoint during this war. Nobody knows how or where the country will go ... the population is still so bitter after the Anglo-Irish war that there is huge anti-British sentiment there. A group of people burned the effigy of Neville Chamberlain in Dublin city centre the day war was declared. There is known to be a number of Nazi sympathisers in the Dublin government. Yet, the close ties between Britain and Ireland remain and we are getting a confidential agreement from Mr de Valera that they will secretly assist Britain in the war as best they can, while outwardly remaining resolutely neutral. There is a risk Ireland may be invaded by the Nazis or indeed there may be a need for us to invade Ireland in order to secure its strategic position."

Karina nodded. It was true that having grown up in Ireland she was very familiar with the sentiments and feelings within the country. From all her typing at the Foreign Office and her attendance at Great Hankerton Hall, she was also acutely aware of the importance of its potential role during the war.

"But – what am I to do to help you in Dublin?" she asked.

"Be our eyes and ears. Be part of the network we are establishing there to assist us. Gather as much information as possible, network as much as possible and report back to us everything you read and see – not only about your colleagues at the embassy but the people you will meet as part of your work with the Irish government. Use the skills you showed in manipulating Alfred Smyth and Sir William

Baxter to find out anything you can. Your relationship with Gabriel Ford will be crucial for us to infiltrate the Irish government and to find out what they are doing and planning."

"My relationship with Gabriel Ford! But I have no relationship with that man!"

"You spent a night with him, that's a start, and with the enquiries he was making about you at Great Hankerton Hall it's clear he was quite taken with you."

"But I heard he was engaged!"

"All the better! He will be open to blackmail already. You have something on him – use it!" encouraged Kendrick with a steely look in his eyes.

"And what – what if I refuse to have any part of this?"

"It's your choice, of course. You will have to live with the knowledge you didn't help your country when you were asked to … and I think we both know that you will never see your lover in Berlin again. This is your one chance, through us, to find him and rescue him."

She sat in silence for a few minutes while she stared at Hugo's letters.

"So when do I go to Dublin?" she asked eventually.

CHAPTER 15

Karina walked down the street to her home that night, holding her handbag tightly to her. It contained all the letters given back to her by Kendrick. She didn't know what to think. There was a maelstrom of emotions whirling through her – from fear to confusion to hope. She had been given hope at last that she could find Hugo. She had finally been given access to the powerful people who could save him. It was an amazing opportunity. She put her key in the front door and walked in. The wireless was on in the kitchen and she went in to find her mother there, cooking a dinner of roast beef.

"That smells nice," said Karina.

"Well, I think I might have got the last piece of roast beef in Chelsea. I thought I would grab it before the rationing begins to take effect. I've done us a nice gravy as well."

Karina took off her jacket and sat down at a chair at the table.

"I had such a day!" said Penny as she stirred the gravy. "These men called from the Gas Board – all business-like they were, with clipboards and pens. They said there was a suspected leak – imagine! Anyway, they searched everywhere for the leak and it turned out there was none at all in the end – can you imagine?"

Karina smiled at her. "Mama, come and sit for a moment. I've got something to tell you. I'm going away for a short while."

"Away? But where?" said Penny, looking concerned as she wiped her hands on her apron and approached the table cautiously. "But where? It can't be to Berlin – not now with the war!"

"I've been offered a promotion at work. To work in Dublin."

"Dublin!" exclaimed Penny as she plonked herself down at the table in shock.

"It's only for a short while – I promise!" said Karina.

"I must say I was most surprised when I heard you were to be transferred to the new consulate in Dublin," said Mrs Potter as Karina sat in her office. "A special request came in for you from the legation in Dublin itself, I understand."

"It took me by surprise myself."

"And not just as a typist, I understand, but a fully fledged secretary – I do hope you are up to the job, Karina." Mrs Potter looked sceptical.

"I'm sure with the wonderful training I have received here from you, I shall be," said Karina.

"It is just as well you didn't get your posting to Berlin. All the staff there have been arrested and interned by the Nazis. So much for diplomatic immunity – we are desperately trying to negotiate their transfer to us," said Mrs Potter, looking very concerned.

Karina nodded. The arrest of all the personnel at the Berlin embassy had shocked everyone at the Foreign Office. She realised that if she had been transferred she would be in custody too. And if the Nazis were willing to arrest diplomats from foreign countries, then she shuddered to think what they would do to their own citizens like Hugo.

"I will miss you, Karina!" said Vera with a little tear in her eye. "Who will provide us with intrigue now? No more tales from the 400 Club. No more entertainment!"

"I don't think there would have been much entertainment to report in any case, now that the war has arrived," said Karina.

"Well – best of luck in Dublin. Keep your head high and your corset fastened!"

"Quite!" said Karina, as she gave her a quick hug and then hurried from the building.

As she jumped on the bus home she was filled with excitement. She had been given a golden opportunity and was determined to use it to find Hugo.

* * *

"I really wish you wouldn't go, Karina," said Penny who looked terrified as she watched her daughter pack.

"I have no choice, Mama. I must go where I am sent."

"But why there? Why to that wretched country?"

"I don't know – perhaps because I'm from there and they feel I can help navigate the waters for the new embassy that is being set up there," said Karina, knowing she must never let anybody, even her mother, know what was happening behind the scenes with her posting.

"You are *not* from there, Karina. Just because you were born there and were there as a child does *not* make you Irish – certainly the Irish themselves will never accept you as one of them."

"Well, that is their concern. I've always felt Irish deep down, whether they want me or not! And, however badly they have treated us in the past, I still feel I am from there!" said Karina, allowing the bitterness to the surface.

"Well, I've written to our friends the Berrys and let them know you are coming over and they are looking forward to seeing you. You can rely on them, Karina – they are old friends."

Karina nodded. The Berrys were indeed old friends. The father, Major Utred Berry, had been her own father's best friend. He had two daughters, Patience and Grace, who Karina was friends with and who regularly came to London for the social scene. They had been presented at court as debutantes a few years ago. Something that had never happened to Karina as they couldn't afford it.

There was a knock on the door and Penny went to answer it. A minute later she arrived in with Julian.

"Hello," he said sheepishly as he came into the bedroom.

She gave him a cold look. "Oh, so you have come to say goodbye, have you?"

"Yes, and not just with you going to Dublin – I am away to France." He took off his coat and she saw he was in uniform.

"Oh!" she said, looking alarmed. She didn't know why she was surprised because of course Julian would be joining the army like the others. He just seemed singularly unsuited to have anything to do with the military.

"Could you ever forgive me for the truly horrendous trick I played on you over Hugo?" he asked, looking very embarrassed.

"It was really all my fault – I put poor Julian up to it all – I practically forced him to do it," said Penny.

"Oh, I know that, Mama," said Karina cuttingly.

"Well – let's just agree to share the responsibility," said Julian, not exonerating himself. "I just couldn't go off to France without putting things right – it would be too dreadful."

Karina managed to smile. "Of course I forgive you, Julian. I love you far too much to ever be mad with you for too long."

He held out his arms to her and she went to hug him.

"Well, this is a turn-up for the books – you in Dublin and me in France – whatever will Club 400 do with us away?" he said, laughing.

"Well, they will just have to keep the champagne on ice for us until we can meet back there … and, when we do, hopefully the war will be over and we shall have Hugo with us," said Karina.

"Of course," said Julian, hugging her tightly. "One thing, with you in Dublin and London expected to be bombed, may I suggest your mother moves to a cottage on my estate? She would be much safer there."

Karina smiled and nodded. "Thank you, Julian."

She knew Julian was making this gesture as much for her as for Penny as she would be fretting nonstop about her once the bombings started.

"A cottage in the country! But whatever am I supposed to do all day long there? I shall die of boredom!" cried Penny.

"Crosswords, Mama! Learn to do crosswords!"

She smiled at Julian and hugged him again.

CHAPTER 16

"Eighteen years since we achieved independence and it takes a war with the Germans before the British begrudgingly award us an ambassador," said de Valera in a meeting with Gabriel.

"They are only doing so for practical reasons so communication with us will be easier during the war, now we are to remain neutral," said Gabriel. "It is a bitter pill for them to swallow."

"We can but hope they will continue to swallow it. We risk provoking the British into launching a fullscale invasion. The reality is we stand with our democratic friends throughout the world in the hope that the Nazis will be defeated and so, even though we must absolutely be seen to be neutral, we will help our British neighbours discreetly, as best we can, to victory."

"The reality is there are sections of the population that do not share that sentiment, Taoiseach. I have real information that there are units of the IRA in Berlin actively working with the Nazis. I am trying to decipher as much information as I can about them – who they are and what exactly they are doing."

"We need to try and bring those under control as quickly as possible," said de Valera.

"When was that ever easy?" asked Gabriel.

De Valera lifted up a letter and started to read it, peering closely at it. Gabriel had witnessed many times recently how de Valera's eyesight was failing quickly.

"This is a letter from Chamberlain," said de Valera. "We have been going back and forth these past weeks trying to settle what title we are to give the new ambassadorial role to Dublin. The British wanted 'Minister', we wanted 'Ambassador' – we could not agree. Then they wanted British Representative *in* Ireland, which is not acceptable to us. Finally we have agreed British Representative *to* Ireland. So finally they have agreed at last to treat us a fully independent nation that deserves an envoy posted to us and not just over us."

Gabriel nodded. With the whole continent about to go up in smoke, he felt it was strange to have such debate on a comparatively trivial matter. But he sighed as he knew that had always been the way in relations between the two countries.

Cynthia had an easel set up at the end of the garden as she painted the view of the sea. There was a wrought-iron garden table and chairs close by and Tess sat there drinking her tea. They had both just had lunch there before Cynthia had returned to her painting. Cynthia's two Labradors lay stretched out on the lawn, enjoying the autumn sunshine.

"Don't you ever get tired of painting that sea?" asked Tess.

"Never! No matter how many times I paint it, it is never the same. There is always a different shade cast from a cloud, a different ray of light changing the colour of the water, a different boat on the horizon."

"Well, it always looks the same to me," sighed Tess.

"That's because you don't understand the sea like I do, Tess. You look out there and just see water. But I see the unknown ... what is going on underneath that calm surface ... will those clouds in the distance bring a storm and turn that calmness into a torrent of angry waves?"

As Tess studied her mother-in-law, she decided Cynthia was very much like the sea – you never knew what was going on under that calm surface.

"Very profound!" said Tess. "Let's hope there are no German submarines under that water, that's all I can say – ignoring our neutrality!"

"I'm sure there are German submarines all over the Irish coast," said Cynthia.

"Cynthia! Don't say that!" said Tess, giving a sudden shiver.

"Why not? It's probably true. We have nothing to fear from the Germans – they came to our assistance during the Easter Rising."

"Well, I'm frightened of them, and I don't mind who knows it! I can't sleep at night because of what they are doing in Poland. They destroyed the place in a matter of weeks! Murder, mayhem, bombs! And as for their treatment of the Jews – shocking, let me tell you!"

"I thought it was Tim's snoring that kept you awake at night, not your touching concern for Poland?" said Cynthia knowingly.

Tess cringed as she realised Cynthia had been listening to her conversation with Gabriel in the garden the night of his engagement party. She'd had too much champagne that night and had spoken too freely which she had regretted ever since. Even more so now it was confirmed that Cynthia had indeed been eavesdropping.

"I'm meeting Gabriel and Siobhán for dinner tonight at the Shelbourne," said Cynthia.

"That's nice for you," said Tess.

"Always nice for me to be in their company. They are so much in *love*. They can hardly keep their hands off each other!"

"I hadn't noticed."

"They are an absolute pleasure to be around. Siobhán has asked me to give a talk to the girls at her school."

"That's nice," said Tess, lighting up a cigarette, causing Cynthia to frown.

"I do love giving talks at the schools to the young people – particularly the girls. I mean, it's all very well for them to read about the Glorious Revolution in books – but the little dears can hardly believe it when they meet me, Rory Ford's widow and an eyewitness to history," said Cynthia smugly.

"Nice for them," said Tess, discreetly raising her eyes to heaven.

"Siobhán has asked me to go bridal-shopping with her – for the dress," said Cynthia.

"Hasn't she got her own mother for that?"

"I suppose but Mags isn't actually big on fashion, let's face it. And I guess Siobhán just has come to rely on me and respect my opinion so much. She has almost become the daughter that I never had."

Tess blinked back tears of frustration, listening to her mother-in-law.

Cynthia suddenly stopped painting and walked to the edge of the garden.

She stared down the beach. "There he is again," she said.

"Who?" asked Tess.

"That man. He's on the beach every other day either painting or taking photos ... I think I'll go and investigate." She turned to the Labradors and called "*Come!*"

The two dogs jumped up and trotted after her as she made her way to the steps that led down to the beach.

Tess again raised her eyes to heaven and shook her head in disbelief.

"Of course, Cynthia! Don't mind me, Cynthia!" she whispered angrily.

Cynthia walked down the beach, approaching the man she had spotted as he painted at the easel he had set up there.

"Hello there!" she called as she walked towards him, followed by the two dogs.

The man turned around in surprise. He was in his early fifties, a similar vintage to herself, Cynthia suspected. Although not stereotypically good-looking, Cynthia found him to have a quirky attractiveness with his intense blue eye, high cheekbones and stocky strong build.

"It's a nice day for painting," she said. "Actually I'm painting the same view as you, from my garden up there." She pointed back to her home.

"*Ahh*, a fellow artist!" the man declared with a foreign accent.

"Quite so!" she said as she came up to his easel and inspected his work. He was painting the view to the south and had recreated an amazing likeness of Bray Head and the Sugar Loaf on his canvas.

"That's very good!" Cynthia complimented him.

"Really? You think so?" He seemed delighted.

"Your contours, your tones – exquisite."

"Thank you – Mrs ...?"

115

"Ford – Cynthia Ford."

"So pleased to make your acquaintance. I am Marc Pietch." He offered his hand and she shook it.

"I have seen you down here on the beach quite a few times this past month. Have you moved to our area?"

"Temporarily, yes – I am from Poland."

"Oh, I see!" said Cynthia, looking concerned.

"I had come here from my home in Warsaw to paint in August and take the sea air. Then suddenly the invasion occurred and I have been stranded here ever since – unable to get home."

"Oh, how awful for you, you poor man! It is tragic what is happening in Poland – it keeps me awake at night thinking about it!"

"I can barely look at the newspapers each morning with what has happened at home." He paused, lost in thought. "So I am trapped here for the foreseeable future. I am renting a house just over there on Bay Road."

"Ah, so near, we are almost neighbours! So would you care to come back to my house and see my painting?"

The man looked surprised. "But I would be delighted!"

"Excellent – and we can have some tea, hot and sweet, at the same time!"

Back at the house, Cynthia gathered a number of her paintings and arranged them around the drawing room. She watched as Marc Pietch inspected them in detail, peering at them over his glasses. Although she never showed it, she was always filled with anxiety when displaying her paintings to anyone. She had harboured ambitions once to be an artist and had brought a selection of her paintings to an art critic in Dublin for his opinion. The experience had been an utterly humiliating one for her. The critic had told her that, although she was a very capable landscape artist, capturing the scene she set her paintbrushes to with detailed accuracy, her art unfortunately was devoid of any passion, emotion or vision. "In short, Mrs Ford," the art critic had concluded, "your paintings are more suited to end up on the wall of a lowly paid bank clerk's dining room than any art gallery of note!"

Cynthia felt the sharp pang of rejection once again as she remembered the critic's harsh words and she quickly dismissed the horrible memory to concentrate on the present.

"But these are really quite remarkable, Mrs Ford," said Marc Pietch as he now held up a magnifying glass to one of her paintings.

"Remarkable?" she repeated.

He turned to her with a flourish. "When did you last exhibit, Mrs Ford?"

"Exhibit? But I have never exhibited," said Cynthia.

"But why ever not?"

"Well ... I did once take them to an art critic but he said my paintings were ..." Cynthia had another flashback to the art critic and his scathing words of assault on her talent – *banal, bland, mundane and terribly mediocre.* She coughed loudly and banished the image of the art critic from her mind. "He said they were unsuitable for the market."

"Well, I do not know what market your art critic was referring to, but clearly he did not know what he was talking about," said Pietch.

Although Cynthia remained utterly cool on the surface, her heart had begun to race excitedly.

"Do you really think so?" She moved closer to the paintings to inspect them.

"My dear Mrs Ford, I have been in the art world all my life and consider myself to be something of an expert and I tell you your work is remarkably good – the accuracy, the precision, the detail – remarkable, I tell you!"

"Well, I am – I am flattered!" She allowed herself to smile.

"It is not flattery I offer you, Mrs Ford, but high praise for a wonderful talent ... if you are interested in selling your work, I am certain I could get you a very good price."

"Sell my paintings!" said Cynthia, now becoming slightly dizzy with excitement.

"Forgive me, let me explain – you see, I also act as an art dealer. I have a number of clients, who are always willing to purchase what I recommend, trusting I am putting a wise investment their way. I have a number of wealthy clients in New York and Boston and Chicago, Irish Americans, who would be delighted to buy such paintings of Ireland and its beautiful landscapes. They would be willing to pay good money for your art."

"How much?"

"Up to ten shillings," said Pietch.

"Ten shillings!" exclaimed Cynthia as she quickly sat down on an armchair to steady herself. "Per painting?"

"Maybe more," said Pietch. "What do you say, Mrs Ford?"

Cynthia recovered her composure and rose to her feet smiling. "Please – call me Cynthia, as I know we are to be close friends. I say your proposal sounds delightful and I suggest we discuss it in more detail over a freshly baked Victoria sponge!"

CHAPTER 17

As Karina sat on the train, gazing at the English countryside on her way to Liverpool to get the boat to Dublin, she wondered would it be a very different England that she returned to when her tenure in Ireland was over. She wasn't sure how long she was expected to be in Ireland but as she had left London there was a terrible feeling of uneasiness and foreboding everywhere.

The blackout had become law on the day war was declared and everybody had to ensure no light escaped from a window or a door each night. People were going to incredible lengths, not just relying on heavy thick curtains but actually painting the glass black and stuffing blankets over the outside doors to make sure not an inch of light escaped. Karina didn't know, but she was sure a pilot up in the sky in charge of a bomber wouldn't be able to see a glimmer of light that escaped from under a front door in a street so far down on the ground. But it didn't matter whether he could or not, the civilian population were not taking any chances. She had typed up reports for the government that said they expected the bombing to be instant and merciless, with perhaps three hundred thousand people killed in the first week which would lead to the breakdown of law and order as the country descended into chaos. It sounded like something from a H.G. Wells novel, Karina thought. When they had first come to London, she used to see veterans from the last war in the streets, who were suffering from shell shock resulting from the bombings on the battlefields. It had upset and frightened her and now the experts were saying this shell shock would be widespread in the civilian population when the air raids began. She shuddered at the thought.

She was just relieved that her mother was ensconced in a cottage on Julian's estate.

"I wouldn't set foot in Ireland if it was the last place on earth!" said Penny. "I'd take my chance with the bombs and the Nazis rather than go there ever again after what they did to us at Inishwood!"

Indeed, that was some 'take' considering Penny was secretly Jewish and so was at a premium risk from the Nazis. But whatever about their bombs at night, everyone was sure there was no real risk of a Nazi invasion of Britain. They would be stopped at France like in the last war.

In a way, Karina felt guilty leaving London for neutral Ireland when everyone else had to suffer at home. But she reminded herself she was going there on a mission – to help Britain win the war in whatever small way she could and to save Hugo. And, no less than Penny, Ireland was the last place she wanted to be. She never thought she would set a foot in the place again. And she felt terribly nauseous and apprehensive about going to a country where her class was so reviled.

After arriving in Liverpool, she got a taxi to the docks and boarded the boat for Dublin. As she walked up and down the decks, she longed to arrive on the other side. The aerial war might not have started but the war at sea was in full swing. Seemingly there were German U-boats cruising the Irish sea looking for targets. There had already been battles in the Atlantic and merchant ships had been torpedoed. No passenger boats had been attacked yet, but everyone knew it would only be a matter of time.

She felt relieved when the boat arrived in Dublin the next morning at Dun Laoghaire. She gathered her two suitcases and walked onto the busy pier.

She was to be met by somebody from the embassy who would be holding a card with her name on it and she desperately searched the crowd but could see nobody.

"Karina? Karina Harper?" said a voice behind her and she turned to see a young brunette woman with crimped hair and a neat sensible tweed suit standing there.

"Yes?"

"I'm Emily Fernsby – Emily from the embassy – gosh, that sounds like a cabaret song, doesn't it? Emily from the Embassy!" said the brunette in a clipped English upper-class tone, giving a wide toothy grin. She held up a card with Karina's name on it.

"Ah, I was expecting a man would be collecting me," said Karina with a smile.

"Most of the men at the embassy have buggered off back to Blighty for their army training, leaving just us gals and the older men!" said Emily, reaching forward and taking one of Karina's cases. "Which leaves the possibility of romantic entanglements pretty limited unless you consider going local – never a good thing, let me tell you! Follow me!"

Karina followed Emily from the port to an open-top motorcar parked on the road outside. Emily took both the suitcases and put them in the backseat, then climbed into the driver's seat.

"With the men being drafted off to war, we women have to roll up our sleeves and get on with it! My aunt drove an ambulance in the last war, you know. The hospital said she was the best man they ever had!" said Emily as she started the engine and tore off down the street. "Right, first things first – a quick tour! Show you to your new abode and then report for duty, I say!"

Karina smiled to herself as Emily was an exact replica of Vera and most of the other girls who worked at the Foreign Office in London. The diplomatic corps obviously attracted a type, Karina thought as she observed Emily's no-nonsense driving.

As Emily drove through Dublin city, Karina was filled with emotion. It all looked so familiar and it felt like coming home. She had hated what had happened to her and her family so much in the final year that she had convinced herself she hated the country too. And yet, as she recognised different landmarks as they drove by, she allowed herself to remember how much she had loved the place growing up. Why would she not have? It was her home.

That was why the rejection when they were forced out was all the more cruel. They had regularly come to Dublin from Inishwood which was why Karina was so familiar with the city. But the last time she had been in the city was when she and her family were evacuating to London after independence had been granted. By then the city had endured years of warfare and was in a sorry state with many of the buildings in ruins. Now, as Emily drove, Karina was mesmerised by how those buildings and streets had now been rebuilt and had recovered much of their original glory.

"It's exciting now that the war has started, isn't it?" said Emily as she perilously took a corner.

"Is it?" said Karina, astonished at this atitude.

"Don't you think so?"

Karina wondered how to respond but luckily didn't have to.

"Ah, here we are! Your new home!" said Emily, swinging the motorcar towards the pavement. They were in Merrion Square, just across from the Irish Parliament.

The two women got out of the motorcar and took a suitcase each. Emily led her up the steps to a grand Georgian door.

Inside was a long ornate hallway and Karina followed Emily to the wide staircase.

"Top floor, I'm afraid – I hope you like climbing!" said Emily, who clearly had no problem, the way she bounded up the steps.

Karina was immediately taken with the flat.

"It's very nice," she said as she walked around the large sitting room.

It had a nice ornate marble fireplace and a chandelier hanging from the very high ceiling. There were wooden floors throughout the flat.

A comfortable bedroom led off the small hallway, as did the bathroom and a small kitchen.

"Really very nice," said Karina as she returned to the sitting room and stood at one of the tall windows, looking out at the park in the middle of the square and Leinster House, the Parliament building, opposite.

"There's a nice view of the park," said Emily.

"Yes."

"And more importantly of the Parliament – or the Dáil, as they call it – which will give you a bird's-eye view to observe the comings and goings. The majestic building beside it is Government Buildings, which is where the Taoiseach or Prime Minister's office is located. You will be watching the activity there as well as part of your role." Emily's voice had changed as she spoke the last sentence, cold compared to her previous jolly tones.

Karina quickly turned from the window.

Emily's toothy grin had now changed to a cold business-like expression that gave Karina a shiver.

Emily sat down on one of the armchairs and lit a cigarette. She looked at Karina coolly.

"*You're* my contact here from the Service?" asked Karina.

"You look disappointed. Were you expecting a man?"

"I – I guess I was," said Karina.

"Women always make better undercover agents – people suspect us less. And they won't suspect you at all, especially the way you manipulate men, from what I've heard."

"I don't know what you've heard, but I imagine it is exaggerated," said Karina.

"We've been trying to get something on Gabriel Ford and his family for years," said Emily. "Now we finally have it and it couldn't have come at a better time. If we chose to reveal it, not only would his personal life with his lovely new Irish fiancée and his hero of a mother be destroyed but his career would be over too. Him having pre-marital sex with a dirty Protestant aristocrat while engaged to another would destroy him in the eyes of the Church and the people if the truth ever came out."

"I really am uncomfortable with the idea of blackmailing the man to get what we want," objected Karina.

"Well, then, make sure we get what we want using different means – blackmailing him can be used as a last resort." Emily pointed to an armchair across from her. "Take a seat and I'll go through the situation we are in with you."

Karina sat down and waited.

Emily threw her cigarette into the fire grate and began speaking. "The reality is Britain is in a precarious position in Ireland. There is huge dislike and distrust among the general population towards Britain and with quite some justification I would say after the War of Independence some twenty years ago. The Irish government are insistent on neutrality yet are our natural allies and are professing they will assist us behind the scenes in any way they can. Their Prime Minister de Valera and Neville Chamberlain actually have a very good and cordial relationship, despite de Valera's central role in the fight for independence. They are a democratic nation, extremely pro-American, and appear to have little in common with the Nazis. De Valera and his cabinet are as wary and dislike the Nazis as much as any other democratic government ... that is our understanding of the situation."

"So why are we spying on them if this is the situation?" asked Karina.

"Because we cannot be confident that is the full story. Half of de Valera's cabinet, including the Minister for External Affairs, are vehemently anti-British. The Church has become an integral part of the state since independence and controls the educational system where again vehement anti-British rhetoric is taught. And our experience of the Irish is that they can say one thing but mean another ... they have indicated to us that they have 'got our back', quite literally as our western neighbour ... but how much can we trust them? What are they saying to the Germans? Thinking you can trust somebody and *knowing* you can trust them are two very different things. Also the Irish army is small and ill-equipped, their intelligence services leave much to be desired. The Germans know all this too and Ireland is a weak spot to our west. We don't want to see Ireland, through their lack of competence, being used by the Fascists as a base to attack Britain or weaken our position in the war."

"So what can I do?" asked Karina.

"Firstly, you can keep an eye on the comings and goings at the Parliament buildings across the square. We can inform you of important events or personnel who are attending the building and you can report on their arrival, how long they stayed etc. Secondly, we need to infiltrate the Irish government and senior civil service.

We have identified your relationship with Gabriel Ford as a major fault line for the Irish government. He has access to everyone in the Irish establishment and the information he could give us would be invaluable."

"As I keep saying, it is hardly a relationship I have with Gabriel Ford," Karina said.

"Kendrick spoke to you already about Ford, Karina. If it's not a relationship then use whatever means you can, blackmail, bribery." Emily reached into her satchel and took out a pair of binoculars which she handed to Karina. She pointed to the Parliament buildings across the square through the window. "So you can keep tabs on who is arriving and how long they stay. First job for you is this afternoon. The meeting between your boyfriend and the German Minister, Dr Eduard Hempel, is taking place. Keep watch and note what time he arrives, how long he stays and what time he leaves."

"But how will I know who he is?"

"That's easy," smiled Emily. "The car will have a Nazi flag flying at its helm and here is a photograph for good measure."

Emily again reached into her satchel and handed the photograph to Karina.

"Right! I'd better get back to the embassy or they will wonder have I been kidnapped!" Emily had suddenly changed persona back to the toothy, grinning, cheery girl she had portrayed herself originally as. "I will see you at the embassy first thing in the morning – nine sharp!" She headed for the door.

"Emily!" called Karina.

"Yes?" asked Emily, swinging around, smiling.

"I just wondered had you managed to find out anything about my friend in Berlin yet? Kendrick did tell you about that aspect of our deal?"

"Oh yes, he did mention. Nothing heard back yet. Our people on the ground there are being hunted like rabbits since war was declared. I'll see if I can find anything out."

"Thank you," said Karina.

"*Ta ta!*" said Emily but gave a cold nod to the binoculars before she swished out the door.

Karina bit her lip and lifted up the binoculars. She went and sat inside the window, using the curtain to make sure she could not be observed from outside.

As she trained the binoculars on the front of the Government Buildings, she sighed, realising it was going to be a long afternoon.

CHAPTER 18

Gabriel drove down Sloperton Road in Monkstown, looking out for the address he had been given as the residence of the German Minister in Ireland, Dr Eduard Hempel. The meeting had originally been scheduled to take place at Government Buildings as de Valera had been expected to attend. As it transpired, de Valera would not be attending and it was rescheduled to take place at Hempel's home. The fact was, the Irish had decided that, as this was the first meeting with the Germans, it might be better for Gabriel to meet Hempel on his own in order to gauge the situation better. If de Valera was in attendance, the Irish might be pressed for decisions by Hempel at the meeting. Whereas, with just Gabriel there, he could not be expected to give any decision or concrete opinion as naturally he would have to refer any demands from Hempel back to de Valera and the cabinet.

Gabriel saw the name of the house, *Gortleitragh*, on the gateway and drove into the driveway. It was a very large two-storey-over-basement semi-detached Victorian villa with a perfectly manicured garden. There were two motorcars already in the driveway, one with a Nazi flag on it. Gabriel felt supremely uncomfortable seeing even that small Nazi flag on show in Ireland. When the Germans were appointing a Minister to Ireland in 1937, de Valera's government had insisted that the appointee must not be a Nazi. After much diplomatic wrangling, Berlin conceded to Dublin's demand and a non-Nazi, Eduard Hempel, was appointed. One year later in 1938, Hempel was forced to join the Nazi party. Despite the Irish government's fierce fight not to have a Nazi in the position, that is exactly what they ended up with and now they could do nothing about it. Gabriel thought it was a valuable lesson to learn – the Nazis were excellent mind-players and would do or say anything to get what they wanted – but, as soon as they got what they wanted, their word meant nothing. Gabriel reminded himself to remain alert as he bounded up the steps to the front door and banged the knocker loudly.

A minute later the door was opened by Mrs Hempel – Eva. Gabriel had met her before at different functions and found her to be pleasant.

"Good afternoon, Mr Ford," she said in English. "I hope this did not put you out of your way – to come to Monkstown to see my husband?"

"Good afternoon, Mrs Hempel. No inconvenience in the least as I live in Monkstown myself – Victoria Terrace," said Gabriel, stepping inside.

"Ah, then we are practically neighbours."

Gabriel saw the Hempel children playing happily in the hallway.

"The children are settling in well, Mrs Hempel?"

"Yes," she smiled. "It is like home for them now."

As Gabriel waved and smiled at them, he thought how lucky they were compared to other children around Europe. The Polish children whose homes and country were being destroyed amidst mass killings, or the British and German children being separated from their parents for who knew how long as they were evacuated from the cities. But there were no such scenes in this leafy South Dublin suburb, only happy children playing in a safe environment with their whole family intact.

Gabriel had to fight a growing feeling of anger as he was led into the drawing room and was greeted by Hempel.

Gabriel reminded himself he was a diplomat representing a neutral country and Hempel was representing a country non-hostile to Ireland. He tried to banish the terrible news reports he read of what was going on in Poland and also the fact that Hempel had a Nazi party badge, even if he was being forced to own it.

The two men shook hands.

"Just in time for tea, Mr Ford," said Hempel. "Do sit down."

The two men sat, facing each other.

After his wife served them tea from a silver teapot, she excused herself and left the room.

The two men studied each other for a while.

"Well, it is a very different world we are in now than when last we met a couple of months ago," said Hempel.

"It certainly is," said Gabriel. "It – very unfortunately – is. It is a great regret to the Irish government that war could not have been avoided in the end."

"A regret to us all," said Hempel. "But some things are unavoidable. Large parts of Poland have German people living there, so our only wish was to unite our people. I'm sure you as an Irishman can understand this with your desire to unite with your people in the north of the country which the British will not allow. It is your territory being kept away from you."

"Hardly the same thing, Dr Hempel, and I would like to think that we would not just roll our tanks across the border and invade the North as you have done with Poland – even if your territorial claims were in any way valid."

"It was not our choice to invade – we were attacked by the Polish first. It was self-defence," said Hempel, who could not even to manage to look as if he believed the lie he was being ordered to retell.

Gabriel arched an eyebrow as his face portrayed scepticism and disbelief. He wanted to ridicule this claim as a falsity that the Nazis had put out to justify the invasion but obviously Hempel had been told to toe the party line and to repeat this untruth, so there was no point in saying anything. Gabriel was here to determine Germany's position towards Ireland and to safeguard the country's neutrality.

"We are very pleased that Ireland has decided to pursue a strategy of neutrality and not join the British in their fight despite the immense pressure I can imagine Mr de Valera's government is under to do so," said Hempel.

"I am glad you understand the pressure we Irish are resisting to join the Allies, Dr Hempel, and the reason for my visit here today is to impress on you and your government in Berlin that we are taking our neutrality very seriously and we hope that you do too."

"But of course!"

"We expect Germany to respect our neutrality and to understand that under no circumstances will we allow German U-boat activity in Irish waters or tolerate our country to be used in any way as a base to spy on Britain."

"It goes without saying," said Hempel.

"We would look on any infringement of our neutrality as a hostile act," said Gabriel.

"You can assure your Mr de Valera that we Germans have no desire to do anything to upset the Irish people. Were we not your friends in the last war? Did we not supply arms to you to try and throw off the British oppression you were suffering under for hundreds of years?"

"I think, as educated men, we both know that was a case of my enemy's enemy is my friend more than any natural affiliation ... and, besides, that was a generation ago ... now things have changed – dramatically," said Gabriel.

Hempel waved to Gabriel from the doorway as he got into his motorcar to leave.

His wife joined him at the door.

"He always seems such a nice young man ... how did the meeting go?" she said.

"As expected – plenty of diplomatic nonsense," said Hempel as he watched the motorcar disappear through the gates. "He attempted to lay down the law with us ... repeated what would not be acceptable to the Irish government and people ... but, at the end of the day, behind our diplomatic niceties, both of us know that it is really irrelevant what is acceptable to the Irish ... they are quite powerless against the wishes of Hitler who will play them along until he decides the time is right to take what he wants."

CHAPTER 19

It was after midnight and Karina sat at the window in her new flat, staring out the window at Government Buildings through the binoculars. She was exhausted as she had been there since Emily had left, waiting for the German embassy motorcar with the Nazi flag on it or a man who looked like the one in the photo of the German ambassador. But she had seen neither. She sighed as she realised she must have missed his arrival despite her best efforts. She looked at her watch and realised there was no way he could be arriving so late. She sat back in the chair and decided to give it another hour just in case.

Next morning Karina walked from her flat in Merrion Square to start work in the British Embassy which was situated at 50 Upper Mount Street. As she walked past the lovely Georgian buildings and people in the streets smiled at her, she had an unusual feeling of having come home. This was the Ireland she remembered from her childhood. The friendly and warm people, the beautiful buildings, the gentle pace of life – before it had all changed during the War of Independence. Now as she continued walking through the streets it felt quite parochial with people riding their bicycles to work and the traffic much less congested than in London.

She got to the embassy, climbed up the steps of the huge Georgian building and knocked on the door.

"I'm Karina Harper – I'm starting work here today," she said to the security man who answered the door.

"Karina!" came Emily's now-familiar voice and the security man let her in.

Karina walked over to Emily who was standing by the stairs.

"Morning!" said Emily who was all bright and cheery.

Karina realised she was in toothy-grin rather than cold agent persona. Clearly, Emily did not let her mask slip even in the safe confines of the embassy.

"Found the place alright, did you?" asked Emily as she began to climb the stairs.

"Yes, the flat is very handy. I had to take quite a long bus ride in London to the Foreign Office each morning," said Karina, following her.

"At least it saves on the bus fare then!" said Emily. "So, we are all quite excited as the new so-called 'British Representative' to Dublin, Sir John Maffey, is arriving today. We'll all be meeting him this afternoon ... and we are all invited to a drinks party at the American embassy next Tuesday which is being given in honour of Sir John by the American ambassador."

"Oh – I'm glad I brought a couple of cocktail dresses!" said Karina.

"I'm wearing green – so avoid green so we don't clash!"

They reached the top floor and Emily swung open the door into an office.

They walked into the small room which had a desk and a typewriter situated in front of a tall Georgian window that looked down to the street below.

"I've never worked in an office by myself before," said Karina, sitting down at the desk.

Emily quickly closed the door and hurried over to Karina, her facial expression completely changed.

"I–I waited at the window until one last night, but I saw no motorcar arrive with a Nazi flag or any man looking like Hempel," said Karina, knowing from Emily's expression she would not be wasting time beating around the bush.

"I know – they rescheduled their meeting to take place in Hempel's home in Dun Laoghaire instead of Leinster House."

"Well, I wish somebody had let me know!" said Karina. "My

back was aching by the time I finally pulled myself away from that window last night!"

Emily looked unimpressed. "I'm sure a girl who can stay out partying until three in the morning every night at the 400 Club can sit in an armchair looking out the window for a few hours without too much issue!"

As Karina shut her mouth quickly in case she was tempted to answer back, she wondered what else Emily had heard about her. She seemed to have been informed of an awful lot.

"Why was the meeting venue changed?" asked Karina, trying to show interest.

"We don't know. De Valera was supposed to be at the meeting but in the end only Gabriel Ford was. We need to find out what was discussed. Why was the meeting deemed so top secret that it was held in Hempel's house without even de Valera being present?"

Karina didn't know what to say so remained silent.

"Gabriel Ford will be at the American ambassador's party for Sir John next week so it is an excellent opportunity to rekindle your relationship with him," said Emily.

Karina's face clouded over. "Look, Emily, there is no relationship between Ford and me to rekindle! As I explained to Kendrick, our night together meant nothing – to either of us! One simple night that meant nothing to either of us. We were in the wrong place at the wrong time and fell into the wrong bed! I have done nothing but regret it since and I'm sure he – with his fiancée – feels the same way!"

"Let's hope he does – then he will not want what he did to come out," said Emily.

"Look," said Karina, "I want to do whatever I can to help with the war but I think you just have the wrong girl in me to do what you expect me to do! I'm no blackmailer – I just wouldn't be able to do it! I hardly know this Gabriel Ford at all, but he seemed decent enough but I don't want to bring that kind of fear and misery into anybody's life. I just couldn't live with myself if I did."

As Emily studied her, she believed it certainly was going against Karina Harper's nature to be doing such things. And yet she had proved herself more than capable of blackmailing Sir William

Baxter and manipulating Alfred Smyth to get what she wanted – which was why she was selected for this job in Dublin. However, Emily realised it was affairs of the heart that had led Karina to do those things in her desperate pursuit to find the love of her life.

"I thought you had agreed all this with Kendrick before coming here," said Emily crisply. "We were going to help you find Hugo in exchange for you going above and beyond the call of duty to help us win the war!"

"Well, yes, I had agreed to that. But you are basically expecting me to be a spy and I'm just not equipped to be one. I'm sorry, I'll do anything to help but I can't do this."

"Well, in that case we can't waste any more valuable time and resources trying to save your boyfriend from the Nazis," said Emily. "He's on his own from now on."

Karina blinked a few times. "Have you managed to find out where he is?"

"Not yet – but I can tell you that his safety – his life – was in danger from the Nazis. He was high on the list of people they classed as enemies of the Reich."

"I just have to find out where he is and what's happened to him!" said Karina. "You have to keep going and rescue him!"

"But, Karina, we have to prioritise. We are risking our people's lives by exposing them as they try to investigate Hugo's disappearance. You can't ask our people in Berlin to risk their safety if you are not willing to do what has to be done here in Dublin."

Karina nodded. "I understand, I completely understand. I'll do whatever I have to do. Alright – leave Gabriel Ford to me – I'll get you what you need from him."

"Very good," nodded Emily before pointing to the stack of papers that were left on the desk. "I'll let you get on with your official work."

Karina watched Emily leave then went to the window and stared out at the street down below.

Her heart was beating fast as she thought about Hugo. She began to shake as she thought of him in captivity. She needed to do anything she could to free him.

* * *

Upstairs in their bedroom at Roxford, Tess had changed into her nightdress and sat at her dressing table putting cold cream on her face while Tim sat up in bed reading through government documents.

"So Cynthia is now embarking on a career as an artist after meeting this Pole on the beach," said Tess. "At her age, can you imagine?"

"She's only fifty-two, Tess."

"Still a bit late for such a dramatic change of direction."

"She's been painting all her life, not that much of surprise." Tim looked up momentarily from his papers. "Just more of a surprise that anybody thinks she is any good!"

"Anyway, another string to Cynthia's bow! She never shut up about it when I met her for lunch today. As for this Polish man she has befriended – his whole country is being bombed and destroyed and he is discovering new talent for the art world! You'd think he'd have more on his mind."

"Everyone still has to earn a buck," said Tim, not looking up from his papers. "Had she anything else to say?"

"Oh, she got in her usual speeches – how brave she was during the Glorious Revolution. Why does she call the Rising that? Nobody else does! Then of course she spoke incessantly about Gabriel and Siobhán's wedding and wouldn't shut up how wonderful Siobhán is – *again*. And then kept saying how she couldn't wait for them to make her a grandmother – *again*!" She looked at Tim in the mirror to search for a reaction but could see none as he concentrated on his papers.

She stood up and went to the bed, folded down the blankets and sat down.

"The way she talks, she has basically written us off as being capable of ever giving her a grandchild," she said.

No response.

"Did you hear me?" she pushed.

He looked up from his papers. "I don't know why you spend so much time in her company if she pisses you off so much. It's like you can't keep away from her! You seem so impressed with her and you're craving her approval. The more she disapproves of you, the more you put yourself in the firing line and the more you crave her approval!"

"Well, family is important, Tim. It's easy for you and Gabriel as you both automatically get her approval as she sees you as an extension of herself. But I don't get that approval, I have to earn it. And being part of this family is important to me and should be important to you. The Ford name is famous throughout the country and we – you and I – are about to be shoved out in the cold when Siobhán marries into the family. We are becoming a laughing-stock at this stage."

"You're talking shit as usual," he said dismissively as he rattled his papers.

She leaned over, grabbed the papers and flung them through the air.

"What the fuck do you think you're doing?" he demanded.

"It's like this, Tim, neither of us particularly fancy the other anymore, if we ever actually did – but we are going to have a baby if it's the last thing I do."

"*What?*"

"Now – get on with the job," she demanded as she got into the bed.

He looked at her through gritted teeth as he leaned over to the lamp on his side table and turned it off.

CHAPTER 20

Gabriel and Siobhán walked down the long pier at Dun Laoghaire. The pier was quiet, despite it being a lovely warm evening. They each had an arm around the other as they strolled along.

Gabriel was gazing out across the sea and seemed lost in thought.

"Are you alright, Gabriel?" Siobhán asked, jolting him back to reality.

"Yes." He smiled down at her. "Of course."

"It's just you seem quite distracted recently – since you got back from England."

"Well, I – eh ..." He became uncomfortable at her words. "Nothing to do with you, Siobhán. Just there's been a lot on with work and the war – it's a whole new world to get used to."

"Of course ... as long as that's all it is?"

"Of course." He squeezed her waist with his hand. "I just hope we're doing the right thing – remaining neutral."

"We've no choice, Gabriel. I mean it would be suicide to join up with the British. We'd be inviting the Germans to come and bomb Dublin and the rest of the country ... sure, we are just getting on our feet after the country was destroyed after the War of Independence and the Civil War. This isn't our fight – we've had enough fighting in this country."

"So we stand on the sidelines and let the Nazis do their worst?"

"Sure if British and French Empires can't defeat the Nazis, what chance has little Ireland got in that case? Besides, if anyone in Ireland wants to go and fight the Nazis then nobody is stopping them, are they? Thousands of Irishmen have already joined the British army."

"Much to Cynthia's chagrin," sighed Gabriel.

"Well, your mother isn't the only one, Gabriel – plenty people cannot forgive the British for what they did during the War of Independence and now they expect us to join up with them? Not likely! But I'm tired of all this war talk, Gabriel, let's talk about something else ... I saw some lovely bridesmaids' outfits yesterday in Brown Thomas, beautiful they were. Máire would look lovely in one as would Mary, and Rita too ... do you think three bridesmaids is an odd number to have? Cynthia says it is – she says to either even it up to four or bring it down to two. But, sure, if I was to bring it down to two, then who would I get rid of? And how would I break it to the girls? Sorry, girls, but one of you isn't needed ... best to even it up to four ... I could always ask Valerie, though she would have to go on a strict diet ... and she and Rita have never seen eye to eye ..."

As Siobhán continued to talk about the politics of the wedding, Gabriel's mind quickly drifted off. He looked out at the sea again as they walked. There were dark clouds over the horizon and he wondered would there be rain. All weather forecasts in Ireland had been suspended since the outbreak of war in case the information was made use of by either the Allies or the Axis to their advantage, thereby compromising the country's neutrality. However, weather reports were routinely but secretly being handed to the British to assist them in the war. This certainly was a strange kind of neutrality Ireland was pursuing. The weather reports were vital to the British as the only real fighting that was occurring so far was at sea, between ships and U-boats on the Atlantic, putting Ireland very near the thick of it. The devastation that everyone was expecting to rain down on London in the first week of the war never happened. The planes with their bombs, so feared and dreaded, had not come as everyone had expected. Life for the most part still went on as normal, with some even calling it the 'phoney' war. Even beer hadn't been rationed.

Gabriel wondered was everyone still flocking to the 400 Club as he remembered his night there. He wondered was Karina Harper still going there at night. Still picking up men or had she settled into her affair with Sir William Baxter? Gabriel thought about that night a lot. And he thought about Karina Harper a lot. He wondered why such a beautiful and intelligent woman was wasting her life on a man like Sir William, already committed to another. It made him inexplicably sad when he thought of her and how he had caught her coming out of Sir William's bedroom at Great Hankerton Hall that morning. And there was also another feeling that he couldn't quite understand. He hated to admit it, but that 'other feeling' when he thought about Karina and Sir William was jealousy. Pure and simple jealousy. Karina had just passed through his life for one night and disappeared the next morning without so much as a goodbye – but when he thought about it he was overcome by a terrible sense of loss. If he had known the impact she would have had on him, he would have stayed awake that night in Claridge's and tried anything not to let her just slip away. And now it was too late, she was gone forever.

But as he looked down at Siobhán still discussing bridesmaids' dresses, he was furious with himself for even allowing any thought of Karina Harper enter his mind again.

CHAPTER 21

It was the evening of the reception at the American ambassador's residence and Karina opened her wardrobe and looked through the dresses she had hanging there. She spied a beautiful green dress which had been a gift from Julian to her from the previous Christmas. She remembered Emily's warning not to wear green and then her mouth set in a defiant line and she began to change into the gown.

"You might be able to tell me what to do, but you cannot tell me what to wear!" she said out loud.

Gabriel inspected himself in his mirror and adjusted his bow tie before leaving his house at Victoria Terrace and getting into his motorcar. He had arranged to collect both Cynthia and Siobhán to take them to the reception at the American ambassador's. He called to Roxford first where he collected Cynthia.

"Oh, you do look smart, Gabriel – black tie always suited you," she said admiringly. "I'm in two minds about going to this drinks reception ... I'm loath to welcome any Englishman to Ireland but, with the appointment of a 'Representative to Ireland' by London, it at last shows they accept us an independent country deserving an ambassador."

"Mother, I do hope you will remember yourself tonight – no cutting comments please!" urged Gabriel as he drove through the roads of Dalkey.

"My dear, I know you have proven yourself as an accomplished diplomat by this stage but I do not need any lectures from you on

140

how to behave publicly. I have been doing it since you were in nappies!"

"Yes, Mother, of course," said Gabriel. He knew his mother was far too seasoned a political animal to let the side down, in public at least. However, Cynthia often didn't need to actually say anything – a withering look from her was all that was needed to crumple a grown man's confidence.

"Of course I won't say anything cutting – but I can't guarantee I will not give a frosty reception."

Karina was putting on her lipstick in the mirror when she heard honking outside. She went to the window and looked down to see Emily waiting in her motorcar below. Karina put away her lipstick and, grabbing a fur stole, hurried from her flat and down the flights of stairs to the ground floor and out onto the street.

"Hello!" she said, jumping into the passenger seat.

"Is that green you are wearing?" asked Emily, horrified.

"I'm afraid it is – I didn't have anything else to wear."

"For goodness' sake! We'll be arriving in like twins!" Emily looked down at her own rather plain green dress.

"Bit of an overstatement," said Karina as she compared her glamorous gown to Emily's rather dowdy one, aware that Emily's rather plain toothy-dominated features could not be more different from her own.

"Well, there is nothing to be done at this stage – too late for me to go back now and change into my dusty-pink frock!" said Emily as she started the engine and tore off down the road.

"Pity – I could see you in dusty pink!" said Karina, causing Emily to glance unpleasantly at her.

As Emily drove through the Phoenix Park the American ambassador's residence, which was called the Chief Secretary's Lodge, came into view. The palatial eighteenth-century white building also housed the American legation. Karina could not help but be blown away by the splendour of the building.

"Some place, isn't it?" said Emily, noticing Karina's reaction. "And the Americans rent it from the Irish government for a nominal fee of one penny a year! That's the closeness of the link between Dublin and Washington. The ambassador John Cudahy is an Irish American whose family hailed from Kilkenny. Before he was appointed to Dublin two years ago, he was the ambassador to Poland so he's been at the thick of it! With America being neutral as well, we can't expect any help yet from the Americans to press their good friends the Irish to join the war ... at least not yet!"

Emily braked to a halt.

As Karina got out, she looked around at all the expensive motorcars.

"The Americans are certainly putting on a show," she commented.

"They're doing their bit to smooth relations between the British and the Irish – the last thing anyone wants or needs is hostility breaking out between these two countries at the moment," said Emily.

As Gabriel stood beside Siobhán, he watched Cynthia work the room and could not help but be impressed by her.

"She's not intimidated by anybody, is she?" said Siobhán.

"She certainly doesn't show it if she is ... she's gone through a lot in life, so she's had to be strong," said Gabriel.

"I never looked at it that way. I guess she has sacrificed a lot, losing her husband and being widowed at such a young age with two young children. I don't know how she did it – I know I could not have coped with that. I'd have fallen apart."

He looked down at her. "Don't put yourself down, Siobhán. You're every bit as strong as Cynthia."

She elbowed him and smiled. "Who're you kidding, Gabriel?"

Gabriel looked around and saw there were people he should be talking to but he didn't want to leave Siobhán's side. He had hoped Cynthia would act as chaperone for Siobhán, but she was too busy promoting herself to worry about anyone else. Tim and Tess were supposed to be there but he hadn't been able to spot them and now realised they were very late.

Almost as if she was reading his mind, Siobhán said, "If you need to go and talk to people, Gabriel, then don't feel you need to look after me. I'll be fine here."

He looked down at her nursing her sherry and smiled. "No, I'm fine just here, Siobhán."

As he studied the crowd in the room he observed Sir John Maffey, the new British Representative. So far they had been lucky in their dealings with him. He seemed anxious not to offend the Irish and appeared accepting of their neutrality, at least on the surface. Gabriel spotted many people he knew but also others he didn't recognise – presumably new staff from the British legation.

As he scanned the crowd, he suddenly did a double take. There was a beautiful woman in a striking green gown who looked just like … as he peered across the room he realised with dread and excitement that it actually *was* Karina Harper.

"I don't know if I like this sherry, it's a bit too sweet … I prefer a dry sherry, but I wouldn't want to make a fuss … I'd put up with a sweet if they have no dry …" Siobhán looked at Gabriel and realised he wasn't listening to a word she was saying. "Gabriel?"

Gabriel was staring at Karina as a thousand thoughts ran through his head. What was she doing here? Why was she in Dublin? Who was she with? And, most importantly, he could not understand the utter excitement he was experiencing on seeing her again.

Karina was standing beside a brown-haired girl, also in a green dress, and they were chatting to a group of people.

"*Gabriel!*" snapped Siobhán loudly, jolting him back to reality.

"Sorry – yes? What did you say?"

"I was *saying* that the sherry is far too sweet for me!" she repeated, exasperated.

"Oh, well – drink something else then!" he said, impatiently.

At that moment Tim and Tess arrived in – Tess looking frustrated and Tim looking a little dishevelled.

Siobhán waved happily over to them, delighted there was somebody now there that she knew.

Tess strode over, followed by Tim.

"Everything alright?" asked Gabriel, concerned.

"Fine!" snapped Tess.

"I was getting worried about you when you hadn't arrived," commented Gabriel.

"We were having a little car trouble," said Tim.

"Is that what we're calling it now?" snapped Tess before folding her arms.

An awkward silence followed.

"Can I get you a drink?" asked Gabriel.

"No! He's had enough!" spat Tess before they fell into another silence.

"I was just – eh – just saying that the sherry is a bit too sweet!" said Siobhán, hoping to break the atmosphere.

Tim reached out, took her glass and downed the sherry in one go.

"There! Problem solved!" he said, before nodding at Tess and giving her a triumphant look.

"I'm going to the toilet!" snapped Tess as she marched off.

Tim promptly grabbed a glass of wine from a passing waiter.

Karina had spotted Gabriel enter the reception room. She experienced a strange feeling when she saw him again. She immediately thought back to meeting him that first time at the 400 Club and how she had been attracted to him. She recalled the night she had spent with him at Claridge's and how she had been impressed by him and his kindness and understanding and easy company. It was exactly what she had needed that night when she had thought Hugo was dead, before rushing off the next morning and coming quickly to regret it. And that strange chance meeting she had with him was now the reason she was in Dublin. Little did he know the impact he'd had on her life … and little did he know the impact she was *about* to have on his life. She observed the woman who accompanied him, a pretty blonde woman who never left his side and looked adoringly at him. If you could tell by appearances, she looked like a nice woman. She could imagine Gabriel being with somebody like her. They looked right together. A handsome couple – likable – stable – respectable.

So what was he doing picking up her in the 400 Club if that was the case?

"He's seen you," Emily said, later on in the evening. "He's staring right at you as if he cannot believe his eyes."

"I'm sure he can't!"

"The blonde is his fiancée – Siobhán Vestry – a teacher."

"How very quaint," said Karina.

"No competition for a femme fatale like you!" said Emily, causing Karina to give her a warning look.

"So how do I get him to come over and talk to me without it looking obvious?" asked Karina.

"No need for you to do anything, Karina – he will come over to you all on his own – they always do. He needs to know that you are not going to expose him."

Tim was standing by the bar staring into space while Tess had gone off to mingle. She was now positioned in the centre of the room with four men around her who were all laughing while she told a funny story.

Cynthia was observing both of them as she stood beside Gabriel and Siobhán.

"Is Tim alright? He seems a little distracted," she said.

"I'm sure he's fine," said Siobhán.

"I'm not so sure. Keep an eye on him, Gabriel. I don't know what's going on between those two but I don't like it," said Cynthia.

"It's none of our business what is going on between them," said Gabriel.

"I'll make it my business if they don't sort themselves out soon," threatened Cynthia.

"How is the painting coming along, Cynthia?" asked Siobhán, anxious to change the subject.

"Very good, Siobhán," she said gleefully. "Do you know Mr Pietch has bought many of my paintings and is now commissioning me to paint more. I'm making a small fortune!"

"Who'd have thought?" said Siobhán.

"I'm driving to Wexford in the morning as he has a client who would like a painting of Hook Head – an Irish American whose family hails from near there."

"You won't stop until you end up being exhibited in the Municipal Gallery in New York, Cynthia!" said Siobhán.

"Well, I wouldn't go quite that far just yet – but Mr Pietch has predicted great things for me!"

"If you could excuse me, I need to talk to some people here," said Gabriel and he walked off.

He cut quickly through the crowd as he made his way towards Karina. He passed by Tess who was now surrounded by six men who were hanging on her every word as she regaled them with a story. He passed by Tim who was now gripping the bar to steady himself as he reached for a gin and tonic. Gabriel didn't give them any thought as he made a beeline for Karina.

When he reached her, she had her back to him and he steadied himself before he spoke her name.

"*Karina!*"

Karina prepared herself and got ready to display a look of shock as she turned around.

"*Gabriel!*" she said, managing to look startled.

He stared at her for a few moments, remembering the impact she had on him before and realising it was not imagined.

"What are you *doing* here?" he asked.

"I'm working here. I got a transfer to the British legation here," she explained.

"I see!" He digested the information.

"Well, with the men all going to war, personnel is short on the ground and I guess they felt I had the right experience after working on the talks at Great Hankerton Hall."

"I'm sure ... well, it's extraordinary to see you! Lovely to see you!" he said, smiling broadly at her.

As she studied him, he seemed genuinely delighted to see her. She couldn't understand why, as she had been so cold and offhand to him at Great Hankerton Hall. She realised it would make it all the easier to manipulate him.

"Who are you here with?" he asked, looking around.

"Oh, just a girlfriend from work. Another secretary – I think we are just invited along to these do's as window dressing!" She gave a little laugh.

"Of course you aren't – you do invaluable work," he said.

"Armed with my typewriter!" she joked and made a face.

He was staring at her and she was feeling uncomfortable as the smile dropped from her face.

"Who are you with?" she asked casually, looking around.

"I'm with –" He stopped abruptly as he was jolted back to reality. "I'm here with my fiancée."

"Oh!" She managed to look startled again. "I didn't realise … have you been engaged for long?"

She wondered if he would lie at this point. He could just say that he had become engaged over the past month since he returned from England. That being so, it would lessen the crime of him being with her in London as he wouldn't have been technically engaged when he slept with her. Having said that, if it did come to her blackmailing him, she would dispute the claim anyway and tell him he was indeed engaged when she had slept with him at Claridge's.

"I've been engaged since July," he admitted as a look of shame came over his face. "And we've been together two years."

"I see!" she said, raising an eyebrow. As she looked into Gabriel's embarrassed handsome features she began to almost feel sorry for him. He was handing all the ammunition to her willingly, not realising the danger he was putting himself in. And by the way he was looking at her, she realised she might not even need to use blackmail but could manipulate him easily by playing him. Either way, by love or hate, Gabriel Ford's goose was cooked.

"I think you might have mentioned that fact before you took me back to Claridge's that night," she said, pretending to look upset.

"I – I have no excuse," he said, looking ashamed. "I don't know what came over me … I wanted to explain when I saw you again at Great Hankerton Hall, but you didn't give me a chance – you were so cold."

"Were you really trying to explain or were you just looking for a repeat performance?"

"No! Of course not!"

"Just another girl that you met on your tours around the world on the diplomatic circuit?"

"No! It wasn't like that, I assure you! I've never cheated on Siobhán before … I hadn't planned to meet somebody that night when I went to the 400 Club. I never expected to meet somebody like you."

"And you were just so blown away by my beauty and charm that you just couldn't resist?" Her voice dripped sarcasm.

"Well ... something like that ..." he blurted out.

She looked at him, surprised, as his expression was genuine.

"I don't know if I believe you," she said.

"It's true! I don't make a habit of just falling into bed with anyone, you know!"

"Neither do I!" she shot back, suddenly feeling the need for him not to think badly of her either.

"Really?" he asked, and now it was his turn to look sceptical.

She cringed as she suddenly had a flashback of sneaking out of Sir William's room and Gabriel catching her doing so. She felt herself go bright red. Kendrick and Emily thought they knew everything, but they didn't know Gabriel had seen her leave Sir William's room. It might make her manipulation a little less assured.

"That night – morning – at Great Hankerton Hall – what you saw – well, it wasn't what it seemed at all," she said.

"It looked pretty obvious to me!"

She wanted to tell him it was really none of his business, but she could not jeopardise this mission. And for some reason she didn't want him to think badly of her – she didn't want him to think she had slept with Sir William Baxter.

"I did not sleep with Sir William that night or any other night for that matter," she stated.

"Very late to be taking shorthand. Look, I really am in no position to judge, so if you are in a relationship with Sir William and you obviously can't speak about it as he is married then I understand. It kind of all made sense to me when I saw you creeping from his room. He's obviously the reason why you were upset the night I met you at the 400 Club. You said you needed a distraction for the night over something that had happened – obviously it was something to do with Sir William ... had he tried to break up the relationship? Is that why you are really in Dublin?

To get away from him or you have been sent here for him to get away from you as it's getting too hot with his wife and family?"

As she stared at him, she felt flabbergasted. She was supposed to be in control of the situation, but instead he was taking control, making quite a lot of assumptions. With all their planning, Emily and Kendrick had not prepared for this as they were not aware of the chink in her armour.

"As you say, Gabriel, you really are in no position to judge and it really is none of your business," she said, trying to take back control.

"I know all that! But I just want to help because you struck me as being in some kind of trouble from the moment I met you, and I think you need a friend."

As she stared into his face, he seemed so earnest. She glanced around and saw Emily across the room, staring at her. She nodded discreetly at Karina. As she looked away Karina suddenly saw Kendrick was there as well. She got a start. She hadn't known Kendrick was in Dublin. What was he doing there?

"Karina?" said Gabriel, forcing her to look back at him.

"Gabriel ... your fiancée is here and waiting for you. I suggest you go back to her before she becomes suspicious."

"All we're doing is talking! What's suspicious about that?"

"So when she asks who I am, you will tell her the truth?"

He looked at the floor.

"Of course you won't! Well, if you have any sense you won't. Stop playing with fire, Gabriel, and keep away from me while I'm in Dublin, for your own sake," she said, her voice as cold as ice.

They stared at each other.

Suddenly, there was a loud crashing sound like a breakage of glass.

The crowd started murmuring and then talking loudly as they tried to figure out what had happened.

Suddenly, Cynthia appeared beside them. "Gabriel, it's your brother. Come quickly!"

Gabriel glanced at Karina and then hurried through the crowd, following Cynthia. They went through one of the French windows onto the patio outside where a crowd had gathered. They pushed through the crowd to see Tim sprawled on the ground as Tess attempted to pull him up. There were upturned garden chairs nearby and broken glass.

Cynthia stared at the scene, her mouth a thin line.

"Get him out of here!" she hissed at Gabriel.

Gabriel rushed over and, putting an arm around Tim, began to pull him up.

"What happened?" Gabriel whispered to Tess.

"He was out here pissed on his own and fell against the chairs, knocking them through the French window," said Tess, who was fighting back tears.

A couple of men came rushing over to help.

"We're fine! Thank you! Just a little trip!" said Gabriel with a big smile.

He began to move off, supporting Tim with one arm.

"We'll take him around the side of the house to the front – less people gawking that way," he said as he and Tess led Tim off through the gardens towards the front.

Cynthia looked around uncomfortably at the crowd as they made their way back inside.

At the front of the house, Gabriel put Tim into the back of his motorcar before turning around to Tess who now had tears streaming down her face.

"What the fuck happened?" demanded Gabriel.

"He's been drinking all day and then kept drinking when he arrived here ... I saw him stumbling outside and, when I followed him to see where he was going, he–he just fell into the garden chairs and sent them crashing into the window!"

"Look at the state of him!" said Gabriel as Tim lay out semi-conscious on the back seat.

"What will we do?"

"Just take him back to Roxford, Gabriel, and let him sleep it off," said Tess.

"Do you want to come with us?"

"No, I do not!"

"OK, will you follow in your car then?"

"No! I'm not going back to Roxford tonight with him, Gabriel! I'm sick of the sight of him after his antics tonight. I don't want to be anywhere near him."

"Tess, you're his wife!"

"Unfortunately!" snapped Tess.

"And what are you going to do? Go back to the party?" He was shocked.

"No! I can't go back in there – I'm too humiliated! I'm driving myself back to my parents'. I'll stay there tonight." Tess marched across to her own motorcar and got in.

A minute later Gabriel watched as Tess's motorcar tore off down the avenue.

He looked down at Tim and decided he had better just 'get him out of here', as Cynthia had ordered. He took out a piece of paper from the front of the car and scribbled a note before whistling for one of the valets to come over to him.

"Hand this to Mrs Cynthia Ford, make sure she gets it," he said to the valet, handing him the note and a tip.

Sighing, Gabriel then got into the motorcar and set off back to Roxford.

Siobhán stood beside Cynthia in a corner of the reception room, too frightened to say anything. Cynthia was not displaying any emotion and smiled and greeted people as they passed by, but you could cut the atmosphere with a knife. Siobhán knew under that cool surface Cynthia was erupting like a volcano.

"Are you alright, Cynthia?" she eventually asked.

Cynthia turned and smiled at her. "Of course, why wouldn't I be?"

A valet came up to Cynthia and handed her a note which she hastily opened and read.

"It's from Gabriel – he's taken Tim back to Roxford."

"Gabriel's gone!"

"Of course, I told him to," said Cynthia.

"But without even saying goodbye?" Siobhán was incredulous.

"He had to deal with an emergency, Siobhán. My Lord, but the amount of times I had to deal with emergencies with two young children and I didn't know where my husband was from one week to the next as he fought the British!"

"I know but that was a different time," said Siobhán, feeling hurt by Gabriel's abandonment.

"Times never change that much – only the people change," said Cynthia as she crumpled up the note and threw it into a plant pot.

"How will we get home ourselves?" asked Siobhán, perplexed.

"That's the problem with the younger generation – spoilt!" snapped Cynthia.

"So you have made contact with Ford – what was said?" asked Emily as she sidled up beside Karina with a cocktail in her hand.

After the disturbance caused outside with Tim Ford, the party gradually had returned to normal.

"He was just very surprised to see me and asking me questions about what I was doing here," replied Karina.

"He looked very happy to see you from what I could observe."

"Maybe."

"Maybe you won't have to resort the blackmail with him after all ... maybe just a little persuasion from you, using your womanly wiles, and he will sing like canary."

"I don't know about that – Gabriel Ford strikes me as a very clever man," said Karina.

"If he was that clever, he wouldn't have left himself as exposed to you as he has. And judging by his brother's performance outside earlier the Ford family are not as clever or perfect as they like to portray themselves in public. If his brother's weakness is drink then Gabriel's weakness is clearly women from his history with you."

Karina felt deeply uncomfortable, having met Gabriel again. It was all very well formulating a plot against him in theory, but now she could not imagine how she could put that plot into action. She turned to Emily.

"I'm still thinking you've got the wrong girl for the job. I'm just not capable."

"Don't doubt yourself, Karina. You are more than capable. War brings out sides of us we never knew existed. Look at me – to think that all I used to care about was the price of silk stockings!"

Perhaps Emily was right, Karina thought. Everyone had a weakness, a chink in their armour that led them to expose themselves, put themselves in danger and in the firing line. Hers was her love for Hugo. It was what had caused her to go to bed with Gabriel in the first place, what had caused her to blackmail Sir William and had what had brought her to Dublin entangled in this dreadful web.

"So – what do I do now? What's my next step?" asked Karina.

"You wait! Just like tonight, he will come to you. He won't be able to keep away. And when he does, you trap him like a fly in a cobweb," said Emily.

CHAPTER 22

In Roxford, Tim was sat on a chair in the back garden with his head in his hands. Gabriel came out carrying another pot of tea and placed it on the garden table beside his brother.

"Oh, no more of that shit, please! I can't drink another cup of black fucking tea!" begged Tim.

Gabriel picked up the teapot and filled Tim's cup to the brim.

"Drink it!" he ordered.

With a shaking hand, Tim reached out for the cup, raised it to his lips and took a gulp, then emptied the contents down his throat.

"Tastes fucking disgusting!" he said, making a face and placing the cup back on the table before putting his head in his hands again.

"How do you feel now?" asked Gabriel.

"How do you think I fucking feel? My head feels like one of those German tanks is doing its very own blitzkrieg through it!" Tim shook his head in horror.

Judging that Tim had somewhat sobered up from all the tea and water he had forced him to drink, Gabriel felt brave enough to broach the subject of what had happened at the American ambassador's residence.

"Do you remember what happened tonight?" he asked.

Tim nodded. "Not all of it, but enough to make me want to vomit again – and again and again!"

"Whatever possessed you?"

"The fucking drink! What else did you think it fucking was?"

"I know it was the drink, Tim, but why did you drink so much?

Why did you act the way you did?"

"I don't know." Tim sighed loudly. "I started drinking in the afternoon and just couldn't seem to stop."

"Did Tess not tell you stop?"

"Of course she did but the more she pleaded and then demanded me to stop, the more I drank!"

"Why?"

"I was enjoying upsetting her ... I was doing it out of spite," Tim admitted, before hanging his head shamefully down.

Gabriel remembered the conversation he'd had with Tess out there in the very same garden the night of the engagement party. How she had indicated the marriage had become unhappy. But Gabriel could never have guessed it had become so unhappy. "But you adored Tess since we were all kids," he pointed out.

"Well, the reality is very different from the fantasy, let me tell you ... we are completely incompatible ... in *every* way." Tim was now staring out at the black sea under the night sky. "How did I get myself into this and how can I get myself the fuck out of it? We can't spend the rest of our lives chained to the other ... that's what it feels like, a fucking life sentence."

Gabriel gave a nervous laugh. "It's drink talking, Tim, you'll feel better in the morning."

"It's the drink that makes it more bearable! I feel *worse* in the morning when the drink wears off fully," said Tim, sighing and looking around. "Where is she anyway?"

"She drove herself home, back to her parents," said Gabriel.

"Telling them what a bastard I am, no doubt!"

"Look, Tim, you need to pull yourself together, man!" Gabriel said sternly. "That spectacle you created tonight – well, it's just not on! You made a show of yourself in front of everyone from the American ambassador to the newly appointed British one! You are a member of parliament – you're not just letting the family down, you're letting the party down and the fucking country to boot! But most of all you are letting yourself down!"

"Fuck's sake, that's a rousing speech, Gabriel – did you ever think of going into politics?" mocked Tim. "Please don't bring

Dad into it next! Don't say he's looking down on me from heaven above with sorrow and shame!"

"Well, he wouldn't be looking down with any kind of pride. And what about Cynthia – hasn't she gone through enough in life without seeing her son showing her up like that?"

"The old girl is as tough as nails. She might pretend to be all aghast but it wouldn't have knocked a feather out of her! If the Germans bombed Dublin, she'd check her hair was in place first before she went for shelter!"

"The reality is, Tim, you can continue to self-destruct or you can face facts. You might feel trapped by your marriage to Tess, but the reality is you *are* trapped! You've made your bed and you have to lie in it. So start speaking to your wife and mending your marriage."

"How can I speak to her when we can't stand being in the same room as each other?"

"Well, that, brother of mine, is just something you are going to have to figure out," said Gabriel as he slapped his hand on Tim's shoulder and stood up. "Come on, you need a good long sleep."

"I wish I never married her!" said Tim, rising to his feet.

As Gabriel looked at him, his smile dropped and his face creased with worry.

"I simply will not let your father's legacy be brought down by such shoddy behaviour!" said Cynthia later that night in the drawing room at Roxford. "It's shameful! I do not know what is wrong with those two but they need to sort themselves out or I'll do it for them!"

"Tess and Tim?" said Gabriel.

"No – Edward and Mrs Simpson!" Cynthia spat sarcastically. "Going on five years married and no children. They barely speak to each other in public – she is too busy tossing her hair in any man's direction while he is tossing the nearest glass of gin down his throat!"

"They do seem to be having problems," said Gabriel, his voice lowered.

"We all have problems! Do you not think your father and I had problems? But did we bring them out into the public arena? Did we ever make a spectacle of ourselves? And we were living under severe pressure compared to those two spoilt brats! No – we always maintained a public image of togetherness and happiness and that is why our family is so respected. And now all that is being jeopardised by your brother's outlandish behaviour."

"I think we all need to go easy on him. He doesn't seem to be happy with the choices he has made."

"There is a simple method that results in a person being satisfied with the choices they make – choose wisely! They were his choices! Nobody forced him to marry her or anybody else for that matter! But marry her he did – he couldn't wait to get her up the aisle. Well, for such a short trip up the aisle of a church it sure is a long journey on the other side!"

"I think he feels he made a mistake."

"A mistake!" laughed Cynthia. "Marriage isn't a mistake, it's for life. There's no room for mistakes when getting married – simple as that! There's no getting out of it, if that's what he thinks! There's no divorce legally in Ireland and no divorce period for us Catholics. If he wants to get rid of her, he will have to murder her!"

"Mother!"

He went and looked out the window as Cynthia sat in silence for a while.

"Who was that girl you were talking to at the party?" she asked then.

"Which girl?" asked Gabriel uneasily.

"The strikingly beautiful girl in the green gown – do you recall her now?" asked Cynthia sharply.

"Oh, she's just a secretary who works at the British legation."

"Well, out of all the important people who were in that room, I'm surprised that you spent so much time focused on a secretary?"

"Eh, we met before."

"How?"

"At Great Hankerton Hall – she was in attendance at the talks I had with the British there. She worked for the Foreign Office at the time."

"Is that a fact?" said Cynthia, even more surprised. "So what could you possibly have in common with a secretary who worked at the British Foreign Office? So you greeted her tonight like a long-lost friend?"

Gabriel felt himself go red under his mother's cross-examination and the fear of the anyone finding out what had really happened in London.

"Why not?" he asked.

"Why so?" she responded.

"She's an interesting person. She's actually from Ireland."

"Is she *actually*? From Ireland? What's she doing working for the British Foreign Office and legation if she's Irish?"

"Well, she's Anglo-Irish from what I understand."

"Oh, I see! A Protestant!" said Cynthia as if it now all made sense to her.

"Her family evacuated to London after their house was burned down during the troubles," said Gabriel.

"What's the name of the family and where are they from?" asked Cynthia.

"The Harper family – their house was in Galway. Did you ever hear of them?"

Recognition flooded across Cynthia's face. "Of course! Their mansion was called Inishwood ... your father gave the order to burn their house down and drive them out of the country," she said with an element of satisfaction. "He'd be horrified to know one of them had sneaked back in!"

Gabriel turned to Cynthia in shock.

CHAPTER 23

The next day, as Gabriel sat in his office contemplating everything that had happened, he felt confused and yet at the same time saw things clearly for the first time in a long while. Seeing Karina again like that had thrown him. She was the last person in the world he had expected to see at the American ambassador's. And yet there she was. And when he saw her, he realised the effect she'd had on him at the 400 Club and at Great Hankerton Hall was more than just an attraction – she stirred something so deep in him that it scared him as he had never felt that emotion before. Last night when he'd seen her at the embassy, it was as if nobody else mattered. He had abandoned Siobhán and Cynthia and all the dignitaries, just to be in her company for a few minutes. For that brief time he hadn't cared about anything. He hadn't even thought about risking exposure, in Siobhán's presence, that he had spent a night with Karina at Claridge's. Nothing else mattered except talking to her. When he saw her, he should have pretended he had a headache and left immediately before she had a chance to spot him. Now he had exposed himself, told her he had a fiancée even. He had put himself in danger and had to be more careful in future.

Seeing and hearing Tim's life come crashing down had jolted him back to reality. Tim seemed set on a course to ruin himself – and the whole Ford family and legacy into the bargain. But he himself had set out on the same journey of self-ruin by cheating on Siobhán with Karina and becoming dangerously transfixed by her since he had met her. Now that Karina was in Dublin, he realised if he had anything more to do with her he would be like a moth flying to the flame.

And then, on hearing from Cynthia that his father had ordered the burning of her home, he realised it was all the more dangerous. If Karina should ever find out, he could only imagine the anger and hatred she would feel towards him and the Ford family. And she now had the ability to destroy them all by disclosing what had happened between them.

The lecture he had given to Tim the previous night was a lecture that was relevant to himself. He was engaged to a wonderful girl and needed to put all his focus on her and making sure they had a happy life and future together. He also had to think of his career and the Ford family name. He would not do anything to bring disrepute on either himself or his family.

As Siobhán stood at the top of her classroom, there was a knock on the door.

The door opened and Gabriel put his head around.

"Gabriel!" she said, surprised and a little alarmed to see him.

"Do you have a minute?" he asked.

She nodded before turning to the class. "Open your books – Page 7 – and start transcribing the passage into French."

She walked out into the corridor and saw Gabriel was holding a bunch of flowers.

"Gabriel! What's this all about?" she asked.

He looked up and down the corridor and, confident they were alone, took her in his arms and kissed her.

"Gabriel! What *is* all this about?" she repeated, looking shocked but delighted.

He handed her the flowers. "I am so sorry about everything … sorry about disappearing last night without coming to find you first to explain."

"I -I know you were under a lot of pressure, but I admit I was a bit taken aback when you just left without even a word of goodbye," she said. "Cynthia and I had to hitch a ride home with a Hungarian diplomat!"

"Can you forgive me?"

"I can forgive you for being a little distracted occasionally or even careless ... but I could never forgive you if you were only pretending to love me." She smiled sadly as she looked down at the flowers.

He looked at her, saddened and shocked. "Can you really think that of me?"

"I don't know what to think sometimes, Gabriel. You seem as if you are not really with me ... as if your attention is elsewhere. Flowers are all very nice, but ..."

"Siobhán!" he said, grabbing her by the shoulders. "I adore you! You mean everything to me!"

"Oh, Gabriel, how I needed you to say that!" she said as she threw her arms around him and he held her tightly.

CHAPTER 24

Time went quickly since Karina arrived in Dublin and suddenly the autumn was turning into winter. She was kept busy with her work in the legation and doing spy work for Emily. But Gabriel Ford had not made contact, much to Emily's consternation.

Being back in Dublin made Karina feel like a stranger in her own home. Everything was so familiar and yet she didn't feel part of it. And in a strange kind of way she wanted to feel part of the country again. She thought if she visited Inishwood it might help her adjust to the love and hate she was feeling for her native land.

As she drove through the Irish countryside in the motorcar she had borrowed from the legation, she realised she had forgotten how beautiful it was. There was much she had forgotten. Since her family had left for England, she would always interrupt her thoughts when she remembered her upbringing in Ireland. She would quickly force herself to think of something else as she could not bear the pain of where those thoughts would eventually lead her. She would remember the wonderful memories of her childhood, so happy they became almost painful to recall. But the real pain came when those memories led her to the night of the burning down of Inishwood. Strangely, she never actually dreamt of that final night at Inishwood. She only dreamt of the good times, almost as if her subconscious had blocked out the attack.

She did not want to return to Inishwood. She did not want to go back there. But she felt she simply had to go back and visit her homeplace, regardless of how painful it would be. She knew her father would want her to return there and see it. So, she continued her journey all the way across the country to the west coast and Galway.

As she neared Inishwood, her heart started pounding. It all looked the same as when she had left all those years ago. There was the little pub and post office on the corner of a crossroads. She hadn't thought of that place in years and suddenly there it was in front to her, the exact same as she remembered it. She used to come riding there on her pony as a child, accompanying her father. She would go into the post office to post the mail.

"I'll just drop in to say hello to Jack – I'll just be a few minutes," her father would say, dismounting from his mare.

Jack was the owner of the pub and her father would head in and inevitably the 'few minutes' would turn into at least an hour. Karina would climb up on the window seat and peer through the window and she would see her father standing at the bar, surrounded by a few locals as he regaled them with his stories as he drank a pint of stout. She would tap on the window until she caught his attention and point to her watch in exasperation, forcing him to leave and rejoin her.

She would be smiling as she waited for him on her pony and he would saunter out.

"Gosh – is that the time? I never noticed!" he would say as he mounted his horse again. "No need to tell your mother I dropped in for a chat with Jack."

"Naturally!" Karina would say knowingly.

"Giddy up, old girl!" her father would say to his mare and the two would set off for a leisurely afternoon ride along the country roads.

Karina smiled to herself at the memory. And the memories kept on flooding back as she kept seeing landmarks she recognised. As she drove through the local village she could not believe how unchanged everything was – almost as if she had stepped back in time. As she continued up the road to Inishwood she began to expect that to be unchanged as well – but she knew that could not be the case. She made her way down the tree-covered road to the entrance of the house, the wind rustling through leaves which had turned rusty in the autumn sunshine.

She slowed the motorcar down and turned off the road into the space before the huge gateway of Inishwood. She brought the vehicle to an abrupt stop as she saw the gates were closed. She got goosebumps as she looked up at the large wrought-iron gates. She felt she was home. It felt like home. But as she looked at the gates she saw they were not the shiny white painted gates she remembered so well. They were now rusted and one was hanging off its hinges while a big sign ordering *Keep Out* hung from the heavy chain that tied the two gates together in the centre.

She got out of the motorcar and looked around. It was eerily quiet. She made her way to the gates and saw the chain had a lock on it. She wondered who had put the chain on and the sign up. She felt angry that somebody had taken control of her family home in that manner. She went to the side of the gate where it was hanging off its hinges and slipped to the other side through the gap.

As she peered up the long avenue she almost didn't recognise it. It was completely overgrown. The once lovingly tended trees on either side of the avenue had nearly closed in over it. The avenue itself was thick with weeds and bushes and briars. She picked up a long sturdy stick and fought her way up the avenue.

She remembered how, at the top, the house itself would suddenly come into view in all its palatial glory. But now, when she reached the top of the avenue, instead of seeing the magnificent three-storey mansion it used to be ... she saw just the burned-out shell of the house. As she stumbled towards the building, her heart ached. She had never seen the house after it had been torched. Her last memory of it was being in the back seat of their motorcar as her father frantically drove them away. She had turned for a final look at the house and had stared in dismay at the sight of it being engulfed in fire, the flames dancing high into the night sky.

Karina continued up the steps and in through what used to be the front door. As she walked down what used to be the great hallway, she realised there was nothing left of the house but the four walls. As she looked up, she saw that the ornate ceiling that had been there had disappeared and all she could see was the blue above – the upper floors and roof of the house all gone. As she walked through what had been the drawing room, the dining room, the ballroom, she realised there was not even a trace of the Harper family left there. Three hundred years of history erased in one fateful night.

It had been a night much like any other. A hot July night in 1922. The previous few years had been certainly full of turmoil. There had been the Irish fight for independence. A vicious horrible war. But that was then over and everyone hoped for a return to peace. But then the Civil War had erupted and the country had been immersed in more bloodshed.

But life at Inishwood had mostly gone on uninterrupted. The Harper family had always enjoyed relatively good relations with the locals and, although they were increasingly made to feel like outsiders, they got on with life as usual.

During the War of Independence there had been a certain number of attacks on the 'Big Houses' – the homes of the Anglo-Irish aristocracy. But during the Civil War and afterwards the attacks on these homes increased. They were seen as a symbol of British rule and they or their occupants were no longer welcome in Ireland. The houses were systematically attacked, set on fire or blown up and now nowhere was safe.

"I understand how the Russian nobility felt during the Russian Revolution!" declared her father one morning over the usual breakfast of bacon, sausages and eggs. He was reading the newspaper which brought fresh reports of the Civil War and the attacks on several more Big Houses around the country.

"I wonder should we go and stay in London for a while – at least until the danger is over?" asked Karina's mother.

They were constantly being urged to leave by their English friends, particularly Karina's aunt and uncle, Lord and Lady Ashton.

"I am not being driven out of the home we have lived in for three hundred years by a bunch of hoodlums!" declared her father.

"But what about the child, Percy? We should at least send Karina away?"

"I've never backed down from a fight and I refuse to back

down now! My daughter, I think you will find, is the same!"

"My friend Caroline said when the Rebels came to their house to blow it up in County Cork, they were very polite!" said Karina. "They even assisted Caroline's mother, Lady Hillary, to take her favourite Persian rugs with her before they detonated the bomb and blew the house to Kingdom Come!"

"Caroline was always such a strange child." Penny shook her head in dismay.

"There you go! You would never need to be frightened of a fellow who helped you rescue your Persian rugs before he blew your house to Kingdom Come!" said Percy as he laughed and winked across the table at Karina who started giggling uncontrollably.

"You two! You never take anything *seriously!*" admonished Penny.

But that night they had come. They came in the night like thieves. Everyone had gone to bed, including the servants, when there was a loud knock on the front door. Karina scrambled out of bed, clutching her doll, and looked out her front window.

There was a group of men standing in the forecourt.

As the loud knocking started again she could suddenly hear screaming. After she hastily got dressed she came out onto the corridor to see that it was the servants who were crying and screaming as they rushed down the stairs carrying their belongings.

"Quick, child – we'll use the back entrance and make a dash down the fields to the village. They won't do us any harm if we don't do them any either!" said the cook as she grabbed Karina and began to drag her along with her.

"Let go of me!" Karina freed herself just as her mother came out of her bedroom. "Mama!" She raced to her mother and embraced her.

"We'll be off, ma'am. I advise you to do the same!" cried the cook as she scrambled down the main staircase with the other servants. "You can post on my wages!"

She and the others disappeared out the back of the house.

"Like rats deserting a sinking ship!" cried Percy who arrived out of the bedroom holding a rifle.

Both her parents had hastily dressed.

"I bet they didn't lock the back door on their way out – the bastards!" Percy said. He raced down the stairs to bolt the back door.

Penny and Karina descended to the great hallway.

"That'll keep them out until the cavalry arrives!" said Percy as he came back into the hall.

Penny and Karina stood staring at Percy who was loading his gun.

"Percy! Have you gone insane! You haven't a hope of keeping them out!" cried Penny.

"Three hundred years my family have been here! We have every right to stay and we are not going anywhere!" insisted Percy.

"They'll burn the house down around us if we don't go!" said Penny.

Karina tugged her mother's sleeve and whispered, "Shall I fetch the Persian rugs?"

"*Shhh, child!*" snapped Penny.

There was a loud knock on the door followed by a man's voice. "Mr Harper, we will give you five minutes to leave voluntarily or else break down the door and have you escorted from the building."

"I demand you leave my property or face the consequences, you–you–you hoodlum!" Percy shouted back.

Suddenly there was a large crashing sound. Penny and Karina screamed. There was a series of crashing sounds as the men outside threw rocks through the windows.

"Percy! Please – we have to leave!" begged Penny.

"I will not be pushed around!" insisted Percy.

Suddenly there was a massive thumping sound at the front door.

"*I'm ready for you – you bastards!*" shouted Percy aiming his rifle straight at the door.

"*Percy! You've lost your mind!*" cried Penny as she started to pull Karina away from the hallway.

Suddenly the front door burst open and a group of men wearing hoods over their heads ran in. They came to an abrupt halt when they saw Percy standing at the bottom of the hallway with a rifle aimed straight at them.

"Now let's see if you are quite so clever!" said Percy as he began to pull the trigger.

Suddenly a man sprang out from the servants' stairs beside Percy, grabbed the rifle out of his hands and threw it away.

Then he raised his arm and gave Percy a thump across the face, sending him flying to the floor.

"*Papa!*" screamed Karina, rushing to him, dropping her doll to the ground.

Percy lay badly hurt on the ground.

"Get him and your daughter out of here, madam, or you will be set on fire along with your house," said the man who had struck Percy.

The other men were now racing through the house, pouring petrol over the furniture and curtains and then setting them on fire.

Penny struggled to raise Percy to his feet. He seemed to be in shock.

"We are leaving," said Penny as she began to help Percy down the hallway to the front door.

"*And don't ever come back!*" the man who had hit Percy growled at them as he reached down to pick up Percy's rifle.

As he bent down, Karina lunged at him.

"*You horrible, horrible man!*" she shouted as she tore the hood off his head.

The man looked at her in shock as she stared back into his handsome face.

The man quickly grabbed his hood and put it back on before marching away.

"*Karina! Come on!*" Penny screamed at her from outside.

Karina turned and ran quickly down the hallway as the men continued to set the house on fire.

Penny managed to start the motorcar. As Percy was still in shock, he was put in the passenger seat. Karina sat in the back seat and, as Penny drove down the avenue, she looked back at the house, now in flames.

It was the last time she had seen Inishwood. The last time she had seen her beautiful home as it disappeared in a gulf of fire.

* * *

As Karina continued walking through the house, all the memories of that terrible night came flooding back. She and her parents had evacuated to London the next day and stayed with Julian's family at their estate in Norfolk. They were all in shock but particularly Percy who refused to see a doctor despite the assault he had suffered. A week later, he had a heart attack and died. Everyone blamed what had happened at Inishwood, particularly the assault he had endured. Karina knew the man who had struck her father had murdered him. And she was the only person who had seen his face. She would never forget that handsome face after she pulled the hood off him. It was hard to believe that such a handsome face could have committed such a vile act.

As she walked to the spot in the hallway where her father had been struck, the memory of the incident felt as vivid as if it had happened yesterday. She suddenly spotted something over in the corner. She walked over, looked down and to her surprise saw it was a child's doll. She bent to pick it up and was shocked to see it was her own doll. She remembered it distinctly from her childhood. The doll she had been holding that night and dropped as she ran to her father after he had been struck to the floor. As she held the doll tightly, the tears began to roll down her face. That doll was the only evidence that the Harpers had ever lived there. The only evidence that the Harper family had lived there for three hundred years.

She sat the doll back in the corner where she had found it. She wouldn't deprive the house of the only thing it had left to remember the Ford family by.

Karina returned down the long, overgrown avenue to her motorcar and sat in. She took one final look through the front gates into Inishwood and then drove away. She had a feeling of overwhelming sadness as she went. Despite everything that had happened that dreadful night seventeen years ago and the terrible way her family had been treated, she now realised that she still considered Inishwood her home. In a way it was the only place she ever felt was home and it was as if she had been searching for a new place to call home ever since. She had been robbed of her home and her father that same night. She had never really been happy since. Oh, she had thrown herself into high society in London, trying to find a new place for herself in this world, in a life of parties and nightclubs. But she never did find a rightful place for herself.

Not until she had found Hugo and begun a relationship with him. When she was with him she felt safe and secure and right – he made her feel as if she had a home with him. And now this new war was going to rob her again of the man she loved and the future she had planned with him.

As she speeded up and passed a road sign showing the direction to Dublin, she was more determined than ever to be reunited with Hugo. She might have been robbed of her past but she would not be robbed of her future.

CHAPTER 25

Back in Dublin, Karina waited to be contacted by Gabriel Ford. The days went by and suddenly it was nearing Christmas. She was busy at work, being given plenty to do and Emily was constantly giving her small spying assignments which usually involved watching the coming and goings at Government Buildings or delivering a package. Karina had met up with Patience and Grace Berry, the daughters of the old family friends, a couple of times for drinks and dinners and had been invited to their home, Berryfield, for Christmas.

"No word from Ford?" questioned Emily in her office at the legation.

"Not a dickie bird," answered Karina.

"I was sure he would make contact with you after the way he ran up to you last time," said Emily, deep in thought.

"He's obviously not as enamoured of me as you imagined," said Karina, looking out the window as the rain pelted down.

"*Hmmm*, playing hard to get doesn't work with him anyway by all accounts," mused Emily.

Karina turned around to face her. "Or perhaps he is actually in love with his fiancée and what happened between us in London is one big source of regret for him."

"If that's the case then we will have to shift to Plan B."

"Plan B?"

"We must resort to blackmailing him. If he is in love with his fiancée then he won't want the truth to come out. If the mountain won't come to Mohamed then Mohamed must go to the mountain ... sit down and write a note to Gabriel Ford."

"Saying what?" Karina was becoming stressed.

"Saying you would like to meet him at the earliest opportunity."

"Is it wise to put something in writing?" asked Karina, sitting down.

"Yes! Hopefully he will put something in writing back to you which will add to the evidence we can use against him," said Emily.

Gabriel hurried back to his office after a meeting with the Chilean envoy. He was in a rush as he was meeting Siobhán for dinner in the Shelbourne that evening,

"Any messages?" he asked his secretary as he walked past her desk.

"The German Minister asked for you to phone him urgently, I left some papers on your desk for you to sign and this arrived by courier," said the secretary, handing him an envelope.

"Get me the German Minister on the telephone, will you?"

Gabriel went into his office and closed the door. He sat at his desk, tore open the envelope and unfolded the notepaper inside. It was official British Embassy paper.

Dear Gabriel,

I was hoping to hear from you after we met at the American ambassador's recently. I was disappointed you left so early that night and we didn't have an opportunity to continue our conversation. Now that I am living in Dublin I would very much like to meet you. I hope you don't find this too forward of me – but please do contact me either here at the British legation or at my address – 54 Merrion Square.

Sincerely,

Karina Harper

Gabriel stared at the letter in surprise. He reread it again and again trying to fathom what it was about. Why was Karina Harper suddenly wanting to see him? She had been as cold as ice to him at Great Hankerton Hall and not much better in Dublin. He was consumed with curiosity and the opportunity to see her again, at her invitation, was too great to resist.

He thought of her face, picked up the phone and held the receiver tightly as he looked at her letter in his hand. Suddenly, he slammed down the phone and at the same time crumpled up the letter and threw it in the bin under his desk. He had successfully avoided Karina Harper since he met her in Dublin and he aimed to keep it that way. He did not know why Karina was reaching out to him but he would not give in to temptation. He would not jeopardise his whole future happiness over this woman.

Karina waited anxiously for a response to her letter. Emily constantly asked if she had heard anything back.

As December moved into Christmas week, Karina was certain that Gabriel would not contact her.

"Maybe he didn't get the note," suggested Emily, standing over Karina's desk in her office.

"And maybe he just had no interest in seeing me. The man is engaged!" said Karina. "Look, Emily, I really need to hear what has happened to Hugo! You keep telling me that next week you will have news, but every week is the same and no news!"

"We are trying our best to find him, Karina, under the most appalling circumstances. While you can't even get to arrange to meet for coffee with a man down the road in a neutral country!" said Emily as she turned and marched out the door.

CHAPTER 26

As Gabriel walked down Grafton Street doing his Christmas shopping, he realised the shops were not stocked with their usual wonderful display of goods. Rationing had begun to hit hard and merchandise usually taken for granted was becoming hard to find. But he had managed to buy a hat for Siobhán which he had seen her admiring when they'd been out shopping a couple of weeks before.

As he made his way back to his motorcar which was parked on Fitzwilliam Square, he kept thinking about the note he had received from Karina Harper. Just when he was trying to forget about her, that bloody note had arrived. As he thought about her, he was filled with that usual feeling she stirred in him. He had never had that feeling before and couldn't explain it. A feeling of loss and jealousy and desire and confusion. As he got in his motorcar and started the engine, he remembered the address on the note – *54 Merrion Square.*

Rather than turning the motorcar to home, he found himself driving towards Merrion Square. He looked at the numbers on the doors as he slowly drove around the square until he found Number 54. He parked down the road, facing the building, and waited. The evening was drawing in and it was dark. He didn't know what he was waiting for but something was keeping him there. He watched each figure appear on the square, hoping it might be her. Then, about an hour later, he spotted the unmissable figure of Karina Harper come round the corner. He watched transfixed as she walked confidently down the street. She was on the opposite side of the road but his mouth dropped open as she neared him and he huddled down in the seat so she wouldn't notice him. As she passed by he studied her intently and watched as she skipped up the steps of her building, took out a key and let herself in. Most of the windows in the building were in darkness and he watched intently to see which floor was hers. Suddenly the lights came on, on the top floor. He sat up straight as he peered up at the windows.

A minute later Karina appeared at a window. She stood there for a while gazing out while she smoked a cigarette. Then she drew the curtains.

Gabriel stayed parked across the street as he stared up at Karina's flat, unable to move.

Upstairs in Karina's flat, she had made herself a quick sandwich and then gone to one of the front windows in the sitting room. She had drawn the curtains but had kept a small gap between them open. She had been told to watch out for a group of four men who were due to arrive at Leinster House that evening in a silver Jaguar. She was to note the time they arrived and keep watch until they left, noting their time of departure. As she settled down for another night of spying, she felt at least she was managing to be of some use to the Secret Service, even if Gabriel Ford had so far ignored her letter.

She wondered what Hugo was doing now. As she thought of the Friedrichs, the family in Berlin, she prayed he would be safe with them. Hugo had said in the telegram that the post was not safe – that meant it was being intercepted and not to send anything. But if she just sent a friendly, casual letter to Charlotte Friedrich without any reference to Hugo, then they would know she had received the telegram and that she knew Hugo was with them. She checked her address book and found their address in Berlin. Then she sat down and wrote a friendly letter to Charlotte, speaking of the great parties she had enjoyed at her house. She enclosed her new address in Dublin and asked her to write to her if she had time.

She hoped she was doing the right thing sending the letter and that it would not anger Hugo. But she figured it was a harmless letter and would at least be some kind of contact with him through the people she hoped were shielding him.

Karina reported to Emily the next morning at the legation with her notebook in her hand.

"The four men arrived at 8 o'clock in the evening and remained in Leinster House until six minutes past midnight. When they left they were accompanied by a woman – who appeared to be young."

"Very good," said Emily, taking down the information before looking up at Karina and smiling. "You are quite wrong about Gabriel Ford, Karina."

"What? In what way?"

"That he has no interest in you. Why else was he outside your building last night, sitting in his motorcar gazing up at your flat for an hour?"

"He did *what?*"

"I'm never wrong on these things – I have a nose for them. The question is, why didn't he come and knock on your door if he was feeling amorous?"

"Who said he was feeling amorous?" Karina's mind was spinning with this news.

"Why else would somebody sit looking up at a building an old flame was staying at?"

"I'm not an old flame of his, Emily," said Karina.

"Well, he has some kind of flame burning for you!"

"You have had him been followed?"

"Of course."

"So you are watching him who is watching me while I am watching through a pair of binoculars for you!" sighed Karina.

On Christmas Eve, Karina made her way to the Berry family who lived just outside Dublin. Their home, Berryfield, was a gothic baronial pile. Karina remembered going there as a child to stay and it hadn't changed a bit. The Berry family, which now consisted of the widower father Major Utred and his daughters Patience and Grace, still managed to live in considerable style. Although they pretended to be broke, Patience and Grace always stayed at the Dorchester when they came to London to do the Season each year. Despite being paraded before London's most eligible bachelors for years, neither had managed to snare one and they were both the wrong side of thirty now. Grace was extremely beautiful while Patience was extremely plain.

"I got the beauty and the brains, *she* got the knitting skills," Grace was often heard saying.

Karina had always surmised their unusually close and often stormy relationship was the reason they were both single as it had scared off every suitor.

As she was greeted in the lobby with hot port served by a butler and hugs and kisses from Patience and Grace, Karina could not help but feel jealous. As she looked around their stately home, it seemed it had just been a matter of luck that Inishwood had been targeted by the rebels and not their home, Berryfield. That turn of fate had meant the Berrys had continued living their life of comfort and privilege whereas Karina and her mother had struggled desperately for near on twenty years.

Inside the vast drawing room, there were a number of guests who were staying for Christmas and they all were drinking hot ports.

"How's your dear mother?" asked the girls' father, Major Utred.

"She is well and has gone to stay at a cottage on my cousin's estate till the war is over."

"She was a stunner in her day, your mother! We were all shocked when your father arrived home from New York with her on his arm. He never had much success with the ladies before then. They used to push him aside in their haste to get to me at the hunt balls!"

Karina nodded and smiled, not believing a word of it.

"They said she came with plenty of money too – banking background, they said," mused Utred.

Karina could see Utred had been jealous of her parents. She believed many had been jealous of them before it was all taken away from them.

"More port, darling!" said Grace as she refilled Karina's crystal glass and then her own.

"Is that wise, Grace?" asked Patience with a disapproving face. "You know how port doesn't *agree* with you!"

"Who says it doesn't agree with me?" asked Grace as she drank her port.

"Last Easter Sunday is all the evidence needed to prove that, I should say!" huffed Patience as she walked off.

"She is always trying to ruin my fun!" Grace whispered bitterly to Karina. "Every year in London she has humiliated every man who wanted to take me out, driving them away! Jealous cow!"

Karina nodded and smiled and realised it was going to be a long night.

Four hours later and Patience and Grace were embroiled in a full screaming match in the drawing room with only Karina and Major Utred as witnesses as everyone else had retired to bed.

"You knew I wanted him! You knew it and it didn't stop you – you went straight after him!" accused Patience at the top of her voice.

"That's a lie! He went after me!" Grace defended herself.

"You couldn't stand the fact he fancied me rather than you and so you locked me in the bedroom that night and seduced him!"

"Fancied you more than me?" scoffed Grace. "I thought the fellow dumb but didn't realise he was blind as well!"

"*Girls! Girls!*" pleaded Major Utred.

Karina put down her port and slipped out of the room to bed.

At Roxford, Christmas passed with the usual festivities and Siobhán joined the Ford family for Christmas Day.

But Gabriel could not get the image of Karina out of his mind after seeing her again walking down the street. It was as if she had cast some strange spell over him. Try as he might to banish her from his mind, she kept intruding. As he saw her face in his mind, he remembered Cynthia's revelation: "Y*our father gave the order to burn down their house and drive them out of the country.*"

BOOK 2

JANUARY TO APRIL 1940

CHAPTER 27

A new year, a new decade and a war that people were calling 'phoney' as the terrible destruction and slaughter predicted had so far failed to be unleashed. Karina hoped that would continue to be the case.

Every evening when she came back from work, she anxiously checked the post, hoping there would be a response from Charlotte Friedrich in Germany to the letter she had sent. But there never was. Karina decided to write another letter, keeping it casual, making no reference to Hugo, telling her again she had moved to Dublin and asking her to write to her. But again there was no response. Karina wondered was it just too risky for the Friedrichs to respond to her in the post. Was the post really not that safe, as Hugo had warned? Karina decided not to write again as not receiving a response indicated it was not the correct thing to do. Nor was there any response from the letter she had sent Gabriel Ford before Christmas.

For Gabriel, it was an awful thought that the father he adored all his life had been responsible for what happened to Karina's family. Cynthia had been quite certain, almost proud, that her husband had given the order to attack and burn down the Harper house, Inishwood. It was a savage order. But it was war, a horrible vicious war, and the Harper family were aristocratic despots who had crushed their people for generations. He felt the need to find out more about what had happened and called in to the archive section of the *Irish Times*.

He explained to the archivist that he was looking for any reports on the burning of Inishwood during the Civil War.

"Terrible times," sighed the archivist as he looked through shelves of old newspapers. "And now terrible times again ..."

Finally he tracked down the newspaper.

"Here we are – the burning of Inishwood House."

As the archivist continued to file, Gabriel sat down at the desk and spread the newspaper out in front of him. The burning of Inishwood had featured on the front page of the newspaper. There was a photograph of the burned-out building with some policemen positioned in front of it.

Gabriel remembered those dark days as a child after independence was achieved. The Anglo-Irish Treaty had allowed for an Irish Free State which was still within the British Empire. It also allowed the six northern counties to opt out and remain in the United Kingdom. This was unacceptable to a great swathe of the Irish people and there followed a civil war between those who accepted the Treaty and those who didn't.

Gabriel stared down at the headline on the front of the newspaper before him.

INISHWOOD HOUSE DESTROYED IN ATTACK BY ANTI-TREATY REBELS

Gabriel read on.

In the seventh such attack this month on property owned by Protestant landlords, historic Inishwood House in Galway was burned to the ground last night. Local police report that a gang of hooded men called to the house in the early hours of the morning and forced their way in before dousing the house with petrol and setting it on fire. The fire that burned was so ferocious that the red glow it caused in the night sky could be seen twenty miles away in Galway City. The owner of the property, Percy Harper, was at home at the time of the attack with his wife Penny and daughter Karina ...

Gabriel broke off reading as he was overcome with nausea.
He forced himself to keep reading.

> It is understood that Mr Harper, whose sister is married to
> Lord Ashton, suffered a vicious assault during the attack.
> Mr Harper is a much-loved local character, enjoying the
> respect and friendship of people in the locality of Inishwood.
> It was with much sadness, regret and anger that the people
> of Inishwood learned of the attack on the Harper family
> who have lived in the locality for three hundred years ...

Gabriel sat back in his chair, feeling shocked and repulsed. He had
been indoctrinated from an early age by his mother and the
education system not even to question what happened during
those years. But, seeing this article and thinking of Karina made
him feel tremendously sad and disillusioned.

"Was there no other way, Dad?" Gabriel whispered as he looked
at the photograph of the burned-out house.

"Sorry, sir, I just came across this – might be of interest to you
as well," said the archivist as he placed another newspaper in front
of Gabriel before walking off.

On the front page in the bottom corner was a photograph of a
pleasant-looking man on a horse with a young girl beside him on a
pony. Gabriel read:

PERCY HARPER, SQUIRE OF INISHWOOD
DIES OF A HEART ATTACK

> Mr Percy Harper who featured in the news last week when
> his house was attacked and burned down by rebels has since
> died of a heart attack, this newspaper has learned. Mr
> Harper suffered a violent assault during the attack on his
> property and, according to reports, had not been well since.
> Mr Harper is survived by his wife Penny and daughter
> Karina ...

Gabriel stared at the photograph of the father and daughter on horseback and whispered "Karina ..."

Gabriel was overcome by a feeling of sadness over the following days and weeks. Every time he thought of Karina, he felt distressed. He also felt guilty. He knew war was terrible and atrocious acts were committed on both sides but, thinking of the photo of Karina as a little girl in the newspaper with her father, he could not help but feel guilty. She had been robbed of her father and her home all in the one night. She had been robbed of her childhood really ... and it was due to an order given by his father. He wanted to know more about her. He wanted to know everything about her. He wanted to know what had happened to her and her family after they had been forced from Inishwood. Had she managed to be happy, despite her loss? Had she ever been in love? Why was she not married with children yet? What was she doing picking him up in a nightclub in London and going to Sir Williams Baxter's bedroom in Great Hankerton Hall? Why did he sense she was deeply unhappy and in some kind of trouble? Did it all stem from the great losses she had suffered as a child, caused by his father? Why did he desperately want to help and protect her? Was it the guilt – the sins of the father visiting the son?

As he sat in his drawing room in his home in Monkstown, looking out at the sea across the road, all these questions came constantly flooding through his mind until tears of sadness crept down his face. She had reached out to him with a note and he had casually thrown it away, frightened she would bring trouble into his life ... instead of meeting her and seeing if he could help her in any way to compensate for what his family had done to hers.

CHAPTER 28

Cynthia had invited Marc Pietch to Roxford for Sunday dinner with the family.

"Well, it's our Christian duty," she said. "The poor man is isolated here – cast adrift from family and friends as his country is torn to pieces by war!"

"But we don't know him," Tess had said.

She was dreading the whole day as it was. Bad enough being trapped with Gabriel and Siobhán whispering sweet nothings to each other at the dinner table while she and Tim scowled at each other. Adding a rather slippery-looking foreigner with bad English into the mix and she'd be the one reaching for the whiskey bottle instead of Tim.

"Nonsense! I have come to know Mr Pietch extremely well. We are the best of friends – he is very sweet-natured," Cynthia had retorted.

"I wonder if there is anything going on between them?" asked Tess as she and Tim got ready for dinner in their bedroom at Roxford.

"What do you mean?" asked Tim as he combed his hair at the mirror.

"Well – you know," said Tess as she looked at herself in the mirror of her compact case, putting on her lipstick. "Are they lovers?"

Tim swung around from the mirror and threw the comb down on the dressing table.

"*Lovers!*"

"*Shhhh!* She'll hear you! Yes! Lovers! It does happen, you

185

know, Tim! People do go to bed with each other for other reasons than just to sleep! Even the sainted Cynthia Ford is a living breathing woman in the middle of the night!"

"*You are disgusting!*" snarled Tim. "To even *think* such a vile a thing about Mother!"

"I'm not thinking it – I'm just suggesting! And what if she is riding the Pole? She's a free agent – she's been a widow for nearly twenty years – and certainly not a merry one so she deserves a bit of comfort if she can find it."

Tim marched over to her, wagging his finger,

"If I hear one more filthy word out of that dirty mouth of yours I'll–I'll–I'll march out of here and not go down for dinner!"

"Oh, great – that would really seal our fate with your family – not showing up for the fucking turkey in front of the foreigner!" snapped Tess.

"I've warned you now! Keep your language fucking clean!" he said before he marched off and began to comb his hair again.

"There was a very large crowd at Mass this morning," said Cynthia as the family sat in the drawing room at Roxford.

Siobhán and Gabriel were sitting on a couch together, holding hands, while Tess and Tim sat at polar-opposite positions from each other, Tim conveniently besides the drinks cabinet. Marc Pietch stood beside Cynthia who was on an armchair beside the roaring fire, a glass of sherry in her hand.

"Gabriel and I spent some time talking to the crowd outside the church afterwards," said Cynthia. "Some of the children presented me with lovely posies of flowers to put on your father's grave. They do so love to see me up close."

Tess raised her eyes to heaven.

"It is so wonderful that your dear departed husband is still remembered and so respected by the younger generations, Cynthia," said Pietch.

"It is no more than I would expect or he deserved, Mr Pietch. Great men leave great memories." Cynthia looked disapprovingly at Tim who was refilling his glass of whiskey.

"I must say, Tim and Gabriel, your mother has been doing sterling work for me," said Pietch.

"So we hear. She was in Cork last week painting for work you commissioned, is that not so?" said Gabriel.

"Yes. Your mother is a remarkable talent. A wonderful landscape artist ... I believe she is on a par with Constable and Turner," said Pietch.

"*What?*" cried Tess incredulously.

"Oh desist, Marc – desist! Please!" said Cynthia, smiling broadly as she patted her hair.

"Well, she's making great money from all the commissions so she must be somewhat good!" said Tim, knocking back his drink.

"Your mother cannot keep up with the demand for her," said Pietch.

"Quite incredible," said Tess.

"Yes, the demand is so much that Mr Pietch has advised me to start doing postcards," said Cynthia.

"Postcards?" asked Siobhán, startled. "But surely you would be only able to get a fraction of the price for postcards as you do for the paintings?"

"Yes," said Pietch, "but you see, Cynthia will be able to do the sketches much more quickly and so I will have a much bigger volume to send to a client of mine who owns a printing firm in new York – and then we can mass-produce the postcards."

"So, actually, it will be much more lucrative commercially," said Cynthia, looking gleeful at the prospect.

"We will be able to sell the cards across America," said Pietch.

"Who would have thought there would have been so much interest in dreary Irish landscapes?" said Tess.

"We never appreciate what we take for granted, Tess. It often takes the foreigner to point out the value of what we ignore under our noses every day," said Cynthia, smiling up at Pietch.

The housekeeper walked in, drying her hands on her apron. "That turkey will be burnt and no use to anyone if it's not served in the next half hour, Mrs Ford. Will I put the vegitible soup out on the table?"

"Ah, yes, please serve the – *vegetable* – soup and we shall all take our seats," said Cynthia, putting down her sherry glass on the table beside her and rising from her chair.

"Allow me?" said Pietch, offering her his arm.

"Wonderful to see that all the gentlemen are not dead and buried," said Cynthia, taking his arm.

As the others followed them out to the dining room, Tess gave Tim a knowing look which caused him to scowl threateningly at her.

"It must be so distressing for you, reading the news and listening to the wireless each day, with the dreadful news from Poland," said Siobhán over the dinner table.

"Most distressing," said Pietch, nodding grimly.

"Have you a wife and children back home, Mr Pietch?" asked Tess, causing Tim to give her a warning look.

"No, I don't. I never met the right lady," said Pietch as he smiled at Cynthia.

"Well, it's never too late!" said Tess.

Tim grabbed the bottle of red wine and refilled his glass to the brim.

"I just hope this war is over soon and doesn't get any worse," said Siobhán. "I don't know why the Polish are being attacked like this."

"Because of land, Siobhán dear," said Cynthia. "War is never about race or religion. It's about one thing – land. Pretending it is about race or religion gets people more impassioned. The reality is that war is about land. The Poles have it and their neighbours the Germans want it. It was the very same here in Ireland. We Irish had land and our English neighbours wanted it. And just like the Germans now, the English did just about anything to get it."

"That's very cynical, Cynthia," said Siobhán.

"The truth is never cynical – it just sounds cynical to people who don't want to accept it," said Cynthia.

"You are a very wise and educated woman, Cynthia," said Pietch.

"I'm sure you Polish will get your country back eventually, Mr Pietch, just like we Irish did. But you will have to fight hard and long and there will be much suffering." She smiled sadly at him.

"I don't think we can quite compare what happened here in Ireland to what is occurring in Poland, Mother," said Gabriel.

"Why not? It's the same thing, only their theatre of war is there for all the world to see through modern media. What happened in Ireland just had a wider time frame, spreading over centuries. But the last bout of savagery committed by the English did happen in front of the whole world, during our final fight for independence only twenty years ago."

"There was savagery committed on both sides, Mother," said Gabriel.

Cynthia looked at Gabriel, stunned. "I *beg* your pardon?"

Everyone looked at Gabriel in surprise.

"Well – I'm only saying what everyone knows. It wasn't one-sided – there was a lot of tit for tat going on. They committed an atrocity then we retaliated."

"Did *we* indeed? As I recall *you* were in short pants at the time so I'm not actually sure who the *we* are that you are referring to?" Cynthia said, her voice like ice.

There was a nervousness around the table as everyone hoped the matter would be dropped now.

"I'm just saying –" said Gabriel.

"*What?* What are you *just saying*?" Cynthia's voice was getting colder and icier with every word.

Gabriel paused as he studied his mother's cold eyes and then chose to ignore Siobhán's warning pinches under the table.

"I'm not going to teach my granny to suck eggs here, Mother – you were there, you experienced first-hand what was going on. The assassination of the policemen who were just going about their business –"

"Employees of the British government," said Cynthia.

"The burning of the Big Houses –"

"Symbols of British imperialistic rule. They should never have been built on our land in the first place," said Cynthia.

"But they were – and those families had been living here hundreds of years –"

"Those *families* stole our land and exploited our people for generations!" spat Cynthia. "Causing the death and emigration of millions of our people during the Great Famine."

"The Famine was nearly a hundred years before the War of Independence came along, and most of those families were keeping their heads down and living quiet lives – their estates long gone back to our people. We could have treated them with a little more kindness."

Cynthia looked at her son in horror.

"Gabriel, please – stop it!" Siobhán whispered to him while Tess grabbed her glass of wine and drank it quickly.

"*Kindness?*" said Cynthia, rising slowly to her feet. "Kindness? What *kindness* did those people in their palaces ever show us?"

"Mother –"

"Has it come to this?" said Cynthia as she held out her hand, palm turned upwards. "Has it come to *this*? Is *this* what we fought the revolution for? Is *this* what our brave heroes of the War of Independence laid down their lives for? *Is this* why your father gave his life so that his *son* would complain that he didn't show more *kindness?*"

"Father wasn't killed in the War of Independence, Mother – he was killed by one of our own in the Civil War," said Gabriel impatiently.

Cynthia's mouth dropped open in shock.

Suddenly there was a loud thud as Tim fell off the chair, knocking his plate and glasses off the table and sending them crashing to the ground.

"For fuck's sake!" whispered Tess under her breath as she put her head in her hands.

Gabriel and Pietch quickly got to their feet and went to Tim.

"Tim! Are you alright?" asked Pietch, alarmed.

Cynthia sighed loudly. "Somebody just take him up to his room where he can sleep it off."

Tess went rushing over to him.

"*Will you pull yourself together, Tim!*" she hissed at him as she shook him.

Tim started grunting as Tess and Gabriel pulled him up from the floor and he half-walked and was half-carried out of the room.

Cynthia stared in stony silence at the half-eaten turkey.

Siobhán coughed loudly before smiling brightly. "I have always wanted to see the Baltic Sea, Mr Pietch ... are you from anywhere close to it?"

That evening Gabriel drove Siobhán back home to her parents' house. He was quiet as Siobhán chatted away. It was Siobhán's gift in life to be able to talk about mundane things during the most serious of crises. A perfect wife for a politician. Never an uncomfortable silence with Siobhán around.

"So Mammy is insisting we go to the races in the morning and Daddy has reluctantly agreed to go. I have my hat selected, navy with a white ribbon ... I thought the races would be abandoned with the Emergency, but they are to go ahead ... are you sure you wouldn't like to come with us, Gabriel?"

Gabriel stared ahead as he drove on in his own world.

"*Gabriel!*"

"Yes – sorry – what?" Gabriel was jolted back to reality.

"The races tomorrow! Do you want to come with me and Daddy and Mammy?"

"Eh, no – I can't. I have too much work to do."

"Pity ... as today was ... was ..." She trailed off.

"A disaster," he filled in for her. "A fecking disaster!"

"What is going on with Tim? Why?" she asked as he pulled into the driveway of her parents' home and slowed to a halt.

"Nothing – he just had a little too much to drink," said Gabriel as he turned and smiled at her. "Nothing to worry about."

"If you say so," she said before leaning forward and kissing him.

"I'll telephone tomorrow," he promised as she got out.

She stood in the driveway and waved at him as he turned the vehicle and drove off.

Then she turned slowly and walked into the house.

CHAPTER 29

As Gabriel entered through the front door of Roxford the next evening he could hear voices in the drawing room. He had been summoned there by his mother.

Preparing himself for what was to follow, he walked into the room.

Cynthia was in her armchair while Tim was on a couch, looking sobered up and completely miserable. Tess was on an opposite couch, her expression shifting between being furious and being amused.

"I was nearly going to ask Siobhán to come this evening as well, but I decided I didn't want to put the poor girl off marrying into this family any more than she probably already has," said Cynthia.

"Oh, you should have let her come, Cynthia," said Tess sarcastically. "Let her see exactly what she is letting herself in for ... I wish somebody had done the same for me before I said '*I do*'!"

"It's too late for you, Tess," said Cynthia, "but not for Siobhán – she still has options. I have put all my hopes for this family's future on that girl and I don't want to scare her off if the rest of you already haven't."

Tess fought back tears of humiliation and frustration on hearing Cynthia's words.

"Clearly things can't go on as they are," said Cynthia. "I had hoped after the spectacle Tim made of himself at the American ambassador's that the trouble his erratic behaviour is causing might have become clear to him."

"Why are you talking about me as if I'm not here?" asked Tim, his face red.

"But that clearly isn't the case," said Cynthia, ignoring him. "It's only a matter of time before he acts like he did today in full view of the public who elected him and then he will be disgraced for good and this family along with him ... so ... I have decided to make a few changes before things get further out of hand."

"Such as?" asked Tess, almost frightened of what was to come.

"Tim," Cynthia addressed her son for the first time, "your political career is all but over. You have lost all respect of your colleagues in the Dáil. I've spoken with the party leadership and you will not be running in the next election. You will be announcing your retirement – early retirement."

"You can't do that! You can't talk about me with the party leadership without my knowledge!" Tim was horrified.

"I already have, Tim, and they were quite relieved I did as everybody has been worried for quite some time what to do with a problem called Tim."

"I'll do no such thing as resign! I refuse to do it! They can feck off! You can all feck off!" Tim was furious.

"We'll do no such thing, Tim. You have no choice. If you don't stand down the party will deselect you – with my full support," said Cynthia.

"You'd do this to me?" Tim was incredulous.

"You did it to yourself, Tim, with your scandalous behaviour. I am merely trying to save the family name before you destroy it and your father's memory along with it."

"But – but – what will he do after he – resigns?" asked Tess, her voice trembling.

"A position will be found for him in the Civil Service where he can drink himself silly every day if he wants to – safely out of view of the public."

Everyone was shocked into silence.

Eventually Tim turned to Gabriel. "Have you nothing to say about this?"

Gabriel opened his mouth to speak but Cynthia cut in.

"Gabriel has nothing to say about your reshuffle and he is to have a reshuffle himself."

"What are you talking about?" asked Gabriel.

"Once Tim has resigned from his seat, Gabriel will be selected to run in the election for the party as his replacement," Cynthia informed them.

"*What?*" cried Tim.

"You can't do that, Cynthia!" Tess protested.

"It's already done. I straightened it out with the party leadership and it's been approved. It's decided Gabriel has the right qualities to run in the election and serve the people in the constituency as they deserve."

"It's out of the question!" Gabriel was laughing. "I have no intention for running for office! I am very happy in my position at the Department of External Affairs."

"Yes, indeed, too happy I would say! Flying to London and Washington all the time, trips to the Continent ... and picking up all kinds of strange ideas along the way. Sometimes I wonder if you are a son of mine at all with some of the strange political views you have, Gabriel."

"Just because I'm not stuck forever in the past does not make my ideas strange, Mother!"

"What's most worrying is when a person who has strange ideas no longer realises his ideas are strange! It's all set up with the party faithful, Gabriel. No point in fighting against it."

"But I will fight against it, with every breath in my body!" Gabriel insisted.

"Gabriel, when your father was killed I wasn't just robbed of the husband I adored – I was robbed of my rightful future. If your father had lived he would have ended up being leader of this country and I would have been by his side ... we would have shown them how it should be done. Ever since your father was shot, I have been grooming you two to take his rightful place in the sun. I will have a member of this family as leader of this country no matter what it takes. Tim – you had your chance and you blew it. Gabriel, with Siobhán by your side you can make it to the top ... and I aim to see you do!"

Cynthia stood up abruptly and marched out of the room.

"What are you planning to do about this?" Tim demanded of Gabriel.

"Tim, it's been a long day – I'm just going to go home."

"You can't let her do this to Tim!" said Tess.

"So – suddenly you care what happens to Tim, Tess?" Gabriel looked at her incredulously.

"You can't rob him of his seat in the Dáil."

"I have no intention of robbing his seat!"

"Well, what are you going to do about it then?" demanded Tim.

"What am *I* going to do about it? Maybe if you stayed off the whiskey for a day or two you might come up with a plan yourself!" Gabriel snapped.

"This is all that fucking little bitch's fault!" said Tess furiously. "That little Miss Goody Two Shoes with her butter-wouldn't-melt act and her phoney act!"

"Don't speak about Siobhán like that! She has nothing to do with it!" said Gabriel.

"Of course she doesn't!" sneered Tim. "Going to lunch with Cynthia all the time, dress fittings ..."

"Crumpet and scones with cream and strawberry jam in the Shelbourne Hotel! I saw them there only last week having their afternoon tea!" Tess announced as if she had spotted some great conspiracy.

"Are you seriously suggesting that Siobhán put Mother up to this? Oh, you are both being ridiculous! Siobhán couldn't contrive something like this if she tried! It's not in her nature!"

"She's a wolf in sheep's clothing!" said Tess.

"A bitch in sheep's clothing!" Tim backed her up.

"I'd better just go before I say something I regret!" said Gabriel.

"Oh, running off, are you?" said Tim. "Come on, Tess." He jumped to his feet.

Tess rose to her feet. "I'd never have believed you could be so underhand, Gabriel! Traitor!"

"Let's go to bed. The air stinks down here!" said Tim.

"*Yeah – from the whiskey on your breath!*" Gabriel shouted after them as they marched out into the hallway and up the stairs.

* * *

"I can't believe it … I can't believe it … *I can't believe it*!" shouted Tim in their bedroom.

He rushed over to the drinks table and poured himself a whiskey.

"That won't save you this time," said Tess as she sat down on an armchair, crossed her legs and sighed loudly.

"That she would do this to me! Her own flesh and blood!"

"There's nothing flesh and blood about Cynthia – pure stone," said Tess.

"She won't get away with it. The party would never treat me like that! They'd never kick me out!"

"I'd say the party were relieved when Cynthia gave them the nod to kick you out, Tim. They only didn't do it until now for fear of offending her."

Tim stared into space as he gripped his whiskey glass, as if all this was a revelation of something he had never considered before. "Well, feck them! Feck them all! I'll stand in the next election as an independent – that'll show them!"

"Tim! Who will finance your campaign? Who will even campaign for you without the party or Cynthia behind you?"

Tim collapsed into an armchair "But – but what will I do?"

Tess bit her lip as she had no answers to give him. She had feared something like this would be the outcome of the way he had been behaving, of the way their marriage was. But she felt there was no reason to get angry with him and blame him for their downfall at this stage – it was simply too late. He looked broken and lost and there was no point in adding salt to the wound. Their marriage was a disaster – but it was still a marriage and, if he went down, then she went down with him.

"Gabriel won't do it – he won't stab me in the back! He thinks too much of me and he is too kind to do that," said Tim.

"You see Gabriel as kind, I see him as weak. Gabriel has never stood up to anybody in his life. He's a good boy who does what he's told. That's why the diplomatic service suits him – he's diplomatic! He likes to please people – that's why he's marrying that dull little teacher – because it pleases everyone for him to marry her."

"When push comes to shove, Gabriel will back me up!" insisted Tim.

"When push comes to shove Gabriel will do what he's told! Oh, he'll make all the right noises and huff and puff and protest and then he'll do what all diplomats eventually do – and just give in for the sake of peace!"

"What the feck are we going to do, Tess?" Tim looked terrified.

"I don't know, Tim." She stood up and walked over to the drinks table and poured herself a large gin before turning and holding the glass up in the air to him. "But for now I'm going to match you drink for drink tonight!"

CHAPTER 30

Siobhán and Gabriel were taking their usual walk down the pier at Dun Laoghaire, arms around each other.

"Our neighbours' son has gone and joined the British army to go fight the Nazis," said Siobhán. "That's the third lad on our street who's joined up with the Brits. Daddy is furious with them – says he will write a poem denouncing them as traitors to their country!"

"That'll teach them!" said Gabriel, aware his sarcastic tone would be lost totally on Siobhán.

"Mammy is praying every night for deliverance from a German invasion … Daddy is praying each night for deliverance from a British one … I'm just praying things will go back to normal!"

"If they can ever go back to normal."

"But they wouldn't really come here, would they, Gabriel? Not the Nazis! Sure, who would have any interest in coming to little old Ireland? Sure, even the weather is shocking here most of the time. They'd be better off bringing umbrellas than machine guns!"

"I'm sure Denmark and Norway thought the same before the Nazis paraded into them," sighed Gabriel.

"I wouldn't know what I'd do if the Germans invaded. I suppose at least the British speak the same language as us if they invaded us – but how would we talk to the Germans? I hope we wouldn't have to postpone the wedding if they invaded … I've heard every couple that gets married in Germany receives a copy of Hitler's book *Mein Kampf* as an official wedding gift from the government … can you imagine that? Whether you want it or not!

But, sure, I wouldn't want a gift like that! What would we do with it? We could hardly read it if it's in German. I wouldn't want to read it anyway even if it was in English ... they couldn't make us read it, could they, Gabriel?"

As Siobhán talked on and on in her intermittent style, Gabriel drifted off into his own thoughts.

Tess and Tim were keeping their distance and Cynthia was in full force to fulfil her plan to have Gabriel replace Tim in the Dáil. Gabriel had tried to argue with her but arguing with Cynthia was pointless. He would just not do it when it came to the time. Although, as he looked at Siobhán, he imagined it would be even more difficult to resist Cynthia's plan when he was married to her as she was in awe of Cynthia and would be frightened of going against her.

As Siobhán tightened her grip around his waist, talking incessantly, he felt overpowered and suffocated. He felt she was crowding in on him and he couldn't breathe. He reached for his collar and loosened it. Then, as the feeling of claustrophobia overtook him, he suddenly pulled away from her.

"Gabriel! Are you alright?"

"Yes – I'm just – I need some air!" He was breathing heavily as he went over to a bench and sat down.

"Gabriel! Are you sick? Do you need a doctor?" she asked, sitting down beside him and putting an arm around him.

"No – I'll be fine. I just need some space!" he said, shrugging her arm off and moving up the bench away from her.

"You don't look very well to me! I think you should see a doctor. Maybe Doctor Feehily is at home and could see you – lovely man – lovely manners – I always thought he'd make a lovely pianist –"

"I don't need a fucking doctor, Siobhán! I just need *quiet*!" he said, throwing his hands up in the air in exasperation.

She looked at him, shocked.

"Oh, I see! My lips are sealed!" she said then, doing a zipping mime with her thumb and forefinger across her mouth.

They sat in silence for a while as he stared at the ground, trying to regulate his breathing back to normal.

"There's a fortune-teller – in that little hut," Siobhán said as she looked towards the end of the pier. "Oh, let's go in, Gabriel! Wouldn't that be fun! Not together, of course. I'll go in first and then we'll wait a while and you can go in – so as she doesn't know we are together. We don't want to give her any clues! What do you say, Gabriel? Will we go in? What do you think?"

"Yes! Yes – go in!" urged Gabriel quickly, delighted to have the chance of a few minutes' peace.

"Right so – I won't be long! Don't move!"

She walked quickly down the pier and disappeared into the hut.

Gabriel sat cradling his head in his hands for a long while before he stood up and went over to the edge of the pier. He stared out to sea. He didn't know what was wrong with him. He couldn't understand himself and the reaction he was having.

He didn't even notice time passing until Siobhán came walking back, clutching her handbag to her breast.

"Well, I don't think much of her! Not very good at all! It was as if she could tell me nothing right about myself and, as for my future – well, she told me a very different future from the one I have planned for myself, let me tell you!"

"We'd better be getting home," said Gabriel quickly, trying to cut off a long monologue from Siobhán about what the fortune-teller said.

"But you have to go in to her first, Gabriel!"

"Ah no, Siobhán, I don't believe in all that nonsense!"

"But you promised, Gabriel! And I want to know what she has to say about you and see if she has any idea of the future at all or is she one of those fraudsters you read about in *Reader's Digest* –"

"Alright! Alright! I'll go in!" said Gabriel, quickly escaping down the pier.

He reached the end of the pier and went into the hut where he saw a woman in her sixties sitting at a small table.

"Can I come in?" he asked.

"Looks like you already have, sir. Take a seat."

Gabriel sat down across the table from her.

"Give me your right palm," she said.

He stretched his hand, upturned, across the table to her. He suddenly felt a bit nervous and regretted coming in.

"Tell me," said the woman, looking up at him, "are you in love with that girl you sent in here before you?"

Gabriel was startled. "I thought she wasn't going to tell you we were together."

"She didn't. I see it here in your palm. Well, are you in love with her?"

Gabriel stared at her and said nothing.

"Because if you are not, then don't marry her. It will be the worst thing you could do for you and for her. Marriage is a long time to be trapped with somebody you don't love. What starts off being endearing quickly becomes unbearable."

Gabriel felt very uncomfortable. "Anything else?"

"You will be led into danger ... but there is danger everywhere these days."

"Well?" asked Siobhán.

"As you say – she's doesn't seem to know that much," said Gabriel as he uncomfortably looked away from her.

CHAPTER 31

Gabriel sat in his motorcar on Merrion Square across the road from Karina's building. It was ten o'clock at night and he could see the lights on in her flat. He was in turmoil as he sat there. A maelstrom of emotions was swirling around in his head.

He had to see Karina again. Try as he might to forget her, he had become obsessed with her. He needed to meet her again and break this spell she had cast over him He needed to prove these feelings he was experiencing for her were an illusion. Hopefully five minutes in her company would jolt him back to reality and he could get on with his life.

He got out of the motorcar and crossed the road. He steadied himself and climbed the steps to the large Georgian door and pushed it open. Inside was a very plush hallway with a glittering chandelier and a grand staircase.

He ascended the stairs to the top floor.

When he reached her door, he was trembling as he raised his hand and knocked. He had no idea what he was going to say but decided to let what whatever was going to come out of his mouth come out of his mouth. An unusual feeling for a career diplomat who rehearsed nearly every conversation he had before he had it.

The door swung open and Karina stood there, her hair tied back in a bun.

She looked startled at seeing him there.

"Gabriel!" she eventually said.

"Hello, Karina, I hope I'm not disturbing you? I know it's late."

"No, I was just about to ... to ... come in, why don't you?" she said, standing back and allowing him to enter.

He walked in and she closed the door.

He looked around the sitting room which was very stylishly decorated and furnished.

She crossed over to a table and picked up a cigarette case. She held it out, offering one to him.

"No, thank you." He shook his head.

She took a cigarette for herself and lit it up before going to stand against the frame of one of the windows.

"Well – this is a surprise," she said.

"Yes – I got your note," he said.

"What – like several weeks ago?" she said, not hiding her sarcasm.

"Yes, I'm sorry it's taken so long to get back to you. It's been very busy what with …"

"The war and everything?" she said cynically. "Oh, dear, I shouldn't mention the word *war*, should I? You Irish don't like to mention that word. It's the *Emergency* as you Irish like to call it … that sounds so much more civil than using the word *war*. Easier to distance yourselves from the horrors of what is happening on the Continent with a clear conscience."

He stared at her in disbelief. The last thing he expected was to be confronted with a lecture on Ireland's neutrality.

"Anyway, I do apologise for my delay in getting back to you … what was it you wanted to see me about?" he asked.

She looked at him with incredulity. "Well, I really, actually, can't remember anymore to tell you the truth – it's been that long since I wrote the note it's gone plain out of my head!"

"I see … in that case. I had better go … it was a mistake to come here in the first place." He began to walk to the door.

"Wait!"

He turned as she walked quickly to him.

"I've remembered what I wanted."

"What? What do you want from me?" he demanded.

They stared at each other in silence, then he suddenly lunged at her and began to kiss her. She grabbed him by the back of the neck and kissed him back.

CHAPTER 32

They lay in the quiet of her bedroom in each other's arms.

Karina was almost too frightened to break the silence as she thought over what had happened that night.

Gabriel arriving at her door had taken her off guard. She had quickly pulled herself together and realised this was what they had been planning for. What she had planned for. But, as she had invited him in, what she hadn't planned for was the huge chemistry that was passing between them. It had been there the night she had met him in the 400 Club and it was why she had gone back to Claridge's with him. It had been there in the back of her mind when she had met him in Great Hankerton Hall. But she had been so shocked at seeing him again and fearing exposure that she had suppressed the feeling. And it had been there during the brief conversation she had with him at the American ambassador's. The difference was that on the last two occasions there had been other people about and so the sexual feeling she had for him had been somewhat diluted.

But there that night in her flat it had bubbled to the surface. Suddenly she was in danger of blowing the whole plan. Instead of gently leading him into her web, she had been hostile to him and he had nearly walked out.

It had never been her plan to go to bed with him again. She was sure it might have been in Emily and Kendrick's plan if the situation arose, but never hers. As she watched him sleeping beside her, she felt sorry for him. He had no idea he was a pawn in their game. There was a sweet or sour way of doing everything, and luckily this infiltration was to be done the sweet way. She would meet him regularly, bring him into her confidence and find out everything they needed to know. Gabriel Ford would be putty in her hands. As she looked at him, she felt the tremendous attraction she had for him. She knew he felt the same for her. She wondered if this lust could have led to something else ... if they had met in different circumstance. But that was all it was, lust on both their parts and a means to an end for her. Hugo would never need to know about this. But she had promised herself she would do anything to rescue him and going to bed with Gabriel Ford was not a particularly difficult thing to do.

She gently moved his arm from around her and slipped out of bed. Putting on her long silk dressing gown, she looked down at him for a minute and then crept from the room. It was half past six in the morning and growing light outside. She went into the kitchen, put on the kettle and waited for it to boil before making herself a cup of tea. She then went into the sitting room, pulled back the curtains and lit herself a cigarette. She hugged the cup of tea close to her as she took a drag of her cigarette and watched the rising sun brighten the sky. She wondered what Hugo was doing. Was he watching the same sun come up while he thought of her?

"Any chance of a cup of tea for me?" came Gabriel's voice from behind her and she turned around to see him standing in the doorway.

She smiled at him. "Of course. I might even stretch to making you a breakfast. Though I'm a dreadful cook, be warned."

An hour later she stood at the window, looking down at the Square. She watched as Gabriel crossed the road to his motorcar. Before getting in, he turned and looked up at her. He smiled and waved, and she returned the wave. He then got in and drove away. She turned from the window and bit her lip, her face creased in thought.

BOOK 3

MAY TO AUGUST 1940

CHAPTER 33

Gabriel could hardly concentrate on anything at work as he was consumed with thoughts of Karina. He knew he should feel guilt and bad about himself, but he didn't. He felt fulfilled and had this glorious feeling of happiness. It was as if he had been looking for something all his life and didn't even know it until he had found it. And what he had found was Karina. As he sat in his office at work, staring out the window, he realised that his life had become a complete and utter mess.

As Karina walked to work she saw a large crowd gathered around a newsstand. People were talking loudly in the street as they read the newspaper. Karina read the headline.

GERMANS INVADE NEUTRAL HOLLAND AND BELGIUM

Shocked by the news, she fought her way through the crowd to get a copy of the newspaper.

At the legation, there was a flurry of activity as staff raced around. Karina made her way up the stairs to her office, closed the door and sat down to read the awful news from the Continent. Her thoughts were on Julian as she read about the terrible casualties being inflicted.

Emily walked swiftly into Karina's office and closed the door behind her.

"Isn't this terrible, Emily?" she said.

"I think we can safely say the phoney war is over. Let's hope our chaps and the French can hold them off from getting any further."

"Any further? But surely they can't invade France?"

"We're entering a critical time, Harper. We all have to concentrate on our jobs. And yours is Gabriel Ford." She sat down opposite Karina. "So the mountain finally came to Mohamed!"

Karina contained her anger as she realised Emily already knew about Gabriel at her flat.

"I'm really not comfortable with being watched by your people all the time, Emily."

"You aren't being watched – Gabriel Ford is. If you hadn't picked Gabriel Ford up that night in the 400 Club, nobody would know or give a hoot about you, my dear."

"How gratifying to know," said Karina sarcastically.

"Get to the point – what happened?" demanded Emily.

Karina felt uncomfortable as she sat back in her chair and crossed her legs "Well, you obviously know what happened ... he arrived at my flat at ten last night –"

"And left at seven this morning. I take it he was in amorous mood?"

Karina shifted uncomfortably. "I didn't need to use blackmail, if that's what you're asking. I think more can be found out by me playing him along."

"Excellent. And the more he becomes involved with you, the more we have to blackmail him with when the day comes that we need to use it."

"I'm not really sure how important he could ever be to us winning the war, Emily. He's just a diplomat in a neutral country."

"And look at what is happening to neutral countries across Europe – they are all being quickly annexed into the German Empire. The last thing Britain can afford is to have our neighbour to the west become part of that Nazi empire and encircle us – we wouldn't stand a chance then fighting on all sides. We were at war with Ireland only twenty years ago and although de Valera's government makes assurances that they are sympathetic to us and actually on our side, well – they are not putting their money where their mouth is. We cannot ignore the fact they got arms from the Germans in the last war and may very well do the same this time. We need to know what they are really up to – and Gabriel Ford knows everything they are up to and you are our key to Gabriel Ford."

"You don't have to tell me anything about the Irish, Emily. I spent my childhood here and lost everything twenty years ago ... but it doesn't feel right using Gabriel like this. He seems to me to be just a straightforward man who is being a bit reckless."

"Oh – Karina, I never had you down as a stupid woman whatever else I had you down as! He's cheating on his fiancée with you! Keep your sympathy for a deserving cause – he's a creep!" Emily took out a notebook. "Now, let's begin – what happened with him last night?"

Karina's level of discomfort became intense as she looked at Emily's notebook and pen.

CHAPTER 34

The news from the Continent continued to get worse as the Germans, having conquered Holland and Belgium, swept into France. And, to everyone's dismay, the British and French troops were making a hasty retreat. The British troops had retreated to a seaside town in northern France called Dunkirk and now over three-hundred thousand troops were marooned there as the British tried desperately to organise an evacuation before the Germans got to them.

As Karina saw Emily rush down a corridor, she managed to stop her in her tracks.

"What is it, Harper? The Minister is waiting for me!"

"Emily, I have a cousin who is in France fighting and I think he must be in Dunkirk – can you find out if he is there? If he's alright?"

"There are over three-hundred thousand men in Dunkirk, Harper! How the hell am I supposed to locate just one man?" demanded Emily.

"He's an officer, Lord Julian Ashton – I'm sure that might make it easier to try and locate him?" Karina said, her eyes filling with tears.

Emily sighed loudly. "I'll see what I can find out."

"Thank you," Karina whispered as she allowed Emily to continue past her.

Karina could hardly sleep at night as she thought of Julian and the other thousands of soldiers trapped at Dunkirk, sitting ducks for the approaching Nazi war machine.

It was chaos at the legation in Dublin as a desperate plan was cobbled together in London to try and rescue the men who were facing annihilation.

Karina was startled to see Emily come rushing down a corridor with a huge smile on her face, under such grave circumstances.

"We are sending a flotilla to get our boys!" Emily almost sang the words.

"A flotilla?"

"Every ship we have, every boat from the biggest to the smallest fishing vessel – straight across the Channel to pick them up and bring them home!"

"Really?" said Karina, excited by the news but wondering if it was an impossible task.

"By golly, I wish I was there myself!" said Emily, rolling up her sleeves. "I used to be a dab deckhand on my uncle's yacht on the Suffolk coast during school holidays! If I was there now, I'd grab that yacht and sail her across to pick up as many of our boys as I could fit on her and bring them home!" She looked at once delighted at the prospect and distraught she couldn't actually do it.

"I have no doubt you would!" said Karina.

"Anyway, must dash – the Minister is waiting!" Emily went to run on but stopped and called back. "Oh, and Harper! We have located your cousin for you. Lord Ashton is at Dunkirk and awaiting evacuation with the rest of our boys!"

Karina's heart jumped with joy and relief as she called after Emily "*Oh, thank you, Emily – thank you!*"

As Gabriel looked at the grave faces gathered around the board table in the heavily guarded office in Government Buildings, he could not remember a time of more tension. He felt you could literally cut the atmosphere with a knife and even de Valera looked in a state of disbelief. The fall of France had shaken Europe and the world to its very core and now as photos of Hitler smiling with the Eiffel Tower behind him flashed from newspapers across the globe it looked like the Nazi war machine was unbeatable. Gabriel's boss, Joe Walsh, the Minister for External Affairs, had been to London the previous month for a top-level meeting with the British government after the invasion of the low countries and France, to discuss the desperate situation on the Continent. Now, just three weeks later those countries were under complete German control. In Dublin, everyone held their breath as to what would come next. Now all eyes at the table were on Joe Walsh as he delivered the news they were all dreading.

"I have been informed by my counterpart in London that they have certain evidence of a German plan to invade Ireland," said Walsh.

Everyone sat in silence as they digested the news.

"Can we trust them to tell the truth?" asked de Valera. "The British could be saying it to force our hand, to get us to abandon neutrality and join the war on their side."

"I would say, given the circumstances on the Continent, we have no option but to believe such an invasion plan exists and is being developed ... as we speak," said Walsh.

"If we ever thought our neutrality would be respected by the Germans," said Gabriel, "the invasion of neutral Denmark, Norway, Holland and Belgium has demonstrated that it is only our geographical position as an island on the far side of Britain that has protected us from such an invasion so far."

"We must face the facts and, with the fall of France, it is only a matter of time before Britain falls as well," said Walsh. "The main focus of the Nazis is the defeat of Britain. I am informed the British are preparing for a direct attack on their country and we must prepare for a direct attack on ours. The basis of the German plan to invade us is that if they occupy Ireland, then the British will also invade Ireland, leading to the British and Germans fighting the war out here ... in effect, Ireland would be providing a stage for them to fight it out ... with the Germans being the final victors."

"So our country is to be a back yard for two major powers to fight out their battle and leave us devastated," said de Valera.

"It happened to Belgium in the last war," said Gabriel.

"So what are we to do?" asked de Valera.

"I suppose we should be grateful that the British have respected our neutrality so far and not just rolled into Ireland like they did last month in Iceland for our 'own protection'," said Walsh.

"They may not find us Irish quite as obedient a race to occupy as the Icelanders after our experience here over the past eight hundred years!" said de Valera.

"The British certainly want to cooperate with us and I think we have no choice but to do so, given the dire circumstances we are now facing," said Gabriel.

"We've seen the horrors of the occupation of Poland and the other countries. It's unthinkable it would happen here in Dublin," said Walsh.

"I imagine the French thought the same just a few weeks ago," said de Valera. "As much as it pains me to say this, we must cooperate with the British and forget about the past. However, we cannot be seen to compromise our neutrality. We cannot risk aggravating the Germans by entering this war. But behind the scenes we must start making confidential war plans with the British that can come into effect once a German invasion is unleashed on Ireland."

"Who would ever have thought of such cooperation twenty years ago when we were fighting to the core to get them out of the country," said Walsh.

"Who would have ever imagined a threat like the Nazis twenty years ago?" said de Valera. "It must remain completely confidential as there would be unrest amongst the Irish people if they knew we were cooperating with the old enemy."

"The problem is," said Gabriel, "cooperating with the British in preparation for the event of a possible attack on Ireland is all very fine ... but what happens if and when the British are defeated? What defence do we have against the Germans if they go for a direct attack on Britain first and, as we can only expect, win victory there? The Germans will simply sail across the sea to us and dictate their terms."

"Well, we brought the British empire to their knees twenty years ago, so the Germans can expect the fight of their lives from us," announced de Valera.

"Fighting talk, Dev!" said Walsh with a proud look on his face and a fist shaken in the air.

Gabriel nodded and smiled as he thought how Holland had been defeated just four days after their country was invaded.

"Meanwhile Paris is in German hands. What of our legation there?" asked de Valera.

"It has closed down – it was the second last embassy to close down in the city just before the American embassy closed," Gabriel informed him.

"That's because the other countries are at war with the Germans and had to flee for their lives before they got there!" said Walsh.

"Our staff are temporarily in Ascain and all are safe," said Gabriel. "We have to wait and see what kind of government is established in France before we can re-establish an embassy."

"As for our relations with Germany, they need more attention and careful handling then ever. We have a new ambassador in Berlin who is doing a very good job –"

"Couldn't do a worse job than our last ambassador who went working for Goebbels at the German Ministry of Propaganda since we relieved him of his duties! Not good for our international reputation!" said Gabriel.

"Gabriel," said de Valera.

"Yes?" Gabriel answered.

"I'm appointing you as a special envoy to deal with our relations with Germany. And not just because you are proficient in German. You're the right man for the job. Keep in constant contact with their embassy here and do whatever is necessary to keep them on side. Ireland does not seem to be of much interest to Hitler so far in any of his speeches ... despite his family connections with the Irish ..."

"Indeed."

"So let us hope for the best."

CHAPTER 35

A new American ambassador had been appointed in April. The man, David Grey, was unusual as an American ambassador to Dublin as he was not blindly supportive of the Irish government. David Grey, an uncle of President Roosevelt's wife Eleanor, did not hide his feeling that he felt Irish neutrality was a mistake and that Ireland should enter the war to fight the Germans. As the Germans advanced towards Paris, Grey was making his opinions on the Irish even more vocal.

Karina was seated with her notebook and pen alongside a secretary from the American Embassy during a visit by David Grey to the British legation. Grey was there for a meeting with the British Representative, Sir John Maffey. Karina was taking the minutes of the meeting alongside her American counterpart.

"I can only say that you British are to be admired for your restraint in dealing with the Irish," said Grey. "The fact you have put up with all this neutrality nonsense and not forced them into the war or just taken back the ports."

"We have had an uneasy truce with the Irish over the past twenty years – we do not want to do anything to upset them," said Sir John.

"The Germans are going to be in Paris in a couple of days and your boys barely got out of Dunkirk – those of them who weren't left behind – who cares about upsetting the Irish!"

"Despite the position of neutrality, the Irish are cooperating with us surprisingly well, considering our countries' past history," said Maffey.

"Or so they would have you believe! I, however, think that the Irish are not entering the war on the British side as they expect you to lose! They simply do not want to be on the losing side."

"There is a danger of that, I concede," said Maffey.

"I suspect that the Irish government are actually pro-Nazi, and that is why they are staying out of the war. I wrote to them and demanded they close down the German Embassy in Dublin. They refuse to do it, saying that as a neutral nation they cannot take sides!"

"Irish neutrality is frustrating, but there is little we can do except continue to try to persuade them," said Maffey.

"Well, I will be trying to persuade – and shame – them into doing the right thing and turning against the Nazis," said Grey. "It's all very suspicious ... they are keeping their embassy open in Berlin as well and communication between the Irish and Germans is flowing. I don't hear much condemnation out of Dublin about the atrocities being committed on the Continent."

"They have appointed a new Minister to Germany and also appointed a senior diplomat, Gabriel Ford, as a special envoy to promote good relations between the two countries," said Maffey.

Karina knocked a glass of water over on her desk when she heard Gabriel's name, causing everyone in the room to pause and look at her.

"Are you alright, Miss Harper?" asked Sir John.

"Quite alright, I apologise!" said Karina, going red as she mopped up the water with a handkerchief.

Karina went rushing into Emily's office. "Have you heard about Gabriel? He has been appointed as an envoy dealing directly with the Germans!"

"Yes, I know," said Emily. "And so it has become even more important to ingratiate yourself with him. We have no time to lose, with the Nazis now in control of France."

"Emily, my cousin – Lord Ashton – you remember he was trapped at Dunkirk?"

"Yes?"

"You said he was waiting with the rest of our boys to be evacuated."

"Yes, he was," Emily confirmed.

"Well, he should be back home in London by now. But I've contacted his house in London and his butler says he has not arrived home yet. None of our family or friends have seen or heard from him. Surely he should have arrived in London by now if he had been evacuated?"

"I'm not going to lie to you, Karina. He should be back on English soil by now if he managed to get out," said Emily.

"But you said before – you *said* – that he was just waiting be evacuated."

"But you know that some were captured by the Germans," Emily said gravely. "And there were casualties."

Gabriel walked along the beach that evening with Cynthia, her two Labradors racing around them in circles. He was explaining what had been discussed that day at the cabinet. Gabriel regularly discussed the political landscape with Cynthia, no matter how confidential. Cynthia herself was part of the inner sanctum of Irish politics and had been for over twenty years and so was privy to the most confidential of political knowledge. Gabriel, like many others in government, found her a wise and experienced advisor. But that evening she could only listen in horror to what Gabriel was divulging.

"Has Éamon lost his mind?" she demanded. "He cannot seriously be thinking of inviting the British back into Ireland after the blood that was shed to get rid of them only twenty years ago!"

"I don't think you quite understand the threat we are under, Mother. If the Germans choose to invade we will not be protected from the mass bombings, executions and deportations that the other countries are suffering."

"And information about this – German invasion – had come from British Intelligence, you tell me?"

"That's correct."

"*Pah!*" she scoffed. "How convenient for the British to tell us this when they've been trying to force us into their war on their side! I don't believe a word of it! Not one word, I tell you. 'Tis a ploy to get control of us again. And this time by Éamon's invitation! And once they arrive back here it will take another eight hundred years to get rid of them!"

"Mother! The intelligence is indisputable. Most of the members of the government cabinet fought against the British twenty years ago, just like you and Father did and they all realise that this time – *this* time – we have to cooperate with the old enemy or we will all perish." Gabriel was becoming desperate to get her to understand.

"The Irish people will never put up with it," she said dismissively. "If the Irish government allow the British back in, then they are betraying the people!"

Cynthia turned abruptly and began to march back furiously down the beach towards Roxford, the dogs following her.

"The Germans invading Ireland! Whatever next!" She swung around, laughing dismissively. "Let me tell you, the Germans would never get an invasion force across the English Channel to Ireland. That sea is one of the roughest in the world! I did the trip on a night boat once – twenty-four hours of sheer hell! I felt I was on the *Titanic!* My face was green when we finally arrived in Cherbourg the next morning! Never again – I was sick the whole time!"

"The invasion is expected to be predominantly airborne. Paratroopers being flown in!" he called.

"And how on earth would they know where they were going, landing in the wilds of Tipperary? We had better hurry home – it's dinnertime and it looks like rain! Come on!"

He hurried after her.

CHAPTER 36

Karina was busy typing in her office when the telephone rang.

"Harper speaking," she said.

There was no answer.

"Hello?" she said, about to hang up.

"Karina, it's me ... it's Gabriel."

"Oh!" She sat back in her chair.

"Sorry to disturb you at work," he said.

"Oh, I wasn't doing anything too hectic. Just typing up countless memorandums," she said. "My life is a series of typing up memorandums!"

He gave a little laugh.

There was a silence for about five seconds, prompting Karina to say, "Is anything the matter, Gabriel?"

"No! Absolutely not! Everything is just great ... I really just wanted to thank you for the other night. Being so hospitable and everything ... the breakfast ... and the tea ..."

She suddenly burst out giggling.

"What? What's so funny?" he demanded.

"Nothing! Nothing at all!" She sobered herself up and stopped laughing. She found the whole situation perplexing and for some reason amusing. If this was his idea of seduction, she wondered how he ever got to the proposal stage with Siobhán.

"I was wondering as well ..."

"Yes?"

"I was hoping we could meet again? Nothing fancy – just

maybe you would like to come to my place for dinner?"

"Oh – yes, I think I would like that very much. When? And what is the address?"

"I have a meeting with the new American ambassador this evening, so unfortunately not tonight ... tomorrow?"

"Yes, that would be perfect," she said as she jotted down on a piece of notepaper: *Gabriel Ford meeting with American ambassador this evening.*

"Seven o'clock? My address is 32 Victoria Terrace, Monkstown."

"Perfect! I look forward to it," she said, and hung up the phone.

She picked up the notepaper and rushed to find Emily, to give her the update.

Karina walked along the seafront in Monkstown, trying to locate Victoria Terrace. She finally found it. It was a row of three-storey Victorian townhouses. On the other side of the street was the sea. She could imagine Gabriel living there – living in this neat row of townhouses – it suited him.

She found Number 32, climbed the steps up to the front door and banged the knocker loudly.

"Hello there!" Gabriel said a few seconds later, swinging open the door.

She smiled at him and walked in. She looked down the stylish black-and-white tiled hallway with the staircase at the bottom.

"Punctual!" he commented as the grandfather clock in the hall struck seven.

"As the Irish say, what's seldom is wonderful!" she said as she took off her coat and handed it to him. "My boss at the Foreign Office would beg to disagree that the word *punctual* should ever be put in any sentence concerning me!"

"You look amazing," he said as he eyed her.

She was wearing her long gold lamé dress. She had decided to go all out and not dress down. Gabriel was obviously taken by an image of her as this glamorous siren, probably unlike any of the women he knew or had been brought up with. She had decided to encourage that idea.

"Thank you," she said as she walked down the hallway. There was a door open to the left. She glanced in and saw it was a study with a chesterfield desk in front of a large ornate fireplace. There was paperwork scattered across the desk.

"Just in here!" he said, indicating an open doorway across the hallway and quickly closing the doorway to the study.

She walked through the door and saw it was a large drawing room furnished in classical Louis X1V style. It had a large Georgian window which looked across the road outside to a wonderful view of Dublin Bay, a large ornate marble fireplace and a double door leading into a dining room. She could see the table had been set.

He stood there awkwardly at the drinks cabinet.

"Drink?" he asked.

As she studied him, she decided this man was not an expert at conducting an affair. Instead of having a repertoire of seductive moves, he seemed uncomfortable with the whole process. She decided she had better take control.

She walked confidently over to the drinks cabinet and gently pushed him aside.

"Let me take over the drinks aspect. Let me see what you have … my mother is American so I am a dab hand at cocktails, not that she ever indulged too much, I hasten to add." She inspected his alcohol selection and picked up a bottle of whiskey. "Have you ever tried a Manhattan?"

Karina sat at the table in the dining room while Gabriel brought in the food from the kitchen. He laid out a feast of chicken, roast potatoes and vegetables, with a steaming sauceboat of gravy.

"Where did you manage to get all this on your rations? Or do you get extra rations working for the government?" she asked.

"No, I get no extra rations but I used a lot of them for tonight," he said.

"How flattering! A man who sacrifices his rations for a woman – well, it is the most romantic thing he could do these days!"

"I also have a couple of friends who are farmers." He winked at her as he opened a bottle of red wine.

"Oh dear, Gabriel! Indulging in the black market!"

"I know – if it got out my career would be over, for sure," he said as he filled her glass.

As she studied him she wondered did he realise his career would be much more in jeopardy if the affair he was conducting got out – especially in Holy Catholic Ireland. He would be ruined overnight.

"Did you cook this yourself?" she asked as he lit the candelabra on the table and sat down opposite her.

"No, I can barely boil an egg! I have a housekeeper who comes in and she did it all. She went to quite an effort for this evening!"

"How good of her... I expect she thought your dinner guest tonight would be Siobhán?"

"I -I expect she did," agreed Gabriel, looking guilty.

"Are you not frightened she may just unexpectedly show up?" asked Karina.

"My housekeeper?"

"No – Siobhán, of course!" Karina said.

"Siobhán would never unexpectedly do anything. It's not in her nature to do anything that is not routine or planned," explained Gabriel.

"How boring!" scoffed Karina as she drank her wine.

"I'd rather you didn't speak ill of her, Karina. Perhaps better we don't speak of her at all?"

Karina was about to say something sarcastic about his loyalty to Siobhán being touching but held back.

"Whatever you wish!" she said with a shrug.

"Thank you."

They sat in silence for a while but she could see the mention of Siobhán had bothered him.

"She thinks I'm working, anyway. She thinks I'm working late tonight so wouldn't come over even if she was the type to turn up unannounced."

"Really? Well, I'm glad we have that sorted then!"

"She knows how busy I am at work with everything going on ... Something new every week ... It's the Irish stuck in France this week are the priority."

"Are there many of them there?" she asked, probing for any information she could get to hand back to Emily.

"Yes, there is a big Irish community living in France. Many have fled their homes in Paris and are now displaced and we are trying to get them back home."

"Sounds horrific. It must be terrible being trapped somewhere and unable to get away," said Karina, thinking of Hugo.

"The main problem is many of the Irish citizens in France, and elsewhere, still have British passports ... they just never bothered to apply for Irish ones after independence which means they are not neutrals officially and are being treated as British citizens, resulting in them being arrested and detained by the Nazis."

"How awful!"

"We are trying to issue emergency one-year passports to them but the whole process is complicated because France is in such upheaval. It is taking a lot of diplomacy."

"Naturally!"

"Even our legation in Paris has closed down and they are operating from some hotel in the Pyrenees!" said Gabriel.

"That must be difficult." She was taking a mental note of everything that he said. Although there was nothing he was saying that was in anyway confidential or ground-breaking, it was all intelligence that she could report back on in order for British intelligence to build a clearer picture of what was happening on the ground.

"I don't know why they never got themselves an Irish passport and stuck with a British one after we got independence!" said Gabriel.

"Habit, I imagine. I fully understand it because I still have an Irish passport," said Karina.

"You have an Irish passport?" Gabriel was amazed.

"Yes, well, I was born here and lived here a child. Once Ireland gained its independence, and after my passport ran out, I applied for an Irish passport even though we lived in London. I don't know why, as I carried great animosity towards Ireland for years but I felt it gave me a tie to the land that I came from, even if that country didn't want me anymore ... and I felt it gave me a connection to my father after he passed away. He loved Ireland and never wanted to leave it and saw us as Irish. He would want me to have an Irish passport."

"Interesting," Gabriel said, studying her.

"In a way, I think it was defiance on my part after my family home was burned down and we were driven out of the country after independence. I remember that night one of the rebels – the most violent one – shouting after us '*And don't come back!*' After my father died the following week – they said it was a heart attack, which was in a way true as his poor heart was broken – I felt the rebels had taken everything from me. My home, my security, my father, my childhood and they had told me I was not welcome in Ireland and not to come back. But who were they to order me not to come back here and deny me my Irish heritage? I am as much Irish as they are, just a different class and creed … so I suppose I defied them, in the only small insignificant way I could think of – by holding onto my Irishness and by having my Irish passport."

"It must have been awful for you, seeing your home burn down at such a tender age," Gabriel said, feeling overwhelmed with guilt that his own father had given the order.

"It was horrific … I'm not sure if I have ever had a happy day since – not really."

"That's very sad to hear you say."

"Oh, I have had my share of exciting days and fun days and amazing days and dramatic days – but happy days? I'm not so sure."

"What was life like for you after your father died, in London?"

"Very difficult. It was just my mother Penny and me. As she was American we didn't have any close relatives on her side in London to support us. So we relied on my father's very glamorous and wealthy relatives. And they were very kind to us but you never stop feeling like a gatecrasher at a ball. I might have looked and acted the part, but everyone knew Mother had to take in typing for us to live. And I followed suit into the typing pool when I came of age. I guess they expected me to match up with a wealthy aristo and then all would be right in their world again. They would not have to feel slightly embarrassed by the downturn of my fortune anymore. The equilibrium would have been restored."

"So why didn't you? Why are you not married to some wealthy aristocrat?"

"I guess I never found one interesting or fanciable or amazing enough to marry! And maybe, if I did, he didn't like me much anyway!"

He laughed out loud. "I sincerely doubt that," he said as he reached over and took her hand.

After dinner they retired to the drawing room and settled down on the couch in front of a glowing fire.

She lay out on the couch, resting her head on his lap, and gazed at the dancing flames.

"I will never forget the day when I was told that my father had been killed," he said quietly. "I could not understand it. My mother told me. She brought me and my brother Tim into the parlour at Roxford and told us. She never cried, you know. Mother never cried when my father was killed, not once. Which was unusual as she loved him very much."

"People show grief in different ways," said Karina. "How was your father killed?"

"During the Civil War. He was shot. I've never seen her cry – over anything. At the funeral she had the whole country's eyes on her and she didn't falter once. She almost took joy in being this beacon of dignity and reserve on the day. I remember feeling very resentful that I had to share my father with so many strangers that day. There were hundreds of people who we had never seen or heard of before, crying in public – lamenting the passing of the great Rory Ford. My mother then threw herself into keeping his memory alive, to keep the flame burning for him and to pass that torch on to me and my brother, the next generation."

He gently stirred the cognac in his balloon glass.

She watched the flames in the hearth reflect in the deep rich colour of the cognac.

"I guess we have that in common," she said. "We both lost our fathers at a very young age, before their time."

"Yes, two children of tragedy," he said and smiled down at her before his face went serious and he bent down to kiss her.

227

CHAPTER 37

Gabriel was a very still sleeper. Karina realised he hardly ever moved when he was asleep. He made a good bed companion in that way. She could sleep away and hardly know he was there. But she didn't let herself go to sleep that night. Not yet, as she had things to do. She looked at her watch on the bedside table and saw it was four in the morning. She checked to make sure he was indeed asleep and then gently removed his arm which was lying across her and slipped out from under the covers. She picked up her watch and put it on, then grabbed his dressing gown from an armchair and slid into it as she crept out of the room.

As she sneaked down the corridor and down the stairs, she was glad he had no live-in maids to detect or hear her. When she got to the bottom of the stairs she crossed over to the door leading into the study, the door he had closed over earlier that night.

Opening it, she crept in, turning on the light and silently closing the door behind her again. She stood there for a few seconds and then walked quickly to the desk.

"Not one of the world's tidiest people," she whispered as she began to sift through the paperwork scattered there. From what she could see there were a lot of mundane letters from different diplomats. To her surprise a lot of the correspondence related to matters as banal as agricultural products and trying to secure safe passage of Irish produce to markets abroad. She sat down on the chair and began to read a letter from an Irish diplomat in Berlin. In the letter the diplomat wrote that the people of Berlin were in wonderful spirits after the victories in Europe. As she sifted through more correspondence she read that the Germans were confident of an all-out victory and were content to put up with the rationing as most people felt it would be short-lived. Karina felt these observations from the neutral Irish diplomats might be invaluable for the British Secret Service to check the morale of the enemy. As she continued to root through the paperwork though, she felt there was nothing of any real significance there for her to report.

As she looked at her watch, she realised she had been there half an hour and decided it was too risky to remain any longer. She tidied things back as much as she could to how they were and then sneaked out of the room and back up to Gabriel's bedroom where she found him lying in the same position, unmoved.

Next morning Karina sat at the dining-room table as Gabriel put a boiled egg in front of her.

"So you weren't joking when you said you could just about boil an egg? I was looking forward to some Irish bacon and sausages." She reached for some toast and began to butter it.

"I'm afraid I wasn't lying about my cooking skills. Besides, even if I could cook I used up all the rations on last night's dinner."

"In that case, you need to do a few more favours for those farmers you know," she said.

He grabbed some toast and quickly ate it with some tea as she kept the conversation light. She saw he had a briefcase on the floor beside him.

"I have an appointment in an hour so I'll have to dash, I'm afraid," he said, looking at his watch.

"You are working today?" It was Saturday so she had expected he might be off work.

"I'm afraid so – duty calls," he said.

As he chattered about nothing in particular, she kept one eye on the briefcase. She had noticed it in his bedroom the previous night. She imagined that was where he kept the important correspondence and not just the ones about dairy produce and the morale of the Berlin population that he kept lying around the table in his study.

After he finished his breakfast, he stood up and put his briefcase on the table.

"I can give you a lift back to your place on my way, if it suits?" he said as he took a key from his pocket, opened his briefcase and began to look for a document inside.

"That would be convenient –"

Suddenly there was a scream and a loud bang.

"What on earth?" said Gabriel.

He rushed from the dining room to the window at the front of the drawing room.

Karina followed him quickly. On the road outside, a milk lorry had hit a motorcar. It looked like a nasty collision and there was a woman getting out of the motorcar with blood coming from her forehead.

Gabriel ran from the room, out the front door and down the steps to the road.

Karina watched as he assisted the injured woman to the side of the road and began to tend to her injury.

Karina turned and raced into the dining room to Gabriel's briefcase which was open on the table. She began to riffle through the paperwork inside. She picked out a letter from the head of the Irish Army ...

... **having learned of the existence of Operation Green, the German plan to invade Ireland, I can report that the Irish armed forces are wholly undermanned and ill-equipped to fight such an invasion. I would imagine, left unaided, Irish forces would be defeated in a matter of days by an invading German force. I urge cooperation with the British at every level to ensure they come to our aid and assistance in the event of a German Invasion ...**

Karina picked out another letter, this one from the Department of Foreign Affairs.

Dear Gabriel,

Further to your appointment as an attaché to the Irish legation in Berlin, plans are afoot for you to the travel to the German capital within the next month to execute a diplomatic mission to try and avert a German invasion of Ireland and establish a good relationship with the Nazi hierarchy for when the war ends. The purpose of your diplomatic mission is to try to impress on the German government the sovereignty of Ireland as an independent country that will not tolerate interference from Germany in the post-war period. Failing this, for you to establish exactly what relationship Germany would expect to have with Ireland after a German victory, paying particular attention to trade, defence, interference in the legal and government process, the Jewish population ...

"The milk cart came from nowhere! It just came straight at me and crashed into me!" said a woman's voice in the hallway.

Karina quickly replaced the papers she was reading and dashed into the hall in time to see Gabriel escort a middle-aged woman, who was holding a hand to her bleeding forehead, into the drawing room.

"Oh, you poor thing!" said Karina, rushing to her and helping her to the couch.

"Crashed right into me, I tell you. The man is an imbecile!" cried the woman.

"There's a lot of spilled milk and broken glass out there!" said Gabriel, giving Karina a worried look. "She hit her head on the steering wheel when she hit the milk cart."

"*He* hit *me!*" the woman corrected.

"I don't think it needs stitches," said Karina, inspecting the gash.

"How would you know?" said the woman, looking at Karina's full-length lamé dress.

"I did a nursing course once."

"Did you indeed!" scoffed the woman.

"I think it might be safest to drop you at the hospital, just to make sure," said Gabriel.

"Won't you be late for your appointment?" Karina asked him.

"Yes, I will," he sighed.

"Order us a taxi and I'll take her – and you go to your appointment," said Karina, standing up.

"Dressed like that?" he said.

"You would be surprised what I have done in the past, dressed like this!" she said and winked at him, causing him to smile.

"I wouldn't be!" said the woman under her breath.

"Thank you!" Gabriel mouthed at Karina as he went to the dining room to get his briefcase.

Later that day Emily sat in Karina's sitting room in her flat with a notebook and pen as she furiously wrote down everything that Karina had discovered.

"Well done, Harper!" said Emily once Karina had finally finished. "Excellent stuff! Rather than the Irish being particularly pro-German as had been suspected, what you read would indicate they are just covering their arses in case there is a German victory."

"And using the British as a back-up if they are attacked. To use an expression – they are running with the hare and hunting with the hounds," said Karina.

"When are you seeing Gabriel again?"

"Well, I suspect it won't be long until he makes contact," said Karina.

"He's been very reckless having you over to his home – it just adds more ammunition if we need to blackmail him. As my dear stepfather used to say – a man can bring his work home but never a mistress! Or in other words – don't shit on your own doorstep!"

"Well, Gabriel seems almost naïve. I am certain he has never cheated before," said Karina.

"Oh, my dear Karina – do not kid yourself! That is what they all say – take it from one who knows!" She stood up.

"He was speaking about his family last night. About his father being killed in the Civil War," said Karina. "He seems very affected by it still. Who else is in the family? He was speaking about his mother and a brother."

"Well, they are actually quite a small family considering their name is so well known. There's only Gabriel and his brother Tim, a rip-roaring alcoholic by all accounts – his political career is all but over, we understand – Tim's wife Tess, a floozy apparently – and the mother Cynthia, who the Irish public revere as some kind of hallowed ground because she waved a tricolour during the 1916 Rising."

"And what of the father? What exactly happened to him?" Karina braced herself for the information.

"Rory Ford was shot dead twenty years ago – not by one of ours but by one of their own during their Civil War. Ambushed while he led a brigade through the back of beyond somewhere. He was one of the masterminds of the War of Independence."

Karina was lost in thought. "Both of us lost so much during the Civil War."

"Stay focused, Harper! We are here to win this war, not lick wounds from one twenty years ago! Anyway, must dash – I've got a date with an Ecuadorian sea captain. His vessel was torpedoed off the coast of Cork and he had to swim to shore. He's stuck here until he can get a lift on a passing ship back to Quito! And there's not too many of those passing by, let me tell you!"

"That all sounds rather exotic," commented Karina.

"He is! Excellent work, Harper! You will have Ford singing like a canary soon!"

"Does it never worry you that we are playing with a man's life here?"

"There are millions of lives at risk from the Nazi tyranny ... we are doing our bit to stop it all. I do not suffer one jot from worry!"

CHAPTER 38

"Two of our senior boys ran off from school to join the British army this week – can you believe it?" said Siobhán as they sat in Stephen's Green. "They are barely turned eighteen and just abandoned their studies to go and fight Hitler ... though I'm not sure what good they'll be – both of them were hopeless at Geography. They wouldn't be able to find their way from one end of a battlefield to another."

"I'm sure they'll get the proper training," said Gabriel.

"I imagine training would just be wasted on both of them ... they had the attention span of goldfish so all the training in the world wouldn't do much good ..."

They had met in the park for tea and a bun and, after they had found a free bench, Siobhán had taken two cups and a flask from a small basket. After pouring two cups of tea, she'd produced two iced buns, each with a red cherry on top. She'd handed him one bun in a napkin and had bitten into the other.

She seemed so unsophisticated compared to Karina, Gabriel thought. She seemed so parochial.

As, between bites of bun, Siobhán spoke on and on about the two boys who had run off to join the army, Gabriel tried to concentrate but was unable. All he could do was think about Karina the previous night and the euphoria he felt when he was with her compared to ... this ... whatever he felt when he was with Siobhán.

"Daddy is furious, of course. He says, what is the point in

teaching them all about the horrors the British inflicted on us for centuries when the next generation runs off to join their army at the first opportunity? There are so many Irishmen in the British army at this stage, you wonder was there any point in Ireland staying out of the war at all!"

"They obviously are hearing the call to fight fascism," said Gabriel.

"More likely they are desperate to escape the humdrum of their boring lives and can't resist the lure of a steady wage and seeing a bit of the world!" said Siobhán, finishing off her bun and draining her cup. "Fighting Hitler is the least of it for them!"

"That's very cynical, Siobhán. I think you are spending too much time with my mother."

"Is everything alright, Gabriel? You seem distracted – even more than usual!"

He stared at her and then put his cup and uneaten bun down on the bench. He felt his eyes fill with tears as he reached for her hands.

"What's this about?" she asked, alarmed.

"Siobhán ... I can't go through with it ... I'm so very sorry," he said as he squeezed her hands.

"Go through with what, Gabriel?"

"The wedding."

"What are you saying, Gabriel?" she asked as tears sprang to her eyes. "Are ... you ... *finishing* with me?"

He nodded sadly. "It just doesn't feel right for me anymore."

"Not right? But ... how can I make it right?"

"You can't. The feelings aren't there ... they never really were, but I only realised it recently, I suppose."

"Is it something I did? Is it because I talk too much? Or my hairstyle? Or the way I dress? I can change all that, Gabriel – I can change it all," she said, becoming desperate.

"But you shouldn't have to change, because you are perfect. You just aren't my perfect fit and I don't want to waste any more of your time, stopping you from finding your perfect fit."

"But you are my perfect fit, Gabriel!"

"I'm really not. That's the problem. You only think you know me but you don't know the real me … if you knew the real me you'd think I was anything but your perfect fit … you would be horrified … the thoughts I have …"

She pulled her hands away from his. "What thoughts?" she demanded.

"When you're talking, Siobhán – I'm not even listening to you! I'm silently begging you to be quiet," he said, putting his head in his hands in shame.

"You're very cruel!" Tears now began to stream down her face. "Where's *my* Gabriel? He would never say something like that!"

"This is the real me, Siobhán. The other person was just somebody you wanted me to be. I'm just flawed like everyone else. If you knew what I had done!"

"Stop it! I've heard enough! I don't want to hear the things you've done! Leave me with some good memory of you – no matter how false it is. I just don't understand and I'm too scared to ask the questions I need to ask because I don't want to hear the answers." She took out a handkerchief and wiped away her tears.

"I hate what I'm having to do here, but I've no choice," he said. "I've seen Tess and Tim and the horror of their marriage and how it is destroying them both … I don't want that to be us in a couple of years. You'll find somebody else who can love you the way you deserve."

"But where will I find him? It took me long enough to find you! And what will everyone say? What will Daddy say? And Cynthia? And all the children at school when they hear Miss has been dumped!" She looked horrified at the prospect of it all.

"You can say you finished with me. We can say you didn't want to go through with it – that way you can save face."

"Oh no! You don't get off that easy, Gabriel! You'd like that, wouldn't you? That way nobody would think badly of you and you would be able to keep your sainted reputation. But no! We'll say it as it is, and everyone can see you for the bastard that you are!"

He was taken aback, shocked as he would never have thought Siobhán capable of swearing like that before.

"As you wish," he agreed.

"Nothing about this is … *as I wish!* Get ready for the backlash,

Gabriel. You've only ever known people say good things about you and liking you – I doubt you are strong enough to cope with being disliked." She threw the tea from her cup on the ground and grabbed his cup and did likewise with it before putting them and the flask back into the basket. She stood up and put on her scarf. "I don't know what is going on with you but one day somebody will do to you what you have done to me and I'll applaud when that day comes!"

"Siobhán!" He was horrified by her bitterness. He had only ever seen a gentle-natured Siobhán before. He had expected floods of tears but not anger.

"I was going to say good luck but instead will say good riddance!" Siobhán said and went to walk off. Then she halted, seeing the iced bun with the cherry on top that she had given him sitting on a napkin on the bench beside him. She reached down, swiped it from the bench and dropped it into her basket before she marched off down the path with her head in the air.

When Gabriel got back to his house in Monkstown that night he went straight to the drinks cabinet and poured himself a large gin and tonic. The overwhelming emotion he felt was relief. He felt as if he had escaped a life sentence. Just at the last minute he had found the strength to untangle himself from what would have been the worst mistake of his life. And a mistake, like Tim and Tess's, that would have been inescapable. As Siobhán had predicted, the fallout would be immense, but he didn't care. He just felt relieved he was free. And he had Karina to thank for it. If he hadn't met her, he never would have had his eyes opened to the fact he was sleepwalking through life nor had the courage to end his engagement with the wrong woman.

There was suddenly a knock on the front door. He put down his drink and went to answer it. It was a courier.

"Yes?"

"A message for Mr Gabriel Ford," said the courier.

"That is me ... thank you," said Gabriel, taking the envelope and closing the door.

He walked across the hall back into the drawing room where he opened the envelope and unfolded the sheet of notepaper inside.

Invoice to Mr Gabriel Ford

One ivory embroidered wedding dress with a twelve-foot train

Ten Pounds

To be reimbursed to Miss Siobhán Vestry immediately

CHAPTER 39

Karina was in her office at the legation typing, when the telephone on her desk rang.

"Harper speaking," she said as she continued to type.

"Good afternoon, Harper," said Gabriel.

Karina stopped typing and sat back in her chair. "Well, hello."

"Busy?"

"Always!" she laughed.

"I was just ringing to ask if you wanted to go out to dinner tonight?"

"Yes, I think I would. What time should I call round?"

"No – I'm asking do you want to go *out* to dinner?" he said.

"Oh!" She started tapping her pencil on the desk while her mind raced. "In public?"

"Yes – in the zoo!" he said, his self-assured sarcasm surprising her.

"It's a bit risky, isn't it?"

"Why? Are you frightened a German bomb might drop on the restaurant?"

She was again surprised by his tone. "I just don't know if that's the wisest thing for us to do, Gabriel. What if someone sees us who knows your fiancée?"

"Well, we will hardly be fornicating in the restaurant. Last time I checked a woman and a man are allowed to have dinner together. We are a free country still, just about."

As she sat there, twirling her hair, she was becoming a little intrigued by this other side of Gabriel.

"Alright then? When and where?" she asked.

"Restaurant Jammet – tonight – nine o'clock."

She didn't know why she was surprised that he was suggesting the internationally famous French restaurant. Maybe she was surprised he was taking her to such a high-profile place where he would undoubtedly know many of the people there. Or perhaps she just didn't see Gabriel choosing a place like Restaurant Jammet. She wasn't sure why that was as she had met him in Club 400 and he had been staying at Claridge's in London. But she had considered he'd been at those venues more by accident than design.

"If you can get a booking," she said.

"It's already booked," he informed her.

"I see … that was rather presumptuous. What if I had said no?"

"If that was the case, then restaurant bookings can be easily cancelled. I'll see you tonight at nine." He hung up the phone.

She replaced the receiver and sat deep in thought.

Her office door swung open and Emily walked in.

"That was Ford – he's asked to meet me for dinner in Restaurant Jammet tonight," Karina informed her.

"He's meeting you in public?" Emily looked surprised and unhappy. "But what about his fiancée?"

"That's what I said but he didn't seem to care."

"*Hmm* …" Emily frowned.

"Emily, I really need to find out about my cousin, Lord Ashton. I'm beside myself with worry."

"We have been trying to trace him, Karina, but he wasn't on any of the ships or boats that arrived back to Britain from Dunkirk. I'm sorry, Karina, we'll keep looking … but if he hasn't been accounted for back in Britain …"

Karina fought back the flood of tears that were threatening as she thought about her wonderful, loyal cousin and the horrible fate that might have befallen him in Dunkirk.

CHAPTER 40

Marc Pietch walked up the steps from the beach to the back garden at Roxford. He had become such a regular visitor there that he never used the front door anymore. He just walked down the beach from his own rented cottage and came up the steps from there.

As he walked through the back garden, the French windows were open and he could hear Cynthia speaking loudly.

He paused at the windows, listening.

"Ich komme aus Irland … das Wetter ist heute sonnig …" said Cynthia's projected voice.

He walked through the door and saw her sitting on her usual armchair, reading from a book.

"Gern geschehen in meinem Land –"

Pietch coughed loudly.

"Oh, Marc! I didn't hear you come in," she said and gave an embarrassed laugh as she put the book face down quickly on the little table beside her.

"Good afternoon, Cynthia," said Pietch as he strolled over, picked up the book and studied it. *German for Beginners*.

"What is this, Cynthia? Learning German?" he asked, with a concerned look on his face.

"Well … yes, I'm afraid so …"

She stood up, took the book from him and put it in a drawer.

"But why?" he asked. "I expect you are not planning a holiday to the Black Forrest anytime soon?"

"Well, no. I'm certainly not planning any visit to Germany, but that doesn't mean they might not be planning a visit to here!"

"But whatever do you mean?" he asked.

Cynthia would never give away any information she received from Gabriel, but she felt she could speak openly about a suspected invasion when the dogs in the street were talking about it.

"Well, we must face facts, Marc. With France gone now, how long can Britain hold out? It can only be a matter of time and, once Britain capitulates, then Ireland will not be long behind. I know this is very upsetting for you to hear as a Pole with what is happening in your country but it's now a whole new Europe and there's no going back to the way things were in my opinion."

"How very sad to hear you say this." Pietch shook his head morosely.

"It is what it is, Marc. There is no point in us ignoring the obvious ... or what's more being unprepared for the obvious, hence my German lessons."

"So sad!" Pietch continued to shake his head.

"Poland yesterday – France today – Britain and Ireland tomorrow! What's really sad is all those thousands of young Irishmen who have rushed off to join the British army to fight a losing war! Fools! They are on the wrong side and what will become of them when Britain is defeated? I can't imagine Germany treating them well just because they come from neutral Ireland when they took up arms against them – and they won't be welcomed back here, having joined up with the old enemy, Britain. It's hard to have sympathy for people who are quite so stupid!"

"All very sad," repeated Pietch.

"Anyway, enough of this! If we hurry we can be at Bray Head and get the best of the afternoon's daylight for the headland you want me to sketch for the next postcard range!"

And she rushed off to fetch her paints and pencils.

CHAPTER 41

As Karina walked down the street towards Restaurant Jammet, her head was filled with thoughts of Julian and horror that he might have been captured by the Germans. She couldn't imagine him as a prisoner of war – he was such a free spirit – but perhaps worse had befallen him. She pushed any negativity to the back of her mind. Julian had to have been rescued, he just had to. He had probably arrived back in England and gone to a party in Scotland or someplace like that and had just forgotten to tell everybody where he was.

"Good evening, miss," said the doorman as he opened the door of the restaurant for her.

"Good evening," she said as she swept in.

As she stood at the reception, she looked down the long restaurant where every perfectly set round able was filled with chattering people being waited on by a small army of impeccably dressed waiters.

"I'm meeting Mr Gabriel Ford," she informed the maître d'.

"Mr Ford asked me to look out for you, Miss Harper. If you would like to follow me to your table?"

Like so many things since she had arrived in Dublin, this place was bringing back memories. It had been her father's favourite restaurant and on special occasions she had been allowed to come there with her parents. She remembered how her father would arrive in and would know nearly everyone who was dining there. He would spend ages walking around chatting to all the people he knew, much to her mother's chagrin. But Karina never minded. She would take delight in seeing how popular her father was, how he could walk into a place and own it. She would be filled with pride as she observed him.

Gabriel waited nervously at the table. For some strange reason he was petrified Karina wouldn't show up. He wouldn't know what to do if she didn't. It was with a sense of relief he saw her being shown by the maître d' towards his table. The second thought he had was how stunning she looked in a long silver gown, topped off with a fur stole around her neck. As she reached the table he stood up.

"Hello, Gabriel," she said as the maître d' pulled out her chair for her.

She draped her stole over the back of the chair and sat down. Gabriel retook his chair.

"You look lovely," he complimented her.

"Thank you," she said as she picked up the menu.

He did likewise and looked at her nervously over the top of it as he tried to concentrate on what was on offer.

Karina sat with her two hands under her chin, listening to Gabriel as he recounted a story from when he was posted to Washington.

"So, I said to the man – in a rather serious tone – 'Sir, I may not be a Brazilian but that does not mean that I do not have a brain. You, on the other hand, are living proof that being born a Brazilian does not naturally entitle you to a brain!'"

Karina fell back in her chair laughing and clapped her hands together.

"Oh marvellous! What a comeback, Gabriel! What did he say to that?"

"Nothing! Well, what could he say? There was no retort to cap that!" he said, laughing.

"Oh, I am so envious of you. It must have been wonderful getting to travel to Washington and all those other wonderful places as part of the diplomatic corps." She sighed with envy.

"Well, I don't get to travel that much. I am mostly stuck in an office in Dublin looking out at the rain and the grey skies. What about you? Did you not want to be posted abroad? Surely there must have been an abundance of opportunities working at the British Foreign Office?"

"Not a for a lowly typist! The only travel I ever got to do was to go down to the stock room to get a new ribbon for my typewriter!" she said with a grimace.

He laughed. "Well, you got to go to Great Hankerton Hall."

"Ah yes – Great Hankerton Hall!"

"And to come to Dublin."

"True," she conceded.

"Which I am very glad you did." He reached over and stroked her hand.

She looked at his hand. "You are taking a very big risk, Gabriel. What if someone should see?" She pulled her hand back.

"I really don't care if anyone sees us, Karina."

"Well, perhaps you should!"

"You see, I've been thinking about you ever since the other night."

"I've been thinking about you as well," she said. "But affairs are not supposed to be played out in public. Discretion is supposed to be the order of the day."

"Karina ... I want to be honest with you ..."

She laughed. "Ah, honesty is certainly not the order of the day when it comes to affairs! By the very nature of what they are, affairs are built on dishonesty."

"Karina, will you be serious for once? Don't you see? I think I've fallen in love with you."

She couldn't think of how to respond.

"I've never felt this way about anybody," he said.

"Not even your fiancée?"

He shook his head.

"I see ... I suppose I'm very flattered," she said, forcing a smile.

She studied him for any sign of manipulation or falseness but couldn't find any. He looked earnest and sincere.

"Just flattered?" he asked.

"Well, this has all come as a bit of a surprise to me, Gabriel. I don't know quite what you want me to say, apart from saying that you should try to keep more control of how you feel as you are engaged to another."

"I've ended my engagement to Siobhán. I had to."

"*Oh no!*" Karina sighed loudly, resting her forehead in her hand.

"This isn't quite the reaction I was expecting from you, Karina."

She looked up abruptly at him. "But what other reaction could you possibly have expected?"

"Some – reciprocation perhaps?"

"I think it's time you got a grip on reality! We hardly know each other! Gabriel, you seem like a very nice man – don't destroy your life over a silly dream that does not even exist."

"I don't understand you!" He was becoming angry. "You blow hot and cold and I never know where I am with you. The first night we met in London you were all over me and then disappeared the next day without so much as a by-your-leave! Next, when we meet at Great Hankerton Hall you treat me as if I'm something unpleasant you stepped into and ignore me! Then you arrive in Dublin and send me a note to meet you and go to bed with me again! And I thought – I just maybe very stupidly thought – that we might have something real going on here! But now I see I mean absolutely nothing to you! That I am just filling in time for you when you have nothing better – or nobody better – to do!"

"This has all gone too far. I never meant for you to ruin your life and finish your engagement –"

"You know nothing of my engagement or my fiancée – ex-fiancée. Staying with her would have ruined my life, not leaving her!"

As Karina looked at him, she didn't know whether she wanted to slap him or hug him. Could anybody be this sincere and this stupid all at the same time? She felt tremendous guilt that his emotions were running wild while all she was doing was using him. And, as she looked at him, she felt a need to protect him – if only from himself.

"If you have any sense, just walk away from me now and have nothing more to do with me," she whispered.

"What?"

"Go back to your fiancée and forget about London, forget we

ever met and refuse to have anything more to do with me. Even if I send you a note in the future or try to contact you, have nothing more to do with me! For your own good!"

"What is wrong with you?" he asked, completely confused. "Why are you always trying to push me away?"

"For your own good! You don't understand –"

"But I want to understand!"

Suddenly he reached over and grabbed her hand and they both looked at his hand holding hers tightly.

She pulled free of him and stood up. "I'm leaving, Gabriel."

"Gabriel! What are you doing here?" said a man's voice beside them.

Karina turned around and, as she looked at the man standing beside her, it was as if someone had punched her in the stomach. Looking into his handsome face, she was suddenly overcome with nausea and felt she was going to be sick as horrific memories from her childhood came flooding back. Memories of the night the men broke into Inishwood to set it on fire. Memories of her father being struck viciously and falling to the floor. Memories of herself as a young girl running at the man who had hit her father, pulling his hood off and staring into his face. Now, all these years later, in this restaurant, that man was standing beside her.

Karina felt the room go black as she collapsed to the floor.

"Karina! Karina!"

A large crowd of diners and the staff of the restaurant had gathered around in a circle.

She opened her eyes and groaned.

Gabriel was kneeling beside her.

The maître d' poured a glass of water which Gabriel took and, lifting her head gently, put to her lips.

As she came round, Karina tried to make sense of what had happened.

Gabriel turned to the crowd. "Is there a doctor here?"

But he was answered with shaking heads.

Karina tried to remember what had happened. She looked at

Gabriel's kind face, full of concern, and she gripped his hand for support.

Then she felt overwhelmed with embarrassment as she realised that half the restaurant was gathered around her.

And then suddenly she saw him again, behind Gabriel. The man who had caused her to faint. She recoiled from him, the very sight of him filling her with terror and horror.

"Karina?" said Gabriel, full of concern.

"*I need to go home – now!*" she hissed at him.

"Do you need a doctor?"

"No. Just take me home!" she insisted.

Gabriel gently helped her to her feet and sat her back on her chair, as the maître d' ushered the other customers back to their tables.

Gabriel turned and to Karina's horror began to talk to the man who had caused her to faint, a whispered private conversation which indicated they knew each other very well.

But, as Karina studied the man, realisation dawned that it could not be the man who had hit her father. This man was barely thirty years old. The man who had hit her father nearly twenty years ago would now be almost twice his age.

Confused, dazed and again feeling she was about to be sick, she grabbed her stole, stood up and hurried towards the foyer.

"*Karina!*" cried Gabriel and strode after her.

She rushed through the front door. She looked up and down for a taxi but there was none.

"Karina! What on earth has got into you? You look like you've seen a ghost!"

"I just need to get home. Where are all the bloody taxis in this bloody city!"

"Karina, I'm parked around the corner. Let me drive you home!"

"*No!*"

"*Yes!*" he insisted, grabbing her arm and leading her down the street.

They sat in silence as Gabriel drove her back to Merrion Square.

"Would you care to tell me what that was all about?" he asked eventually.

"I just must have eaten something that didn't agree with me," she said.

"Really?" he asked incredulously.

They sat in silence again for a while.

"That man who came to the table – who is he?" she asked.

"Man?"

"The man you were speaking to just before we left."

"Oh, you mean Tim! My brother."

She felt as if she had been hit by lightning as she looked at him, shocked.

"Your *brother*?"

"Yes. What's the matter?"

"Nothing."

"Well, it must be something or you wouldn't have asked!"

As a hundred thoughts raced through her head, she realised she needed to throw him off the scent while she tried to figure out what was going on.

"Nothing – he's just very handsome," she said quickly.

Gabriel glanced at her curiously "I guess he is … good looks run in the family."

He pulled up outside Karina's building.

"Shall I come in with you?" he asked.

"No! I need to go straight to bed." She quickly opened the door and got out.

"Karina –" he began but she slammed the door shut.

He watched, mystified, as she raced up the steps to her building and, rushing inside, closed the front door after her.

Upstairs in her flat, Karina raced to the whiskey bottle and poured herself a large drink. She knocked it back in one. She then poured herself another and took it to the couch with her. She sat down while she lit a cigarette with trembling fingers.

That was a face that she had never thought she would see again. But suddenly there it was – the face of the man who had murdered her father. But, as she had realised earlier, this man was far too young to be that man. But he was the very image of him. He must be a relative. A very close relative.

Memories of that awful night of the burning of Inishwood kept flooding through her mind. That face under the hood that had haunted her dreams ever since. And now, through a bizarre twist of fate, she had been led to that man again.

CHAPTER 42

The next day Emily grilled her in her office at the legation.

"He says he has broken off his engagement and that he has strong feelings for me," said Karina.

Emily sat opposite her, speechless, which was a first for her.

"Broken off his engagement!" she repeated.

"Yes."

"Do you believe him?" asked Emily.

"I can't see any reason not to believe him. He says he has fallen in love with me."

"What a fool!" exclaimed Emily. "If he is the best in the Irish diplomatic corps then God help them!"

"I thought you would be pleased. It gives me a further chance to spy on him with the fiancée out of the way."

"But the whole point of this exercise was that it was to be secret and that people wouldn't know about you and him, so that he would have so much to lose if it did ever get out. So we would always have the upper hand. But now – if he is going public with the relationship and parading you around restaurants like a prize cow, it puts him in the driving seat."

"But if he trusts me to this extent then I will have access to classified information so much more," said Karina.

"I will need to discuss the situation with Kendrick as soon as possible. It was never meant to go this far, Harper! You are in danger of blowing the whole fucking cover!"

Karina steadied herself. "His brother happened to be there and stopped by to say hello."

"Oh great! Tim?"

"Yes, he didn't stay long. He's an TD, isn't he?"

"For now at least until he is booted out!" said Emily.

"Gabriel was talking about his father again. His death affected him terribly," said Karina.

Emily raised her eyes to heaven. "Are you offering him therapy into the bargain?"

"No, I'm just trying to understand him better so I can ingratiate myself more with him. If I can find out more about his family, then I have better chance of manipulating him. His said his father was adored by the Irish public – had a huge funeral when he died?"

"Despite the awe Rory Ford is held in throughout this country, he was a thug and a terrorist in mine and many others' opinion!"

"I see," said Karina. "Tell me, is there a photo of his father somewhere?"

"Why would you want to see that?"

"I'm just curious," she said.

"You are here to spy, Harper, not to be curious! I'm sure there are plenty of photos of him about but I don't make a habit of carrying photos of Irish terrorists in my handbag, let me tell you! I'm sure there's a portrait of him hanging in the National Gallery. That's where they hang all their dead war heroes."

On her lunchtime, Karina walked the short distance to the National Gallery. She enquired from the curator and, true for Emily, there was a portrait of Rory Ford there. The curator directed her to where it was.

As Karina walked through the hushed floors and looked at the fabulous paintings adorning the walls, she was overcome with a feeling of apprehension. She did not want Rory Ford to be the man who had caused the death of her father. She hoped when she saw the portrait that Rory Ford would look nothing like the man who had led that gang of men into her home and burned it down all those years ago. She prayed it was just a coincidence that Tim Ford resembled the man. Or that they were just distant relatives. As she neared the room where the painting was, her heart started pounding.

She entered the room and stared up at the huge painting of Rory Ford painted in resplendent colours.

She began to shake uncontrollably. Rory Ford was indeed the man who had torched Inishwood and killed her father. She began to cry as she saw the face that had haunted her for twenty years stare coldly down at her from the portrait.

CHAPTER 43

"You're very quiet this evening, Gabriel," commented Cynthia over dinner at Roxford. Gabriel and Tess were also present.

"Just a lot on at work," said Gabriel.

He was lost in thought. He had tried to make contact with Karina a few times during the week but there had been no reply. He had telephoned her at the legation but the receptionist always said she was away from her office. He had called to her flat but there had been no reply when he knocked on the door. She was obviously avoiding him and he wondered had he scared her off when he told her he had broken off his engagement. It seemed she had never viewed him as a serious relationship and he was just somebody to occupy her time while he was stationed in Dublin.

"Say – that was a bit of commotion at Restaurant Jammet last week! Who was that woman you were with who fell to the floor?" asked Tim.

"What's all this?" demanded Cynthia.

Gabriel frowned at Tim's indiscretion. Having said that, as Tim was convinced Gabriel wanted to steal his political career, it was obvious this line of conversation was purposeful.

"Nothing – nothing at all," said Gabriel.

"Well, it must be *something* – a woman falling to the floor can hardly be dismissed as nothing!" said Cynthia.

"I was just having dinner with a person from the British legation," began Gabriel.

"A person? That's an unflattering description of her. She was a very beautiful young woman, let me tell you, in actual fact!" said Tim.

Cynthia was staring at Gabriel, her eyes alert.

"Then – in the middle of the restaurant – she faints! – collapses to the ground in front of Gabriel!" announced Tim gleefully.

"Women are always falling at your feet, Gabriel," Tess said sarcastically.

"Well, it makes a change from *you* falling to the ground, Tim!" said Cynthia scathingly, giving him a warning look before she turned her attention back to Gabriel.

"And what does Siobhán make of your new friendship with this raving beauty from the British legation?" asked Tess.

"It's really none of Siobhán's concern anymore because I have – I have – I have broken off our engagement," Gabriel blurted out.

"I don't fucking believe it!" said Tim loudly and he began laughing loudly.

"You finished with Miss Goody Two Shoes!" Tess exclaimed, her eyes wide with delight and shock all at the same time.

"I ended it last week," said Gabriel before mustering the courage to look at his mother.

She looked like a volcano about to erupt.

"I do hope this is some sort of unsavoury and unkind joke on your part, Gabriel?" she said.

"It's the truth," Gabriel whispered, looking down at the table, ashamed.

"Well, how did Siobhán take it?" demanded Tess.

"How do you think she took it?" snapped Gabriel.

"That'll give her father something to write poetry about!" laughed Tim.

"I mean, I never had anything in common with the girl, but I wouldn't wish that on her – dumped at the altar!" said Tess.

"Hardly the altar!" objected Gabriel.

"Nearly! She had the dress bought!" said Tess. "She'll probably end up a spinster now. Miss Havisham all over again."

"You didn't let the grass grow under your feet, Gabriel! Off with the old and on with the new!" guffawed Tim.

"What's got into you, Gabriel?" said Tess.

"Siobhán had the whole thing arranged right down to how many currants she wanted in the wedding cake and an extra layer of marzipan!" said Tim. "I'd say she must be fierce pissed off!"

"Poor Siobhán! I mean she could be dull – let's face it – but no girl deserves this!" said Tess.

"Or fella either!" said Tim.

"Could you both leave us, please?" Cynthia sternly. "I wish to speak to Gabriel alone."

"I've really nothing more to add," said Gabriel.

"You may have nothing left to add, Gabriel, but I have plenty. Tess – Tim – time you were going were going to your room to bed," ordered Cynthia.

Tim and Tess stood up reluctantly.

"Goodnight," said Tess as she headed to the door.

"And good luck!" said Tim as he winked at Gabriel and followed her out.

Once Cynthia heard they had gone up the stairs, she began to speak.

"Now, Gabriel, kindly start from the beginning and tell me what is going on," ordered Cynthia.

"There's really nothing further to add, Mother. I called the engagement off last week."

"But the poor girl must be devastated?" Cynthia face was clouded with concern.

"She wasn't happy of course. It came as a shock to her and –"

"To us all! Will she take you back if you hurry and explain it's all been a terrible misunderstanding?"

"But I've no intention of doing that!" he insisted, looking horrified at the thought.

"It's perfectly natural for a groom to get nervous as his wedding day approaches. It's a big step and the whole thing can be daunting. But, Gabriel – you can get over this hiccup and get back on track."

"I don't love her. I never did. I was only kidding myself that I did."

"There's more important things in marriage than love sometimes," said Cynthia.

"Mother!"

"Well – it's true! Love is fleeting and overestimated in my opinion."

"Well, Siobhán deserves somebody who will love her and I've every belief she will find the right man who will."

"I wouldn't be so sure. Who will want her now – somebody else's cast-off? Gabriel Ford's spoiled goods!"

"For goodness' sake, it's not the Edwardian era, Mother!"

"A terrible thing you have done to poor Siobhán! You were never that cruel – what's become of you?"

"As touching as your concern is for Siobhán, admit that this upsets you more because it upsets your plan for me and the Ford family and our image!"

"Well, I won't lie and say that is not my priority. How will this affect your career?"

"It won't affect it! I'm not getting a divorce!" said Gabriel.

"But she would have been perfect for you – the perfect political wife," said Cynthia.

"Mother – I'm not going into politics! As I said before, I have no intention of running for Tim's seat in the parliament. It was an awful thing for you to suggest in the first place, setting brother against brother!"

"But you are my only hope, Gabriel! Tim just isn't cut out for a life in politics. If you don't go into politics the Fords will never be powerful again!"

"Well – if that's the way it is to be then that's the way it will be! I love my job at the Department of External Affairs and I have no intention of leaving it."

"But, Gabriel – you could be so much more! You have what it takes to go to the top. I've always wanted this for you and expected it for you. Your father was robbed of his rightful destiny – that he would lead this country – and I was robbed of being by his side while he led. But you could fulfil what we were robbed of!"

Gabriel shook his head sadly. "But I don't want it, Mother. I never have."

Cynthia's eyes filled with tears. "I don't know what to say to you. You've thrown away your future happiness with Siobhán and your future political career. You were always my favourite, my true hope. Now I have not just one, but two sons who have thrown their opportunities and destinies away! What was it all for?"

He reached over and placed a hand on hers. "I'm sorry, Mother."

She pulled her hand away and stood up. She went to the window and looked out.

"And I take it this woman you were having dinner with last week has something to do with your break-up with Siobhán? The one you said worked at the British legation – of all places!"

"Yes – she does," he admitted.

"I wasn't aware there were any female diplomats stationed at the British legation."

"She isn't a diplomat, she's a secretary," said Gabriel.

"I see!" said Cynthia, turning around and arching her eyebrows in shock.

"I'd met her before she came to work at the legation in Dublin. She was working at Great Hankerton Hall when I was there last year."

"*I see!*" said Cynthia.

"She was the woman at the American ambassador's last year that you asked me about – in the green dress, if you remember?"

"American ambassador's?" repeated Cynthia. Suddenly a look of realisation spread across her face. "But – but – you said she hailed from the family who had lived at Inishwood?"

"That's right, she's a daughter of the family – a cousin of Lord Ashford in England. Yep, that's right … she's one of them! A true blue-blooded Anglo-Irish aristocratic Protestant!" Gabriel said, getting it all out in one.

Cynthia was horrified. "But you simply can't!"

"I can and I have. I have fallen stupidly and ridiculously in love with Karina."

"*Ka-ri-na,*" Cynthia repeated the name as if it were a sin.

"I know this is so hard for you to understand and accept, Mother. And I'm not saying it's a fait accompli and that I will end up with Karina because she's quite complicated and I don't know what if any feelings she might have for me. But I know what I feel for her and it's very strong and powerful."

"It's unthinkable," Cynthia whispered before her face suddenly became animated. "But-but, Gabriel – I told you about what happened during the Civil War – I told you your father ordered the burning down of her family's house! Does she know – did you tell her?"

"Of course I didn't tell her!" said Gabriel, becoming angry. "And I never will. She must never know that!"

"But – if she knew, Gabriel! If she knew!" Cynthia looked uncharacteristically alarmed.

"She will never know! Because nobody will ever tell her! Do you understand me, Mother? *Nobody will ever tell her!*"

Cynthia stared at Gabriel's angry threatening face. She had never seen him like that before. Never seen him look so determined. He almost looked frightening in his intensity.

"Do you understand, Mother?" he repeated the question again.

She nodded and whispered, "I understand."

CHAPTER 44

Cynthia walked down the narrow country roads of Dalkey towards Pietch's house. It was a warm cloudless day – ideal for painting. She and Pietch had arranged to go for a drive up the coast to Dundalk for the day. He had a number of picturesque beauty spots around Carlingford he wanted her to sketch for postcards. She was looking forward to the day. He was such charming company. She loved how he would watch her painting and sketching, complimenting her on her talent. He never criticised her work or even offered any advice – he always declared it as perfect. She often became annoyed when she thought back to that art critic all those years ago whose scathing attack on her art had put her off pursuing a life as an artist. So many years wasted, she thought sadly. How easy it is that we can take a wrong turn or meet the wrong person in life – and that stops the life we were meant to have. It was now happening with Gabriel and this woman he had met. Cynthia could hardly believe it. Sensible, dutiful, dedicated Gabriel throwing his whole life into turmoil overnight. Discarding his wonderful fiancée, jeopardising his wonderful future for a woman he hardly knew. They said love was blind, but was it insane as well? She kept telling herself that it was a silly phase Gabriel was going through. A rebellion, as it were, that would be short-lived. That Gabriel would wake up and realise how stupendously stupid he had been and return to normal. The worst thing was Cynthia didn't know how to deal with it. She had never been able to manipulate or bully Gabriel in the way she had

Tim and others. That said, she had never needed to as Gabriel had never done anything she had disapproved of before. But now she realised how dangerous that independent streak in Gabriel had always been. When he decided to do something she utterly disapproved of, she literally had no power over him.

She sighed as she turned into the gateway of Pietch's house. He was renting a very pretty two-storey cottage, perched on the side of a cliff, looking down at the sea. There always seemed to be seagulls calling as they glided through the sky above the cottage.

She walked past his motorcar parked in the driveway and up to the front door which she knocked on. There was no answer and so she knocked again, only louder this time.

There was still no answer. Looking at his motorcar in the drive, she thought he must be home so tried the door handle and found it locked. She went and peered through the windows but could see nobody there. She became worried as he was a stickler for punctuality and she couldn't imagine him being late for her. She looked at his motorcar parked in the driveway and became concerned. That staircase was very twisty and old and he could have easily fallen down it.

She walked around the side of the house and peered through the kitchen window. To her horror saw blood on the kitchen floor. Fearing he'd had a terrible accident and was unconscious inside, she began to bang at the back door but there was no answer.

She ran back to the front door and pulled two hairclips from her hair. Opening out one into a straight line, she bent the other into a little lever and inserted it into the lock. Then she inserted the lengthened one into the lock and began to pick it. Sweat broke out on her brow and her hands as she fumbled but she forced herself to calm down and focus. It was a trick she had become expert at during the War of Independence but she was now a little rusty. Minutes passed but then there was a click and it was open.

Heaving a huge sigh of relief, she pushed open the door.

Expecting to find Pietch lying at the bottom of the narrow winding stairs, she was relieved not to find him there.

In a moment she was inside the kitchen, inspecting the small pool of blood on the floor. There was no trail to follow.

She went back to the stairs.

"*Marc! Marc!*" she shouted up but there was no reply.

The house was in a hushed silence, apart from the seagulls cries above.

She ran upstairs but there was no sign of him there.

She went back down to the front room and stood there, uncertain what to do.

She looked at the beautiful view of the beach below and the sea from the wide windows. Her curiosity was caught by a telescope set up at his desk – it hadn't been there on her previous visits. She went over to it and examined it. Looking down on the desk she saw there was a number of her sketches there.

She picked one up. It was of a harbour in Wexford she had drawn the previous week. She saw her own name scribbled at the bottom corner of the sketch. Soon it and the others would be on their way to the buyers in New York and Boston. There were several packages wrapped in brown paper on the desk. One wasn't yet sealed. She pulled back the paper and saw a number of her sketches inside. Glancing at the other packages, she was startled to see that they were all addressed to different names and places in Berlin.

She turned the unsealed one upside-down to see if it was addressed. It was.

It read:

> *Herr Gerhard Schneider*
> *1562 Gartenstrasse*
> *Charlottenburg*
> *Berlin*
> *Germany*

Confused, Cynthia studied the address.

"Berlin?" she whispered. "What is going on?"

She picked up another package and tore it open. Several of her sketches fell to the ground. She picked them up and studied them. She remembered doing them over the past few weeks. Different locations around Ireland that Pietch had asked her to draw. She grabbed the other packages and tore them all open. Each one contained her drawings, paintings and sketches. And all had been destined to be posted to Berlin and not America as she had been told.

Bewildered and confused, Cynthia suddenly felt very uncomfortable – and scared as she thought of the blood on the kitchen floor. She didn't know what was going on, but she needed to get away from there quickly.

"*Guten Morgen, Cynthia*," came Pietch's voice.

She swung around to see him standing in the front doorway, observing her intently. He was not wearing his normal friendly affable expression. Instead, his face was cold and unpleasant. And she saw his hand was bandaged.

"Marc! What happened to you?"

"I stupidly cut my hand with a knife in the kitchen. A very bad cut. I had to rush down to the doctor at the bottom of the road," he said, his eyes cold as ice.

"I saw the blood on the kitchen floor through the window and was concerned about you, so I ... I picked the lock and came in ..."

"I see! How touching that you cared so much! And how very talented you are!"

"I – I thought you might be unconscious or something," she said.

"I see you have been opening my post ..." He closed the door behind him.

Cynthia's eyes widened in fear as he then locked it.

Pietch walked slowly towards Cynthia whose mind was whirling in many directions.

"Why have you locked the door?" she asked.

"We do not wish to be disturbed, do we?"

Cynthia could not fathom what was going on but realised she needed to get away. She remembered her training for the Easter Rising – to always remain calm and not alert your adversary that there was anything out of the ordinary going on.

She coughed loudly and, holding her head high, walked confidently towards the door as she spoke breezily. "We should really be making a move without delay. The sun is wonderful today and I don't want to waste any daylight for sketching. I can drive if you are unable because of your injury ..."

Pietch stepped quickly in front of her, blocking her.

"Marc?" she asked, her voice becoming strained.

"I think we can drop the façade that everything is normal, don't you?"

She stepped back abruptly from him and walked over to the desk.

"Why are my sketches and drawings being posted to Berlin and not New York, Marc?" she asked, her voice now cold and uncompromising.

"If I said I had customers there who wanted to buy your work?"

"I would reply that I think you have played me for a fool for long enough, Marc." She picked up one of her drawings and studied it. "I'm beginning to think that the art critic was correct all those years ago when he dismissed my art ... and that your – enthusiasm – for my work has to do with a little more than my brushstrokes."

"Do not put your talent down, Cynthia. As I've always told you – you are an excellent landscape artist. The artwork you have supplied to the Führer –"

"The *Führer!*" cried Cynthia in shock.

"All the landscape paintings, drawings and sketches you have done have been sent to Berlin and are providing excellent details as the German Intelligence compile the invasion plan of Ireland."

Cynthia stared at him in horror.

"Maps are all very good but having the actual visuals of the places will provide so much more preparation. We were relying on postcards and photos taken by German tourists to Ireland but they were proving inadequate. That is why I was sent here, in order to do the work on the ground and provide up-to-date images for the invasion."

Cynthia tried to comprehend what she was hearing.

"But – you are Polish! Why are you helping the Germans?" she demanded.

"I am from Poland, yes. But I am ethnically a German."

"No!"

"Before the Germans invaded Poland, I gathered sketches and drawings of Poland in order to prepare for the invasion. I was sent here to do the same thing. I am a very good painter and artist but then, when I heard about you, the frustrated artist with a passion for landscapes, I realised you would be perfect. Especially after the outbreak of war, I would arouse suspicion going around painting and drawing, even as a Pole. But you! The great Cynthia Ford – well, who would doubt you?" He smiled.

"You targeted me! You targeted me and used me! Used me to betray my own country!" she said, horrified and furious.

"Oh – you suddenly don't look frightened anymore, Cynthia," he said.

"I'm not frightened of *you*! It would take a lot more than the likes of you to scare me! Don't let this coiffured hair fool you. At the end of the day, Mr Pietch, I was a freedom fighter. I dodged bullets and bombs to deliver messages and don't underestimate what I am capable of!"

"But, that's my whole, point, Cynthia. I don't underestimate you in the least. I know your past and everything about it and have been studying you these past weeks and months ... and determined this vital role you would play in your country's security."

"My country's security!" she exclaimed before pointing to her sketches. "By providing the road map for the Germans to invade!"

"But don't you see? This invasion is only to protect you from your enemy. The British are devising a plan for the invasion of Ireland. Are you aware that your government is working in conjunction with the British on those invasion plans? That they are willing to sell out the independence won by the heroes of your revolution?"

"I – I –"

"Only twenty years ago you finally got rid of the British and now they are to be allowed in through the back door! By your own government!"

"The Irish people would never stand for it," Cynthia said.

"And neither would the Germans. We came to your aid during your fight for your independence, didn't we? We Germans have no argument with you Irish. We are your natural allies. And you can be part of our new strong future together, Cynthia."

"I? But what part could I play?"

"It is only a matter of time until Britain loses," said Pietch.

"I suppose," said Cynthia.

"Then don't you want to be on the winning side? You've always struck me as a winner, Cynthia. You believe what we believe in – so let us join forces."

"But an invasion!" she said, looking at her sketches.

"I thought you were already expecting it any day – with your German lessons," said Pietch, giving her a knowing look.

"What makes you think that I won't go straight to the police once I leave here and tell them what you have been doing?" she demanded.

"But what good would that do? I would be long gone before they get here. And I am very confident you would not do such a thing."

"What makes you so sure?"

"Firstly, you would be showing yourself up as being an accessory to the invasion," Pietch said.

"But I had no idea what you were getting me to do those drawings for!"

"So at worst you will be accused of treason and at best of outright stupidity. I'm not sure which is worse! But your reputation will be in tatters. Cynthia, I am offering you an opportunity here to be with us when we win."

"With you?"

"With the final victory we will need families like yours here in Ireland to oversee things for us and run things the way we want."

"You mean in the way they are doing things in France with the new government being set up under German supervision?"

"Precisely."

"But are those people not being seen as collaborators by most French people?"

"They may be seen as collaborators, but I see people who deal in realpolitik," said Pietch with a smile as he moved over to a cabinet and took from it a bottle of wine. "Why don't we abandon our plans of painting today and enjoy this splendid bottle of French red wine instead, Cynthia? We have so much discuss and this wine is from a very good year." He took up the corkscrew and began to open the bottle.

* * *

That evening, as Cynthia walked back along the beach to Roxford, she felt a little tipsy. She and Pietch had spent the day drinking red wine as they discussed politics, ideas, plans. They had both come to the conclusion the world had gone very wrong and needed to be put right. Pietch was quite a remarkable man, Cynthia thought. So intelligent and aware of the world. So unusual to meet a man like that. She should have known there was much more to him that just being an art dealer. Little did anyone suspect he was so high up in the Nazi party. So modest as well. And he had faith in her. Pietch had full faith in her. He respected and admired her and what's more believed she had a central role to play in Ireland's future. She had always felt robbed of that important role by the assassination of her husband. She had watched as other politicians' wives were given status and prestige that was rightly hers and knew that she would have been so much better at conducting their roles than they were. She had put all her hopes and dreams into her sons. But now Tim was a disaster and Gabriel was intent on throwing it all away. All her hopes and dreams had come crashing down for the second time in her family.

But now Pietch was offering another chance. He was offering her a central role in Irish government once the war over. He was assuring her of a place so powerful that she could ensure Tim would reach the top, regardless of his inadequacies. Pietch was offering her hope.

As Cynthia sat in Pietch's sitting room one afternoon later in the week, she listened intently to what he was requiring of her.

"We are trying to find out about the Jewish population in Ireland," said Pietch.

"What about them?"

"Oh, just general information. Where they live, their addresses, what do they work at – a kind of a census," said Pietch.

"But why? Why would you want to know that?"

Pietch smiled at her. "I think we both know, like everyone else, that the Jews do not want a German victory. And, as we have discussed, a German victory is inevitable. So we just need to prepare for that victory by being able to locate the enemy –"

"The Jews?"

"Yes, the Jews, so we can make sure they do not disrupt life after the victory."

"I've heard that in Germany the Jews have been excluded from public life and their property taken. Is that what you plan to do to them here?" she asked.

"We aim to stop them having as much control as they have, Cynthia. But surely you – as a great Irish freedom fighter – can understand that? You didn't drive out the British twenty years ago for the Jews to take all the senior positions now, did you?"

"Well, I had never given them too much thought, to be honest. But, no – Ireland is a Catholic country and I dearly – *dearly* – wish it to remain so!"

"Well, then, we are on the same side! Help me control their power by finding out all about them so we know where to act when the time comes to act," he said.

Cynthia sat in thought for a long while.

"Nobody would ever know my involvement in this, would they?" she asked eventually.

"Of course not! Except our people in Berlin who will reward you amply when the time comes," he promised.

"You are asking me to be a collaborator, Marc," she whispered.

"I am asking you to be a friend, Cynthia," he said, smiling back at her.

Converted to Pietch's cause, Cynthia set about assisting him in compiling a list of Jewish people living in Dublin and around the country. As she was so well connected it was easy for her to make enquiries through casual conversation with friends and acquaintances to discover who might be Jewish and where they lived. She knew of a Jewish family that lived in Ranelagh but was not sure how many were in the family. She went and sat in the park across from their house for an afternoon and counted the family members as they returned home from work and school. She knew of a street in Terenure that had a concentration of Jewish people living there. She went there and saw all the houses had post boxes at the bottom of their gardens. She went there early one morning just after the postman had been and checked all the mail in the post boxes, noting the Jewish-sounding names and then did further investigations on the families. She felt all the training she had received during the Easter Rising and the War of Independence had never really left her, and she brought it to the fore now as she gathered information on the Irish Jewish population. She had always found a propensity for gossip amongst Irish people and so it was easy to get information from them.

"I've heard about a Jewish family living in your vicinity?" she would ask a housewife at a sale of works or garden fete.

There was nearly always was some Jewish family the housewife thought Cynthia was referring to and she would gossip away about them – what the husband worked at, what the wife looked like, where the children went to school.

Cynthia noted it all down for Pietch.

CHAPTER 45

Karina walked up the stairs to her flat in the evening after work and, putting the key in her door, she opened it and entered. She was deep in thought as she closed the door behind her and locked it. Turning around she let out a scream.

"For goodness' sake, Harper, calm down!" snapped Emily who was seated on a couch beside Kendrick.

"What the fuck are you both doing here?" she demanded as she marched further into the room.

"We had to see you on urgent business," said Kendrick.

"I don't care how urgent it is – you have no right to just walk into my flat!" She was furious.

"I think you'll find it is *our* flat," said Kendrick.

"I don't care whose name is on the lease, it is my home and you have no right to just walk in!"

"We apologise. We did knock and when you didn't answer ..." said Kendrick.

"You just walked in? Well, don't ever do that again!"

"If we can get down to the urgent business we are here to discuss?" said Emily who looked bored with the issue. "It's about your cousin, Lord Ashton."

"Julian? You've heard from him?" she said, startled.

"Not from him – but about him," said Kendrick gravely and he and Emily exchanged grim looks.

Seeing how solemn they looked, Karina's eyes began to fill with tears.

"Oh, no, please don't tell me," she whispered, fearing the worst.

"He's not dead, Harper – it might be better if he were," said Emily.

"Will you just tell me what is going on?" Karina insisted. "Has he been injured?"

"No, he is fighting fit, Harper," said Emily. "He has defected to the other side."

"Defected?" repeated Karina, confused.

"Lord Ashton is a Nazi," said Kendrick. "When we thought he had been either killed or taken prisoner at Dunkirk, he had in fact taken advantage of the situation and gone to join his comrades. He is in Berlin as we speak."

"You are playing some kind of horrible joke!" Karina gave a little laugh. "Julian a Nazi? It's unthinkable."

"Why?" said Emily. "Many members of the peerage have been suspected of leaning towards the Germans in the lead-up to the war. Why would not some of them now jump ship when they believe a Nazi victory is imminent?"

"But Julian – not Julian!" Karina shook her head in horror.

"Did you ever get any indication of his Nazi sympathies?" asked Kendrick.

"No – absolutely not! Julian was hardly political in any way!"

"But you would have known if he had Nazi sympathies. You were very close?" asked Emily.

"I would have. We were both only children so we were like brother and sister growing up."

"The question is then, Harper – are you cut from the same cloth as your cousin?" asked Emily.

"I?" She was shocked.

"The fact you were so anxious to get posted to Berlin before the war started – well, your cousin's defection really put another angle on your anxiety to get there," said Kendrick.

"But you know that was to get to Hugo! We went through all this before you recruited me, Kendrick, for God's sake!"

Kendrick and Emily exchanged glances.

"You are to return to London with me right away, Harper," said Kendrick.

"London! Are you mad? What about Gabriel Ford?" demanded Karina.

"Lord Ashton's defection has changed things. We can't have you in Dublin anymore, it's too much of a risk," said Emily.

"You mean *I'm* too much of a risk!" said Karina.

"Please pack your things," said Emily.

"I don't know why you are asking me to go back to London when I've been doing everything you wanted here in Dublin! When I've made much progress with Gabriel Ford to now throw it all away?"

"Please hurry, we have a plane waiting and don't have much time to waste," said Kendrick.

"But what about Hugo?" Karina demanded.

"We'll continue to search for him," assured Emily.

"No, you won't! Have you been searching for him at all? You have just been using me!"

"Come along, Harper, we can discuss it in the motorcar on the way to the airfield," said Emily who was now walking across the sitting room.

Karina followed her into the bedroom and watched her take one of her suitcases from under the bed, open it on the bed and wait there impatiently.

"Quick as you can," urged Emily as she tapped her foot impatiently on the wooden floor.

Karina wondered how Emily knew exactly where the suitcase was, without searching first.

Karina went to the chest of drawers and opened the top drawer. To her surprise she noticed her clothes had been moved slightly. Karina was neat and could tell the slinky satin slips she had in the top drawer had been disturbed. She opened the second drawer and could tell the same had happened there.

She turned around to Emily. "Could I have some privacy please while I pack?"

"What on earth do you want privacy for?"

Karina grabbed a handful of her underwear and threw it on the bed beside the suitcase.

"I just would like some privacy, if you don't mind!" she insisted and, going to the door, held it open for Emily to leave.

"For goodness' sake! You obviously didn't go to an all-girls boarding school – no place for privacy there, let me tell you!" said Emily as she marched out.

Karina closed the door and rested her back against it, her mind whirling in confusion. Julian – a Nazi! She just couldn't believe it! She walked slowly to the bed and sat down on it beside the opened suitcase. But why did they now want her to leave Dublin and return to London? What was the urgency? Why was there a plane waiting for her at an airfield? She suddenly felt very frightened and alone. Ever since the fall of France, the secret service in Britain had been rounding up suspected fascists and enemies of the state and putting them in prison without trial. They were now enforcing the special powers that had been brought in at the beginning of the war. Karina had only just read how Diana Mitford, the wife of the British fascist Sir Oswald Mosley, has been arrested that month just after having given birth to a baby, and was in Holloway prison. People who were deemed to be a threat to national security during these desperate times were being rounded up and imprisoned without trial or explanation. Now with Julian's defection and exposure as a Nazi, it was obvious that as soon as they got her back to Britain she would be interrogated and most probably imprisoned. And she would have absolutely no rights or opportunity to legally defend herself. What's more, she could spend the future indefinitely languishing in a prison where she would have no opportunity to ever find Hugo. If she went back now to London, not only would her own liberty be gone, but that would be the end of her search for Hugo. He would be lost forever. She just could not face that.

She stood up and steadied herself then went to the cigarette case on her dressing table. Taking one, she lit it as she thought hard. What she did now would affect the rest of her life. She could go with Kendrick and face an unknown fate and probable interrogation and imprisonment. Or she could stay here and continue on her mission to get to Hugo, using Gabriel as her route. Now, with Julian's arrest, she and her mother would suffer further degradation and humiliation. They would be completely ousted from society and shunned by all their friends and associates. At the end of the day, Julian had been their only ticket into society and with his disgrace they would quickly be shown the door. But if she consented to go back to Britain and found herself put in prison, it would destroy her family name forever. Her mother would not be able to survive the scandal. Karina herself would not be able to survive the scandal. Ever since the burning down of Inishwood and the killing of her father, she had felt she was a charity case amongst her set in London. With Julian about to be disgraced and her being interned, she wouldn't even have that. She would be a pariah.

As she thought of Patience and Grace in their genteel house, she was overcome with bitterness and anger. If Inishwood had not been randomly selected by Rory Ford to be burned down, her family could have lived a comfortable and safe life all these years. The Ford family had destroyed her happiness all those years ago, but now bizarrely were offering the only chance to happiness in the future. Now Gabriel Ford could be her only route to Hugo. With his new appointment as an envoy to Berlin, she could use him directly to try and locate Hugo. She could travel to Berlin with him. She just knew if she got to Germany, she would have a fighting chance to get to Hugo. As for Gabriel, he looked as if he was putty in her hands. What's more, when she thought of the terrible time her family had had at the mercy of his family, it would be a sweet revenge to use him to get what she needed. As she thought of the handsome face of Rory Ford, she was consumed with hatred and bitterness towards him.

She had been pushed around all her life and she was not going to allow it to happen anymore. She needed to be on the winning side for a change.

"Harper!" came Emily's shrill voice from the other side of the door. "How long does it take to pack a few pairs of frilly knickers and frocks?"

Karina put out her cigarette and swung open the bedroom door.

"What is going on? Why are you not packed?" asked Emily seeing the open, still unpacked suitcase on the bed.

"I'm not packed because I will not be going," announced

Karina as she walked into the sitting room.

"We really don't have times for your shilly-shallying, Harper! The plane won't wait forever," said Emily.

"I don't care how long or short it waits as I shan't be on it," said Karina.

"Shall!" insisted Emily.

"*Shan't!*" Karina said with a loud and determined voice.

"But why won't you come with me back to London?" asked Kendrick.

"Because I don't see the point. I have come here to Ireland, which I hated to do, and I have done everything you asked and expected of me. I have even broken up Gabriel Ford's engagement and, just when I am about to get close to him as he is posted to an important new role with Germany, you are dismissing me from my mission. Well, it's just not on. I'm tired of being at your beck and call. I'd do anything to help fight the Nazis, but I fear I am now – after Julian's defection – not trusted by you anymore. I fear I have become too much of a risk for you to trust."

"You were always too much of a risk in my opinion," snapped Emily. "Harper, go and pack! That is an order from your superior!"

"Well, you are no longer my superior as I resign from the embassy," said Karina.

"You can't!" exclaimed Emily in horror and frustration.

"It's better this way for us all. With Julian's defection my position is untenable," said Karina.

Emily and Kendrick looked at each other, their eyes expressing some unspoken communication Karina could not read.

"You're being a very silly girl, Karina. You aren't helping yourself with this behaviour," said Kendrick. "Come back to London and we can talk about it."

"There's nothing to talk about! I'm not going back to England. I'm staying here in Ireland for now until things become more clear."

"But where will you live, where will you go?" demanded Emily.

"I'll figure it out. I am from here after all so I have as much right to be here as anyone else. I even still have an Irish passport."

"An Irish passport!" Emily was horrified.

"I've always had one as I consider myself Irish," said Karina.

"Good Lord!" exclaimed Emily.

"I'm afraid I am going to have to ask you both to leave now," said Karina as she crossed over to the door and opened it. "I shall be gone from here tomorrow and you can have the flat back then."

Emily looked at Kendrick who nodded at her and they both moved towards the door.

"You are just like your treacherous cousin, aren't you?" said Emily as she walked past her. "I really feel the need to tell you that I never liked you in the first place anyway!"

"Goodnight, Karina. I hope you know what you're doing. It can be very cold out there in your own, you know," said Kendrick as he followed Emily out.

Karina closed the door and quickly locked and bolted it. She then sank down to the floor and realised she was shaking uncontrollably.

CHAPTER 46

Karina was hardly able to sleep that night after Emily and Kendrick had left. In one way she couldn't believe what she had done – quitting her job on the spot, losing her flat into the bargain and, as Kendrick warned, losing the protection of the British Secret Service. And yet she felt, without a doubt, she had done the right thing. She would be going back to an uncertain future in Britain. She could not go back there until her safety and freedom was guaranteed. And, with Julian's defection, that just was not the case right now. She was horrified and disgusted by his actions. But she was angry too, angry that he had not only destroyed his own name in Britain but sullied his family's name as well, including her own.

During the night she went to the window of her flat and peeped out through the curtains. She could see nobody out there in the street, but that didn't mean they weren't there. She knew the Secret Service were out there watching her flat now, after her quitting and refusing to go back to London that night. Julian's defection might have made her a security risk, but her own refusal to return to London had confirmed her status as a high security risk, she imagined. Now they would not trust her in the least. They would be extremely nervous that she would expose the fact she had been spying on Gabriel Ford to the Irish. But they could rest assured that she would do no such thing. Gabriel was now her one and only route to finding Hugo and she would continue with the plan they had conjured to use his position for access to confidential material. She felt nervous and uneasy as she quickly stepped away from the window. She would have to leave the flat first thing in the morning. She went to the bedroom and began to pack.

As soon as it began to get light, Karina put on her coat and scarf and, taking her heavy suitcases, put the key on the coffee table and left the flat, closing the door after her. She wondered if Emily and Kendrick would be back that morning and would be trying to get her to change her mind in a more aggressive fashion. Perhaps they might even send somebody else around to fetch her. She reminded herself that they could not touch her, not as long as she was in Ireland. She was in a neutral country and was officially an Irish citizen. She was out of their jurisdiction. That didn't stop her from feeling extremely nervous as she walked down Merrion Square, carrying her suitcases. She kept her eyes alert looking for a taxicab. The streets were still deserted as it was only 6 o'clock in the morning. Across the street by the park she saw a man standing on his own under a tree, looking across at her. She hurried her pace and turned the corner and walked up in the direction of the Shelbourne Hotel. With relief, once she got there she saw a taxicab waiting outside the hotel and she went to it.

"Monkstown, please – Victoria Terrace," she said, feeling relieved to be getting away.

The loud knocking drifted in through Gabriel's dreams. His subconscious attempted to ignore the loud banging but it was too persistent, and as he struggled awake, he realised the knocking was not a dream but a reality. He sat up in bed, turned on the bedside lamp, looked at the clock on his bedside table and saw it was only half past six. The knocking was becoming even more persistent so he got out of bed and, putting on his dressing gown, went to the window and drew back the curtains. He looked down but he couldn't see anyone at the front door. He opened the window.

"*Who the fuck is down there making all that confounded noise?*" he called down.

Suddenly a woman stepped out from the doorway and looked up at him.

"*Karina!*" he exclaimed in shock. "*Wait there! I'm coming right down!*"

Karina could not help but smile to herself. It was such a typical Gabriel thing to say in such a situation – *wait there!* She had been banging on the door for five minutes – she was hardly going to rush off as soon as he appeared!

She stood anxiously at the doorway and looked out at the grey sea in the early-morning light. It was cold and she pulled her fur coat closer around her as she could see the air from her breath turn into short spurts of fog in the cold morning air.

The door was unbolted and there stood a shocked Gabriel in a satin dressing gown.

"Well – may I come in?" she asked eventually.

"Of course! Of course!" he said, reaching down to take her suitcases and beckoning her in.

As he closed the door behind them and she looked down the tiled hall, she felt immediately safe and secure after all the turmoil of the previous evening.

"What on earth are you doing here at this time of the morning?" he asked as he led her into the drawing room.

"I'm sorry, Gabriel, I just wasn't sure where else to go," she said as she sat down on the ornate Louis XIV gold couch.

He sat and took her hands.

"You're freezing!" he said.

He went to the fireplace where embers were dying in the grate. He put some kindling in and set it alight, then added some logs. Soon there was a big roaring fire.

"I'll get you some tea to warm you up," he said, rushing off to the kitchen.

Karina held the teacup in her hands and blew the steam away before taking a sip.

"Better?" he asked.

She nodded and continued to drink.

"Karina – what is going on?" he asked.

"I'm sorry, Gabriel, for just showing up like this," she said, putting down the teacup on the side table beside her and turning to him. "I've quit the legation and left my flat." She got it all out in one sentence.

"Quit! But why?" He was enveloped in confusion.

"They wanted me to go back to London, straight away. They wanted me to leave Dublin – so I quit."

"But why did they suddenly want you to leave?"

"Well, there was a number of reasons. I have a cousin, Lord Ashton – he has defected to the Nazis. I guess they needed me back in London due to the sensitivity of that."

"I see," he said, shocked.

"And, also, I couldn't keep working for the embassy and continue to see you, Gabriel. Questions would have been asked – about the two of us. It was all very well when we were having a clandestine affair – but – at Restaurant Jammet when you told me you have broken off your engagement I realised you were taking our relationship much more seriously."

"Why did you act the way you did that night? You were telling me it was over between us and to forget about you ... then collapsing like that and being so cold when I took you back to your flat."

"I got ... scared. I just got very scared ... I'm afraid my first instinct has always been to run away when I get scared and that's what I was doing that night. Trying to run away."

"So why didn't you keep running?" he asked.

"Because I couldn't run away from you. You mean too much to me," she whispered.

"Karina – do you know how much I've wanted to hear you say that?" he asked as he took her into his arms.

They lay in bed as the sun shone through the window.

"Don't you have to be in work?" she asked.

"I'm going to take today off. I've more important things to attend to," he said as he kissed her forehead. "I can't believe you left your job for me – your career."

"Well, it wasn't much of a career for me to leave, Gabriel. And look what you have left for me – your fiancée!"

"The best decision I ever made," he said.

"When we went to the restaurant that night and met your brother I realised if I stayed working at the British legation my bosses would not be happy about the relationship. And your position would have been compromised as well."

"I would like to think I have too many friends in government for that to happen," he said with a laugh. "And, besides, not being offensive, but seeing a you're a typist – how would anyone think I was being compromised? However, that said, it certainly makes things simpler for me that you are no longer at the British legation. What are you planning on doing now?"

"I have no idea. I'll need to get a job and a place to live. I shall go and stay with my friends Patience and Grace Berry for now."

"But you can stay here!"

"I don't know, Gabriel. I don't want to impose and it's too early in our relationship."

"Karina, I felt from the first time I met you that we were meant to be together and here we are – together. And it has been quick, but sometimes that is the way things are meant to be."

"But what would people say? If we were living together without being married?"

"Nobody will know. We will be discreet. Besides, the world is changing rapidly with this war. Society is changing."

"Even in Ireland?"

"Yes, even here!"

"I can't see that happening somehow ... so perhaps we just remain discreet for now, Gabriel?"

"As you wish," he said, reaching forward and kissing her.

Karina came down the stairs the next morning wearing her cream silk dressing gown.

She saw Gabriel in his study on the telephone. She waved to him from the doorway and he grinned back at her.

"Alright – I'll be there in an hour," he said as he put down the phone.

"Something important?" she asked.

"Unfortunately so. I'm going to have to leave you today for a few hours." He stood up and put papers in his briefcase.

"That's alright, I honestly never expected you to baby-sit me."

"But I had planned to work from home today so we could spend some more time together," he said.

"It's honestly fine, Gabriel," she said with a smile.

"I've told my housekeeper to stay away this week so you won't be disturbed."

"Probably for the best. In that case, as you cannot cook, I shall cook us something tonight."

"If you can find anything to cook with in the larder," he said with a grimace.

"Oh, I'll find something, don't you worry. It comes from being brought up with frugal means after we left Inishwood. You would be surprised how resourceful I can be."

"I don't think I would be one bit surprised," he said as he put on his jacket.

He walked towards her and kissed her.

"Oh, could I ask a favour?' she said. "Would I be able to use your telephone? I need to speak with my mother. I won't be long with the call, I promise. Short and sweet is the best way to handle my mother!"

"Best way to handle all mothers!" he said with a laugh. "Of course telephone her – take as long as you want. And I wonder could I ask you a favour?"

"Of course."

"I'm expecting a delivery in the post – could you answer the door to the postman and take in the package for me? Just leave it on the sideboard in the hallway along with the rest of the post, if you wouldn't mind?"

"Sure."

He went back into the study, picked up the telephone and disconnected it before carrying it into the hallway and putting it on a stand there. He bent down and reconnected it to the socket there.

Then he closed the study door and locked it.

He turned to her. "I'm not locking it because of you. I always lock it when I leave the house. It makes me feel better – not that there is anything important in there."

She smiled at him. "Of course. You mustn't change any of your routines because of me – I insist!"

A car horn beeped outside.

"That's my lift! I had better go," he said.

He leaned forward and kissed her lips. "See you tonight."

She watched him walk out the front door and close it.

She went into the drawing room and from the front window watched him get into the passenger seat of the motorcar waiting for him. She wondered who the driver was and where Gabriel was going and felt a sense of relief that she didn't have to report back on his every move to Emily. She bit her lip as she headed back out to the hallway and the telephone.

She got through to the operator and waited to be put through to Julian's country manor house. Once she had finally been put through, she spoke to the butler there and he said he would fetch her mother from the cottage she was staying in and for her to telephone back in half an hour.

Karina sat on the stairs smoking a cigarette as she thought how best to handle her mother. She had always adopted a motto with her mother that seemed to work. That motto was: *Tell her the truth, some of the truth, but not all of the truth*. This policy ensured that she wouldn't alarm, worry or antagonise her mother unnecessarily but allowed her to receive just the amount of information necessary.

Half an hour later Karina phoned again and true to the butler's word, her mother answered.

"Karina darling, so wonderful to hear from you! I am going daft with boredom here on Julian's estate – I shall never complain about London again. The cottage is cold and draughty! I think I'd risk whatever bombs come to London rather than put up with this draughtiness much longer!"

"Mother – shut up and listen to me.! I don't have much time."

"Whatever is the matter?"

"Julian has defected to the Nazis – he is somewhere in Germany in bed with them!"

"Julian! A Nazi? There must be some mistake! Julian couldn't be

283

a Nazi even if he wanted to be – he was always such a nice boy!"

"And I have left my position at the legation in Dublin," continued Karina.

"*What?* Is there anything else you need to tell me to shock me to my very core even more – have the Germans won the war? Have the Martians landed on Wimbledon Common?"

"Mother –"

"Are you coming back to Britain if you have left your job?"

"No. I'm staying here a while longer."

"But whatever for? Where are you staying? What will you do?" Penny was becoming distressed.

"I'm moving around a bit at the moment, so not actually at any fixed abode."

"Typical of you!" snapped Penny.

"But I'll be in constant contact with Patience and Grace, so contact me through them when you need me."

"It sounds like you have run away to join the circus!"

"Be serious, Mother! This – Julian's defection – is going to be difficult for us all. My position at the legation was just no longer tenable after he joined the Nazis."

"Your papa would be disgusted! His favourite nephew."

"He was his only nephew, Mama! Anyway, I don't think you should stay at Julian's estate any longer. Once the press find out, the place will be swarming with newspapermen, I daresay, and you don't want to be associated with it."

"What should I do then? Go back to London?"

"I think it's going to be too unsafe there. I was going to suggest you go and stay with Papa's cousin Agatha in Scotland."

"Oh, Agatha! Scotland is so far away and always cold and Cousin Agatha is even colder than the weather once you arrive!"

"Well, why don't you come to Dublin then? I would love that."

"I shall never set foot in that place again, you know that … if the choice is Scotland and the cold or Ireland and the rain – Scotland wins every time! I'll pack today and leave tomorrow."

"This evening if you can?" said Karina.

"Oh, alright then!" said Penny.

"And don't speak to anybody about any of this."

"Of course not."

"And I miss you terribly, Mama. And I wish I was with you now. I miss your breakfasts in the morning and – and – everything about you!" Tears sprang to Karina's eyes.

"Are you alright, Karina?"

"Yes – it's just a terrible shock about Julian. Everything that is happening is a terrible shock."

"I know – but we must be brave, darling. We have been through worse. We are survivors."

There was a loud knock at the door.

"Listen, I have to go, Mama. I'll telephone you again over the next couple of days. I love you."

"I love you too, Karina. Please do take care."

"I'd better go, the postman is here with a delivery – I'll speak to you soon again," said Karina as she replaced the receiver and wiped away the threatening tears.

There was another loud knock.

Karina ran a hand through her hair as she crossed the hallway and pulled open the front door.

To her surprise, it wasn't the postman. It was an immaculately dressed woman in her fifties.

The woman looked startled to see Karina.

"Is Gabriel home?" she asked, looking Karina up and down.

Karina pulled her dressing gown tighter over her chest. "No, he's at work."

"Are you a new housekeeper?"

"No, I'm a friend … may I ask who is enquiring?"

A wave of recognition dawned on the woman's face as the penny dropped with her.

"I'm Cynthia Ford – Gabriel's mother."

She walked past Karina into the hallway.

Stunned and mortified, Karina closed the front door.

Cynthia stood there in the tiled hallway, looking Karina up and down.

"I'm a friend of Gabriel's – Karina Harper."

"Yes – yes – Gabriel did mention you. I hasn't realised – I just hadn't realised ..." Cynthia's voice trailed off.

Karina wished with all her might she was wearing something other than a dressing gown.

"Was Gabriel expecting you?" she asked.

"No, I was in the area and I saw his motorcar in the driveway so I thought he was not at work today ... so I dropped by to – to collect a scarf I left behind here last week." Cynthia cast her eyes around as if looking for the scarf.

"I didn't see any scarf ..."

"Oh – have you been staying here long enough to have noticed? Gabriel never said he had a house guest."

Cynthia walked into the drawing room, her eyes darting everywhere as if looking for further evidence of what was going on between Gabriel and Karina. Although Karina wondered what further evidence she needed with her standing there in her dressing gown.

"It's blue with a cloud pattern on it," Cynthia said.

"Sorry?"

"The scarf!"

"Oh, of course." Karina made a show of pretending to search the room.

She stopped and turned to Cynthia who was scrutinising her.

"Would you like some tea?" she said, to break the horrible silence.

"Yes – two sugars – a thimbleful of milk, if you would," said Cynthia.

Karina nodded and smiled at her and quickly exited the room. She walked down the hallway and into the kitchen.

Cynthia sat down slowly on the couch, feeling dazed. She couldn't remember when she had last received such a big shock.

She had been in the area gathering information for Marc Pietch's report. She knew of a Jewish family who lived close by in Belgrave Square. They had been wealthy jewellers and the daughter of a friend of hers had bought her engagement ring from them. She knew the family name and had found out what number the house was from her friend in casual conversation. That morning she had gone and sat in the park in the centre of the square and pretended to be reading a book while she watched the house as the household got ready for their day's events. The husband going off to work, two teenage daughters left together in school uniforms and then finally a young son left with his mother. She jotted down the facts in her notebook to be added to the list she and Pietch were compiling.

As she left the park she decided to walk past Gabriel's house on the off-chance he might be home and she could call in to try and persuade him to go back to Siobhán. She had been delighted to see his motorcar in the driveway and called up to the front door with a big smile on her face, determined to sort out her favourite son's life once and for all. A few minutes later, she was doing anything but smile as she was confronted with the sheer horror of finding this woman semi-naked in her favourite son's house.

Once in the safety of the kitchen, Karina shook her head in despair. The whole thing was beyond awkward and humiliating. As she thought what to do, she realised there was very little she could do except try and charm the woman. But she suspected this woman was incapable of being charmed.

The kettle finally boiled and Karina filled the teapot and set a silver tray.

"Sorry it took so long," she said as she walked back into the drawing room.

She stopped abruptly as she realised Cynthia was not in the room. As she wondered had Cynthia just walked out, she heard someone walking around upstairs. Karina put the tray down on a table and went out into the hallway and up the stairs.

"Mrs Ford?" she called but there was no answer.

She saw the door to Gabriel's bedroom was open. She hurried down to the open door and walked into the room.

She found Cynthia standing there looking at the unmade bed which was showing clear signs of much activity.

As Karina realised her clothes and undergarments from the night before were strewn around the room, she went red with embarrassment.

"I thought I might have left my scarf here so I came up to check," said Cynthia whose voice was like ice as she stared coldly at Karina. "But I can't see it here."

Karina just nodded. "Your tea is ready downstairs," she said.

"I'm afraid I can't stay for it after all. I must leave. Good day, Miss Harper."

Cynthia marched past her and down the stairs.

A few seconds later, Karina heard the front door open and slam shut. Karina went to the bed and sat down. She felt mortified and embarrassed. But she also felt something else – anger. That was Rory Ford's widow. And, as she went swanning around Dublin like a queen, her own mother was being shuttled around feeling lost and insecure. Karina became more determined to avenge the Ford family.

But, she reminded herself, Hugo was her priority. She needed to remain focused. This situation with Gabriel could not be allowed to go on indefinitely nor did she wish for it to go on for much longer. Now she had direct access to his power as diplomat, she needed to use it quickly to locate and rescue Hugo.

When Gabriel was on that plane for Berlin later that month, she needed to be on that plane with him.

CHAPTER 47

Gabriel sat in de Valera's office as he digested the news he was being told. The Germans had bombed Wexford, in the south-east of Ireland, that morning, killing three people. The reality of a direct attack on the country was terrifying.

"Three people – all women – were killed in the bombing. Two Luftwaffe planes flew over Wexford and attacked the creamery," said de Valera. "Many more could have been killed had it been lunchtime and the creamery restaurant full of workers."

"The question is, was the attack on purpose? Are we at war with Germany?" asked Gabriel.

"The German legation in Dublin are denying the attack was by their planes. I have no doubt it was their planes, but we need a full investigation to produce evidence it was their bombs that were dropped."

"It could have been pilot error. The intended target could have been Britain and the pilots mistook our south-east coast for the British one," said Gabriel. "But whatever they come back with, can we believe a word they say? They constantly tell lies and untruths to justify their attacks on other countries. This could be a prelude to an invasion – a test drive, as it were. Without doubt, there are agents working here for the Nazis, gathering information for an invasion."

"Or it might be simply a warning to us not to be helping Britain as much as we have been. We do not have much time to waste to find out, Gabriel. We need to investigate the bomb site in Wexford and then I want you to travel to Berlin sooner than you had planned to meet with the Nazi government and assure them of our neutrality. Try to smooth this over and hold off any further aggression from them. If they caused this destruction in a small village in Wexford with two fighter planes, imagine what the result of an attack on Dublin would be?"

Gabriel nodded as he digested what was being said. He thought of Karina at home in Monkstown. He had just managed to get their relationship on a sure footing. How could he leave her now to go to Berlin? He was sure she would not wait around for him. She would be gone by the time he got back which he could not bear to contemplate.

There was a knock on the door.

"Excuse me, Taoiseach, Cynthia Ford is here and says she needs to speak to Mr Ford urgently," said the secretary.

"My mother?" asked Gabriel, shocked.

"We are finished here in any case. If you can start making the arrangements to travel to Berlin?" said de Valera.

"Of course, Taoiseach. I'll keep you informed of the arrangements."

Gabriel quickly rose to his feet and left the room.

"Where is she?" he asked the secretary outside.

"She's waiting outside in the front gardens," said the secretary.

As Gabriel quickly made his way to the front gardens he was overtaken with anxiety. What was Cynthia doing there? She had never shown up at work before like this and he began to fear the worst.

"Mother, what's wrong? What's happened?" demanded Gabriel, his face tortured with worry.

"I went to find you at your office and your secretary said you were here at Government Buildings and so I came straight over," she announced.

"Yes, but what is wrong?" he demanded.

"I called to your house in Victoria Terrace this morning – and I found a half-clothed woman answering the door to me! A half-clothed British Protestant woman by the looks of her at that!"

Gabriel's face went bright red with embarrassment.

"Never in all my born days did I think I would have to face the shame of a son of mine – *fornicating* – with the enemy! Is this how

I brought you up? Is *this* the result of the shining example of virtue I have given to both my sons all my life? Is this my reward? To have one an alcoholic and the other a fornicator!"

"Mother –"

"For the first time in my life I am glad – glad, I tell you – that your father is not here to see this show of immorality you are displaying for all to see!"

"Mother, *please!*"

"It's easy to see now why you were so anxious to get poor old Siobhán out of the way – so you could turn 32 Victoria Terrace into a whorehouse!"

"*Cynthia!*"

"A whorehouse, I tell you! You need to get yourself down to Confession and plead for forgiveness for the mortal sins you have knowingly and energetically committed under your own roof and then you need to get back to your house and throw that prostitute out into the street and back into the gutter where you found her!"

"*Will you be quiet!*" Gabriel shouted, causing her to jump with fright.

Some civil servants who were passing by looked over, startled.

Gabriel looked around, embarrassed, before he hissed, "*Will you just be quiet?*"

"How dare you speak to me like that!" she said, seething.

"How dare *you* speak to *me* like that! You must not speak about Karina like that. I will not have you call her those names and speak of her with such disrespect!"

"How else am I to speak of a woman who answers your door with hardly any clothes on?" Cynthia demanded.

"I am certain you are exaggerating. But, even if it were the truth, it is none of your business!"

"Gabriel!"

"What Karina and I do is none of your business. You know nothing of what is happening between us."

"Oh, I think I've a very good idea of what is happening between you!" said Cynthia, her voice dripping in sarcasm. "I know everything that is going on between you two!"

He stared at her, his blood boiling. "Well, you didn't know that we are engaged, did you?"

"*Engaged!*" she shrieked.

"We are to be man and wife as soon as possible."

"*No!*" She was aghast.

"I'm glad you met Karina this morning, Mother, because she's going to be your daughter-in law!" He smiled triumphantly at her before he turned and marched away, leaving her standing as still as a statue, stunned and horrified.

As soon as Gabriel got out of view, the smile fell from his face.

Cynthia sat in her drawing room at Roxford, staring out at the sea that evening with Tess sitting on one side of her and Tim on the other.

"I can hardly believe it!" said Tess.

"Shocking behaviour, all the same!" said Tim. "Naked, you say?"

"Apart from a dressing gown," said Cynthia.

"He's a disgrace to the family!" declared Tim.

"He'll ruin our good family name!" said Tess.

"I need some air to clear my head," said Cynthia as she suddenly got up and walked out the French window.

As they watched Cynthia walk across the garden and down the steps to the beach, Tim and Tess looked at each other.

"Not her golden-haired boy now, is he?" said Tim, taking a sip of wine from his glass.

"Whatever is he thinking of, shacking up with a woman from her background?" said Tess.

"They say love is blind," said Tim.

"I just always thought he was too level-headed to be so reckless and careless. He really must be in love, the fool. Regardless, this is our opportunity to save your political career, Tim."

"I know!" he said, taking another sip of wine.

"There is no way Cynthia will continue with her plan now for him to stand in the election and take your seat away from you."

"I know that too!" he said, taking another sip.

"We just have to play the old girl right. Keep undermining Gabriel to her."

"Though he's so headstrong we won't need to do much work – he'll do it all himself," Tim, said, taking another gulp of wine. "He was always like that. When he wanted something, nothing would get in his way."

"And all we have to do is keep on the right side of her and keep our reputations sparking clean, at least until Gabriel has completely self-destructed."

"Yes!" agreed Tim as he went to take another gulp of wine.

"Which means –" she said, grabbing the glass from his hand, "staying off this stuff for the foreseeable future!"

Tim's face dropped in anguish as he looked at his stolen glass of wine.

Gabriel put his key in his front door and paused for a moment before he let himself in.

"Karina?" he called. For one awful moment, he had this expectation that she would not be there. That she would have absconded after her encounter with Cynthia that morning. That she would have been horrified by Cynthia's rudeness and judgemental attitude and have packed her things and run. That's what Karina did in life, Gabriel figured – ran. She had admitted it to him herself. When she didn't want to be bothered with something or someone anymore, she simply left. She did it the first time they had met in Claridge's. She had even, seemingly, been doing it – running away – from someone else that night when he met her in the 400 Club. She had run away from London and then she had run away from the British legation in Dublin. It was his overall fear – that she would simply run without an explanation or giving a reason. He would turn around and she would simply be gone. That thought filled him with fear and a form of terror. A terror he did not know how he would deal with when the day came.

"Hello!" said Karina as she walked out from the drawing room into the hallway.

He was filled with relief to see her still there. He went to her and embraced her and kissed her.

"Gabriel, I've something to tell you about what happened this morning after you had left," she said.

"I know what happened already. My mother came to see me," he said.

"Oh!" She raised an eyebrow and pulled away from him. She walked back into the drawing room and lit up a cigarette from the pack she had left on the fireplace.

He followed her in.

"I'm so sorry," she said. "I had been on the telephone to my mother and then there was a knock on the door and I knew you were expecting a parcel, so I opened it without thinking, without dressing properly …"

"You're sorry? But you have nothing to be sorry about!" He went to her quickly. "You did nothing wrong!"

"It was unfortunate I was in my dressing gown. I just never expected your mother!"

"You can answer the door any way you want, Karina," he said impatiently. "I don't want you to ever feel embarrassed or ashamed and don't let anyone make you feel that way either!"

"But she sneaked up to the bedroom, Gabriel, when I went to make tea. She knows what's going on –"

"I don't care! I don't care what she thinks!"

"But, Gabriel, this is Catholic Ireland – I don't need to tell you what is the done thing and not the done thing around here! You were brought up with it! You are part of it!"

"But I don't think I ever was, not deep down, not in here." He touched his heart. "I was always searching for something other than the way we are constrained to live here. I think that's what I was doing going out on my own to the Club 400 that night – looking for something else – some kind of freedom – and I found you."

"A sorry day for you." She raised her eyes and blew out smoke from her cigarette. "What did your mother say anyway?"

"What didn't she say!" he said, looking out the window. "She said some really horrible and disgusting things."

"I guess she had a right," Karina acknowledged.

He swung around angrily. "She had no right! And I told her so. I told her to mind her own business and I told her … I told her … I told her …" He couldn't get the words out.

"Yes?"

"I told her we were engaged!" he blurted out.

Karina dropped her cigarette on the carpet as her mouth dropped open.

They stared at each other.

"I had – I had no choice! She was calling you all kinds of names and I had to let her know that you were not some passing woman to me – that you meant something to me – that I loved you – that I love you," he said as he stared at her stunned expression.

The smell of burning drifted up from where Karina's cigarette was burning a hole through the carpet.

"Oh, your carpet!" she exclaimed as she dropped to her knees, picked up the cigarette and threw it in the fireplace. She remained kneeling as she began to pat the singed carpet.

He came over quickly to her, raised her to her feet and took her hands, gripping them tightly.

"I know I shouldn't have said such a thing," he said. "So many things were going through my head as I had just met Dev – as we call him – and I am to travel to Berlin very soon because of the worsening situation and I don't know how long I'll be away. It might be for a long time and I just can't bear the thought of leaving you behind or you leaving me."

"You are going to Berlin soon?"

"Very soon. And I just know you will forget about me once I'm gone and then when my mother said those things I told her we were engaged. I wanted to show her and reassure myself, I guess, that this will not be over soon."

Karina reached out and grabbed his face and kissed him passionately.

"So when are we going to Berlin?" she asked as she lay in his arms in bed.

"We – Berlin? Us?" He looked at her, confused.

"Well, if we are engaged – you are hardly going to leave me behind if it might be an extended stay there?"

He was speechless for a long while before he whispered, "So we are actually engaged? I was only saying it to my mother to shut her up!"

"Oh, well, if you didn't mean it ..." she said, pulling away from him.

"I did mean it – I just can't quite believe it!" he said, as a smile crept across his face.

He kissed her.

"Mrs Gabriel Ford – it has ring to it, doesn't it?" she asked, with a smile.

"It certainly does. I'm going to get a bottle of champagne and open it to celebrate. Don't go anywhere!" He jumped out of the bed and hurried to the door.

He stopped when he reached the doorway and turned around and said, "I know this may sound like a cliché – but you have made me the happiest man alive!"

"Don't forget to bring two glasses!" She smiled at him and blew him a kiss.

He grinned back before disappearing out the door.

The smile disappeared from Karina's face as she rested back on the pillows, deep in thought.

"You're right about one, thing, Gabriel," she whispered to herself. "It does sound like a cliché. A rather bad one at that."

Karina had been shopping in O'Connell Street for a gift for Gabriel. She had bought him a cashmere scarf from Cleary's Department Store.

She had him eating out of her hand and that's what she needed to continue to do. He was an easy man to manipulate – a little kind gesture here, a small compliment there and he was grinning like a fool from ear to ear. She almost felt sorry for him, he seemed to have fallen so badly for her. He would be like an overexcited puppy when she handed him the scarf, beautifully wrapped by one of the Cleary's staff. But she had to remain focused. She was nearly there. After all this time battering her head against a wall trying to get to Berlin, trying every ruse available, she was now getting a diplomatic escort there where she could finally – finally – find

Hugo. The excitement, combined with this anxiety she felt over it all, was almost too much to bear.

She got onto a tram and went up the stairs and found a seat there. As she looked down at O'Connell Street it was packed with black motorcars and hundreds of people on bicycles. It was a city of bicycles, Karina thought. So many more bicycles than in London and she imagined it was because there was no underground system in Dublin so it was the easiest and cheapest way for getting around.

There was a different feeling in the city that day. An undercurrent of fear and uncertainty of what might come after the German bombing raid in Wexford.

There was a middle-aged man reading the *Evening Press* in front of her.

"Strange times! Strange times indeed, Mrs O'Mara!" he said to the middle-aged woman sitting beside him as he folded away the newspaper.

"They certainly are, Mr Dwyer! They say the bombing in Wexford was a mistake and the Irish goverment are looking for compensation from the Germans."

"That bombing was no mistake, Mrs O'Mara, make no mistake about that!"

"Really, Mr Dwyer?"

Mr Dwyer leaned towards Mrs O'Mara and lowered his voice. "I have a nephew who runs a guesthouse on the coast in Wexford. And he tells me there are a lot of strange goings-on there – at night!"

Karina leant forward a little, straining to hear. It had become a habit to listen since she'd had to collect information for Emily.

"At night, Mr Dwyer?" asked Mrs O'Meara.

"A huge increase in the traffic of passing ships at night ... and not just that, but lights, Mrs O'Mara!"

"Lights, Mr Dwyer?"

"Lights flashing on and off from those ships at sea and somebody up on the headland flashing back at them. Signalling them ... enemy agents here in Ireland sending signals out to the Germans at sea."

"Enemy agents! Oh no, Mr Dwyer!"

"Only last week an odd fellow booked into my nephew's guesthouse late at night. He said he had got lost."

"Was he a foreigner, Mr Dwyer?"

"No – he was from Cork. He said he had got lost because all the roads signs have been removed ... but who ever heard of Corkman who couldn't find his way home like a homing pigeon – signs or no signs? In any case, my nephew reported him to the Guards the next morning!"

"I hope they hang him!" spat Mrs O'Mara.

"Mark my words, in anther few weeks the Germans will land an invasion force in Wexford and blitzkrieg their way up the coast to Dublin and the Storm Troopers will be goose-stepping down O'Connell Street as if they own the place!"

Mrs O'Mara blessed herself quickly. "What will become of us at all, Mr Dwyer!"

Karina sat back, troubled but glad she didn't have the burden of reporting anything to Emily and Kendrick.

CHAPTER 48

As Cynthia walked down the beach under the darkening sky, she felt her life was being thrown upside down. She had always thought she could bank on and trust Gabriel. On his sense of duty and obligation and his need to do the right thing. But now he had fallen under a spell. The vicious, sinful, lustful spell of this woman. And this spell was going to destroy him and the whole Ford family. Cynthia was certain there was more to this than a simple love story. The woman was dangerous, Cynthia could see that straight away and Gabriel was blind to how dangerous she was. And it would be too late for him by the time he realised that, as his life would be already destroyed by then. She stopped walking and went and sat on a nearby rock, staring out at the sea. Suddenly, tears were falling down her face. She never cried. Not since she was a child. And then suddenly here she was crying deeply. She had a fear of crying, for she felt that if she allowed herself to, she might never stop. But now as she saw all her life's work, all her hopes and dreams slip away from her and all the sacrifices she made turn out to be in vain, the tears flowed easy. She suddenly stood up and wiped away the tears. She would not be destroyed. She would not allow herself and her family to be dragged down to the gutter that this woman had crawled out from. She was a survivor. She knew how to survive. She had survived all her life and she would not let Karina Harper cause her downfall. She would destroy Karina Harper first. She would use her intellect to find a way to get Karina Harper out of their lives.

As she looked up to the sky she began to speak to her dead husband.

"You should have finished off that Harper family when you got the chance twenty years ago, Rory. But, as ever, it's been left to me to clean up the mess you left behind. One of those Harpers has come home to roost and now I have to finish what you started. And this time, I'll make sure none of them ever come back!"

Cynthia drove through the country roads of Galway. She had become quite accustomed to navigating country roads during all her painting and sketching for Pietch. She had also become quite accustomed to spying on people. She hated that word – spying. She was not spying on people for Pietch, she was researching. And she was very good at it. She had been trained to research people in her role during the War of Independence. She had discovered then that nobody is as they portray themselves to the world. There was always something else hiding behind the veneer. And the very fact that something was being hidden usually meant the person was ashamed of it. Once you found out what each person was hiding, then you had them in the palm of your hand. And Cynthia knew the best way to find out what was behind the veneer was to start at the beginning. Right at the beginning where the person was born and brought up.

As she turned into the gateway of Inishwood, Cynthia knew this was where the story started for Karina Harper. She parked the car and looked up at the huge gates, half locked and half hanging off their pillars. She edged through the gap and peered up the long wild, overgrown avenue. She carefully made her way up the track until she came to the ruins of the great house. As she walked up to the ruins, she imagined why Karina Harper felt such pride in herself. She imagined her as a young girl there being brought up in such wealth and privilege. As she entered the ruined house, she felt a huge sense of pride that her husband had been responsible for its destruction and for forcing the family to flee.

"You did a good job, Rory – but not good enough!" she said as she took a final look around the house and made her way back to the motorcar.

* * *

"You are a relative of the Harper family, you said?" asked the vicar as he continued to plough through the ledgers of births, deaths and marriages in the parish archives.

They were in the vicar's study, in his house located in the grounds of the Protestant church in Inishwood.

"A cousin – once removed," said Cynthia, with the sweetest smile she could give.

"Yes, I remember the Harper family when I came here as a young curate some twenty-five years ago. There was the father Percy, the mother Penny and the most delightful young girl." He paused to think back.

"That's right – Karina – whose birth certificate we are searching for," said Cynthia, wishing he could talk and work at the same time.

"We never saw them again around here after the – the – tragedy." He gave Cynthia a sorrowful look.

Cynthia returned an understanding sorrowful look.

"Penny and the daughter fled to London after the great house fire and we heard of the subsequent death of Mr Harper. I did wonder what happened to them since?"

"Alive and well, I am glad to report. And we are just looking for a copy of Karina's birth certificate for her," said Cynthia, reminding him again of what he was looking for and nodding down at the archives for him to continue his search.

"Yes ... she was an American, the mother," said the vicar.

"Really?" said Cynthia, very surprised by this news. "Yes, she was – she is!"

"Not a bad-looking woman," said the vicar as he began to drift off again.

"Did they get married here?" asked Cynthia.

"I'm not so sure. That would have been before my time. I'm sure they got married in some big cathedral as a society wedding. They were very well connected, you know. Were you not there?"

"I–I lived in South Africa at the time and had lost contact with the family for years and have only been reacquainted recently ... I wonder should I get a copy of Penny's marriage certificate while I'm here? In case they decide that they want one sometime in the future – so we'd best we take a look for it while I'm here! So – *sharp, sharp* – vicar! Stand aside and let me assist you in the search!" She pushed the surprised vicar out of the way and began to riffle through the archives at an alarming pace.

Cynthia held a copy of Karina's baptismal certificate and studied it intently.

In accordance with the rites and tradition of the
Church of Ireland Church at Inishwood
the following baptism took place
on the 1st of May 1910

Date and Place of Birth – 12th of April 1910,
Inishwood House, Galway

Name (if any) – Karina Alexandria Harper

Sex – Female

Name and Surname and Dwelling House of Father

Percy Rupert Harper, Inishwood House

Name and Surname and Maiden name of Mother

Penelope Curtis Harper

There was nothing remarkable about the baptismal record. But Cynthia did find it intriguing that Penny was an American. She needed to find out more about this side of the family. As for her father's side, they were a well-known gentry family who had lived in the same house for three hundred years before it was burned down – she felt if there was anything scandalous there it would already be known. The only interesting thing that had ever happened to the Harpers was the fact Rory had burned their house down, Cynthia thought wryly.

As she continued to sift through the archives, the vicar looked on confused.

"Can I be of any more assistance?" he asked.

"No, thank you, I can manage fine!" said Cynthia.

Now she had Karina's parents' names she was going to check to make sure they did not get married at that very same church. It was true, as the vicar said, that as Percy Harper was a well-known member of the peerage it would be normal to have a grand society wedding. But the fact that Karina's mother was American might have made them do something a little unconventional.

With delight, Cynthia finally came across the marriage cert. They had indeed been married at the local Protestant church at Inishwood.

"*Yes!*" she cried as she held up the archive, the bemused vicar staring at her.

Marriage Solemnized at the Protestant Church of Ireland Chapel of Inishwood in the Registrar's District of Killa in the County of Galway

*

Name and Surname – Percy Rupert Harper

Age 38

Condition – Bachelor

Residence at time of Marriage – Inishwood House, Galway

Rank or Profession – Farmer

Father's Name – Bertram Harper

Rank or profession of Father – Farmer

*

Name and Surname – Penelope Ruth Curtis

Age 27

Condition – Spinster

Residence of time of Marriage – Astoria, New York

Rank or Profession –

Father's name – Joseph Curtis

Rank or Profession – Banker

Cynthia took out her notebook and jotted down the details.

"Is there anything else I can help you with?" asked the vicar as he showed her to the door.

"No, I won't take up any more of your time. Thank you for all your assistance."

"Oh, it was my pleasure. It kept me busy. I am so quiet these days. The days of the births and marriages in my parish are few and far between now. I only seem to get the occasional death to register and funeral to preside over," he sighed.

"There aren't many Protestants living in the area still?" asked Cynthia.

"Very few. Most left since independence."

Cynthia nodded her understanding and then spotted an opportunity to do some work for Pietch.

"Tell me, vicar, are there any Jewish families living in the area?" she asked with a big smile.

As Cynthia drove back to Dublin that evening she felt satisfied with her day's work. Satisfied but with many more questions to be answered. She was getting a whole picture of Karina's family background from the marriage certificate. Karina's mother had a blank space for her profession or rank. Her father, Joseph, had been a banker. She came from a place called Astoria in New York. It sounded very posh and wealthy. Cynthia decided that Karina's mother had been an American heiress who had married into the peerage. That happened a lot – American millionaires' daughters marrying into aristocratic families in Britain and Ireland. One got the other's money in exchange for offering a position in society through marriage.

Cynthia continued on her journey home, feeling she had made significant progress.

CHAPTER 49

"But, my darling – in all honesty – do you *really* want to come with me to Berlin!" asked Gabriel as he and Karina walked down Grafton Street arm in arm.

"But of course! Why not?" she insisted.

"Because it's far too dangerous with the war going on."

"But from what I hear Berlin is operating absolutely as if times were normal. Other than there being a frustration that the British have not capitulated yet and the war is dragging on longer than they feel it should." She was recalling what she had read in the correspondence from Berlin she had spied on in his study. "As I told you, I have an Irish passport as I was born here, so I will be travelling there as a neutral, just like you."

He stopped walking and stared at her.

"As much as I'd be breaking protocol taking you with me, I can't bear the thought of leaving you behind," he admitted.

"And, as I am fluent in German, I will be of great assistance to you over there," she teased him.

"I do believe my German is better than yours, madam," he said.

"In your dreams!" she said, laughing.

Arm in arm, they continued to walk.

In truth, he did not want to leave her behind. Even now that they were engaged, he couldn't quell the fear that she might disappear.

The telephone rang and Gabriel walked into the drawing room to answer it.

"Hello, Ford here."

"Gabriel, it's your mother," came Cynthia's voice on the other end of the phone.

He paused as he did not know what to do. He was tempted to hang up.

"Don't hang up ... I've telephoned to apologise. I have been atrocious – truly terrible. I feel ashamed of how I spoke," she said, sounding contrite.

Gabriel was astonished. He had never heard his mother apologise before.

"Well – your behaviour and language were very shocking," he said.

"I know. I am so embarrassed. I guess I just got a shock meeting Karina in such an unconventional way."

"The timing was bad, but that still gave you no excuse to speak of her the way you did."

"I can't apologise enough. I'm not condoning the fact that Karina appears to be – living with you – before marriage. But the fact you are engaged does possibly throw a different light on your relationship with her."

"I'm glad you see it like that."

"Oh, I do! I would like to meet Karina in more normal circumstances. I would like for you both to come to Roxford for dinner and give us all a chance to meet her properly. I'm sure she is a lovely girl, we just got off to a bad start."

"I appreciate what you are trying to do. I would have to check with her."

"Of course. I want us to be friends, Gabriel. I just want all of us to be friends. Speak to Karina and I'll telephone you tomorrow to check," said Cynthia and then she hung up.

Gabriel replaced the receiver, hoping he could take Cynthia at her word.

CHAPTER 50

On the evening Karina and Gabriel were due to come for dinner at Roxford, Tess and Tim were getting ready in their bedroom.

"I don't know why the old girl is having Karina Harper over for dinner – she despises everything about her," said Tim as Tess fixed his tie.

"Knowing Cynthia, she isn't having her over to welcome her into the family! She's up to something for sure."

"Karina Harper is walking herself into a trap," said Tim.

"Let her walk! Gabriel meeting Karina Harper is the best thing that ever happened for you and me, Tim. Gabriel is being destroyed through his relationship with her."

"I nearly feel sorry for him," said Tim.

"Don't feel one bit sorry for Gabriel. He didn't feel sorry for you when Cynthia was ending your career and throwing you to the wolves – now, it's payback time."

She stood back and inspected how he looked.

"Now tonight, you just remember – no drink! No matter how much alcohol is flowing – do not take a sip, Tim! Do you hear me?"

"Yes, I hear you!" he said grumpily.

Karina was filled with trepidation as Gabriel drove them through the narrow roads of Dalkey for dinner with the Ford family. She really did not want to go, but she saw how much it meant for Gabriel and she did not want him disturbed in any way in the lead-up to their trip to Berlin. Besides, she was curious to see the home of the man who had killed her father.

"Are you alright?" Gabriel asked as they drove through the large gateway of Roxford.

"Of course. I'm looking forward to getting to know your family," she said with a smile. As she looked up at the medium-sized pretty manor house she felt her resentment build.

Gabriel brought the motorcar to a stop and they both got out of the vehicle.

Karina's high heels crunched along the gravel driveway until they reached the front door. Gabriel knocked and a minute later Cynthia swung the door open and stood there resplendent in a cream sequined gown.

"Gabriel!" she said as she reached forward and kissed his cheek and beckoned both of them into the hallway.

"Mother – this is Karina. I think you already met," said Gabriel.

"Good evening, Mrs Ford," said Karina.

"Ah, Karina – you are so welcome to Roxford," said Cynthia as she shook her hand.

She began to usher them into the drawing room.

"I hardly recognised you with your clothes on," she said under her breath, just loud enough for Karina to hear.

Karina realised in an instant that she had walked into a lion's den. Cynthia Ford had no intention of ever accepting her as a daughter-in-law and the whole evening was to be a charade to pretend to Gabriel that the family were accepting her. Karina realised she would have to be extra vigilant as Cynthia would try her best to either put Gabriel off her that evening or put Karina off marrying into the family. As she had no intention of ever marrying into that family, she really didn't care how they might try to turn her off. But she had to be careful they did not try to derail Gabriel. She hadn't waited this long to finally have her chance to go to Berlin scuppered by Cynthia Ford at the final fence.

As she walked into the drawing room she was immediately struck by a giant portrait of Rory Ford hanging on the wall, staring right down at her. She immediately felt queasy and dizzy at the very sight of his face. She felt claustrophobic and fought the need to run away from this place, the home of her father's murderer.

"So – this is Karina – Karina Harper," announced Cynthia as she placed a hand on Karina's back and pushed her further into the room.

Karina saw there were three other people waiting in the room. A good-looking brunette in a red cocktail dress, an older man who was dressed as a priest and the man she had met in Restaurant Jammet that night. Tim, Gabriel's brother.

As she stared at Tim, the uncanny likeness he bore to his father was overwhelming for her again and she felt herself become nauseous. She glanced up at the portrait of Rory Ford and then to Tim's identical features in front of her and she was transported back to that night in Inishwood, seeing her father being viciously struck and falling to the floor.

"You met my brother, Tim, before, Karina," said Gabriel.

"Indeed she did!" said Tim, coming forward with a big smile and grabbing her hand and shaking it.

His very touch made her shiver in horror.

"I hope you don't faint on us this time!" Tim said with a wink.

"And this is Tim's beautiful wife, Tess," said Cynthia.

"I have been hearing all about you!" said Tess with a big smile as she stepped forward and shook her hand. "Every last detail!"

"And this is a very good friend of our family, Bishop Roche," said Cynthia.

Gabriel was surprised the bishop was there. It was only supposed to be the family and he wondered what Cynthia was up to.

"Pleased to meet you, my child," said the Bishop as he stepped forward and, instead of shaking her hand, started to bless her over her head.

Karina glanced at Gabriel who widened his eyes but gave her a slight nod to accept the blessing.

As the Bishop stepped away from Karina, Cynthia smiled broadly. "Now, we have the introductions out of the way, I wonder will we start off the evening with the Rosary? Your Excellency – would you be so good as to lead us?"

"Of course, Cynthia. It would be my pleasure," said the Bishop and he got down on his knees.

Cynthia swished her long gown to the side as she got down on her knees and joined her hands in prayer.

Tess and Tim exchanged surprised looks then Tim reluctantly knelt down followed by Tess beside him.

"What's she doing? We never say the Rosary before a meal," whispered Tess.

"*Shhh!*" Tim hissed back.

As Gabriel got down on his knees as well, Karina looked at them all in bewilderment.

The Bishop began to recite the first decade of the Rosary.

Karina looked at Gabriel who with a slight nod indicated that she should kneel down as well. She gathered up her long gown, knelt down and joined her hands together.

The saying of the Rosary seemed to last forever.

By the time it was over, Karina felt exhausted as she staggered up from her kneeling position, her knees aching.

"I need a drink," Tim snapped at Tess as he got up.

"*Shut up and stay away from that drinks cabinet!*" Tess hissed back.

"Poor Karina," said Cynthia as she came and put an arm around her. "You'll have to get used to all this now when you are married to Gabriel. It must be a bit of a culture shock for you."

"Yes, Cynthia tells me you are one of *them*? Is that so?" asked the Bishop.

"I am a Protestant, if that is what you mean, Your Excellency," said Karina.

"For now anyway! We'll drum that out of you!" said the Bishop.

"Yes, the Bishop has very generously offered to personally instruct you on your road of converting to Catholicism, Karina," said Cynthia.

Karina's eyes widened.

"Don't look so worried, my dear, I shall go easy on you!" said the Bishop with a chuckle.

"It's not an exorcism you are conducting on the poor girl, Your Excellency – just remember that!" said Cynthia who laughed as well.

Gabriel found his voice. "Well, I'm not sure – we hadn't discussed – that is – Karina has said nothing about converting."

"Well, it would be expected, Gabriel." The Bishop's tone was suddenly stern. "And the children of course would have to be raised as Catholics – that is without negotiation, you do understand that, don't you, Gabriel?"

"Well, yes, but that doesn't mean Karina would have to –"

"Ah, and dinner is about to be served if we can all make our way to the dining room!" said Cynthia.

She grabbed Karina's arm and led her out of the room and across the hallway to the large ornate dining room.

"You can sit beside me so I can keep an eye on you," she said as she sat at the head of the table, seating Karina to her right.

"And I'll sit here, Karina, so I can keep an eye on you from the other side!" said the Bishop as he sat down next to her.

Karina felt suffocated squeezed in between the two and was grateful at least that Gabriel was seated opposite her.

"Will I serve, Mrs Ford?" asked the housekeeper who was standing at the end of the room.

"Not yet, Joan. I think we'll say Grace first. Bishop, would you be so good?"

"My pleasure!" said the Bishop, clearing his throat and saying the prayer.

As the Bishop droned on, Tess and Tim looked at each other and raised their eyes to heaven in despair. Gabriel made an apologetic face across the table to Karina who just gave a small smile back.

Finally, Grace said, Joan the housekeeper began to serve a dinner of roast beef.

"I'll fetch some wine, shall I, Mother?" said Tim.

"Oh, no, no, no," said Cynthia, shaking her forefinger. "The Bishop doesn't approve of alcohol."

A silence fell and Karina noticed three sets of raised eyebrows around the table.

"Eh, Mother mentioned you just got back from the Vatican, Your Excellency," said Gabriel.

The Bishop sighed loudly. "I did indeed, Gabriel. I am involved in many different organisations within the Vatican, trying to help the refugees from this terrible war. Trying to negotiate to bring the persecuted to some sort of sanctuary away from the Nazi menace."

"You mean the Jews, Your Excellency?" said Tess.

"Mainly, Tess, yes. Any Jews left in Germany at this stage are all in these dreadful concentration camps where I believe conditions are appalling. And they will be deporting German Jews who fled to France and the other occupied countries back to Germany to face imprisonment soon, I have no doubt. We are trying to get them to safety first."

Cynthia shifted uncomfortably in her chair before smiling broadly. "Have some more gravy, John."

"This beef is wonderful, Cynthia – so tender!" said the Bishop.

"I cooked it myself earlier today," said Cynthia. "Do you cook, Karina?"

"I'm afraid not very well," said Karina with an apologetic smile.

"Well, no doubt you had an army of servants growing up so had no need to learn the basic necessities of domestic life," said Cynthia. "Karina is a member of a very distinguished family, Your Excellency."

"So I believe, Cynthia ... an army of servants ... in other words poor Catholic people exploited by the Protestant overlords," said the Bishop.

"Actually, we had no servants once we left our home at Inishwood when I was a child. None at all – we had a very modest life in London. I would go so far as to say we lived very frugally," said Karina, hiding her anger and fury.

"Why did you leave your home at Inishwood, dear?" asked the Bishop.

"We didn't leave, Your Excellency, we were driven out. Our beautiful home was burned down after Independence," said Karina coldly, fighting the desire to shout at the Ford family that they had committed that crime. That their husband and father was responsible for ruining her life.

"And how long had you lived there?" asked the Bishop.

"Our family were there three hundred years, Your Excellency," she said, through gritted teeth.

"Imagine – three hundred years and you still have an English accent!" said the Bishop with a laugh.

"There is nothing to laugh about when an innocent family is terrorized by a bunch of hoodlums in the middle of the night – and they are forced to watch their home and all their possessions being destroyed, Your Excellency. I would have hoped you could understand that."

Gabriel and Cynthia exchanged a quick uncomfortable look.

"Of course! Very upsetting, it must have been, for a child to see," nodded the Bishop.

"Was your mother from Inishwood as well?" asked Cynthia.

"No, she's actually American, from New York," said Karina.

"How very exciting for you!" smiled Cynthia. "Have you many relatives in New York?"

"No, my grandparents on my mother's side died before I was born so I never knew them. And my mother was an only child so there really is no connection with New York anymore."

"Your mother is an only child and you are an only child too – how sad – not big breeders, are you?" said Cynthia. "And how did your father and mother meet?"

"My father was on holiday in New York and they met while he was there. It was love at first sight, or so they said," she said with a smile, causing Gabriel to smile back at her.

"How very romantic! I do like a nice romantic story with a happy ending!" said Cynthia as she clapped her hands together before her face turned sad. "Which is more than poor Siobhán got – bless her broken little heart!"

As the night wore on, Karina endured a constant trail of subtle insults, remarks, comments and underminings. She had often wondered about the men who had burned her house and struck her father. She wondered what kind of families they had and what lives they led. Now that she had met the Ford family, she realised they were every bit as hateful as she had imagined.

If she had actually been in love with Gabriel and planning a life with him, she would have run out the door in tears, heartbroken by the reception she received. But she wasn't, so their comments were like water off a duck's back to her. In fact, their ugly behaviour only strengthened her resolve to use her relationship with Gabriel to get what she wanted for a happy life.

As the Ford family talked down to her for the night, they might think they were in control and superior. But one day soon she would just walk out of their lives when she had what she wanted and leave them dealing with a heartbroken and destroyed son. As she looked at Gabriel's face, she did feel sorry that he would have to rely on these people when that time came.

"I really feel I got to know you tonight," said Cynthia as she showed Karina and Gabriel to the front door.

"And I you," Karina smiled back.

"I just feel you will fit into our family like a hand into a glove," said Cynthia.

"So do I!" agreed Karina.

"Thank you, Mother," said Gabriel as he kissed her cheek.

As Gabriel and Karina walked across the gravel driveway Cynthia waved goodbye and called goodnight before closing the door.

They sat into the motorcar.

"I am so sorry about all that," said Gabriel, turning to her. "The prayers, the politics, the conversation – it must have been hard for you."

"Oh, it was fine, Gabriel! It was a lovely evening! I always knew marrying a Catholic was going to be slightly different from what I am used to," she said.

"Slightly different! But my family aren't usually like that! We don't pray all the time and drink water with our dinner with a Bishop! I'd say Tess and Tim were more horrified than you!"

"It was fine. It was lovely – I enjoyed it," she reassured him.

"Really? You are amazing, Karina," he said as he reached over and kissed her.

Cynthia and the Bishop sat on armchairs opposite each other as they drank a large glass of red wine each.

"Well?" asked Cynthia.

"Oh, you are very right to be concerned, Cynthia. She has

bewitched him, that's plain to see," he said, taking a drink from his wine.

"Bewitched is the right word, as she is a little witch in my opinion. I have to get rid of her, John. I can't let Gabriel make the biggest mistake of his life."

"She didn't falter once there this evening despite the pressure we heaped on her. What can I do to help?"

"I need to find a crack in her armour. I went searching at Inishwood, where her family hailed from, and found nothing. I was hoping she was illegitimate or had a different father than the one she claimed or something. My only hope is that there might be something in New York on her mother's side that will destroy her. Could you use your contacts there to investigate the family?"

"Of course! I am very good friends with the Bishop of New York and have many contacts there."

"Thank you, John. So, her mother's name is Penelope Ruth Curtis – known as Penny according to the vicar in Inishwood – and she was from Astoria in New York. Her father was called Joseph and he was a banker. From the marriage cert Penny was twenty-seven when she married Karina's father in 1909, which means she was born in 1882."

"In New York?" checked the Bishop as he wrote all the information down in a notebook.

"Yes, I presume so," said Cynthia. "Do you really think you could help, John? Do you think you could locate the family in a place as big as New York?"

"Well, you have given me quite a lot of information to go on here, Cynthia. And we do have one of the biggest and most powerful networks at our disposal to help us with our search."

"Network?" said Cynthia.

"The Catholic Church," said the Bishop with a smile as he reached his glass over and clinked it against hers.

CHAPTER 51

Cynthia sat at the table in Pietch's cottage as she typed up the names and addresses from her notebooks which were laid out in front of her.

"You have done excellent work, Cynthia, collecting all these details for our records," said Pietch. "The information we are providing here will allow the authorities in Berlin to establish the numbers we are dealing with in Ireland and begin preparations. Then, once there is a German victory, we will have access to the official records and censuses in Ireland and we can use this list to cross-reference. The same process was followed in Norway and is proving very effective there."

"It's been an interesting project."

"I'm glad you've enjoyed it. I couldn't have hoped for a better partner." He handed her a piece of paper. "Could you add this name to the list as well?"

"*Mrs Anouska Levinsky, 37 Roundwood Road, Terenure,*" Cynthia read out from the paper and typed the name onto her list. "Is she an Irish Jew?"

"No, I believe she fled here from Berlin back in the thirties. A widow with two young children."

The thought of a widow with two young children reminded her of her own circumstances in life. "So ... would she be sent back to Germany after the German victory?"

"I'm not certain yet. It depends on whether she has an Irish passport now or continues to have a German one," he said in a matter-of-fact fashion.

"I see …" she said, concerned.

Pietch suddenly noticed Cynthia's troubled expression. "But I'm sure she will be allowed to stay here."

"It's just … I've heard that the Jews who are returned to Germany end up in these concentration camps that the newspapers speak so badly of," said Cynthia.

"That the *British* newspapers speak so badly of, Cynthia. It is in the British media's interest to portray the German system in as negative a light as possible. Rest assured, the camps are just detention centres that are properly managed to detain undesirables for indefinite lengths of time to keep them from causing trouble for the general population."

She nodded and continued typing.

"When is your son due to go to Berlin?" asked Pietch.

Cynthia stopped typing and looked up at him. As much as she trusted and liked Pietch, something was holding her back from divulging too much information about Gabriel's visit to Germany.

"Next week, I believe … it's a peace mission, to foster good relations between Ireland and Germany."

"Of course, isn't that what we all want? He will receive a warm welcome, no doubt," said Pietch with a smile.

Cynthia continued typing.

"But now that we have nearly finished compiling the list, we have a problem, Cynthia," said Pietch.

"Oh?"

"How do we get this document, this very important document back to Germany?"

"Why can you not just post it? As you did with my drawings and paintings?"

"It would be far too dangerous to do so. If your drawings and paintings were opened by the authorities here, they could easily be explained as just art being posted to art dealers abroad … but a list of some four thousand Jews living in Ireland – that would open up very uncomfortable questions."

"Can you not just sneak it out with one of your agents?"

"It's become far too difficult with the war worsening. Everything and everyone is being searched thoroughly at Customs ... but I think *you* have the solution to our problem."

"I have?"

"Your son. Gabriel."

"Gabriel?" Cynthia was alarmed. "But how could Gabriel help?"

"We simply wrap up the papers in a parcel and hand it to Gabriel and tell him they are your drawings to be delivered to an art gallery in Berlin. I'll provide you with the details of the gallery acting as a front for us."

"But-but ..." She was alarmed at the idea of involving Gabriel.

"It is an ideal cover. He will be flying out on a private plane no doubt as a government diplomat on an important mission. Nobody will check his luggage or anything he is carrying. Then he will deliver it safely into the right hands in Berlin. It could not be more ideal."

Cynthia looked at the lists of names she had typed up and became more disturbed as she digested Pietch's plan.

Cynthia poured tea from the silver teapot into Bishop Roche's china cup as he sat in an armchair in the drawing room at Roxford. She had laid out a display of cakes and buns on the low table before him.

"You always have the most delicious confectionary, Cynthia," he said as he gleefully took in the display before him.

"Thank you, John. I baked it all myself."

"I don't know where you put your hands on all the ingredients during the rationing."

"I have my contacts," she said, winking at him as she sat down opposite him.

"And I have mine, Cynthia, in New York amongst other places," he said and winked back at her.

"Oh! Have you found out anything about our new friend, John?" She leaned towards him.

"Indeed I have, Cynthia, indeed I have," he said as his face became grave.

"Well?"

"Karina's mother was not an American heiress as you supposed, Cynthia," he said.

319

"But her father was a banker and they lived in Astoria – was that area not named after America's richest man, Mr Astor?"

"Yes, but Mr Astor never set foot in the place. Penny grew up in an exceptionally ordinary house on an exceptionally ordinary street."

"Really!"

"As for her father, Joseph Curtis, being a millionaire banker, he was a lowly banking clerk at the Chase Manhattan Bank."

"I see!" she gasped.

"And I don't think Penny had much of a career apart from typing before her marriage."

"Why ever did Harper marry her?"

"As Karina said, it must have been love … but there is more, Cynthia."

"Pray continue, John!"

"It wasn't just Penny's lower-class background that was kept hidden at the time … Penny's family are Jewish, Cynthia – on both sides. Penny is Jewish and so were both her parents."

Cynthia sat in silence, staring in shock.

"But it can't be," she said eventually. "They are Protestants!"

"Karina was baptised a Protestant but she is half Jewish," said the Bishop as he reached into his pocket, took out some documents and handed them over to Cynthia.

She unfolded them and read them, studying every word. They were the birth certificates for both of Penny's parents and their marriage certificate which had been carried out at a synagogue.

"I cannot believe it!" Cynthia was stunned.

"I have been carefully checking into the Harper family and everybody has always thought that Penny was a Protestant. She has been passing herself off as one ever since she left America to marry Karina's father."

"But why would she do such a thing? I mean it might be understandable now with everything happening on the Continent. But back then?"

"To avoid the anti-Semitism that is present in the British and Irish aristocracy, I imagine. So that nobody would be able to look down on the Harper family."

"But how has she got away with this for decades?" asked Cynthia.

"Quite easily. She left behind everyone and everything she knew in New York when she left to come and live in Europe. Her mother was already dead, her father died a year after the marriage. She was an only child. There was nothing to connect her with the Jewish faith anymore and she let it go and disguised herself as a Protestant to fit into her new aristocratic world."

"The woman has lived her life as a lie!"

"And so has Karina," added the Bishop.

"But this changes everything! I mean, how could Gabriel marry her now? The Jews in Europe aren't allowed civil service jobs, or bank accounts or to own property – and that's just in the recently occupied countries like France and Norway and Holland. As for what is happening to the Jews in Germany and Poland ..." She trailed off uneasily. "When the war is won by the Germans, the same thing will happen here. Gabriel's life will be destroyed!"

"I know, Cynthia. It's not even legal for a so-called Aryan to marry a Jew in Germany."

Cynthia stood up abruptly in a panic. "I have to stop him. He will end up in prison or one of those camps if he goes through with this!"

"Calm down, Cynthia!" The Bishop stood and put his hands on her shoulders "If you say anything of this to Gabriel, it will only strengthen his resolve to marry Karina. You know how stubborn he is and he is quite clearly besotted with her."

"But what shall I do, John?"

"Use your intellect, Cynthia. You'll figure this out with that brain of yours – you always have before," said the Bishop reassuringly.

CHAPTER 52

The telephone on Gabriel's desk at work rang and he answered it.

"Gabriel? It's your mother," came a calm, sweet voice down the phone line.

"Oh, hello, mother," said Gabriel, sitting back in his chair.

"Just phoning to say thank you for bringing Karina over to meet us for dinner," said Cynthia.

"Well – thank you for having us!"

"I hope it wasn't too much for her?"

"Too much?"

"Well, perhaps it was a mistake to invite the Bishop along. I hadn't realised he would be quite so intense talking about converting Karina to Catholicism and whatnot."

Gabriel smiled to himself. He knew Cynthia knew exactly what she was doing bringing the Bishop that night and the Bishop had fulfilled his role superbly.

"Oh, it didn't knock a feather out of Karina. She's quite resilient, you know," he said.

"Yes, she looks it. All that typing obviously hardens the soul!"

Gabriel smiled as he heard his mother unable to resist getting a dig in.

"Anyway, I just wanted to ask you when are you travelling to Berlin?" she said.

"We are leaving Wednesday morning. We are flying to Stockholm first and then on to Berlin. It's the safest route for now," said Gabriel.

"We?"

"Yes, Karina and I."

There was silence on the other side of the phone.

"Mother?" Gabriel said eventually.

"I didn't realise Karina would be going too."

"Well, yes, I would have preferred not. But she insists!" He couldn't admit that he was afraid to leave her behind in case she disappeared.

"Yes, I see … anyway, I'm sure you know what you are doing. The purpose of my call really is to ask a huge favour."

"Of course – if I can."

"You see – it's quite a coincidence actually – a fairly lucrative order for my work came in from a distinguished art gallery in Berlin of all places! It's not a large package – just sketches and postcards – no paintings. But I got a shock down at the post office when they told me how much it would cost me! And, in any case, I'm a bit nervous it might go astray in the present climate. Could you find space in your suitcase to take them over and deliver them?"

"Yes, I can do that for you, Mother," said Gabriel.

"Thank you, Gabriel, you are so kind. Where are you staying in Berlin?"

"The Hotel Kaiserhof – it's in the heart of the government area so good for my meetings."

"Alright. Well, I shall see you before you leave."

"Yes, of course," said Gabriel.

Cynthia replaced the receiver on the telephone in the sitting room of Pietch's cottage and turned around to face him.

"Well?" asked Pietch.

"Gabriel said he will carry the package for me to Berlin."

"Excellent!" said Pietch, smiling broadly.

Cynthia sat back down at the table and continued typing the last list of names and addresses they had accumulated.

"Well, I think that is our work nearly done here, Cynthia. Nearly four thousand names in total," said Pietch. "We will package the papers this evening and you can give them to Gabriel tomorrow. Are you certain he can be trusted to do what he says and deliver them to the gallery in Berlin? He won't forget to do it – or lose the package – or open it out of curiosity – will he?"

"Gabriel would never do any of those things. When Gabriel says he will do something, he will do it. It's what I have always loved – and sometimes despaired of about him."

"Excellent!" said Pietch. "This work we have done together will be of enormous benefit to the Führer – and to Ireland after the war is won. You won't be forgotten for what you have done here, Cynthia."

Cynthia stopped typing and looked up at Pietch. "What will happen to the names once Gabriel hands them over to your contact?"

"They will be transferred to Gestapo headquarters where the names will be analysed and checked. They will see which Jews are foreign nationals living here and whether there any names on the list that are political activists, communists, enemies of the people. They will all be filed away for future reference."

"It would never be – it can never be revealed that I had any part in this, can it?" said Cynthia.

"Absolutely not, Cynthia! You can trust us – we appreciate our friends and would never betray them."

Cynthia nodded and stared at the page still sitting in the typewriter.

"I'll just make us a cup of tea," said Pietch as he walked into the kitchen.

Cynthia continued to stare at the paper in front of her and then she began to type.

To the bottom of the list she added one more name:

Karina Harper, 32 Victoria Terrace, Monkstown
Staying at the Kaiserhof Hotel, Berlin

The pages with all the names and addresses were neatly stacked on Pietch's table in the sitting room, ready to be wrapped in brown paper.

"What time is Gabriel's flight tomorrow?" he asked.

"Early in the morning. So he is expecting me this evening, to say goodbye and give him the package."

"Excellent."

"I'll fetch some glasses and that bottle of wine I brought so we can celebrate!" she said.

"Yes, we must!" He laid out two layers of brown paper on the table, placed the typed pages on top and began to wrap.

"*Tut-tut!*" said Cynthia. "I always find men are so clumsy at wrapping. Let me do it!"

She stepped forward and waved him away.

"If you insist! Though I assure you I am not clumsy at anything!"

"You fetch the wine!" she said.

"With pleasure!"

As he went into the kitchen, Cynthia reached into her pocket and quickly took out Karina's baptismal certificate along with her mother's birth and her parents and grandparents' marriage certificates and slipped them in amongst the papers about to be wrapped. Then she folded the brown paper around the entire stack, picked up the scissors and began to cut the excess paper away.

"Make sure it's secure!" urged Pietch as he returned with the wine and two glasses. "Use plenty adhesive tape!"

Cynthia began to apply the tape and then cut string and tied up the package securely.

Once Cynthia had finished, Pietch inspected it and, happy with the job done, he took up a fountain pen on the table and wrote the address on the brown paper.

> *Günter Durchdenwald*
> *Durchdenwald Art Gallery*
> *Josefstrasse*
> *Michaelkirchplatz*
> *Berlin*

"And we are finally done, Cynthia," said Pietch as he lifted up the package held it out to her.

Cynthia tentatively reached forward and took the package into her hands.

"And now let's celebrate!" said Pietch.

CHAPTER 53

It was the evening before their departure for Berlin and Karina could hardly believe it was finally happening as she packed her suitcase in their bedroom at Victoria Terrace. She felt extremely nervous about travelling into the heart of the Nazi empire. But this was overtaken by the utter excitement that she would be able to finally track Hugo down. She wouldn't be relying on Julian or Emily or Kendrick to drip back information or lie to her. She could go to the Friedrich family who were hiding him. She wondered if he would still be with them or would have been moved elsewhere by now. In any case, they would know where he was and take her to him. She took Hugo's precious British entry permit and placed it carefully in her handbag. This was Hugo's ticket to freedom. With it, he would be allowed entry into neutral Switzerland and from there fly to Barcelona, there being no flights to Britain because of the war. He could then transit neutral Spain and Portugal to reach Lisbon, the main point of exit for refugees from the Continent. From there he could get a boat or possibly fly to Britain. Exiting Germany would be the problem. Without an exit permit it might involve a perilous illegal crossing. She had great hopes the Friedrich family would be able to assist.

Her main concern was to find him first.

"Nearly packed?" asked Gabriel as he walked into the bedroom.

"Just about!" she said as she closed over her suitcase.

"Darling," he said, taking her by the hand and sitting her down on the bed beside him. "I have something to show you."

He produced a ring box and handed it over to her.

She blinked a few times as she took it and opened it to see a stunning diamond engagement ring inside it.

"Gabriel ..."

"Do you like it?" he asked as he took the ring out of the box and placed it on her finger. "A perfect fit! Just like you are for me." He leaned forward and kissed her.

"Gabriel ... I don't know what to say ..."

"Say you like it!"

"I love it – but it's too much," she objected.

"It's no more than you deserve but because we got engaged so quickly and under unusual circumstances, I hadn't time to get a ring. But now it's official – we are engaged!"

She looked into his face and her forehead creased. "You really love me, don't you?"

"Of course. I wouldn't be marrying you if I didn't!" he said with a laugh.

"Well, you were marrying Siobhán and you didn't love her!"

"You bitch!" he said in mock horror.

There was a knock on the door.

"I think that's Mother – she was dropping over to say goodbye," said Gabriel, kissing her.

Karina watched him go before she looked down at the diamond ring and bit her lip.

"You will be careful over there, Gabriel?" said Cynthia anxiously. "It's not like a normal diplomatic trip. There's all kinds of things happening in Germany these days."

"Of course I will," said Gabriel.

"And let's hope you can secure peace between our two countries."

"Why does that make me feel like Chamberlain in Munich in '38?" frowned Gabriel.

"Well, as long as you don't come back waving a piece of paper assuring us of peace in our time like he did!"

"Is that the package you want me to deliver for you?" he asked, indicating the large brown-papered package under her arm.

"Yes ... yes, it is," she said as she held it out. "The delivery address is written on the front. The Durchdenwald Gallery. You are to give it to Mr Durchdenwald himself. He's expecting it."

"Will do," he said as he reached out to take the package.

She pulled it back. "You will be careful with it, Gabriel? You won't leave it lying around a hotel suite or anything? Take it as soon as you can to the gallery."

"First opportunity I get I shall go to the gallery and hand it to Mr Durchdenwald personally," he assured her.

"Make sure you give it to nobody else ... I'd hate for it to go astray. I put so much work into this."

"Artists and their work!" he said as he prised it from her hands. "I will put it straight into my suitcase now."

"Good evening, Cynthia," said Karina from the doorway.

Cynthia gave an uncharacteristic startled jump at hearing her voice. "Hello, Karina."

"Can I get you a tea or coffee?"

"No, I was just going ... I only dropped in to say farewell to Gabriel ... and to you, of course."

"Come here, darling," said Gabriel and, when she did, he took her hand and raised it to show off the ring.

"Oh!" said Cynthia.

"Do you like it?" asked Gabriel, with a big smile.

"Very ... very nice," Cynthia said, trying to hide the whirlwind of emotions she was feeling.

"He's very kind," said Karina, embarrassed by the size of the diamond.

"Yes, he is ... he deserves the best ... goodbye, Karina ... it was nice meeting you."

With a quick nod, Cynthia hurried out.

As Gabriel followed her, Karina wondered at Cynthia's strange choice of words

BOOK 4

SEPTEMBER TO DECEMBER 1940

CHAPTER 54

As the small plane crossed over the North Sea on its way to Stockholm, Karina looked out the window at the water below. Gabriel was engrossed in paperwork beside her. So many thoughts were rushing through her head and she was filled with anxiety and stress. Travelling to the heart of the Nazi empire was filling her with fear. Suddenly, she was acutely aware of her Jewish ancestry. And now, as she was going to a place that was persecuting and imprisoning Jewish people, she felt frightened. She dismissed the fear. Nobody knew of her Jewish ancestry and she was travelling as a neutral. She was completely safe, and she must concentrate on now finding and rescuing Hugo.

She glanced at Gabriel who looked up from his paperwork and smiled at her. She wondered when he would become surplus to requirement. Would she abandon him in Berlin once she had found Hugo and they had the opportunity to leave together? Or would she continue to play Gabriel along in case she needed his diplomatic status over there or he was of some other use to her? She wondered how he would cope when he found out she had been using him and had no intention of ever marrying him. She was suddenly overcome by a feeling of deep shame at how she was treating him. As she felt consumed with guilt, she forced herself to think of what his family had done to hers. Whatever upset he would feel when she jilted him was a drop in the ocean compared to the destruction and pain his family had inflicted on hers.

After landing in Stockholm, Gabriel and Karina were transferred to another plane which flew them south over the Baltic Sea to Germany. As their plane flew over Berlin, Karina looked down at the massive metropolis of four million people stretched out below. There had been an air raid on Berlin two weeks earlier on August 25th which had mainly targeted the Tempelhof Airport. This meant the plane they were travelling in was diverted to a small airfield north of the city.

As they disembarked, she thought it strange that she had campaigned so long to get there and now she just wanted to get out of Germany as quickly as possible.

A motorcar was waiting for them and, as it drove them into the city, she viewed the familiar sights of Berlin. As she studied the busy streets, life in Berlin did not seem that different to her from what it was before the war. Unlike London and the other British cities that were now being bombarded each night by the Luftwaffe, the Berlin bombings had been sporadic and had not inflicted much physical damage. Berlin was at the very far reach of the flight ability of the British air force, making an attack on the city difficult to carry out. Also, the civilian population had not been the target of the air raids so there had been few civilian casualties.

As their motorcar pulled up outside the majestic Kaiserhof Hotel, Karina felt that Berlin was a city at the zenith of its power, bursting with confidence after all the military victories. A city waiting impatiently for a final victory in the war, so it could be established as the new undisputed capital of Europe.

As Karina stepped out of the motorcar, she looked at the Nazi flags hanging over the doorway of the hotel and hid the shiver that ran through her body. The hotel was beside Hitler's Reich Chancellery and across the street from the Ministry of Enlightenment and Propaganda in the heart of the government district. As such, it was a favourite of the Nazi elite, and had established itself as the epicentre of the Nazi social scene.

As they went through the doors, they passed a Gestapo officer walking out with a blonde woman on either arm as they all laughed uproariously at something he had said.

The foyer was gigantic and luxurious and filled with people. As Karina looked around, she realised that the majority of the men were wearing high-ranking military uniforms and there were members of the Gestapo everywhere. There were beautiful women, dressed glamorously, drinking champagne with them at the different tables while a fleet of waiters continually served them. A blonde woman was singing a seductive song in a throaty voice while a pianist accompanied her on a grand piano in the corner of the foyer.

Karina looked through the doors into the hotel bar which was full of people in party mood while, on a landing up a central staircase, impeccably dressed waiters were hurrying in and out of the restaurant, holding aloft trays of food. It was all so different from the atmosphere and mood in London, a city under siege. The war had already been won in German minds.

At reception, they filled in the forms provided and handed them back.

"Thank you so much," said the receptionist. "And may I can have your passports, please?"

Karina looked at him. "Why do you need my passport?"

"It is our policy to hold the passports of our guests during their stay. They will be quite safe – they are held in the hotel safe."

Karina hesitated as all her instincts were telling her not to part with her passport. The idea of being in Nazi Germany without it seemed unwise – to the point of being dangerous if her secrets were ever revealed.

"Passports, please!" repeated the receptionist as he held out a hand.

Gabriel reached into his inside pocket. Taking out his passport, he handed it to the woman.

Karina nervously opened her handbag, took out her passport and handed it over.

"Thank you!" said the receptionist.

He went to the safe and put the passports in, before returning to the service desk and ringing the bell loudly for a bellboy to take their suitcases to their room.

Their suite was large and luxurious with a black-and-white tiled bathroom. They had made a booking in the hotel restaurant for dinner and, as Gabriel had a bath, Karina stood at the window in the bedroom looking out at the Chancery building across the street. It was hard for her to comprehend that she was near the heart of all the decision-making that was bringing Europe to its knees. More importantly for her, as she looked out at the Berlin skyline under the darkening sky, was Hugo looking out at the same scene? She planned to visit the Friedrich house the next day and could barely contain her excitement at the thought of seeing Hugo again.

As she looked around the hotel room, she knew she'd had enough of this life. She was coming to the end of the lifestyle she had lived for so long. The clubs, the parties, the swanky hotels, the short-term relationships – she wanted more than that. She wanted her own home with Hugo and to have her own family. She didn't want to be at the mercy of others, staying in a flat provided by the strangers in the Secret Service or at Gabriel's house.

Gabriel came out of the bathroom in a hotel dressing gown, drying his hair. He came up behind her, put his arms around and hugged her.

"The city looks very romantic, doesn't it?" he whispered as he kissed her neck.

"How?" she snapped. "How the hell does it look romantic when there are Nazi flags hanging from every building?"

He pulled back from her and looked at her, startled.

"Are you finished in the bathroom?" she said. "I need to get ready or we shall be late for our dinner reservation."

He watched her walk across the bedroom and into the bathroom where she closed the door. A few seconds later he heard her turn the lock in the door.

Feeling confused, he turned and stared out the window at the city's skyline.

An hour later, Karina and Gabriel stepped out of one of the lifts into the foyer which seemed even busier than it had been earlier. Gabriel was wearing black tie and Karina was dressed in a silver dress with a pearl necklace and pearl bracelet, her blonde wavy hair loose. As they walked into the restaurant a couple of Gestapo officers walked out and nodded admiringly to Karina. She ignored them.

As Gabriel studied Karina while she spoke to the maître d', his confusion continued to intensify. She seemed like a different person since they had arrived in Berlin. She suddenly seemed cold and offhand with him, the way she had been with him in Great Hankerton Hall. He wondered was it just the shock of being in Berlin and the stark reality of being surrounded by so many Nazis. He was beginning to regret bringing her. They were shown to a round table in the very centre of the restaurant. A band was playing lively music and there were couples on the dance floor in front of the stage. The maître d' pulled out a chair for Karina and she sat down.

Gabriel sat opposite her. He took up the menu and began to study it. When the waiter arrived, Karina took charge as she ordered the duck for herself and the pork for Gabriel.

As they finished their starters, the plates were cleared away and the main courses were served. Karina seemed in a world of her own, Gabriel thought, and not that interested in conversing beyond the bare minimum.

Karina observed that the mood in the room was getting merrier and louder as the night wore on and the drink flowed.

"Right about now, our air force is dropping tons of explosives on what was once the great city of London," announced an Oberführer in full military uniform to the small audience of six who sat at his table. The four men were all senior military men, the two women glamorous blondes in spectacular evening wear.

"How many nights this week is that?" asked one of the blondes.

"Every night, my dear! And every night they will be receiving the same present from the Führer until they realise their resistance is futile."

"But why have they not surrendered yet, Klaus? Why are they continuing this defiance?"

"It's hard for a once great nation to admit they are finished. The French had to be taught the hard way and so it is with the British. But if they don't surrender soon, there will be no country left for them to surrender after it is flattened by our air force!"

The whole table laughed heartily.

Karina tried to contain her anger. She became anxious and upset as she thought of everyone she knew in London suffering such terrible bombardment day after day, night after night.

At the table on the other side of them were members of the Gestapo.

"We have already started to seize all the property owned by wealthy Jews in Paris. They are powerless to object," said one of them.

"Are the French authorities objecting?" asked another.

"They have no power to object to anything. The Jews in France must learn the same as the Jews in Germany did that they can no longer expect privileges – they have no future in Europe."

Karina suddenly stood up, knocking over a glass of red wine on the white linen tablecloth.

"Karina?" asked Gabriel, concerned.

"I need to leave," she said as she marched away from the table towards the exit.

Then a Nazi officer stood in front of her, blocking her.

She pulled back in fright.

"Would you care to dance, my pretty?" asked the officer.

Karina shook her head and quickly hurried from the restaurant.

Gabriel hurried out after her and saw her disappear into the lift.

"Karina!" he called after her.

But she was gone.

"Would you like to explain to me what all that was about?" Gabriel demanded as he let himself into the suite and found Karina sitting at a window, smoking a cigarette.

She ignored him.

"*Karina!*" he demanded as he walked crossly over to her.

"What?" she snapped at him.

"What the fuck has got into you? You are being cold and unpleasant, and you are acting like a split personality!" he said angrily.

She fought the overriding desire to tell him the truth about everything. But she knew it was too soon. She couldn't blow her cover yet. Not until she found Hugo.

"There is nothing the matter with me," she said coolly. "I am just tired after the long journey."

He stood away from her and stared at her.

"I can do difficult, Karina – but I can't do impossible!" he warned as he turned and walked towards the door. "I'm going to the bar downstairs."

He left the room, slamming the door after him.

She inhaled on her cigarette and turned to stare out the window.

Gabriel sat at a bar, downing another whiskey. It was now midnight. After the altercation with Karina he had left the hotel and gone walking through the streets until he found a tavern. Everyone looked happy and people were singing and dancing.

He didn't know what was wrong with Karina. They had been getting on so well in Dublin. He felt they had really connected. Then were engaged for God's sake! Then since they arrived in Berlin she was acting like a stranger.

Suddenly the bar manager jumped on the bar and started shouting to the crowd.

The band stopped playing.

He spoke energetically, pointing to the exit.

Gabriel found it hard to understand his accent and idiom but the words "air raid" were explanation enough.

Suddenly everyone was leaving the bar, looking angry and fed up. Gabriel grabbed his coat and quickly followed suit.

As Karina sat in darkness at the window of the hotel room, she wondered where Gabriel had got to. Suddenly she heard a buzzing sound. The sound was getting louder and louder.

Then she saw a plane flying over the city, coming in her direction. As she slowly stood up, she stared at what turned out to be a series of planes as they began to drop bombs and the air-raid sirens began to sound.

By the time Gabriel arrived back at the Hotel Kaiserhof, the place was being evacuated.

"Please leave the hotel, sir – you cannot come in," said a concierge who blocked him from entering. "Please follow the crowd to the nearest air-raid shelter."

"My fiancée is still here," said Gabriel.

"I'm sure she has already gone to the shelter," said the concierge.

Karina came running down the stairs at that moment, still dressed in the gown she had worn to dinner with a jacket around her shoulders.

"*Karina!*" Gabriel called and she came running towards him.

He put an arm around her as they ran from the hotel and hurried down the street with the rest of the people.

The sound of bombing began to thud in the distance.

"Don't worry, it's still a distance away," said Gabriel but they quickened their pace.

The air-raid shelter was a U-Bahn underground train station.

Karina and Gabriel wound their way through people who were seated or huddled on the platforms. They found a spot at the far end of the platform in a corner and sat side by side on the ground.

As the bombs being dropped sounded louder and nearer, Gabriel realised that Karina was shaking. He put his arms around her.

"The British are doing strategic bombing, only targeting industrial and military areas," said Gabriel, trying to reassure her. "We should be safe here as it's residential."

But his words didn't seem to soothe her and she grabbed him tightly as the sound of a bomb going off sounded way too dangerously close to be aimed at an industrial target. As they held each other tightly, Gabriel was aware that tears were falling down her cheeks.

"I wish I could understand you, Karina ... I wish you would let me know what is happening in that mind of yours ... I wish you would trust me and let me in," he whispered to her.

The next morning Gabriel was up early as he had an appointment with the Irish Minister to Berlin. They had been allowed back into the hotel in the early hours of the morning and had fallen into an exhausted sleep.

Karina seemed sheepish as she got out of bed and put on her dressing gown.

"Any plans for today?" Gabriel asked as he put his tie on.

"Just to take a look around the shops," she said as she opened the window and looked out. "There doesn't seem to be much damage from last night."

"As I said, the British weren't targeting the civilian areas. As yet their aim is to destroy industry and the military." He came over to her and kissed her. "I'll see you this evening."

She nodded and smiled.

Once he had left she sighed loudly. Her intention may have been to wreak revenge on the Ford family, but she was not enjoying the process. She remembered Gabriel rushing back to find her during the air raid the previous night and how he had comforted her for the night in the shelter.

What she was doing to him was beginning to feel unforgivably cruel. She now just wanted to find Hugo, leave Gabriel as quickly as possible and allow him to get on with his life. And, as she began to quickly get dressed, she hoped that today would be the day that she could do that.

Karina got the U-Bahn out to Charlottenburg. As she walked through the wealthy suburb, memories came flooding back to her – how she had attended parties there at the Friedrich house in the summer of '38.

She turned onto the street they lived on, Delbrückstrasse. The Friedrich house was a large three-storey villa up a gravel driveway – a perfect place for Hugo to remain hidden with the Friedrichs' cooperation. As she walked up to it, she marvelled at how little it had changed. As she reached the front door, she steadied herself then pulled the doorbell and waited.

A minute later the door opened and a man Karina remembered as being the butler stood there. She could see he also remembered her and was startled to see her.

"Good afternoon," he said.

"Good afternoon. Could you please tell Frau Friedrich that Karina Harper is here to see her?"

"Please come inside," he said.

"Thank you," she said as she went in.

He walked off down the long carpeted hallway and up the stairs.

Karina wandered down the hallway. Everything was as she remembered. It was a bright spacious house. The carpet on the floor was thick, luxurious and gold-coloured. Expensive paintings hung on the cream panelled walls. She remembered the Friedrichs were wealthy industrialists. They had been connected with everyone in Berlin society.

A maid came walking down the hallway carrying a huge vase of flowers and went through an open door. Karina wandered down to the doorway and looked in. It was a dining room where the staff were busy preparing for what looked like a large luncheon party. As the footman polished the silverware on the table and a maid arranged the flowers, it looked like the Friedrichs were expecting important guests. She remembered being a guest at that same dining table the night she met Hugo. She felt goosebumps thinking he was probably somewhere in the villa and she would be with him in a few minutes.

"Karina?" came an uncertain voice as a woman descended the stairs at the bottom of the hallway.

"Charlotte!" said Karina as she walked towards her with a big smile.

She remembered Charlotte Friedrich as being impossibly glamorous and chic with a pencil-thin figure. She had not changed.

"It *is* you! I was certain that Karl had misheard you or got the name wrong." She stared at Karina as if she were seeing a ghost.

"It is good to see you again, Charlotte," said Karina, who instinctively leaned forward and gave her a kiss on the cheek.

"But whatever brings you to Berlin? It's been an age since we heard anything of you!" Charlotte led her into the front drawing room across the hallway, closing the door behind them. She sat down and gestured to Karina to take the armchair opposite.

"How did you get here from London?" she asked.

"I'm actually living back in Dublin now. I'm doing some work for the Irish legation here."

"Ah, yes, of course – your family were Irish originally, were they not?"

"I wrote to you a couple of times earlier in the year, telling you

I had moved to Dublin and was working for the British legation there – did you not receive my letters?"

"Oh – yes, I did receive them now you mention it," said Charlotte.

"Oh!" Karina was perplexed.

"Sorry, I meant to reply to you – but you know how busy it is now."

"Yes, indeed."

"At least you have no bombs in Dublin. The Irish have cleverly remained neutral."

"As had the Danes, Norwegians and Dutch – alas, to no avail."

"Indeed," said Charlotte as she studied Karina intently. "How long will you be here?"

"I'm not sure yet, but it won't be that long."

"Who are you staying with?"

"At the Kaiserhof," said Karina who was becoming impatient with the line of questioning. "I am actually here today – to try and find Hugo."

"Hugo?" Charlotte suddenly looked concerned. "But why ever have you come to me over a matter such as that?"

"Because you are such a good friend of his," said Karina.

"Hardly a good friend!"

"Well, I met him at a party here at your house," said Karina.

"So have many people met at parties here – that does not mean I am close friend with them all – or any of them, for that matter! I like to fill my house with writers and intellectuals and artists and politicians and even society girls, but it does not mean I like or even approve of any of them!" Charlotte gave a little laugh.

"Well, I'm glad we have all managed to provide you with some evening entertainment, if that be the case!" Karina said, not hiding the sarcasm in her voice.

The door suddenly opened and a smart-looking man in his late thirties walked in. It was Felix, Charlotte's husband. He looked startled to see Karina there.

"Felix, do you remember Karina? She has come to pay us a visit – unexpectedly," said Charlotte, her tone cautious and measured.

"Ah – yes, of course, I remember you," he said, staring at Karina.

"Hello again, Felix – you are looking well," said Karina.

"As are you." He turned to his wife. "Charlotte, our guests are arriving very shortly!"

Charlotte nodded and he smiled at Karina before leaving and closing the door after him.

"It is so nice to see you again, Karina, but I'm afraid you have caught me on a bad day as I am expecting guests for lunch shortly."

The sound of motorcars coming up the drive cut through the silence.

Charlotte stood up. "Perhaps we can meet again before you leave Berlin."

Karina felt she was being dismissed and panicked. "I appreciate you don't have time for chit-chat, Charlotte – but I need to know where Hugo is."

"How on earth should I know?" asked Charlotte, looking aghast.

"When did you last see him then?"

"I can't recall – well over a year – before the war."

"I don't believe you!"

"What is wrong with you?"

"You were very good friends with Hugo and now you are denying that and pretending you hardly even knew him!"

"Hugo made it very hard to remain good friends with him. He did not help himself in any way," said Charlotte as the front doorbell echoed through the house.

"Over a year since you saw him! But that doesn't make any sense!" Karina's brow creased as she tried to figure it out.

"Why would that not make sense?" Charlotte looked exasperated as there were now loud voices in the hallway outside.

"Because I received a telegram ..." said Karina.

"A telegram? A telegram from whom about what?" demanded Charlotte.

"A telegram from Berlin ..." said Karina.

Suddenly the door was pushed open and Charlotte's husband Felix stuck his head around it.

"Charlotte! Our guests have arrived. *You must come and greet them at once!*" he hissed urgently before disappearing and closing the door.

Charlotte smoothed down her dress, looking as if she were at a loss as to what to do. "Could you excuse me for five minutes, Karina. I need to greet my guests."

She walked out of the room, closing the door behind her.

Karina stood there, trying to figure out what was going on. Something was very wrong.

Why was Charlotte lying?

She stood up and went to the window. Outside were three highly polished Mercedes. To her shock she saw Nazi flags on the fronts of them.

She gasped as she hurried over to the door, pulled it slightly ajar and peeped out. Across the hallway she could see into the dining room where there were several men dressed in senior military uniforms talking and laughing with Charlotte and Felix as the butler served them drinks.

As Karina watched, Charlotte stopped laughing and chatting and leant towards Felix and one of the officers. She appeared to be speaking to them in a hushed conspiratorial way while she nodded over to the drawing-room door. Karina saw both Felix and the officer look in her direction. She quickly closed the door and leant against it as she thought what to do. She ran across the room to a window, pulled it up and then climbed out onto the grass below. She looked around and didn't see anyone, then darted across the lawn towards some trees and hid there. Careful not to be spotted by any of the chauffeurs chatting by the motorcars at the front of the house, she edged around the garden to the front gateway and escaped onto the street.

Once outside, she hurried back to the U-Bahn station.

Gabriel sat in the office of William Warnock, the Irish Minister to Germany, in the legation building in Berlin.

"Well, I am glad you have arrived," said Warnock. "I am constantly telling Dublin that I need back-up and more support ... do you know how many secretaries I have here? One! One for the whole legation! No support staff! The Germans call us the cheap legation!"

"Budgets are so tight," said Gabriel.

"Aren't they always? However, there seems no shortage of funds and personnel for the Irish embassy in London ... it looks bad, Gabriel. It looks like the Irish are not taking Berlin's new importance seriously."

"I doubt anybody does not take Berlin's new importance seriously, William. Anyway, for now I need to concentrate on trying to get the Germans to accept responsibility for the bombing of Wexford, get a firm commitment they will not come into Irish territory again, and start building good relations."

"Well, asking them to compensate for a bombed creamery in Wexford is not the best way to build good relations with them. The Germans are categorically denying they did it," said William.

"Well, I have brought with me material evidence that it was German planes and bombs. The fallen bombs have been inspected and show German crests and markings. One of the bombs was unexploded and is clearly of German manufacture. And witnesses on the ground identified the bombers as being Heinkel 111 planes. I can't see how the Germans can continue denying the air raid was theirs."

"Oh, the Nazis can deny many things," said Warnock, shaking his head sadly.

Gabriel opened the hotel-suite door.

"Karina?" he called as stepped inside and closed the door behind him.

But she wasn't there. She was probably still out shopping. It was nearly four o'clock in the afternoon and he had finished his meetings at the Irish legation earlier than expected that day. He had hoped to spend some time with Karina and try to find out why she was so unhappy since she arrived in Berlin. He felt they had grown close again during the air raid the previous night as she had held him tightly and he had assured her everything would be alright. He wanted to build on that closeness. He hated when she went cold on him and he could not reach her.

He picked up his suitcase, laid it on the bed, and began to unpack some things that were still in it. Then he spotted Cynthia's package in the suitcase. He sighed as he picked it up. He had forgotten about it and now realised he had better deliver it immediately as he had promised to her.

As he walked down the hotel corridor he saw a large crowd waiting for the lift and went down the stairs instead.

The lift door opened and Karina stepped out. She passed the people waiting to get in and slowly walked down the corridor to their room.

She let herself in, locking the door behind her. She went and sat down on the sofa as a thousand thoughts ran through her head. Her biggest feeling was crushing disappointment and despair that she had not been reunited with Hugo. And now she was back to square one and had no idea where he was. But what had happened to him and what part had the Friedrichs played in that? She took his telegram from her handbag and read it once again. He said he was going to stay at the place when he met her. That had been at the Friedrichs'. So he had gone to the Friedrichs for sanctuary as the Nazis were closing in on him and ... and the Friedrichs had betrayed him. Judging by what she had witnessed that day with their luncheon party, the Friedrichs were very well connected with the Nazis. When Hugo had turned to them for help, they had obviously turned him over to the Nazis and now they were denying they had ever even been friends with him. They had wanted to be his friend when he was a famous and successful writer, but when he stopped being an asset and became a liability, they had betrayed him. She became consumed with anger at the Friedrichs ... and with despair.

Gabriel walked down Josefstrasse in the Michaelkirchplatz area of Berlin as indicated on the front of the package. As he peered up at the different names over the shops, he stopped abruptly when he saw the name *Durchdenwald* inscribed over a shop window. He peered in and saw it was indeed an art gallery. He pushed open the front door and a little bell sounded at its top, announcing a customer had arrived.

"Hello," said Gabriel as he approached the bespectacled man behind the counter who looked like he was in his sixties.

"How can I help you?" He peered at Gabriel over his spectacles.

"Are you Günter Durchdenwald?"

"Yes."

"I was asked to deliver this to you – it is from Dublin – from Mrs Cynthia Ford." Gabriel held the package out to him.

A smile lit up Durchdenwald's face. "*Ahhh*, I have been waiting for this!" He took the package from Gabriel. "Thank you!"

"You are welcome. Good day to you," Gabriel said with a smile as he turned and walked out, setting off the little bell at the top of the door again as he opened and closed it behind him.

CHAPTER 55

As Karina sat opposite Gabriel in a little tavern that evening, she was barely listening to what he was saying.

"The air raid last night didn't do much damage to the city centre from the looks of it. I wish the same thing could be said for London, it got blitzed again last night... just as well your mother is in Scotland."

Karina wondered what she could possibly do now to track down Hugo as she had drawn a blank with the Friedrichs. She was racking her brain. Was there anybody else she could contact in Berlin who used to know him? She decided she had to go to his flat and see what was going on there. Maybe if she managed to get into it she could find some clue as to what happened to him and where he went, however she could manage that.

"I have a meeting in the morning with the Department of Foreign Affairs here," he said.

"Yes?"

"To request compensation for the attack on Wexford."

"I can't see you having much luck getting that!" she scoffed.

"Why not? We now have proof that the planes and bombs were German."

"And who is going to compensate the Danish and the Dutch and the French for the wholescale destruction of their countries?" she said incredulously.

"Well, they will have to make their own claims for any damage they perceive as done," he said.

She shook her head and laughed derisively. "Oh, Gabriel – you are priceless! A diplomat through and through! Don't you ever think with your heart? Don't you ever want to cut through this diplomatic red tape you live your life in and shout out at the German Foreign Office tomorrow that they are committing monstrous activities across Europe?"

"I think I would be letting down my country if I do that, don't you? Making an enemy of a country we cannot afford to make an enemy of."

"So like the school kid who is scared of the bully in the playground, you are pretending to be Hitler's friend?"

"Not his friend, Karina, but reasserting our position of neutrality. Of course I would like to tell the German Foreign Office what I think of them tomorrow, but I am unable to … it is called realpolitik," he said.

As a singer began to sing a low love song in the corner of the tavern, the other diners listened. The atmosphere was very different from the Hotel Kaiserhof the previous night. The people were more subdued and there weren't any Nazi officers present. But like everywhere else that Gabriel had since arriving in Berlin, there was a huge sense of pride in the people here, almost a disbelief that they had achieved so much during the war.

As Karina studied Gabriel across the table, she wondered what was going through his mind.

"Why do you put up with me, Gabriel? What possible reason do you have for having me in your life when all I bring is disruption and confusion and uncertainty?" she asked.

"I must be in love with you," he said with a grim smile.

She sighed. "I warned you to keep away from me for your own good, Gabriel."

"Well, now it's probably too late."

CHAPTER 56

Over breakfast in the dining room at Roxford, Tess was reading the morning newspaper as Cynthia buttered her toast and Tim poured tea into his cup.

"Shocking ... disgraceful," tutted Tess as she read.

"What is it?" asked Tim.

"I am just reading about the shocking treatment of Jews in Poland. They are being stripped of their property and herded into ghettos where there is a severe lack of basic food and medical facilities."

"The same thing is beginning to happen in France," said Tim. "The seizing of Jewish property and money. Robbing people of what they own and calling it 'expropriation'. Just because a government gives something a fancy name does not make it right – it's just still plain robbery! Thugs!"

"You shouldn't read the British press, Tess – it obviously gives a one-sided view," said Cynthia.

"It isn't a British newspaper I am reading – it's an Irish one!" said Tess, holding it up.

"Even worse, then,' said Cynthia. "I've heard the German government are very displeased with the way the Irish press are reporting the war, saying it is very anti-German and should remain neutral."

"The press's job is to report the facts, Cynthia, not to remain neutral!" said Tess.

"It won't be long until the Jews in Poland and the other occupied countries will be rounded up and put into concentration camps the way they are in Germany," sighed Tim.

"Mr Pietch says the way the press present the concentration camps is unfair and that most of them are civil places – more like detention centres," said Cynthia.

"Mr Pietch doesn't know his arse from his elbow, Cynthia!" Tess was unable to help herself from snapping. "You only have to think of the atrocities that were committed on Kristallnacht in '38 to see how the Jews are treated in Germany. That was before the war, so how they are being treated under the cover of war in these 'detention centres', as you call them, doesn't bear thinking about!"

Cynthia looked down at her half-eaten breakfast and stood up. "I think I need to do some gardening. Those bushes at the back need pruning before the autumn comes in."

Cynthia patted her hair as she walked out of the room.

As Cynthia walked down the road towards Pietch's cottage she tried not to think of the harsh things Tess and Tim had said that morning. What did they know? They had never even been to Germany and were hardly intellectual giants. It was unusual to hear Tim express anything more serious than the rising price of alcohol due to rationing. And all Tess ever really cared about was which Hollywood movie star was divorcing her husband next. They were typical of the kind of people who got manipulated by the British establishment and press, and by extension the Irish press by all accounts. People who could not think for themselves.

As she turned the corner of the country road and Pietch's cottage came into view, she was surprised to see a man in the garden putting up a sign. As she neared the house, to her shock she saw the sign read 'To Let'.

She felt dismayed that Pietch might be moving. He had never mentioned even a thought of doing so.

"What are you doing, young man?" she said as she opened the garden gate and walked in.

The young man looked at her as if he was about to give her a smart answer.

"Just putting up this sign, missus," he said then.

"But why are you doing so?"

He looked up at the sign which clearly stated the reason he was putting it up and looked again as if he was going to make a sarcastic reply.

"Because the house is going on the market for rent, missus ... the house is – *to let!*" he said, reaching up and tapping the words on the sign.

"But you have the wrong house, young man. I know the occupant of this house and he has no intention of moving out – I was only here yesterday evening having a tea of ham sandwiches and scones with him!"

She marched up the path to the front door which was open.

"*Marc? Marc!*" she called as she walked inside.

She got a shock as she saw the interior of the house had been stripped of all Pietch's personal possessions.

"*Marc!*" she shouted in a panic up the stairs.

"The tenant vacated the property this morning, missus, and left the keys back at our estates agent's," said the young man who was now standing in the doorway dangling the house keys in front of her.

CHAPTER 57

Gabriel was up and dressed and gone early the next morning. As Karina dressed, she tried not to think of him so she could focus all her attention on finding Hugo, but it was hard. Despite herself, she'd had a change of heart. She couldn't act more coldly to him but now she was doing it not out of revenge but in order to protect him against future hurt when she did abandon him. She was preparing him for the fall.

As she walked through the city centre, groups of German soldiers marched down the wide boulevards and people greeted each other with 'Heil Hitler' salutes.

She caught the U-Bahn to the Mitte area where Hugo flat was. As the train sped along underground, she noticed people looking at her. She felt uneasy and wondered did they know she was a foreigner. Did they think she was English? Or could they detect she was half Jewish? When the train stopped at the station nearest the flat, she quickly left the carriage and ran up the steps to the fresh air above ground.

Walking along, she was overcome with nostalgia when she thought back to when she had stayed at Hugo's flat when they had come back from his villa in Bavaria in the summer of '38.

It had been the happiest time of her life.

She turned the corner into the street where he lived. On one side was a park with a small beer garden at the end. On the other was a series of three-storey nineteenth-century buildings that had been converted into flats. As she looked at the park she shivered as she thought it had provided an ideal place for the Nazis to spy on Hugo. She arrived at his building and looked up at his flat which was on the top floor. As she peered up she was astonished to see the windows were open and music from a gramophone was coming from the open windows.

"Hugo!" she whispered as she ran to the heavy front door of the building and pushed it open.

Racing across the hallway and up the steps, she could hardly breathe from excitement as she reached his front door. There was somebody in Hugo's flat. She could hardly believe it could be him, but if not it would be somebody who knew him! Somebody who he would have given the keys to and could tell her where he was. She began to knock loudly on the door.

Across the hallway the neighbour's door opened and the white-haired old lady who lived there peeped out. Karina remembered her and she could tell she remembered her too as she stared in disbelief. As the front door of Hugo's flat began to open, the old lady quickly pulled back into her flat and locked the door.

Karina held her breath as Hugo's front door opened and her mouth dropped open when she saw a Nazi officer standing there. As the music continued to blare from the gramophone, she saw there was a very pretty young woman stretched out on Hugo's chaise longue, dressed only in flimsy lingerie.

"Who is it, Eric?" asked the woman.

"I don't know!" said the Nazi officer. "Who are you?"

As Karina took in the whole scene before her, she knew she needed to get away quickly.

"Oh, excuse me, I think I have got the wrong building!" she said with a smile.

"Who are you looking for?"

"A Frau Weber. I was sent by the hairdressers I work for to do her hair – she's had a fall you see, so can't get out to get her hair done."

Eric gave a laugh and turned back to the woman. "Do you want to get your hair done, Helga? It looks like you may need to – after last night!"

"No! I only had it done yesterday for you – you ungrateful pig!"

"Sorry, I can't help you," said Eric with a smirk as he closed the door over.

Karina turned and quickly left.

As she walked hastily down the street outside, she tried to calm down after the shock of seeing someone wearing that uniform answer Hugo's door. She was desperate to find out why those people were in Hugo's flat.

She thought of the elderly woman who lived across the landing. She could tell the woman remembered her from her expression when she saw her. The way she had retreated quickly back inside her flat when the Nazi officer had opened Hugo's door made her think she did not like him being there and was not acquainted with the new occupants. Karina reckoned the woman might be safe to speak to in that case. And that woman was her last chance to try and find out what had happened.

At the end of the street, Karina crossed the road and went into the small beer garden there. She took a seat. The table she occupied offered a good view down the street to the entrance of the block where the flat was. She would just have to wait there until the old lady made an appearance. If she did. She ordered a small beer, lit up a cigarette and with the leaves in the trees rustling in the breeze above her, she kept her eyes trained on the front door of Hugo's building.

As the hours passed in that beer garden, Karina was grateful for all the hours she'd had to wait at the window of the flat in Dublin spying on the comings and goings at Government Buildings for Emily and Kendrick. It had built up an immunity to boredom that was proving useful.

The beer garden was half empty and Karina remembered going there with Hugo often. They would while away the afternoon there talking about everything under the sun.

She reached over and took another sip of her beer. Then, as she placed the glass back on the table, she suddenly saw the old lady come out the front door of the building and head off in the other direction. Karina stood up and, trying not to draw too much attention to herself, hurried down the road after her.

As the old lady turned the corner into the next street, Karina caught up with her.

"Hello – excuse me – I'm sorry for bothering you, but we met before. I'm Hugo's friend, do you remember me?"

The old woman looked stunned to see her there and set off walking down the street again, ignoring her.

Karina quickly followed her. "Please, I do need to speak to you. Can you not spare me a few minutes?"

"Go away!" whispered the old woman as she continued on.

"I can't without speaking to you first! I'm trying to find Hugo and I have no idea where he is! You are my only hope to find out what became of him. Who are those people in his flat and when did you see him there last?"

The woman continued walking, ignoring her.

"*Please!*" begged Karina.

"I need to get to the shops quickly and home. I have no time to talk," said the woman.

"I remember Hugo used to go the shop for you when you weren't feeling well – don't you remember? And once I went for you. Don't you remember? You had a bad cold, so couldn't go out yourself."

The old woman stopped walking, turned and looked at Karina before sighing. "Yes, I remember ... but it can't be known that I was speaking to you. I can't have any trouble, not at my age."

"I understand that. Nobody will ever know we spoke – but please, I desperately need to find him. If I could just find out when he was here last?"

The old woman began to walk slowly down the street again and Karina walked alongside her.

"He had barely left his flat for many months. This was last year, before the war started. It was as if he had become a recluse. I even offered to do his shopping for him! I thought he might be ill – he looked terrible and had no visitors. We never really spoke except pass the time of day but he looked frightened any time I saw him ... then, all of a sudden, last year – around August – he left the flat and I did not see him since."

"He hasn't been back at all?"

"Not once – and I would have known if he had." The old woman nodded her head assuredly.

As Karina thought back to the telegram she had received from Hugo in August, she realised he had indeed done what he said he was going to do in the telegram. He had left the flat. But to go where? According to Charlotte Friedrich, he had never gone to them as the telegram seemed to indicate. Charlotte Friedrich then must be lying.

"He left early one morning, seven in the morning as I remember. I watched as he walked down the road carrying a suitcase," said the old woman.

"He never said goodbye?"

"No." The old woman shook her head. "His flat was empty for months. And then last month this Gestapo Officer arrived with keys to the place and let himself in ... and a week later he moved his whore in!"

"I see," said Karina.

"He comes and goes as if the place is a brothel – but she is there all the time! He seems quite senior. I don't speak to them – especially not to *her*!"

"*But where did Hugo go to?*" Karina whispered, thinking out loud.

The woman studied Karina intently. "I was very fond of him – he was always very kind to me," she said.

"I just need to find him," said Karina, despairing.

The old woman looked around and then leaned forward and grabbed Karina's arm, pulling her close.

"The day before he left, his window was open and so was mine," she whispered. "I could hear him speaking on the telephone. I heard him enquiring what was the earliest train to Munich the next day." She squeezed Karina's arm tightly before turning and walking quickly down the street, holding her shopping bag close to her chest.

As Karina watched her, she digested what she had just heard.

She turned and walked back past Hugo's block and across the road to the beer garden again where she lit a cigarette and ordered another beer.

She reached into her pocket, took out Hugo's telegram and studied it.

I AM LEAVING THE FLAT IN THE MORNING BEFORE IT IS TOO
LATE. I AM GOING TO WHEN WE FIRST MET. POST NOT SAFE.

HUGO

The old lady had confirmed Hugo had indeed left the flat with a
suitcase in August, as he had said he intended to do in the telegram.
And he had not been back since. So he had not been arrested before
he had a chance to leave. He hopefully had got to where he had
intended to go – which she had always assumed was the Friedrichs'
house. But according to Charlotte Friedrich their friendship was all
but over, and he did not or would not have gone to them. Karina had
no reason to believe she was telling the truth and not trying to hide a
betrayal of Hugo. But the old lady had now said she had overheard
Hugo enquiring about times of trains to Munich.

Was Hugo trying to get as near to the Swiss border as possible
with the intention of crossing it? Or ... was he possibly going to
stay at the villa in the Bavarian Alps? Where they had spent that
wonderful time together?

To *when we first met.*

When not *where.*

And she suddenly realised that was what Hugo had meant all
along. They may have met for the first time at the Friedrichs' but
the time they spent together in Bavaria was *when* they had been
together and had truly fallen in love.

She stood up quickly and began to hurry back to the U-Bahn station.

Coming back from the German Foreign Ministry, Gabriel was a
little dazed as he thought back on the meeting he'd had that day.
He had made no progress on the matter of the Wexford bombing
but an extraordinary thing had occured.

"You have been cordially invited to meet the Führer and his
senior staff," he was informed by a German diplomat.

"To meet the Führer?" said Gabriel, suddenly finding himself
overcome with nerves. In his position he had learned to deal with
every kind of leader. But the thought of meeting Hitler was daunting.

357

"The Führer has always taken a great interest in Ireland and Irish affairs and he sees an important role for German-Irish relations after the war is over," said the Minister.

It was a golden opportunity for Gabriel to impress on Hitler Ireland's position and determination to remain independent and neutral. But the fact Hitler wanted to meet him unnerved him greatly as it indicated Hitler had his eyes set on Ireland and it featured in his plans.

Gabriel was not surprised that the venue was to be Hitler's Alpine home. The Berghof, as it was called, was where he spent much of his time and he regularly hosted politicians, diplomats and royalty there.

As he got out of the taxi at the Kaiserhof, he wondered how he would explain this to Karina. She seemed already so unhappy in Berlin and uncomfortable there. He could only imagine her reaction to visiting Hitler's home.

CHAPTER 58

Karina studied a map of Germany back in the hotel suite at the Kaiserhof. She remembered the little town near the villa that Hugo owned – Hausham. She remembered the beautiful lakes and mountains around there. Now she was sure that was where Hugo had gone when he left his flat. Perhaps with the stress he was under he had simply forgotten that they had initially met at the Friedrichs', but more likely Hugo was being cryptic and relying on the fact that she would think about their first romantic interlude – which nobody else knew about and could not be deciphered by anyone but her. She could hardly bear to think that he had been waiting in the Alps all this time. But as she looked at the map, she wondered was Hugo using the villa as a stepping-stone to get over the border into Switzerland. Although the Swiss border was notoriously hard for people trying to escape Germany to cross, it did make sense that Hugo, sick and depressed from the threat he was under in Berlin, would try to escape that way when he had a villa in the same region. But she knew he had not in fact managed to cross that border as he would have made contact with her immediately if he had and was free to do so.

As Karina folded away the map, she was possessed with the desire to travel to Bavaria as quickly as possible and go to the villa. She could hardly dare to think he was there, but, if he was, now she had a British entry permit for him. They could travel through Bavaria to the Swiss border and there would be no reason why he, with a visa for Britain, and she with her neutral passport would not be allowed access to Switzerland from where they could fly to Barcelona and

359

travel on to the port of Lisbon.

She thought about Gabriel and realised she had come to the end of the line with him. He had served his purpose. Whatever horrible actions his father had committed on her and her family, she no longer wished to pursue revenge on him or the Ford family. In a way, she felt they were even now. She would write him a note saying she had made a mistake and did not love him but wished him the best for the future. She imagined the letter would break his heart. She also imagined that deep down he always knew this day would come. Ever since she ran out on him after their first time in Claridge's, she guessed he suspected she would do the same again to him one day. He was a smart man and knew deep down she did not love him – he was just refusing to choose to believe it.

As she looked at her watch, she saw it was nearly four. She needed to pack quickly and leave for the train station before he got back from the legation.

She went to the bureau and took a sheet of the writing paper. Taking up the fountain pen lying there she began to write.

Dear Gabriel,
I must

The door suddenly opened and Gabriel walked in.

"Oh! I thought you might still be out shopping," he said as he closed the door behind him.

"I had been out earlier, but got bored," she said.

He smiled at her. "I don't think you will ever come rushing back to Berlin, do you?"

She shook her head and smiled. "Not while the Nazis are in charge in any case."

"Well, we're not going to be here for much longer, you will be glad to know," he said.

"Why not?"

"I have to travel to Bavaria for diplomatic talks with Hitler himself. I'm travelling to his home, the Berghof in the Alps."

"What? Bavaria?" She was astounded.

"Of course, I don't expect you to come. I can arrange a plane through the legation to take you back to Ireland," he said.

"But why would I want to do that?" she asked.

"You mean you want to come with me?"

"Yes, why not?" She smiled as she approached him and took his hands. "I know I have not been the best of company on this trip and you probably regret bringing me. I don't blame you – I can be a tiresome bitch! To be honest, I think Berlin was just too much of a shock for me. I think I should be very glad to get out of the city and into the fresh countryside!"

"Are you certain? To Hitler's home?"

"Should be interesting! And Bavaria is beautiful. I can do some sightseeing while you have your meetings."

He looked at her, shook his head and smiled. When she was like this, happy and relaxed, he didn't want to be anywhere else in the world except with her.

"I'll go down to the concierge and ask them to arrange tickets on the train to Munich tonight," he said.

"Tonight? So soon?"

"I'm afraid so. Hitler's a busy man. I can't miss my allocated slot with him. Start packing and I'll be back as soon as I can," he said and leaned forward to kiss her.

Karina felt elated. Her head was spinning with excitement.

"Oh, and Gabriel – make sure he arranges to hire a car at Munich for us as well. We'll need it to get to the Berghof."

"Yes, I do know that, darling!" he said and smiled sarcastically at her.

She nodded and smiled at him as he left.

Karina felt fate was taking her back to Hugo. She walked over to the writing bureau, took up the page that she had begun writing on and crumpled it up before throwing it in the bin.

It was nearly midnight and Cynthia was in the back garden with a clippers, pruning back the bushes in the full moonlight. She had been there most of the day since morning, ruthlessly trimming away the foliage.

Upstairs in their bedroom Tess was getting ready for bed, putting on her face cream as usual as Tim sat up in bed going through paperwork – as usual.

"Do you think Cynthia has been acting a little strangely these past couple of days?" asked Tess.

"No more than usual!" dismissed Tim. "In what way do you mean?"

"I don't know – a little distracted – lost in her own world," said Tess.

"Maybe a little," agreed Tim as he put his papers on the side table and put out the bedside light.

Outside in the back garden, Cynthia now had a rake and was raking the soil in the flowerbeds in the dark.

"I have to do everything myself, Rory! Why is everything always left to me and I have to do everything myself! And never any gratitude for all I do!" she spat as she continued to rake the ground furiously.

CHAPTER 59

They got a taxi to the main train station in Berlin and got on the night train to Munich. Gabriel had managed to get them a sleeper and, after having something to eat in the dining carriage, they went to bed. Though Karina found it hard to sleep and looked out the window as the German countryside whizzed by under the moonlight.

The next morning they arrived in Munich and the hired motorcar was waiting for them to collect. As they sat in, Gabriel smiled, leaned over and kissed her. Then they set off from the city south towards the Alps.

Karina felt her anxiety rising as they drove up the narrow steep mountain road that led to the front gates of the Berghof. The area was heavily militarized with soldiers in evidence everywhere. She fought an overwhelming desire to beg Gabriel to turn the motorcar around and head back to Munich as quickly as possible. She had never been more aware of her Jewish blood and she felt she was walking deliberately into the lion's den. But, as they reached the front gates and the soldiers there put their hands up to stop them, she reminded herself she was safe. Nobody knew about her Jewish background, not even Gabriel. She was there as the fiancée of a neutral country's diplomat. She was untouchable.

What's more, tomorrow she would make the journey to Hugo's villa and hopefully be reunited with him.

"*Heil Hitler!*" saluted the officer at the gates.

Gabriel nodded back. "*Heil!* I'm Gabriel Ford and this is my fiancé, Karina Harper. We are guests invited to the Berghof."

The officer looked through the paperwork he had on a clipboard before asking for passports.

Gabriel reached into his glove compartment to retrieve his while Karina got hers from her handbag and passed it to Gabriel. The officer examined both passports and then studied Gabriel and Karina. Karina, feeling uncomfortable at his scrutiny, looked up at the mountain tops above her.

The officer nodded and handed back the passports. "Follow the road up to the main house. They are expecting you. *Heil Hitler!*"

The officer gave the command to his colleagues to raise the barrier in front of them on the road.

"Thank you," said Gabriel as he nodded and drove past the barrier.

They drove up the mountain road. Even within the compound, there were soldiers around the grounds.

"Imagine living like this by choice as Hitler does!" said Karina.

"It's probably one of the most guarded places in the world," said Gabriel. "Impossible to get in without an invite."

Karina frowned as she thought it would be impossible to get out without permission as well. The car continued up the heavily wooded mountain road and she had a growing sense of foreboding as the sun was blocked out by the high fir trees.

Suddenly the Berghof came into view, a sprawling villa, built in traditional German architectural style, perched high on a ledge. Karina admitted to herself the house with its location was breath-taking.

"Does Hitler own this himself?" she asked as they neared the building.

"Yes, along with a flat in Munich and a house in Berlin, but this is his main home," said Gabriel.

"So he is a very wealthy man?" asked Karina.

"His wealth is mainly from the sales of his book *Mein Kampf*. It has sold millions and not only that but courtesy of the German state every soldier is given a courtesy copy of the book as are every couple on their wedding day, boosting the sales by many more millions."

"That would be, I imagine, the ultimate unwanted wedding gift," said Karina as the motorcar pulled up in the forecourt in front of the villa.

Gabriel and Karina stepped out of the vehicle and stared at the stunning views across to the mountains.

"It's hard to think a place so beautiful could be harbouring someone so bad," whispered Karina.

Gabriel gave her a warning look. "Remember what I told you before we came, Karina. We have to put on an act here. They cannot detect any negativity from us – this is a diplomatic mission."

"I do know that, Gabriel. I did work in the Foreign Office in London, you know... I know what is expected of me."

He nodded at her and went to the back of the motorcar to take out their suitcases.

"Good morning, Mr Ford," said a voice as two male servants came down the steps. "We trust you had a good journey."

"Very good, thank you," said Gabriel as he handed the suitcases over to one of the men.

"If you could follow me, please," said the other man.

Gabriel and Karina followed them across the forecourt and up the steps towards the front door which was inside a long arched porch. As Karina walked under the cool porch and through the front door she shivered.

As one servant carried their suitcases down a corridor in one direction, Gabriel chatted away in his usual diplomatic style to the other as Karina followed them behind. They were being taken to be greeted by Hitler and Karina almost felt in a trance as she looked around. Strangely, the interior of the house looked vaguely familiar to Karina. Then she remembered she had seen it featured in a number of magazines over the years – *Town & Country* and *Vogue* amongst others – as Hitler liked to show off his glamorous home to an all-too-eager international press that was always ready to be seduced by the illusion of glamour.

They were led into the great hall which was the showpiece of the Berghof. A giant room furnished with elegant furniture, there were clusters of different couches around it that enabled the numerous guests staying there to spread out in separate groups. But the centrepiece of the great hall was the picture window – a giant window that took over nearly one whole wall of the room, affording a panoramic view of the Alps, with mountains meadows that stretched up into snow-capped peaks. It was breath-taking. Seated in a cluster of very modern-style armchairs and sofas gathered around a coffee table at one corner of the window, a group of people were gathered.

Amongst the men there, Karina recognised Hitler. He was sitting beside a young blonde woman.

"*Heil Hitler!*" saluted the servant once they reached the group. "Mr Gabriel Ford from the Irish legation with his fiancée Miss Karina Harper, Führer."

As Hitler rose from his chair and greeted Gabriel, Karina could hardly concentrate on what they were saying. She watched as Gabriel turned on the charm with Hitler but she felt overwhelmed and nauseous being so near this man who was now turning his attention to her.

"Welcome to the Berghof, Miss Harper," said Hitler as he held out his hand.

She looked down at his hand and forced herself to smile as she shook it.

"So nice to have guests from Ireland – I hope to go there one day," said Hitler.

As Gabriel smiled back at Hitler, he sincerely hoped he did not mean to go there by means of an invasion.

"My brother is in fact married to an Irishwoman he met while working in Dublin," said Hitler.

"So I believe," nodded Gabriel.

The blonde woman rose and came to Hitler's side.

"I'm Eva Braun," she said with a big smile. "Welcome to the Berghof." She suddenly looked down at Karina's hands. "Oh, your ring! May I see it?"

"Of course," said Karina.

She stretched out her hand and Eva took it in hers and studied the diamond engagement ring.

"It's beautiful! Oh, to have such a ring as that!" said Eva as she glanced at Hitler.

"We have some very interesting other guests staying at the Berghof during your stay with us – an Italian Minister and a Swedish Industrialist," said Hitler.

"And two Argentinian journalists!" said Eva excitedly. "We like to have a good mix of people so nobody gets bored!"

"We look forward to meeting them all," said Gabriel.

"We will be having drinks on the terrace this evening before dinner. So we will see you there," said Hitler.

"We will look forward to it," said Gabriel.

The servant took his cue and stepped forward. "Follow me, if you please."

They followed the servant away from the great hall through a series of corridors until they reached their bedroom.

It was large and luxurious, the windows offering more wonderful views.

"Drinks will be served on the terrace at six," said the servant before leaving.

Karina went quickly to the door and locked it.

"Are you alright?" asked Gabriel, seeing she had paled.

"Oh Gabriel!" she said before rushing to him, embracing him and holding him tightly.

He soothed her and, like the time in Berlin when the bombs were falling, she felt safe and secure with him.

"I know it's daunting meeting him and being here, my love," he said as he stroked her hair. "I have to stay and do what is required of me – but you could leave if you wish. If it's too much for you, then we can make an excuse and I can make arrangements for you to fly back home from Munich."

She thought of how close she was to Hugo's villa and how she would be there the next day. She only had to get through that night and then all her dreams would come true.

"No, I'm fine. I just need to pull myself together," she said as she drew back and smiled at him.

They lay down for a nap in the afternoon but Karina fell in and out of a troubled sleep. As she looked at Gabriel sleeping soundly, she imagined he would be beside himself with worry the following night when she didn't come back to the Berghof. He would imagine she had met with an accident or otherwise come to grief. She realised she must somehow prevent him from raising the alarm, which would lead to a search for her and the car in the area and eventually to Hugo.

CHAPTER 60

As Karina and Gabriel got dressed late in the afternoon to go to the terrace for drinks, as invited, Gabriel said, "I'm afraid the fact the Hitler was not on the steps to greet us shows that we are considered low-ranking guests."

"Who is the girl? Eva?" asked Karina.

"That is Hitler's girlfriend. She basically acts as his wife and mistress here at the Berghof."

Karina, stupefied on hearing this, swung around from the dressing-table mirror. "But there is no mention of her in the press!"

"She's kept out of the way," said Gabriel, fixing his tie in the mirror on the front of the wardrobe.

"She's very young for him," observed Karina as she put on her lipstick.

"Well, she had been around Hitler for quite some time," said Gabriel.

As he looked at her standing there in a long blue chiffon dress, he thought she had never looked so lovely. Then he noticed she was trembling.

"You're shaking!" he said as he came over to her and put his arms around her.

"Yes, I am," she admitted as she allowed herself to sink into his warm embrace.

"Maybe take a stole with you?" he suggested as he ran his fingers over her bare shoulders.

"Yes, I shall – although I'm not cold in the least," she said. "It must be just the mountain air. Speaking of which, as you are busy tomorrow I'm going to take the car and take a tour around, if you don't mind. Visit some of the tourist spots."

"Oh, yes. It will probably do you good to have some time to yourself and a break from being here."

She gathered up her stole and evening bag, took his arm and they left for the terrace.

A number of international dignitaries had gathered on the terrace which had sweeping views down the valley.

A servant was making his way among the guests with a tray of champagne and Karina took another glass as she continued to smile fixedly at Eva Braun who was telling her who her favourite movie stars were.

Gabriel was across the terrace in conversation with Hitler and two senior military officers.

"We have our own projection room and cinema here at the Berghof," said Eva. "The Führer used to watch a film every single night but since the war started he does not have the time anymore." She sighed.

"I can imagine," said Karina.

"The war is so demanding on his time – the sacrifices he makes daily for the German people."

"It must be difficult." Karina nodded.

"Of course, they – most of them – appreciate his sacrifices. We had to cordon off the whole area at the Berghof because the people would come and gather on the entrance roads, tourists, to try and just get a glimpse of him. There had to be extra barriers put up as there were crowds gathering and it was causing security risks."

"Can I smoke here?" asked Karina, reaching for her packet.

"Yes, the Führer does not smoke himself but he allows smoking on the terrace."

"How lucky for us smokers!" said Karina as she lit up. "Do you ever get lonely up here, Eva?"

Eva gave a little laugh. "Of course not! Why would I? The

Führer is here most of the time and we have constant friends and guests. We have so many parties here – we've had the Duke and Duchess of Windsor visit us here and the Aga Khan and the likes of Diana Mitford."

Karina wondered what Eva and indeed Hitler would think if they knew of her own connection to the British aristocracy. She had wondered a lot about Julian since coming to Germany. She wondered where he was. She was surprised, but grateful, that nothing had appeared in the British press about his defection and imagined the British goverment had a hand in covering it up in case it affected morale at home. It was also surprising that the Nazis hadn't paraded him out as part of their propaganda war. No doubt they were just biding their time, waiting for the right moment to announce to the world their latest recruit – the British peer Lord Ashton.

"I think I would get lonely here. I would feel the need to leave and meet people outside," she said to Eva.

"But when you are with the man you love, you are never lonely – you must know that from being with your own fiancée." Eva smiled as she looked over at Hitler and Gabriel. "I have a feeling that the Führer will wish to see a film tonight. What fun!"

Karina inhaled from her cigarette as she looked from Eva's happy face to Hitler who was now petting a German Shepherd dog.

Gabriel watched Hitler make a fuss of his pet dog as they chatted.

"I was very pleased when Ireland appointed its first president in 1937 and wrote a new constitution," said Hitler. "It is the biggest step Ireland has taken since gaining independence to pull itself further away from Britain."

"It certainly has helped us maintain our staunch position of neutrality through the war," said Gabriel. "If we hadn't made those moves three years ago, we might not have been strong enough to resist the British wishes to fight with them."

"Which would have been a travesty – not just for Ireland but for Germany as well. Why should two old friends be dragged into a war against each other because of an old enemy like Britain?

371

Your prime minister Mr de Valera fought Churchill during your war of independence and here I am now fighting Churchill too."

"Yes, but that was a long time ago now," said Gabriel.

"And the Irish have very long memories, I hear."

Gabriel, choosing his words carefully, said, "We have been alarmed in Dublin at reports that Germany has drawn up plans to invade Ireland."

"British propaganda to try and stir up anti-German feeling in your country. No such plans exist," said Hitler.

"I am very glad to hear that. If such a plan did exist and was ever executed we would defend our sovereignty to the last and by whichever means we could, even allying ourselves with Britain."

"It would be very stupid of Ireland to ally itself with a country that will lose the war. But what we must now already start thinking about and talking about is life after the war. It will soon be over with a complete German victory and what we need to discuss is what kind of relationship our two countries will have in the new peacetime."

"Yes, that is very important to us – to establish that relationship," said Gabriel.

"I must tell you that I am very anxious about the way the Irish press is reporting the war. There is a very strong anti-German feeling about it."

"But we cannot censure our press – it is a free press in Ireland," said Gabriel.

"Maybe Ireland needs to have a Ministry of Propaganda as we have in Germany. I believe you actually used to have one once?"

"Yes, we had a Ministry of Propaganda during the first couple of years of independence but it was abolished in 1922."

"Perhaps it is time to re-establish it," suggested Hitler. "Perhaps you could put your former envoy to Berlin in charge of it. We admired him greatly and were disappointed when your goverment replaced him last year."

"Yes, indeed. I believe Charles Bewley has now gone to work for your own Ministry of Propaganda," said Gabriel curtly, relieved they were finally free of their pro-Nazi former envoy.

***

In the dining hall Karina and Gabriel sat at one end of the table while Hitler and Eva sat at the other with the other guests in between. As Hitler had said, there was an Italian politician present, a Hungarian diplomat and two Argentinian journalists. The rest of the guests were high-ranking Nazi officers and some women who were their wives. They seemed a tight intimate circle and Eva sitting to Hitler's left hosted the table eloquently as they discussed music and books and art and opera. But, as Karina realised, they were only speaking of such works that were approved by the Reich. Other works, such as Hugo's books, were burned in the streets. All the time Karina tried not to think of their reaction if they knew the woman at the end of the table was half Jewish.

"The Führer is a strict vegetarian and would like me to be one as well, but I enjoy my bacon far too much!" laughed Eva as she sipped from her champagne glass.

"I do not blame you, Eva. I too could not give up my pork!" said one of the officers' wives as she accepted a large slab of pork from one of the perfectly groomed and uniformed staff.

"Such wonderful writers have come out of Ireland – George Bernard Shaw, William Butler Yeats, James Joyce," said the Italian diplomat as he smiled down at Gabriel and Karina.

"We are indeed blessed with our rich literature," agreed Gabriel.

"My favourite is Bram Stoker," said Karina before muttering to Gabriel in English, "And I am beginning to feel like we are in Dracula's Castle."

Gabriel gave her a quick swipe under the table to be quiet.

The dinner wore on in a sea of champagne and wine until apple strudel was served for desert.

"The thing is, people criticise Germany for not wanting the Jews here. But we offer them to the rest of the world and nobody else wants them either!" said Hitler.

Karina began to feel herself tense and forced herself to remain calm.

"How many countries throw open their doors to them? Britain? America? Ireland?" said Hitler.

Gabriel became uncomfortable.

"Tell me, Mr Ford," said Hitler, "how many visas did Ireland give to Jews seeking them in the last five years?"

"I don't have that information to hand," said Gabriel.

"But I have! One hundred! One hundred visas for Jews between 1933 and the start of the war!"

Gabriel saw Karina flush and squeezed her arm under the table in warning to keep calm.

"And that is me done with apple strudel for tonight," said Eva as she pushed her plate away. "Or else my waist will be lost for good!"

Everyone laughed except for Karina.

"Gabriel, I am going back to the room," said Karina as they were all walking towards the great hall for after-dinner drinks.

"*You have to show your face for at least a while after dinner!*" Gabriel hissed back at her.

"I can't – I'm sorry, Gabriel," she said as she broke away from him and turned down one of the corridors. She rushed through the corridors until she reached their bedroom and entering quickly closed the door behind her.

Only when she was inside did she begin to calm down and start breathing properly again.

CHAPTER 61

Tim stirred in his sleep and woke. He yawned and sat up, switching on the bedside light. He looked at his watch on the side table and saw it was three in the morning. Tess was sleeping soundly beside him. There could be an air raid from the Luftwaffe overhead and Tess would sleep through it – nothing ever woke her up. He got out of bed, left the room and was walking down the corridor to fetch himself a glass of water downstairs when he spotted Cynthia's door open. He looked inside. The light in the room was on but there was no sign of her and the bed looked as if it hadn't been slept in.

"*Mother!*" he called, but there was no answer. Feeling confused and a little concerned he walked down the staircase and into the hallway below and saw the light was on in the drawing room. He walked in but there was no sign of her there either. He then spotted that the French window was ajar. He walked over and peered out into the back garden. There was no moon that night and he could just about see a figure standing at the bottom of the garden.

He picked up the poker from the hearth and crept out onto the terrace, down the steps and across the lawn, ready to strike if it was a burglar. But as he neared the figure he saw that it was somebody painting at an easel. He gasped as he realised it was Cynthia, in her nightdress, painting on a canvas.

As he drew near, to his bewilderment, he saw she was just painting black strokes of paint across the canvas continuously.

"Mother! What in God's name are you doing?"

She didn't even look away from her work.

"Oh, hello, Tim. I'm just trying to get this painting finished before the sun comes up."

Tim looked out at the black landscape and then at the black canvas she was painting.

"But, Mother – there's nothing to paint! It's nearly complete darkness!"

"Where some see darkness, others see light," said Cynthia as she continued to paint.

"Mother, you're going to get your death of cold! Will you come in!"

"Yes, I'm nearly finished, dear. You see, I have a new buyer in Berlin. He wants my paintings and I can't let him down – Mr Durchdenwald."

"He's not going to have much of a market for a black canvas!"

Tim grabbed the paintbrush out of her hand, threw it down and started directing her back inside the house. He was relieved when she didn't put up any resistance.

"Do you know how much you look like your father? You're the image of him ... the very image ..."

He watched her as they walked up the steps into the house.

"I have to do everything myself ... everything myself," she muttered as they went.

Tess listened in amazement the next morning over the breakfast table as Tim described how he had found Cynthia painting in the garden in the middle of the night.

"I told you she was acting strangely," said Tess.

"Well, there is strange and then there is bloody bonkers! There was nothing to paint! No moon! The sea, the sky was all dark!"

"I wonder what on earth is going on with her."

"I put her to bed and made her promise not to leave the room for the rest of the night."

"Maybe she was sleepwalking?"

"She didn't appear to be. She was aware of everything. Will you try and have a word with her? She might tell you what's going on. She would confide in you before me – she always thought more highly of you than me!"

"I'll try, but you know how private and tricky she is," sighed Tess. "Thanks, Tess."

At the Berghof the next morning Karina made sure she had her passport and Hugo's entry permit in her handbag.

"I'm sorry about last night, Gabriel," she said. "I just had to get away from them."

"Will you join us for breakfast?"

She shook her head. "I'll have something when I'm out sightseeing. I'll stop off at a café."

"Will you be alright driving here?" he asked. "The roads are pretty steep and treacherous."

"Of course. I'm a better driver than you!" she said with a laugh.

He grinned, nodding. "What time will you be back?" he asked.

"I'm not sure yet." She hesitated. "Gabriel, don't be alarmed if I decide to drive back to Munich and wait for you there. I find this place so oppressive. Make some excuse for me if I don't turn up. I'll phone you and let you know where I'll be staying."

He sighed. "You're really not cut out for this role of diplomat's wife, are you?"

She shook her head and smiled. "I'm probably the worst person in the world for the job, Gabriel ... you should have stuck with Siobhán. She would have done you proud last night and since you came to Germany."

"But she didn't make me happy," he said, smiling at her.

She looked at him and smiled sadly. "Goodbye, Gabriel."

"See you later."

As the barrier lifted at the entrance of the Berghof, Karina drove past the soldiers on guard and continued down the road. Once out of view of the soldiers she picked up speed and began to drive down the twisty Alpine road as fast as she could without going so fast she would miss one of the turns and go hurtling down the mountainside.

She felt free from the nausea she was feeling at the Berghof as she sped on to Hugo and her new life with him.

* * *

Tess had some errands to run and she got back to Roxford at lunchtime. As she walked into the drawing room, she saw Cynthia sitting in her armchair, staring into space.

"Good afternoon, Cynthia," she said. She was surprised to see Cynthia's usual perfectly coiffured hair was somewhat dishevelled.

"Oh, hello, Tess."

"Can I get you anything – tea or coffee?"

"No, I'm fine, thank you."

Tess pulled up an armchair and sat down beside her. "Tim is a bit worried about you, Cynthia. He says you are not quite yourself."

"Has anyone heard from Gabriel in Berlin?" asked Cynthia.

"No," said Tess.

"I do hope he's alright ..."

"Of course he is. Gabriel is well able to look after himself," said Tess.

"You never stop worrying about them, you know ... it never stops ..."

"I can imagine. It's been extra hard for you to stop worrying as you were left on your own to bring them up," said Tess, shocked, uncomfortable and yet somewhat relieved to see Cynthia showing some sign of vulnerability for the first time since she knew her.

"Yes ... it was very cruel what happened to us ... and I was so young ... I had to be both mother and father to them. It made me strong – I had to be strong, for the boys."

"You did a wonderful job," said Tess as she reached out and patted Cynthia's hand.

"I'm not so sure about that. I might have been ... kinder ... along the way," said Cynthia.

"You made sure they wanted for nothing," Tess assured her.

"Except kindness, perhaps? They were all I had after Rory was killed and I just wanted so much for them ... maybe too much."

"You have to be kind to yourself now, Cynthia. You did the

best job you could under difficult circumstances. Now it's time to stop expecting so much from yourself and from Tim and Gabriel."

Cynthia stopped looking at the fireplace and turned to look at Tess.

"I think I may have done something unforgivable," she whispered.

Tess barged into Tim's office in the Dáil, slamming the door behind her.

"What the fuck has got into you?" asked Tim, startled.

"I've been speaking with Cynthia," said Tess, a look of fear on her face.

"Did she say how she got to be in the garden playing Picasso last night?"

"No, but she said a lot else! Tim, I don't know what Cynthia has got herself mixed up in, but it's something to do with Pietch. I couldn't get the full details out of her, but she has discovered that Karina Harper is half Jewish and she has somehow fed this information through Pietch to the authorities in Berlin."

"*What?*"

"She's told them where Karina and Gabriel are staying and everything. Seemingly Gabriel has no idea of Karina's Jewish heritage. Karina has kept it hidden all her life. Karina's over there thinking nobody knows – but they do now thanks to Cynthia."

"She needs to be warned straight away," said Tim.

"What will we do?" asked Tess.

"I need to get on to the Irish legation in Berlin to have Gabriel contact me urgently." He reached for his telephone.

CHAPTER 62

Driving through the Alpine countryside, Karina's memories of her time with Hugo came flooding back. It seemed so peaceful there, so tranquil. It seemed impossible to imagine it was the centre of a continent at war. It seemed impossible to think also that the architect and tyrant of that war was living just fifty miles away. As she drove into the village of Hausham near Hugo's villa, it looked like the buildings and houses had not changed for hundreds of years. The traditional rustic-style buildings even had the year they were built inscribed in the gables – some from the seventeenth century. There wasn't a Nazi officer or a soldier in sight and Karina thought this must have been heaven for Hugo to come to following the dreadful pressure and scrutiny he was under in Berlin. She turned left at the crossroads in the centre of the village and up the hill that looked over a sprawling lake where the Alps rose high on the other side.

After about ten minutes she turned off the quiet road onto the dirt track that led down to Hugo's villa which was perched on the edge of a hill overlooking the lake. Hugo had told her the property had been in his family for two hundred years and, as an only child and last of the Von Caspars, the property had come to him. Karina remembered at the time making a promise that he would not be the last of the Von Caspars as she planned how many children they would have together.

Now her heart sank when she saw all the wooden shutters on the windows had been closed and locked. She got out of the motorcar and went up to the front door.

She knocked loudly and waited but there was no answer. She wondered if Hugo could be hiding inside, not wanting to betray his presence. She went to the windows and peeped in through the cracks in the wooden shutters but she could not see anybody inside and the house looked empty. She walked around the side of the house and to the back where again all the windows were shuttered and locked.

She stood on the large veranda at the back of the house and looked out at the lake with the mountains behind it. She remembered how they had eaten their dinner each night on the veranda. She had loved how that little valley seemed cut off from the rest of the world. She had wanted to stay there with Hugo forever.

She fell down to her knees and, overcome with the emotion of the past few months and feeling despair, she began to weep softly as she realised he was not there and she had reached the end of the rainbow to find nothing there.

"I thought it was you!" said a voice behind her, giving her a start.

She jumped to her feet.

The speaker was a man in his fifties.

"I don't think you remember me? Blaz? I'm the farmer from up the road," he said.

"Of course I remember you!" She was so glad to see somebody smiling at her, an acquaintance of Hugo, that she rushed to hug him and held him tightly.

"I hope my wife doesn't see us like this!" said the man with a laugh.

Karina laughed too as she pulled away from him and quickly wiped away her tears. She remembered the friendly farmer and his wife who lived up the road. Hugo would get milk and eggs and bread from them and Blaz looked after the land around the villa for him.

"You've come looking for Hugo," said Blaz.

"Yes," she nodded enthusiastically. "Where is he – do you know?"

Blaz shook his head sadly. "He was here. He came here last year in the autumn."

"He's *was* here? Where, Blaz?"

"He was a broken man when he arrived here from the stress of living in Berlin and being followed all the time. He told me he was getting constant threats. So he came here and lay low. He said he was waiting for some kind of miracle that would come along and save him. He wanted to try to get over the border to Switzerland, but he feared he would be turned back without a permit to show the Swiss he was in transit to somewhere else. He said you were working to get him to London – but then the war started and I think he lost hope you would ever come to succeed."

Karina was too afraid to ask what happened as she realised Blaz was speaking about Hugo in the past tense.

"One day, about two months ago, they came for him. The Gestapo drove up the road and arrested him as an enemy of the Reich. They said they were putting him in Dachau. He is still there as far as I know. I try to keep an eye on the place for him and look after the land. But, to be honest, I'm not sure he even owns it any more." He leaned forward and whispered, "They came one day and put a Nazi flag flying on top of the building. I waited a few days and then climbed up and took it down. If anyone asked I'd say the wind must have blown it away."

"I came too late," Karina said, defeated.

Gabriel sat in Hitler's study in the Berghof with Hitler himself and several of his military officers.

"We simply have no record of any of our aircraft having flown into Irish airspace and so this unfortunate bombing in Wexford cannot be blamed on us," said one of the officers.

"We have undertaken a full investigation of the bombsite and the bombs that dropped bear German markings. There was also one unexploded bomb that is clearly identifiable as a German one and people on the ground have identified the planes in the air as German through photos of different aircraft shown to them."

"Forgive me if I don't take the word of a village boy in Ireland on his expert knowledge of aircraft!" said one of the officers with a sarcastic laugh.

There was a knock on the door and one of Hitler's secretaries entered.

"Excuse me, Führer, but there is a phone call for Mr Ford," said the secretary.

"For me?" said Gabriel, surprised.

He stood up and excused himself.

Gabriel made his way to their bedroom, lifted the telephone there and waited for the switchboard at the Berghof to put through the call to him.

"Gabriel, it's Tim in Dublin."

"Tim! What's the matter?" demanded Gabriel, stunned to be getting a call from his brother.

"Everything is fine here, calm down. I contacted the legation and they said you were in Hitler's home in the Alps and they tracked down the number for me. I don't have much time – is Karina there with you?"

"Yes – no – she is staying here but she has gone off sightseeing for the day."

"You must get her out of there and out of Germany as quickly as possible – she is in terrible danger!"

"Danger? What kind of danger?"

"Mother has got herself embroiled in something untoward with that Pietch guy. She went rooting around in Karina's past and discovered she's half Jewish – on her mother's side."

"*What?*"

"She fed the information through Pietch to the Gestapo and gave the hotel address you were staying at in Berlin and everything. She's gone a bit mad, Gabriel."

"Karina is half Jewish? But she never said!"

"The family never told anybody, according to Cynthia. I don't need to tell you Karina shouldn't be in Germany and in Hitler's actual presence. Get her out of there as quickly as possible, Gabriel, for both your sakes and safety."

CHAPTER 63

It was a few hours later and Karina still was sitting on the veranda of Hugo's villa, looking out at the lake. Blaz had asked her to have lunch with him and his wife but she had declined. She was filled with enormous sadness to think of Hugo in Dachau concentration camp. He would be destroyed in a place like that. After all this time of not knowing, now she wished she did not know the truth. The guilt she felt was tremendous.

"I came too late," she repeated over and over again.

As she realised it would soon be getting dark, she stood up and made her way back to the motorcar.

She made her way back to the Berghof, almost in a daze. She didn't know where else to go or what to do. All along she had not given up hope, confident that she would find a way of rescuing Hugo, only to know now it was all for nothing and he was beyond rescue.

She drove up the mountainous road to the Berghof and was waved in by the soldiers. She parked the car and made her way up the steps to the front door where a servant let her in.

As she walked back to the bedroom she could hear much merriment from the terrace where she imagined they were all drinking champagne. It was hard to think of them freely enjoying life and being immune to the suffering of Hugo in Dachau and millions of others across the continent. She reached their bedroom and opened the door.

To her surprise, Gabriel was there, sitting in an armchair with their two suitcases beside him, obviously packed.

"Karina, I thought you weren't coming back when you didn't phone!" he said, getting up.

"Sorry ... I'm here now. But what is going on? Why are the suitcases packed?"

"We have to leave here as quickly as possible."

"What is going on, Gabriel? *Tell me!*" she demanded.

"Karina, I got a telephone call from Tim today telling me ... informing me that your mother is Jewish."

Karina's mouth dropped open.

"I do not know why you in your wildest imaginings thought it safe to come to Germany," he said. "We must leave here at once."

She was astounded. "But how – how did he find out? Nobody knew that. Nobody ever has!"

"It doesn't matter how he found out – we just need to get out of here!"

"Tell me, Gabriel! How did he come by this information?" she insisted, grabbing his hand and stopping him from reaching for the suitcases.

"Cynthia ... Cynthia went rooting around in your past as she didn't like you and found this out about you and your mother ... and has passed on the information to Berlin through that charlatan Pietch. She even said where we were staying – at the Kaiserhof, so they will be able to trace us here soon enough."

"*Cynthia!*" Karina shouted in anger. "Cynthia went rooting around in my past and alerted Berlin! Who the hell does she think she is! How dare she do that!"

"I know. Words fail me. She is completely out of order."

"Out of order! She is trying to get me killed! Your family! Have they not done enough to me over the years!"

"What do you mean by that?"

"What do I mean? Your father led that brigade of terrorists into my home at Inishwood and burned it down twenty years ago and he – your father violently struck my father who died a week later from a heart attack – your father killed my father!"

Gabriel stared at her in shame and shock.

As she stared at him, she reeled back from him. "You knew!

385

You knew all along what your father did!"

"I knew of my father's involvement in the burning down of Inishwood, but I had no idea he had assaulted your father. He wouldn't – *wouldn't* – do such a thing."

"I saw it with my own eyes! And your mother wouldn't shop me to the Gestapo either, would she?" she spat.

As he stared at her a hundred questions ran through his head.

"If you knew this about my father then why did you get involved with me?" he asked quietly.

"I didn't know at first. Not till I met your brother in the restaurant that night. He is the spit of your father. That was why I fainted."

The questions kept whirling through Gabriel's mind – if she had known what his father had done, why had she never said anything? Why did she even continue the relationship with him? Was this why she was always blowing hot and cold with him? Why did she never tell him about her Jewish background? Was it not something she should share with the man she was marrying?

But, as he looked at her, he realised she was about to explode like a volcano. She looked like a woman who could not deal with much more.

There would be time for the questions and the explanations later. But for now, they just needed to get away as quickly as possible.

"Karina, you are in terrible danger here. I can understand the frustration and anger you feel towards my family, but for now just think of yourself. We need to get you away from here as quickly as possible."

As she tried to calm down, she looked in his pleading eyes and realised she had to listen and trust him. She remembered how he always made her feel safe.

"Where can we go?" she asked.

"I'll leave a message saying I've been called away for a family emergency. Then we'll just drive out of here and get back to Berlin and home to Dublin as quickly as we can."

Karina nodded her agreement.

Gabriel quickly wrote a message on a sheet of notepaper and put it in an envelope.

Then they grabbed their suitcases and left the bedroom. They walked down the corridors towards the front entrance. They could hear the laughter and merriment from the terrace as they passed. Gabriel gave the message to one of the servants who was at the front door, explaining why they had to leave. Then they hurried down the steps and across the forecourt to the motorcar.

Karina's heart was thumping as he turned the car in the forecourt and set off down the driveway, passing through the thick forested area until they reached the entrance of the compound. The soldiers there lifted the barrier and Gabriel drove through with a smile and a wave.

Out of sight of the soldiers, he put his foot down and gathered speed.

"We'll get the night train to Berlin – that way I can get the legation to arrange a plane for us early tomorrow, to take us to Stockholm," said Gabriel.

Suddenly an army unit appeared in front, barricading the road.

One of the soldiers held up his hand for them to stop.

Karina's heart began to pound.

"What are they doing here? There were no checkpoints on the road earlier when I was coming back," said Karina.

"Just remain calm," insisted Gabriel as he slowed down.

Karina tried not to show her fear.

The soldier came over to the car.

"Passports!" he demanded.

Gabriel reached into his pocket for his as Karina took hers from her handbag. Gabriel handed them both to the soldier who passed them to another soldier who studied them both before walking over to a black Mercedes parked alongside the military vehicles.

"Is there a problem?" Gabriel asked the soldier who continued to stare silently at him. "We have been guests at the Berghof, but we needed to leave because of a family emergency."

But the mention of the Berghof didn't seem to have any effect on the soldier.

Moments later, the back door of the Mercedes opened and a woman got out.

Karina squinted at the woman as she approached their motorcar.

"*Emily!*" she gasped.

"Well, well, Harper – fancy meeting you here!"

Karina could hardly believe her eyes. It was Emily standing in front of her in this remote spot of Germany, familiar toothy smile on display.

Emily Fernsby … Emily from the Embassy.

Karina could not fathom it.

"Who are you?" demanded Gabriel, registering the shock on Karina's face.

Emily opened the back door of the motorcar and sat in, then closed the door.

"We don't want the whole mountainside to hear our business, do we, Gabriel?" she said.

"How do you know my name? Who the hell are you?" demanded Gabriel as he and Karina turned around to face her.

"Shall I tell or will you, Harper?" asked Emily.

Stunned to see Emily and terrified as to why she was there, Karina turned to Gabriel and whispered, "I'm sorry."

"Could somebody tell me what the hell is going on here?" Gabriel demanded.

"I'm an old friend of Karina's, Gabriel. I heard she was in Germany so decided to pay a visit," said Emily.

"What are you doing here, Emily, with these soldiers? Are you here as part of the Secret Service?" asked Karina.

"No, I'm not here as part of the Secret Service," said Emily. "Never was for that matter. You see, Karina, you were duped – neither I nor Kendrick was ever part of the British Secret Service."

"But of course you were! That's why he sent me to Dublin. You were working at the legation in Dublin!"

"As a German spy, as is Kendrick. We were using you, Karina. When Gabriel came to London last year we were following him and the other Irish delegates to see if Ireland would enter the upcoming war on the side of the British. When we saw him pick you up that night and take you back to Claridge's, we did some investigation of you and were thrilled to find out you were a typist at the British Foreign Office. We began to follow you and intercepted your post and when we discovered all about this doomed love affair you were pursuing in Berlin, we decided we could manipulate you."

"What love affair in Berlin?" demanded Gabriel, looking at Karina.

"We put in a request for you, Karina, to be transferred to the legation in Dublin, in order for you to be able to continue to spy on Gabriel Ford and tell us what the Irish were up to."

"But how could you infiltrate the legation and it not be noticed?" cried Karina.

"The German intelligence service is very sophisticated and we get into every nook and cranny. We even had a waiter spying on proceedings at the conference in Great Hankerton Hall."

Karina could hardly look at Gabriel as she whispered again, "I'm sorry, Gabriel."

"You have been used, Gabriel. Karina has been using you all along to gather information to feed back to us. She thought we were British Intelligence and she was trading information with us about you in order to try and locate her lost love in Germany. She thought she was feeding the information to British Intelligence, but everything she told us was passed on to Berlin."

"Tell me this is nonsense!" begged Gabriel, as tears sprang to his eyes.

"She is in love with another man – a writer, no less – a German – Hugo Von Caspars. I believe she has come to Germany with you to try and track him down. Correct me if I'm wrong, Harper?"

Karina remained silent as she stared at Gabriel.

"Everything she has done – entering into a relationship with you, coming to Germany, was to try to find Hugo, the love of her life! Isn't that right, Harper?" She looked mockingly at Karina. "The situation in Dublin had become too risky for me and so I was being called back to Germany. We were closing down the operation using Karina before I left for Berlin and had arranged for her to return to her post at the Foreign Office in London, where they would be none the wiser about the role she had played in our covert mission. We told her that her cousin had defected to the other side after Dunkirk as an excuse to send her back to London. But then you refused to go, Karina – we hadn't banked on that! And she continued using you, Gabriel, as a means to get to Germany to rescue Hugo."

"*Julian?* You lied that he had defected?" Karina asked incredulously.

"Yes, he's actually a prisoner of war. And a rather insolent one at that! He has tried to escape twice so far, let me tell you!"

Tears sprang to Karina's eyes – tears of relief and pride at Julian not having defected and fury at Emily, Kendrick and their network for the cruelty they had used to try to manipulate her.

"So did you manage to find Hugo?" sneered Emily.

"No – he is in Dachau," whispered Karina.

"I know. When he was finally tracked down to his villa here in Bavaria, we had him arrested straight away before he could slip away again."

Gabriel was trying to think clearly and not allow himself to be overcome with emotion. "But what are you doing here with these soldiers on this mountainside? Why are you bothering us?" he asked.

"Well, we, at German Intelligence, had no idea Karina had come to Germany. We thought she was stuck in Dublin pining away. Then information was fed through to us from Dublin about people of interest and Karina's name was there. A lot of information about Karina, about her being Jewish and even that she would be staying at the Kaiserhof Hotel in Berlin."

Gabriel and Karina looked at each other, knowing that Cynthia had been the source of the information. Karina thought Gabriel looked as if he had aged ten years in ten minutes. He looked like a broken man.

"Could you leave, Emily now, please? You have done enough damage," said Karina.

"I'm afraid it's not quite as easy as that, Harper. You see, we never knew that you were Jewish." Emily reached into her pocket and produced Karina's baptismal certificate, her parents' and grandparents' marriage certificates and Penny's birth certificate which Cynthia had enclosed in the package that Gabriel had delivered to the Durchdenwald Art Gallery.

Karina looked at the paperwork with astonished horror.

"I am not Jewish – I am christened Protestant," said Karina, fear taking over her body.

"It's of little interest to us what you call yourself – this paperwork proves that your mother was Jewish and you therefore are."

"So what if she is?" said Gabriel, anger and frustration overtaking him. "It's of no concern to you what religion she is! She is an Irish citizen – you have no jurisdiction over her."

"Gabriel! After all she has done to you, you still try to defend her?" asked Emily, amazed.

"I'm not trying to defend anybody. I'm just stating the facts," said Gabriel.

Emily reached into her pocket and took out the passports that the soldier had taken from them when they stopped the car.

"You can see for yourself – she has an Irish passport," Gabriel stated.

"Oh, yes, I know. She told me in Dublin and I had it checked out. But Karina's passport is several years old. She never updated it after you Irish adopted your own constitution and appointed your own president in 1937."

"What does that matter?" demanded Karina.

"Ah, but it does, Karina! Your passport says the holder is – *one of His Majesty's subjects of the Irish Free State.*"

"I don't understand what you are implying," said Karina.

"Do you want to explain it to her, Gabriel?" Emily asked, seeing a look of revelation on his face. As Gabriel sat in silence, she continued. "After Ireland adopted its own constitution and established its own presidency three years ago, it also changed the wording on their passports to simply 'Citizen of Ireland', removing the statement they were also subjects of the British Monarch."

"But I still have an Irish passport!" insisted Karina.

"But your passport clearly states you are also a subject of the British King," said Emily. "Before 1937 Irish citizens were still the King's subjects. So, as far as the German government are concerned, you are not a neutral citizen but an enemy alien."

Emily got out of the car and signalled to the soldiers who raised their guns, pointing them at Gabriel and Karina.

"What's going on?" demanded Gabriel.

"We are putting Harper under arrest. She will be taken to the Ravensbrück camp."

"But for what reason?" asked Karina, terrified.

Emily gave a sarcastic laugh. "As an enemy alien – and a rather dangerous one at that. An ex-British Foreign Office employee who has slipped into Germany to try and spring a dissident dangerous individual and who manages to infiltrate the Führer's home!"

"The real reason that you are targeting her is because she is Jewish," Gabriel accused her.

"The fact that that she is Jewish as well just confirms how right we are to be careful of her kind. Now get out of the motorcar."

She signalled to a soldier who came up, pulled open Karina's door and shouted at her to get out.

Gabriel was looking on in horror.

"Come along quietly, Harper – show some dignity at least!" said Emily.

Karina could barely look at Gabriel as she wiped away her tears. She took off her engagement ring and, without looking at Gabriel, handed it to him.

"Come on, Harper! Don't dilly-dally as usual!" insisted Emily.

Karina stepped out of the car and was brought to the boot to retrieve her suitcase before she was marched over to the Mercedes and placed in the back seat.

Emily leaned in through the still-open passenger door of Gabriel's motorcar.

"I've done you a huge favour. She would have destroyed you, Gabriel." She slammed the door shut and went to join Karina in the back of the Mercedes.

Gabriel watched as the soldiers quickly got back into their vehicles and they all departed down the mountain road until they had disappeared from view.

"She has already destroyed me," said Gabriel quietly to himself.

* * *

Karina sat in the back seat of a Mercedes beside Emily, staring out the window at the mountains under the moonlight.

"I really don't understand you, Harper," said Emily. "There you were in the safety of the Foreign Office in London, typing away, and you threw it all away by continually courting danger and insisting on getting to Germany – no matter what danger it put you in."

"Somebody like you will never understand, Emily. Because you have no heart and you can never understand love. You can't even understand loyalty or friendship."

"I never won any popularity classes at school, that's for sure! Then I was always an outsider at the English boarding school I was sent to. My mother is German and my father was English, you see. He died when I was young and we lived in Germany and my mother didn't really want me. So she shipped me off to England to be minded by relatives who didn't really want me either – so I ended up in that school where I learned all the very worst traits of the English, let me tell you."

"Well, your education at that English boarding school provided you with an excellent cover, Emily. I had no idea you were anything else but the horsy, home-counties twit you portrayed yourself as!"

"No need to be rude, Harper!"

"And what about me, Emily? Why do you hate me so? Why have you gone to such lengths to hunt me down? Is it just the fact that I'm half Jewish? Your dislike of me seems so personal. It always has, even before you knew of my Jewish connection."

"I have been acting under orders, Karina. Well, at the beginning you were extremely useful to us, with the information you could provide on Gabriel Ford. But, also, as Hugo Von Caspar's lover you were a danger. Hugo is an enemy of the Reich, a very dangerous one with his writings, and you are dangerous as his partner. You also proved to be a cunning, devious lying manipulator along the way. You got all the way into the Führer's home. I, for one, will be very happy to see you finally put out of the way."

"Do you know what I think?"

"Do tell!"

"I think you have a personal hatred towards me because I represent what you grew to hate in that English boarding school you were imprisoned in. Because I am related to the aristocracy, a member of the peerage – I was the real thing in your eyes, like those other girls at that school who all made you feel inferior. Who made you feel like the plain, toothy unpopular outsider you always were until you found a place to fit in back in Germany along with the other misfits in the Nazi party."

Emily blinked several times and tightened her lips angrily. "Well, you just keep saying that to yourself at Ravensbrück, if that makes you feel any better about your fate. I believe the inmates there are forced to do slave labour. I shall put in a special request that you are shown no leniency. We'll see how long you last there with your smart mouth and pretty face."

Emily turned away from Karina and stared out the window.

CHAPTER 64

Gabriel sat in his hotel suite in the Kaiserhof Hotel in Berlin, staring out the window. He had been almost in a state of shock since leaving the Berghof the previous night. As Karina was taken away and he had been left alone on that quiet dark mountainside, he kept thinking he was having a nightmare and he would wake up any second. He didn't know how much time had passed, but eventually he had started the car's engine and continued his journey down the mountain and on to Munich. He had missed the night train back to Berlin and had spent the night at the Hauptbahnhof, the main train station in Munich, walking up and down the platform, staring out at the dozens of rail lines that came into the station. He had got a ticket on the first train back to Berlin the next morning and slept from exhaustion in the carriage all the way.

Now back in the Kaiserhof, he felt his life had been turned upside-down since he had left there a short while ago to travel down to the Berghof. He had left with the woman he loved and adored. He had returned without her, having discovered their whole relationship was a sham, a joke from start to finish. She had merely been using him to get to the real love of her life. Gabriel felt worthless and stupid. He had known there were cracks in the relationship, but he had thought he could deal with them. He knew Karina blew hot and cold and could not understand the cause of her mood swings, but thought he could live with them. Deep down he had known something was not right, but he had chosen to ignore that instinct. He was so besotted with her he had ignored what was staring him in the face all along. She did not love him and never had. He was so angry with her and so angry with himself for being so stupid.

Siobhán's words after he had jilted her came back to haunt him – when she had said the same thing would happen to him one day and that she would be there to applaud when it did. He felt Siobhán would not be just applauding when she found out what had happened but laughing too. And the whole world would be laughing alongside her.

Karina stared at the walls in the small police cell she was in. She had always been good at coming up with plans, ideas – ways to get out of tricky situations. But she felt there was no way out this time.

After her arrest in the Alps, she had been brought to Munich train station where she had been put on a train with Emily and two soldiers. She had then been brought to Berlin where Emily had handed her over to the secret police and she had been put into a cell. It had only been twenty-four hours since she had been held at the cell but it seemed like a lifetime. Her passport had been confiscated, her suitcase taken from her. She was now an enemy alien about to be put into Ravensbrück concentration camp. And in her captors' eyes a Jewish enemy alien at that. She was sure what they were doing was not legal – her passport still said she was an Irish citizen even if it was the old one that also said she was a subject of the British King. But did it matter in Nazi Germany whether something was legal or not? Who would fight her cause? Who could she ask for help? If she demanded to see someone, they would just laugh at her. The Irish legation would certainly not fight her case, not after what had happened with Gabriel. Despite the terror and fear she felt at being in that cell and what awaited her in Ravensbrück, she still managed to feel the shame of Gabriel knowing what she had done to him. As she thought of his eyes when he found out about her deception, their hollow emptiness haunted her. Her mission to get revenge on the Fords had backfired. Her entry into their lives had only provoked Cynthia to go after her mercilessly and throw her to the wolves.

She should have learned from twenty years ago, with the burning down of Inishwood and the death of her father, that nobody won or got the better of the Fords. They were cold, calculating assassins. And yet when she thought of Gabriel's broken expression, why did *she* feel like the assassin?

She thought about her mother. If Germany won the war, it would be now on record that she was Jewish and Karina wouldn't be there to protect her. As she thought of Emily's cruel words, Karina realised she was speaking the truth. She had stubbornly and relentlessly pursued her desire to save Hugo, and now it meant danger for her mother and a dark future for herself.

CHAPTER 65

Karina was jolted awake as the cell door slammed open.

"*Up!*" shouted one of the policemen who marched in.

She quickly got to her feet and was frogmarched from the cell and out to a courtyard to a waiting car, where she was shoved in the back. Two policemen got in the front and they drove out of the courtyard.

Karina was shivering as she realised that the time she was dreading had arrived and she was being transported to the camp. She was petrified at what awaited her at Ravensbrück. She had heard so many horrific stories, about being stripped on arrival, hosed down, starved and eventually worked to death. She also expected an interrogation. She had worked at the British Foreign Office. Even though she had only been a typist there, they would not let the opportunity pass to find out what she knew. And their methods of extracting information could be brutal.

As the city began to slip away and they entered the countryside, Karina pulled her jacket closer around her as she tried to prepare herself for what was to occur over the next hours and days.

Then the car pulled off the road and into a field. As Karina looked out the window, she saw it was an airfield and a small propeller plane was waiting there.

The car came to an abrupt halt and the policemen got out.

One of them opened the back door. "*Out!*" he shouted at her.

She climbed out of the car.

One policeman took her suitcase from the boot of the car and handed it to her. The other handed her a passport.

She looked down at it and saw it was a new Irish passport with her name on it. Confused, she opened it and saw it was a temporary one-year passport.

"What is happening?" she asked the soldiers.

"You are to go on this plane and it will fly you to Stockholm," said the soldier.

"Gabriel ..." she could hardly say the word as she realised he was behind all this.

"Gabriel!" she said more loudly and then began to smile. "Is he on the plane?"

They ignored her and she went running across the airfield and up the steps into the plane.

"*Gabriel?*" she called loudly.

There was a man sitting there. But, as she squinted at him, she realised it wasn't Gabriel.

"*Hugo! Is it you?*" she cried as she scrambled into the spare seat beside him. "*It is really you?*"

They stared at each other disbelievingly and then fell into each other's arms. The door of the plane closed and the propellers began to rotate as it began to run down the airfield.

Down at the edge of the airfield, Gabriel stood watching as the plane taxied down the runway. It was only when it lifted off and began rising high into the sky that he began to breathe normally again as relief flooded his body.

He thought back on the swift action he had taken since arriving back in Berlin from Bavaria. First of all he had lodged a complaint with the German Foreign Ministry that an Irish citizen had been wrongfully arrested, demanding they stop Karina Harper's transportation to Ravensbrück concentration camp. As the matter was being investigated by the German authorities, Gabriel had quickly issued a one-year temporary Irish passport for Karina from the legation in Berlin. The Irish Department of Foreign Affairs had been issuing many of these temporary passports to rescue Irish citizens who were stranded on the Continent since the war had begun, either because their passports were out of date or they were travelling on British passports they were still using even after independence. Gabriel had then ordered a second one-year temporary emergency passport to be made for Hugo Von Caspars. He had then presented both passports to the German Foreign Ministry and demanded the immediate release of Karina and Hugo.

"But Von Caspars is not an Irish citizen, he is German through and through, and has no permission to leave Germany," said the angry officials at the Ministry.

"The passports I have given you show otherwise and both have been put under the protection of the Irish government. I want these two neutral Irish citizens released without delay. I have just been a guest of the Führer at his Berghof and I will be bringing this issue to him directly if my request is not agreed to. There will also be serious repercussions between the good relations between our two countries with my personal recommendation that the German legation in Dublin is closed down and the personnel there expelled, as the Irish government is constantly being pressurised to do by not only the British but the American government."

The official had left the room with the passports and ten minutes later arrived back to tell Gabriel his request had been accepted.

Gabriel had then arranged a plane to take Karina and Hugo to Stockholm.

As he watched the plane disappear into the clouds, he thought how Karina finally had what she wanted – Hugo freed and with her. She had done practically anything to achieve that and Gabriel had given it to her. As he watched them fly away he felt he had atoned for what his father had done to her and her family. He had redressed what his mother had did to her, betraying her to a near-certain death. And he had managed to rescue just one victim of the Nazi system with Hugo.

As he turned and walked back to his motorcar, he hoped he would never see Karina again. She had destroyed his life and he could never forgive what she had put him through, regardless of what reasons she believed she had.

"Is it really you?" asked Hugo as he and Karina clasped each other's hands.

"I can hardly believe it myself," she whispered, gazing into his face.

He had aged, he was greyer, but she was surprised he did not look worse considering where he had been. She reckoned it was because he hadn't been there that long.

"They suddenly came to me yesterday in Dachau and told me that I was leaving. I feared the worst when they escorted me to a train. But then they brought me to Berlin, handed me an Irish passport and said I was flying to Stockholm. I knew when I saw the Irish passport it had to be you that arranged it all."

"In a very roundabout way, it was," she nodded.

"How did you manage it all?" he asked, perplexed.

"Let's just say I have friends in high places," she said and kissed him.

Karina wondered where Gabriel was. Had he stayed in Berlin or already left for Dublin?

When their plane landed in Stockholm, they were informed that there was a connecting flight waiting to take them to London. Karina was amazed that Gabriel had arranged it all with such precision and yet she knew if Gabriel was doing anything he didn't do it by half measures.

And, by the fact that the flight was to take them to London rather than Dublin, she realised Gabriel did not want to see her again. He had rescued her, rescued her lover and now he was making it clear they were going their separate ways. But as she looked out the window of the plane at the North Sea as they flew over it, she knew it could be no other way. What was the point in Gabriel and her having anything to do with each other anymore? He must feel destroyed by her actions as she knew how much he was in love with her.

As she looked at Hugo sleeping beside her, though, she didn't regret what she had done. As despicable as her behaviour was, she had saved Hugo's life and now they could be together and live their lives quietly and obscurely.

CHAPTER 66

Karina felt she could kiss every brick in every building and every paving in every pathway when they arrived in London. She never wanted to leave there again.

Soon they were sitting on the Tube, heading home. *Home –* what a wonderful word, she thought, as she grabbed Hugo's arm and squeezed it tightly.

Hugo was looking around in a dazed fashion, looking like somebody from Mars who had just been planted in this strange city. Karina realised it would take him a long while to adjust after what he had been through. Even sitting on a train must be strange after being imprisoned.

Her mother had stayed in Scotland so she and Hugo would have the house to themselves for the foreseeable future. She was delighted as it would give them the space they needed to be together.

She opened the front door and stepped in.

As she looked around she realised how stupid she had been all these years. She had always felt she had no home since Inishwood was burned down and that she had been frantically searching for a place to belong. But as she closed the front door of the small terraced house in Fulham behind her, she realised this had been her real home all long.

"Oh, I never realised how much I loved this place!" she said as she walked down the hallway into the small kitchen, Hugo following her.

She turned to him, smiling.

He was standing there, staring around him.

"Is this it?" he asked incredulously.

"This is our home, yes ..."

"I – I just expected so much more," he said glumly.

"What? What were you expecting?" she asked.

"I don't know – with your background and being Lord Ashton's cousin – something more stately, I suppose."

"But you knew our original home was burned down in the War of Independence in Ireland!"

"I did, but I hadn't realised you had been reduced to living like this," he said.

Karina's face could not hide the hurt she felt.

"Oh, I'm so sorry!" He threw his arms around her. "How stupid of me! After where I have been, it doesn't bother me in the least where I am snow. I am just delighted to be free and away from Germany."

"It might not be much, but I was never as glad to be anywhere as here today when I think where I would have been if I hadn't got out of Germany."

"Of course you are," he said as he rocked her while he held her.

Over her head he continued to look around the modest kitchen. "I just get so angry when I think of those Nazis stealing my beautiful flat in Berlin and my stunning villa in Bavaria and I have to be grateful to be living here."

A cloud overshadowed Karina's happiness at his words but she realised she would have to be patient. He had been through so much.

The next day Karina called to the Foreign Office. She spoke to her old bosses and informed them about Emily and what had happened to her at the legation in Dublin. She barely mentioned Gabriel's name as she did not want to drag him into it. Her bosses had become aware of Emily's infiltration in Dublin after she had absconded to Berlin and that she had been part of a wider network that stretched back to London. Karina was questioned over and over again about what had happened but by the end of the week she found herself back in the typing pool, at her old desk by the window looking out at the park with the same girls around her.

"Well, we thought you would have been made a special envoy to Washington by now!" said her old adversary Diana at the next desk.

"No – I'm just happy to be back here, I never want to leave again!" said Karina as she typed away.

Vera, who still occupied the desk in front of her, turned around and smiled. "Good to have you back, Karina."

Karina grinned at her and continued to type through the stack of paperwork that had been left there for her.

CHAPTER 67

Two weeks later Gabriel was sitting in front of Cecil Brolan, the head of a disciplinary committee which had already questioned him at the Department of Foreign Affairs.

"You completely abused your position and power, Ford," said Brolan. "You were sent to Germany on a highly secretive confidential diplomatic trip. You took with you a woman who was a former employee of the British Foreign Office and legation in Dublin who we understand you were in a personal relationship with."

"As you said, she was a former employee," said Gabriel. "I believed she was no security threat."

"It does not matter – you needed permission to take her with you and to take her especially to such a high-level location as the Berghof," snapped Brolan.

"I accept I did wrong by not getting clearance first," said Gabriel.

"Which would have been denied, as you were well aware!" said Brolan. "Then you issue the said woman with a temporary passport and this other person – Hugo Von Caspars – also a temporary passport without going through the proper channels."

"Miss Harper had an Irish passport – I was merely updating it as the Nazis were trying to imprison her. What is the difference between this and the other temporary passports there is such demand for?"

"The difference is you were in a personal relationship with this woman and you should have used the proper channels. And because this Hugo Von Caspars is not Irish, was never Irish and will never be Irish! He was a political prisoner who –"

"Was saved from certain death, I imagine, by the passport," concluded Gabriel.

"We cannot just hand out passports like that! If we handed a passport out to everyone who claims to be fleeing Nazi persecution, where would that leave us? Sunk in the Atlantic from the weight of everyone who would flock to our shores!"

"You will have my resignation by the end of the day," said Gabriel.

"And I will have no option but to accept that resignation," said Brolan.

Gabriel stood up and began to walk to the door.

"Why, Gabriel? Why all this? You were always so dependable, so correct, always knew the right procedure to take. Why have you thrown caution to the wind?"

"Because these times don't require procedures, they require action." Gabriel opened the door and left.

CHAPTER 68

Karina's routine fell back into the way it had been before she ever left for Dublin. Except this time she did not head out to the 400 Club and other chic places every night. Now, she went straight back to Hugo in the house. He was traumatised by his time in hiding in Germany and from being in Dachau. She was becoming worried about him as he rarely left the house. He sat writing or reading the newspapers all day long. When she asked him what he was writing he would say "some stories" but he never seemed to be able to finish them.

One night they were sitting in the front room by the fire. She sat gazing into the fire, thinking about the last year, while he sat doing crossword puzzles.

"Hugo?"

"Yes?"

"After you sent the last telegram from Berlin – why did you not try to contact me again? Why did you not try to send another telegram or a letter from Bavaria to let me know you were there and alright?"

"Because I was terrified of somebody intercepting a letter or a telegram and finding out where I was."

"I just feel the telegram you sent me was misleading as I immediately thought of the Friedrichs' as we had met there."

"But we really met when you came to the villa in Bavaria. I thought you would figure that out – that I would certainly leave Berlin – I guessed you would be smart enough to realise that."

"Well, I guess I wasn't … maybe if you had given a better clue I wouldn't have wasted so much time," she said defensively.

"But what time did you waste? It took you over a year to get to Berlin anyway – I was already in Dachau by then. My giving you a better description wouldn't have got you to Germany any quicker."

She looked at him, startled, as he seemed to be attacking her because of the length of time it took her to find him.

"But you always told me *not* to come to Berlin before you fled to Bavaria," she said and heard her voice rising. "You insisted I would only draw more attention to you!"

Suddenly the air-raid sirens started sounding loudly.

"*Oh, not again!*" shouted Hugo despairingly. "*Does it never stop! Night after night!*"

Karina got up and went to put on her coat and get a blanket.

"That smelly underground with all those awful people – I just can't bear to be down there anymore!" said Hugo.

"I know it is not ideal," said Karina quietly, trying to exercise patience.

"Ideal! It's unbearable! In fact, I'm not going tonight – I'm going to stay here!"

"But you can't! It's too dangerous!" she said.

"A bomb hasn't hit the house so far so I have no reason to think tonight will be any different!" he said, folding his arms.

"Hugo! Don't be stupid – you have to come!" she begged.

"I don't have to do anything anymore. I'm sick of being told what to do. I'm staying put!" He crossed his legs while his arms remained folded.

"Hugo! Please!" she begged.

She tried to drag him up off the sofa as the sound of bombs blasting in the distance began to pound.

It took her half an hour to convince Hugo to go to the shelter. As they made their way through the deserted streets, bombs began to fall close by with huge explosions.

Hugo ran into a shop doorway and knelt down, shaking.

"*Hugo! Will you come on – we have to get to the shelter!*" she screamed, pulling him up off the ground.

Suddenly a bomb dropped across the street from where they were, causing a shop to explode.

Hugo was transfixed, staring at the flames.

"*Will you come on!*" Karina screamed at him as she pulled him down the street to the safety of the shelter.

Down in the underground station it was packed with people who were settling down for the night as the bombs could be heard being dropped overhead.

Karina found a space in a corner and she laid the blanket down for them to sit down on.

"*I can't stand it! I can't stand it!*" Hugo whispered as he looked around at all the people.

Karina wasn't sure if he couldn't stand the sound of the bombs overhead or being down in the underground with all the 'rabble' as he sometimes called the people.

As she tried to comfort and calm him, she remembered when she and Gabriel had taken shelter during the air raid in the U-Bahn station in Berlin. How they had held each other, giving support in silence. He had made her feel safe during such a terrifying ordeal.

He had never asked or expected anything from her, only offered his support.

CHAPTER 69

After he had tendered his resignation, Gabriel had barely gone out except to the local shop to get supplies. He did not answer the door or the telephone. He threw out any clothes or personal items Karina had left there before they went to Berlin.

It was late afternoon, a couple of weeks after he had resigned, and Gabriel sat in the drawing room in Victoria Terrace, twirling the engagement ring between his fingers.

He could hear voices outside and then loud knocking on the front door which he ignored.

Outside Tess and Tim were on the front steps, looking up at the house while Tim slammed the knocker on the door. It was the third time they had been there that week. And, again, his car was there.

"Maybe he's not home," said Tess. "He might have taken a walk."

"Maybe – but I bet he's in there hiding!" said Tim. He had heard everything that had happened to Gabriel at work and they had desperately tried to telephone him and call to the house but there was no response.

"Maybe he has taken a short holiday," mused Tess.

"No – he's in there licking his wounds! He was always like that – even as a child!" Tim then knocked loudly on the door again and, opening the letter box, shouted through it. "*Will you open this bloody door, Gabriel! Mother is very sorry for what she did! Beside herself with sorrow over it all! It wasn't her fault! She got sweet-talked into doing it by that Pietch fella!*"

"*Will you shut up!*" Tess hissed, hitting his shoulder. "The neighbours will hear you!" She smiled at a passing woman who was pushing a pram.

She pushed Tim aside and, bending down to the letterbox, hollered nearly as loudly as he had. "*It's true, Gabriel! Cynthia is beside herself with guilt! She knows she shouldn't have done what she did and she's very, very sorry! I've never seen her like this before – crying even! Tears – real tears! Would you not come back to Roxford and we can discuss it over a nice dinner this evening? Your favourite – roast chicken!*"

But no response came.

Tess stood up straight and shook her head at Tim.

"C'mon, we'll head home … we'll try again tomorrow."

They walked down the steps to their motorcar.

Over breakfast the next morning, Cynthia said, "I always knew that girl was trouble. I always knew she would bring ruin to Gabriel's door."

Tess and Tim looked at each other across the table and raised their eyes to heaven in unison.

"I was just trying to protect him, as any mother would," said Cynthia.

Cynthia saw Tess and Tim's accusatory looks directed at her.

"I'm not saying what I did was right," she quickly added. "I'm not saying that at all … but I knew she was bad news from the start."

The post came through the letterbox and Tim went into the hallway to get it.

"Maybe try and telephone him again today," urged Tess to Cynthia.

"I will – I will, Tess – that's what I'll do, I'll try him on the telephone again today," agreed Cynthia eagerly.

Tim walked in, reading a letter.

"It's from Gabriel," he said, looking up shocked. "He says he's gone to England to join the British army."

"*What?*" shrieked Cynthia as she blessed herself.

"It can't be!" said Tess.

"Read it for yourself," said Tim, handing her the letter and sitting back down at the table.

"He says there is nothing left here for him ... he's going to join the fight to make the world free again ... we are not to worry about him ..." Tess said, scanning through the letter.

"I can't believe it!" said Cynthia. "I just cannot believe that he would do this to me! That a son of mine would join the British army!"

"Oh shut up, Mother, just shut up!" Tim begged, shaking his head in despair at her.

Gabriel pulled the collar of his overcoat up as the ship made its way out past Dublin Bay towards England. He stood on deck, looking at Dublin as it slipped into the distance. It was true what he had written in his letter – there was nothing for him there anymore. He needed to carve out a new life for himself and he needed to forget the past. Fighting in the war would do that for him.

He gripped the handrail of the ship as the city disappeared over the horizon.

EPILOGUE

JULY 1941

Karina dashed down the stairs of the double-decker bus as it pulled up at her regular stop near the Foreign Office. As she walked down the street in the autumn morning sunshine, she glanced over across the street to a building that had been obliterated the night before in another German air raid. It had become such a usual occurrence to see buildings disappear that had been standing tall the previous day, that she hardly paid attention anymore. She, like the rest of London, just went about her daily business as best she could, just grateful that the risk of direct invasion that had been so feared and expected the previous year had now passed.

She climbed up the steps of the Foreign Office and as ever it was a hive of activity as she made her way to her office which was on one of the upper floors.

"Good morning, Pam," she said to her secretary as she passed by her desk.

"Good morning, Miss Harper. I've left your telephone messages on your desk for you," said Pam.

"Thank you," said Karina as she went into her office. She closed the door behind her and went to sit at her desk.

In the previous few months, Karina's promotion up the ranks had been fast and deserved. When she had come back from Germany the previous year, she had thrown herself into her work at a staggering pace. When she thought back to what she was like before she went to Dublin and Berlin, she marvelled at herself. A self-obsessed society girl intent on her own pleasure and desires, regardless of what the consequences were for others. She had even put her own pursuit of a personal relationship ahead of the contribution she should have been making to the war against the Nazis. But going to Germany had changed everything for her. Seeing and experiencing what the Nazis were capable of doing first-hand had made her determined to do her bit, whatever that entailed, to defeat them. She worked tirelessly at the Foreign Office to locate and help refugees, soldiers and prisoners of war and to liaise with their families, not just to give information but hope. She knew from the personal experience of looking for a loved one that hope was everything.

Her mother was quite content to stay in Scotland away from the bombs and so Karina had slipped easily into the habit of living alone and throwing herself into her work.

Every day, when she finished at the Foreign Office, she headed to the Red Cross where she worked tirelessly trying to get food and clothing to Jewish refugees around Europe. When she thought of how close she had come to nearly being one of those people trapped and imprisoned on the Continent, it drove her on to help others. She didn't have any distractions from her work since her relationship with Hugo had ended four months after they arrived back to London.

Hugo was unable to settle into life in London. He could not cope with the Blitz, his nerves were shattered. As the weeks went by, Karina also suspected he could not cope with her. And as the weeks turned into months, she reluctantly and depressingly realised she could not cope with him. She felt she was a constant disappointment to him. She could see the disappointment in his eyes all the time. She slowly and sadly realised they had built each other up into something neither of them was. Being kept apart by the Nazis and the war had allowed their imaginations to run wild. But here in the humdrum of a small dowdy London kitchen or making their way to an air-raid shelter night after night, the reality of their life forced them to see the reality of each other. He tried to write his next book, but no words seemed to be able to flow anymore which filled him with a sense of loss and frustration.

Eventually, Hugo left London and moved down to the countryside where he had found some patron to fund him to write his next book. A book, Karina feared, that would never be written.

It had been a blow to realise that the great love of her life had in fact been nothing. She had been in love with an illusion, a mirage that vanished in the cold light of day.

But Gabriel Ford ... she had thought about him regularly since returning to London and about the unbelievable thing he did for her and Hugo, rescuing them from Germany. And then he had disappeared from her life – not wanting anything back. But then he had never wanted anything from her except to love her. When she remembered the love and admiration that constantly shone from his eyes, how could that compare to the dull look of disappointment that Hugo continually bestowed on her. And, although she could not regret what had happened as it had resulted in saving Hugo's life, she at the same time regretted everything. She hated herself for how she treated Gabriel and was haunted by the feeling that she had never given him the chance he deserved, and that Gabriel so desperately tried to get her to give him. As she thought back now to how she had coldly discarded all his overtures, she felt she would give anything to just have a chance to be with him again.

She had started a letter many times to him to try and explain and apologise for her actions, but the words did not come. And she was sure, even if they did come, she would be the last person on earth Gabriel would want to hear from.

Karina was sitting at her desk, writing up a memorandum, when the telephone on her desk rang.

"Harper," she answered.

"Hello, Karina, it's Joey here on the front desk. There is a gentleman here who wishes to see you."

"Who is it, Joey?" she said, not looking up from her paperwork.

"A Mr Ford, from Dublin."

Karina looked up abruptly as she nearly dropped the receiver.

"Tell him ... not to go anywhere and I'll be down in a minute!"

She hung up the phone and sat back in her chair, putting her hands to her face. She could scarcely believe it. He was there ... he was downstairs after all this time. Her heart began to pound with excitement as she jumped up and, taking a mirror from her drawer, quickly checked her appearance.

She forced herself to calm down and steadied herself as she left the office.

She hurried past her secretary and down the stairs.

In the ground-floor foyer a man was standing, studying a painting as he waited for her.

When he heard her approach, he turned around and she saw it was Tim Ford.

Her face dropped on not finding Gabriel there.

"Hello, Karina," said Tim.

They left the building and went across to the park for a walk.

"You seem well, Karina," said Tim.

"I am, Tim. For a while, I wasn't. But now I'm focused on my work – doing my utmost as we all are in these times. But what about you? How are you?"

"I'm good. Better than I was."

"And Tess? How are you two getting along?"

"Well, we haven't killed each other yet." He gave a rueful smile, then glanced at her. "I've been off the drink now for six months."

"Well done," she said.

He halted and turned to her.

"Karina, I hope you don't mind me just showing up like this. It's just that I'm at my wits' end and I didn't know who else to turn to. I knew you had worked here so dropped in to see if anyone knew where you had got to ... and they told me you were upstairs!"

"What's happened?" she asked, concerned.

"It's Gabriel ... after he returned from Berlin that time last year, he turned his back on all of us and didn't want to know us anymore."

"Not even Cynthia?"

"Especially not Cynthia after what she did." He looked at her pointedly. "He resigned his post at the Department of Foreign Affairs."

"I – I didn't know any of this," she said, shocked.

"He didn't contact you all this time?"

She shook her head.

"After resigning, he left Dublin and joined the British army," said Tim.

"*What?*"

"Yes. And we were contacted a month ago by the army to say he had been injured in combat in East Africa," said Tim.

"Is he alright?" Karina stopped walking abruptly.

"He was evacuated back to England and has been recuperating in Goodfield House in Sussex."

"But he's alright, Tim?"

"He was badly injured, Karina. He was shot in the leg," said Tim.

"Oh!" Karina paled as she blinked back tears.

"There was quite a lot of damage but he'll be able to use the leg again eventually. He will just need time to recover. But it's his mental state that I'm worried about, Karina. I was just down visiting him yesterday. He has shut off from everyone and everything."

She sighed as she continued walking. "He never spoke about what happened in Germany?"

"No, not a word."

"All I can say is I behaved appallingly towards him. I wish I could change how I behaved, but I can't," said Karina.

"It was obvious how much he thought of you." Tim stopped walking and faced her. "Karina, I came to ask you – could you go see him and try to get through to him?"

Karina looked frightened at the thought. "I think he wouldn't want that. Tim. I'm the last person he wants to see."

"But it's worth a chance, isn't it? Don't you owe him that?"

"I owe him far more than that. He's the kindest person I ever met."

Karina could not concentrate on her work for the rest of the day. That night, she sat alone in the front room, thinking of Gabriel and feeling depressed that he was as Tim described and that it was all her fault. She needed to see him. Tim was right, he did deserve that.

As she drove up the long avenue through the parklands Goodfield House was set in, it was a bright sunny day. She parked the car in front of the building which was an old stately mansion that had been taken over by the government and converted into a rehabilitation centre. She walked up the steps to the white-painted door and, on entering, enquired after Gabriel. She was directed to the parklands at the back of the building.

She walked through a large drawing room, passing soldiers being tended by nurses, and out through French windows onto a long terrace where others were resting in deck chairs watching a game of cricket on the green behind the house.

"Excuse me, I'm looking for Gabriel Ford," Karina said to a passing nurse.

"Ah, yes – Gabriel is –" her eyes looked around the park and then she pointed to a man sitting on a bench in the distance, "over there."

"Thank you," said Karina and she walked down the steps from the terrace and around the green towards the lone figure. As she neared him, she saw he was not looking at the cricket match but facing in the opposite direction, looking out at the countryside. *Gabriel.* She felt overjoyed to see him again. She saw that he was dressed in casual clothes but had one leg in bandages and two crutches rested on the ground.

But he wasn't looking at the beautiful view of the countryside as his eyes were closed. She wondered was he sleeping as she stood in front of him and stared at him.

She sat down beside him and reached over and took his hand in hers. This action stirred him from his slumber and he opened his eyes.

He looked at her as if she were a dream. Then his face filled with surprised joy.

"Hello, Gabriel," she said, and she leaned forward and kissed his cheek. "What kind of mess have you got yourself into this time?"

He smiled at her and she touched his face as his eyes welled up.

She forced herself to smile and not cry. "Fine thing you did, running off on me like that without so much as a goodbye."

"I did?" he said and managed a smirk.

"You didn't even give me a chance to explain anything."

"Could you have explained anything?"

"Only that I was biggest fool in the world and I've only realised that since I lost you."

She gazed in his eyes and saw only warmth there – no reproach.

"When are you being released?" she asked.

"I don't know," he said.

"Well, I'll find out this afternoon and as soon as you are released you are coming to live with me in my small little home in London – and not a complaint or an objection from you, do you hear me? I have to keep a close eye on you from now on and make sure you get fully better because I really can't live without you, you see ... and, Gabriel, I'm so sorry for what I did to you." She reached forward and hugged him tightly.

"You're smothering me," he said as put his arms around you.

"Oh, you have no idea how much you are going to be smothered, Gabriel. I'll never let you out of my sight again."

As the afternoon wore on Karina took Gabriel for his exercise through the parklands. He had an arm around her shoulders while she held him tightly around his waist. They walked very slowly as he used a crutch for support.

She chatted away, telling stories from the Foreign Office.

"And then we had a new typist – a pretty girl called Millie – and she had applied for the job as a typist but had never actually used a typewriter before!"

"Well, how did she get the job?" asked Gabriel.

"I don't know. I didn't interview her, but I presume it was a man who did!"

"She told me she thought typing would be the same as cycling and once you learned you would never forget! I told her that might be true, but – you needed to learn how to do it first!"

"Where is she now?" asked Gabriel.

"She's still at the Foreign Office, typing away with two fingers.

I guess we all have to start somewhere ... and then we all have to learn from our mistakes."

They stopped walking a moment and looked at each other, tightening their grip around each other. Before they continued to walk in silence for a while.

THE END

A GREAT BEAUTY

A. O'CONNOR

It is 1920 and, as the War of Independence rages throughout Ireland, Michael Collins is the most wanted man in the British Empire. He lives a life in hiding, conducting guerrilla warfare, outsmarting the authorities, a figure of mystery and intrigue. Very few know even what he looks like. He occasionally finds rest and comfort with the family of Kitty Kiernan, his best friend's sweetheart. Then Michael finds himself falling in love with the complex and enigmatic Kitty.

Lady Hazel Lavery, wife of famous artist Sir John Lavery, is considered the most beautiful and charming society hostess in London. An American of Irish descent, haunted by a tragic past, she sets out to use her friendships with men like Winston Churchill to bring peace to Ireland.

When Michael, recently engaged to Kitty, arrives in London as part of the Irish peace delegation, he finds himself the centre of intense public fascination. Hazel Lavery takes Michael under her wing and navigates him through London high society. They form a close bond and soon are engulfed in rumours of an affair and accusations that Michael has been seduced by the glamour of London and by Hazel. Kitty all but despairs at the situation but is determined to fight for him.

After the infamous Anglo-Irish Treaty, Ireland veers towards civil war. As Michael, Hazel and Kitty arrive in Dublin that fateful week in August 1922, the war is at its zenith – and this love triangle is about to implode with devastating results.

ISBN 978-178-199-797-0

The LEGACY *of* ARMSTRONG HOUSE

A. O'CONNOR

2017 – At Armstrong House, Kate and Nico Collins are looking forward to a bright future with their young son Cian.
When archaeologist Daniel Byrne arrives in the area to investigate life there during the Great Famine, he soon crosses paths with Kate. Through Daniel's work, Kate is horrified to discover that a vicious sexual assault occurred in their home in the 1860s when the occupants were Nico's ancestors Lord Edward and his wife Lady Anna. Kate sets out to use all her investigative skills to discover the circumstances of the crime, the identity of the victim and the guilty party.

1860s – After Lawrence, the long-awaited heir to the Armstrong Estate, is born Lord Edward and Lady Anna take great joy in watching him grow up. But somebody else is watching – Edward's cousin Sinclair who has always felt cheated of the Armstrong legacy by the unexpected birth of Lawrence. As Anna's past comes back to haunt her, life at the house is a tangled web of deceit, blackmail and betrayal that shatters in the summer of 1865.

2017 – As Kate's detective work edges closer to discovering the truth behind the assault, she and Daniel uncover a mystery that goes much deeper. Kate realises that if the truth is ever revealed it will not only destroy the legacy of the Armstrong family but also her marriage to Nico.

ISBN 978-178199-821-2

$\mathcal{O}n$ SACKVILLE STREET

A. O'CONNOR

1869 – When Milandra arrives to live on Sackville Street as a young widow, she becomes the talk of Dublin. Firstly, she scandalises society by refusing to wear the mandatory widow's weeds. She then sets her sights on marrying young solicitor Nicholas Fontenoy, despite the fact he is already engaged to Bishop Staffordshire's daughter, Constance.

But is there something darker behind Milandra's professed love for Nicholas? As she attempts to lure Nicholas away from Constance, a chain of events is set off that leads to bribery, blackmail and murder.

1916 – Now in her seventies, Milandra is one of the wealthiest and most respected women in Dublin. Back in her mansion on Sackville Street, after spending Easter with family, she is astonished to be confronted by a gunman. She fears he has come to rob her, but quickly realises she has been caught up in something much bigger.

Then, as Dublin explodes with the Easter Rising, Milandra's granddaughter Amelia desperately tries to reach her grandmother who is trapped in her house at the very centre of the conflict. Meanwhile, events unfolding on Sackville Street will unravel decades-old mysteries, secrets that were to be carried to the grave.

ISBN 978-178199-868-7

ALSO BY POOLBEG.COM

By ROYAL APPOINTMENT

A. O'CONNOR

In 1861 nineteen-year-old Bertie, Prince of Wales, began an affair with the Irish actress Nellie Cliffden. By Royal Appointment *is a fictionalised account of their story, based on true events.*

In the years following the Great Famine of the 1840's, Queen Victoria has become deeply unpopular in Ireland. In 1861, as an official visit from the monarch is planned to win over her Irish subjects, her son Bertie is dispatched to County Kildare for military training as part of the charm offensive.

Bertie has undergone a life of duty, protocol and a harsh educational regime. As a frantic search is under way to find him a suitable princess to marry, he relishes the prospect of freedom from court life in Ireland. There, he is quickly introduced to a life of decadence and soon presented to the notorious actress Nellie Cliffden.

Nellie is as famous for her shocking behaviour as her beauty. A famine orphan who has climbed the ladder of society by any means she could, even she is shocked to find herself in the company of the Prince of Wales.

When Bertie and Nellie fall in love, the royal family is engulfed in a scandal threatening the future of the monarchy and Nellie becomes a pawn in a dangerous world of power, politics and blackmail.

ISBN 978-178199-807-6